A Universe of Wishes

ALSO AVAILABLE FROM TITAN BOOKS

Vampires Never Get Old
Edited by Zoraida Córdova and Natalie C. Parker

A Universe of Wishes

A WE NEED DIVERSE BOOKS ANTHOLOGY

Edited by
DHONIELLE CLAYTON

TITAN BOOKS

A Universe of Wishes
Print edition ISBN: 9781789098006
E-book edition ISBN: 9781789098013

Published by Titan Books
A division of Titan Publishing Group Ltd
144 Southwark Street, London SE1 0UP
www.titanbooks.com

First Titan edition: July 2021
10 9 8 7 6 5 4 3 2 1

A CIP catalogue record for this title is available from the British Library.

Printed and bound by CPI Group Ltd, Croydon CR0 4YY.

CONTENTS

FOREWORD

Dear Reader,

I was a mess as a teenager. Brimming with wishes and wants. Spoiled and grumpy. A misfit loner. Tiny, mad, and full of so many unanswered questions about this weird world. I'd always felt like I'd ended up in the wrong place. The wrong planet. The wrong time. That one day, I'd find my true home.

The only thing that made me happy was reading. I'd hide beneath my grandmother's mahogany table with a stack of books, a plate of perfect pink-frosted animal cookies, and a glass of sun tea—with the *right* amount of sugar to suit my taste buds. I found my safe space in stories, away from all the other teens in my school, away from the mirrors, away from the comments.

I fell into fantasy and science fiction books to quench my thirst for other worlds and read as much as I could get my hands on during weekend trips with Dad to the bookstore and the public library.

But after a while, I started to notice that kids who looked like me didn't get to save the world, didn't get grand adventures through fantastical landscapes, didn't get to go to magic camp. My imagination started to shrink. My love of reading dwindled. It felt like a light going out. I was losing the very thing that made me *me*. All because I was desperately looking for myself in the pages of the stories I craved.

For far too long some of us have been missing from magical worlds. But not any longer. Because the true secret I learned from books is that we all have magic inside us. We all possess the ability to command the failing spaceship, to break the powerful enchantment, and to change our worlds—both fictional and not—for good.

The universe is better because we are here. Because *you* are here. So let's get started. Your grand adventure awaits.

Love,
Dhonielle

A UNIVERSE OF WISHES

TARA SIM

H e had taken to making wishes whenever he could.
At the last morning star, on the edges of tarnished coins, along the cracks of bones that split in fires.

It was never enough. No matter how often or how aggressively he wished, his words were never heard, his pleas went unanswered.

And then one day, he learned why: wishes could not be made on innocent things, innocuous things, like stars and coins and clovers.

Because wishes were granted only by the dead.

The city of Rastre was pumping like a heart, people moving through its streets as blood flows through veins. It was the end of the day, and the sun burned copper on the horizon, casting long shadows out of the spires and rooftops around him.

Thorn waited in the shadow of a cathedral's bell tower, crouched on the slanted roof with his arms braced on his knees. The wind blew, and he huddled deeper into his threadbare jacket. He'd have to get a new one soon.

Eventually the door across the street opened, emitting a tall, slender boy who couldn't be much older than he was. The boy closed the door behind him, locked it, and headed toward the eastern sector.

Thorn waited several minutes to be sure. When the sun had bled fully into the earth, the sky deepening into a two-day bruise, Thorn slid to the edge of the roof. Jade lanterns flickered to life, casting Rastre in a glowing, starry light.

That light didn't reach the street below. Thorn hopped down into that welcome darkness. Beyond he could hear the sounds of passersby, a child screaming in delight, the tinny first notes of a street musician.

Thorn popped the collar of his jacket and crouched before the door. He tickled the lock with his pick until it gave way and he could slip inside.

His breathing was loud in the silence that greeted him. Thorn swallowed and willed his heart to slow. He usually prowled the cemetery in the western sector, but one too many close calls with the groundskeeper had made him leery enough to try another approach. That, and he was getting tired of constantly washing grave soil out of his clothes and from the beds of his fingernails.

Not like this was much better—but at least it was cleaner.

The building was modest in size, large enough to contain two stories. The ground floor was used for receiving and accommodating customers. Upstairs was a collection of coffins and caskets.

But he knew, after a week of observation and more than his fair share of peeking through the window, that there was actually a third story. It was just underground.

Thorn moved past an open display coffin and a reception desk, around to the back, where a smaller desk sat covered in papers and parchment and pens. And animal figurines, of all things. Beyond that stood a door, and jiggering the lock rewarded him with a waft of cooler air.

A familiar eagerness filled his belly, the taste of magic already on his lips. He licked them and crept down a wooden staircase, feeling his way through the dark until he found a jade lantern at the bottom. It flared to life when he tapped it, illuminating a couple of autopsy tables and a rack of tools that could have doubled as torture devices.

And rows and rows of crystal capsules.

That was what gave off all this cold. Crystals were used for storing perishable goods, or keeping houses cool in the height of summer . . . or keeping dead bodies fresh.

Thorn approached the nearest capsule. They were built into the wall like drawers. He fumbled with the frozen handle until he could yank it open, pulling out the capsule's sole occupant.

The man was waxen and stiff. His skin had become a light blue. Thorn had heard people speak of the dead, had heard words like *sleeping* and *peaceful,* but this man didn't fit either of those. He seemed troubled even in death, his thick eyebrows lowered over sunken eyes, his mouth flat and unimpressed.

Thorn paused, looking at the freshly sutured Y-shaped line

running down the man's naked belly. He wasn't used to this. Touching the dead, yes; digging up bodies, yes. He'd grown accustomed to the smell of earthy ozone and decay, the creeping mold and mulch of graveyards, the chill of stone and nights without moonlight.

This, though, was something altogether different. This was clean and clinical. It was crystal and chalcedony.

It was . . . wrong.

Thorn took a deep breath. He felt that breathing was somehow disrespectful, standing above a body that was no longer capable of the task. And what a strange concept, for this man to have existed only between the span of two breaths—his first and his last—to become merely a *thing*.

Well, there was still *some*thing inside him. And that was the whole point.

Thorn took out his pocketknife and flipped it open. It gleamed in the jadelight, deceptively clean despite its grisly purpose. He ran the knife over the autopsy incision, popping sutures and unraveling flesh. Much easier than hacking his way through dead tissue and muscle.

He peeled back the man's skin, exposing a torso that had been hollowed out like a pumpkin. The organs had been detached and taken . . . somewhere. Thorn didn't want to know, and didn't care. Instead, the man's body was lined with cotton, as if he were being turned into some morbid doll.

His ribs were still there, however. They curved up like anxious smiles, or the claws of a forgotten beast.

And there, residing between the fourth and fifth rib on his left side, was what Thorn had come here for. It was invisible, but he *felt* it, a tiny swirling galaxy of potential. It drew him in like a promise. A secret.

Thorn took the obsidian from his pocket and held it against the man's ribs. The little galaxy continued to swirl between his bones, confused and directionless, but the lure of the obsidian finally caught its attention. It seeped into the black, glassy rock, joining the other little galaxies Thorn had already taken. His own pocket-sized universe.

He wondered if he finally had enough. But maybe, just to be sure, he should—

"What are you doing?"

Thorn whipped around. Standing at the bottom of the stairs was the boy he'd seen leaving the funeral parlor.

He had only a moment to take him in: skin a couple shades browner than his own, hair dark and curling at the ends, eyes that were the gray-green hue of moss. They were wide and spooked, darting between Thorn and the inelegantly opened corpse.

Thorn shoved the obsidian back into his pocket and did the only thing he could think of: he pushed the man's body off its crystal slab.

The boy cried out in dismay and hurried forward to fix the mess. Thorn took his opening and darted for the stairs, his boots thundering on the wooden planks. He crashed into the desk up above, rattling the little animal figurines on its surface.

He was almost to the front door when a hand clawed at his shoulder. Thorn twisted and reached for his pocketknife, but the boy was stronger than he looked, and one purposeful shove made Thorn stagger farther into the shop. The backs of his knees caught the edge of something, and he fell, landing with a hard *thud* that winded him.

The lid to the display coffin fell shut on top of him.

Panic welled in his throat. Thorn dropped his pocketknife and banged on the lid, shoving his shoulder against it, but it wouldn't budge. A creak above told him the boy was likely sitting on top of it, his weight rendering the lid unmovable.

"Who are you?" the boy demanded, voice muffled through the wood.

Thorn didn't answer. He was breathing fast; the coffin smelled like cedar and linseed oil, and something herbal— maybe rosemary. He tried pushing the lid again, but it gave only a mere centimeter.

"How dare you come in here and deface the dead," the boy went on. "You realize that brings bad luck, don't you?"

Thorn was surprised by the rasping laugh that escaped him. "I'm used to bad luck."

Silence. He could hear his own heart pounding, as if his body wanted to assure him that he was alive, despite his immediate surroundings.

"I'm not going to let you out until you explain yourself," the boy said after a moment. "Poor Mr. Lichen didn't deserve what you did to him."

Thorn was inclined to agree, but sensing the little galaxy in his pocket, he didn't regret it. He couldn't say that, though; he'd never be released from this wretched coffin if he did.

When Thorn didn't reply, the boy drummed his fingers against the lid. "If you don't explain yourself," he said softly, almost too softly for Thorn to hear, "I'll call the city guard."

Dread pooled in his chest. He'd been evading the guard for

two years; he couldn't allow all his hard work to unravel in a single night.

But he couldn't easily explain what he'd been doing either.

"I . . ." His face flared hot, though the rest of him burned cold. "I was harvesting magic."

The boy above him was silent. *Thump thump* went Thorn's heart, and *Fool, fool* went his mind. He worried his lower lip between his teeth and blurted: "It's for wishes. This magic, it's not something people understand, so they can't access it while they're alive. So it just stays inside them, even after they die. It's a waste. So I . . . I was collecting it from the bodies. For wishes. It's what I do." Then softer, pleading: "Please let me out."

More silence. Thorn's breaths were absorbed by the coffin walls. Finally, the boy slid off the lid and opened it. Thorn blinked at the moonlight that spilled through, staring up at the morgue boy. His expression was a slurry of confusion, annoyance, and fascination.

Thorn wondered if it was enough to win his freedom. But then the boy said, almost imperially, "Prove it."

Thorn blanched. His hand twitched toward his pocket. "Why? Why should I waste a wish on you?"

The boy's eyebrows rose. "There's a guard patrol just around the corner, you know. They should be able to hear me shout for help."

Thorn grimaced, sitting up. "That won't be necessary."

"Oh, good." The boy smiled, and it offset a dimple on one side, a perfect little divot in his cheek. He stepped back to allow Thorn to climb out of the coffin, reversing his momentary death.

"What's your wish?" Thorn grumbled.

The morgue boy thought, running a hand through his thick, dark hair. His gray-green eyes took in Thorn's own hair—white, like snowfall and ash, like starlight on water. A rarity in Rastre, when most sported hair in darker shades.

The boy snapped his fingers and gestured for Thorn to follow him. Thorn glanced at the front door—too far to make a run for it, especially if what the boy had said about the patrol around the corner was true—and followed him to the desk in the back of the shop. The morgue boy picked up one of the ceramic animal figurines. It was of a little tiger, painted orange with black stripes, its eyes shining jet.

"Make it come to life?" The boy phrased it like a question, almost shy about it.

Thorn frowned. "I can't make it *live*."

"No, no—I meant make it sentient. Make it move."

All that hard work to get a wish, and the boy was going to waste it on *this*? Thorn sighed and rubbed his face, eyes gritty from lack of sleep, hands smelling like Mr. Lichen's clammy skin.

But then a thought occurred to him, and it was like opening a basement door into sunlight.

"I have a proposition," Thorn said.

The morgue boy tilted his head slightly. "Are you really in a position to be making one?"

"Look—I need a way to harvest wishes, and you obviously want some of your own. So how about we strike up a deal? I get to come here at night and take the magic from these bodies, and in return, you get three wishes from me."

The boy's eyes widened, whether greedy at the idea of more wishes or stunned by the outlandish request. Maybe both. He looked at the figurine in his hand, turning it around in his fingers. "Would this count as one of those three wishes?"

"Yes."

The boy thought some more, biting his lower lip. Finally, he sighed.

"If you make this wish come true," the boy said, holding up the figurine, "then yes."

Thorn smiled in victory. He slipped the obsidian from his pocket and felt the dance of magic inside, his prized universe of wishes, a handful of potential and possibility.

He pulled on a thread of magic, teasing it from its swirling shape and out through the glassy rock. He wrapped that thread around the little figurine, never taking his eyes off it. His lips moved soundlessly, crafting the shape and size of his wish, the parameters of its probability. The magic flared, no longer dormant as it had been between Mr. Lichen's ribs, but glowing now with purpose.

The boy gasped as the figurine stretched like a housecat and sat back on its haunches in the center of his palm, looking up at him as its striped tail swished from side to side. He lifted it to his eyes and grinned, a world of amazement on his face. Wonder, Thorn realized, was beautiful; it banished what was impossible and made room for belief. When he thought about it, he supposed that could very well be a force stronger than most things—even wishes.

He met Thorn's gaze with all the weight of that wonder. Thorn felt a quiver of it in his chest, and it was warm.

The boy held out his hand, the one not holding the tiger. Thorn hesitated, then took it in his own. They shook.

"Welcome to Cypress's Funeral Parlor," the boy said.

The boy's name was Sage. His family owned the parlor, and he'd grown up among coffins and caskets, scalpels and forceps, crystals and incense. The dead did not bother him. In fact, they were considered something sacred, making Thorn's treatment of poor Mr. Lichen all the more atrocious. Sage made him help stitch the body back up and return it to its capsule before he was allowed to leave for the night.

But Thorn returned the next night, and Sage was waiting for him. The little tiger prowled on his shoulder, occasionally batting at a curl of his hair.

"How many wishes do you have stored in that thing?" Sage asked, referring to the obsidian.

Thorn made a face. "Why, so you can haggle more out of me?"

"I think three is quite enough." He reached up to pet the little tiger, who allowed it a moment before biting Sage's finger. "Ow. No, I'm only curious. I'm not sure why you harvest them if you don't plan on using them."

"I'm going to use them," Thorn mumbled. "That's why I'm saving them."

For a wish that was bigger than any other he'd made before. A wish that in all likelihood was too improbable, a thing not even belief could conjure.

But he had to try.

Sage shrugged his unoccupied shoulder. "All right, then."

Thorn frowned at Sage's back as they made their way down into the morgue. He'd never met someone like this before, all curiosity and no calculation. Who else on earth would think three wishes was "quite enough"? For that matter, why waste one of those precious three wishes on a tiny tiger that bit you if you petted it too much?

Sage tapped the jade lantern on and lit the incense inside a thurible. Its cloudy perfume rose in thin ribbons, infusing the morgue with a dark, hazy scent, like a night without stars. Thorn caught hints of anise and cedar, and the musky, earthen undertone of myrrh.

He followed Sage to a capsule at the far end of the room. Sage opened it to reveal an older woman with long silver hair.

Sage donned gloves of fine black leather and wheeled over a tray of tools. "Where is the magic located, exactly?"

Thorn told him, and he watched as the morgue boy got to work. He was quickly bewitched by him: the focus that hooded his gray-green eyes, the steady, methodical way in which his hands worked. The tiger was still sitting on his shoulder, peering down as if it were just as enraptured as Thorn.

When the woman's torso was exposed, her ribs standing stark against the incense-tinged air, Thorn felt a curious trickle of self-consciousness go through him. No one had ever observed him do this before. Sage stood on the other side of the crystal slab and looked on just as intently as Thorn had been watching him, which he guessed was only fair.

He licked his lips, tasting the first vestiges of magic as he pulled the obsidian from his pocket. The woman's magic was weaving across her ribs; unlike Mr. Lichen's, it seemed restless, and Thorn wondered if she'd been more attuned to the secret power within her than most people tended to be. He'd noticed that women's connection to magic was always a little stronger, a little more prominent.

Easing the magic across her ribs took a few minutes. It was stubborn, but eventually it gave in and curled itself within the safety of the obsidian. Thorn stepped back and nodded, signaling that he was done.

Sage looked confused. "That's it? But I didn't see anything."

"Did you feel anything?"

"Maybe a bit of goose bumps, but it's cold down here."

Thorn shrugged. "Most humans don't know how to pay attention to magic. If you focused, you'd probably be able to sense it better."

Sage glanced behind him, at the jade lantern and its steady emerald glow. "So . . . you say that humans don't know about magic. But the stones are magic, aren't they?"

"In a sense. At least, it's the only form of magic that's readily accepted. We excavate the stones and use them for their different properties, but it's chalked up to rich soil or unique mining conditions." Thorn snorted. "If only."

"What do you mean?"

"This." He held up the obsidian. "This is what makes the stones magical."

Sage looked between the body and the rock in Thorn's hand. "I don't understand."

"People go on living with this inside them. Different abilities, different strengths." He touched his side, where he could feel his own little galaxy, warm and sleeping within him, primed for wish making. "Most don't know about it, or they can't tap into it. So when they die, what happens? They're buried in the earth. As they decompose, that magic strays from them and is absorbed into the earth around them. That's what makes the stones, like lapis for water dowsing, and ruby for heat." He gestured at the lamp. "Jade for light. They're just different abilities we carry."

Sage's brows furrowed as he thought. "I suppose that makes sense," he said after a long moment. "But if it's true, then how do *you* know about it? How come no one else does?"

Thorn hesitated. Thankfully, he was spared by the sudden growling of his stomach. He flushed as Sage gave him that dimple-inducing smile.

"I figured you might be a little starved," the morgue boy said.

They cleaned up the body and returned it to its capsule, then ascended from the incense-choked morgue to the cooler, cleaner air of the ground floor. There, Sage produced a basket from under his desk. They sat on the floor by the display coffin, and Thorn watched him carefully set out jars and napkin-wrapped foods. His stomach ached with eagerness.

He didn't want to admit that, yes, he was more than a little starved. Living on the streets tended to have that effect. Thorn had been lucky enough to find places to sleep: first a derelict apartment (which was, unfortunately, now being repaired), then the bed of a pretty girl who shared the leftovers from the inn where she worked (until she found another pretty girl who showered her with prettier presents), and now he holed up in a small office within an abandoned warehouse.

His mouth watered as Sage uncovered each item. Before Thorn could tell himself to wait, he was tearing into it all: slabs of thick bacon with mint and tamarind jellies, slices of rosewater-soaked apples, soft herb-encrusted cheese, crusty brown bread slathered with fresh butter and sprinkled with black salt.

Sage leaned back on his hands and watched him with a small smile. When Thorn realized he was making a spectacle of himself, he swallowed his mouthful and quickly wiped his fingers on a napkin.

"Sorry," he mumbled, blushing.

Sage laughed. It was a strangely lively sound for the space they were in, a clear, ringing song. He leaned forward and dug through the basket, pulling out two green bottles. Thorn perked up at the sight of honey beer and eagerly took the bottle Sage handed him.

The first sip was like slipping into a cool lake in the height of summer. "I haven't had this in so long," he said.

Sage leaned forward, resting his elbows on his knees. The little tiger was prowling around their picnic, occasionally batting at crumbs. It found a large kernel of black salt and began to play with it, knocking it about like a ball.

"The city guard's been on the lookout for a grave robber," Sage said quietly. "A boy with white hair."

Thorn lowered the bottle of honey beer and stared at him. Sage stared back. Thorn felt oddly vulnerable; exposing your hunger, your thirst, could do that to a person. But it was more than that—he was at this boy's mercy, kept safe only by the promise of two more wishes.

And when those wishes were granted, then what?

"I won't report you," Sage said, reading the despair on his face. "That's not what I was implying. I just meant that you should be careful."

"I've survived this long," he muttered.

Sage nodded. He picked up his bottle and clinked it against Thorn's.

"To wishes."

Thorn hesitated, then clinked his bottle with Sage's again. "To the dead."

It became a routine: Thorn spent his days sleeping and his nights harvesting wishes with Sage. The morgue boy would open the bodies, and Thorn would extract the magic from within them. Sometime in the night they'd have a picnic, which was usually Thorn's only meal.

Thorn also told Sage more about magic. "You've heard the legend of the titans, haven't you?" he asked after Sage inquired about humans having magic in the first place.

"They were gods, right?"

"In a sense. They were great beings of magic. One of them died and fell to Earth, and the Earth swallowed him."

"And his skeleton makes up the core of the Earth." Sage nodded. "I've heard the story."

"Well, it's not a story. When the titan decomposed, he released all the magic within him into the soil. Humans ate the plants and crops that came from that magic-enriched soil." Thorn gestured at the balsamic-glazed tomato slices before them. "The magic found a place to sit inside them, unused and dormant."

"So you're saying my garden is magic?"

Sage had told him about the overgrown garden he kept behind his family's house, crawling with tomatoes and grapevines, wild with patches of strawberry and pumpkin. It was where most of the fare for their picnics came from.

"Yes, to some degree."

Sage's eyes were wide, and his mouth perked up like a child

who's learned a secret. "Fascinating."

Thorn wasn't sure if Sage actually believed him, but he seemed happy to indulge the possibility, which was enough.

Days passed, until eventually, Thorn began to worry about when Sage would demand his second wish. The morgue boy didn't seem eager to call it in yet, content with his first wish. But it still put Thorn on edge. What would he ask for next? Something innocent, like the little tiger, or something sinister? Or maybe he was secretly greedy and would ask for money or jewels or power.

But still they crept down to the morgue and ate their picnics, and still Sage kept his second wish to himself.

They were eating sugared berries one night when Thorn thought to ask, "When did you start doing this?" He nodded toward the morgue door.

Sage licked the sugar from his fingertips. "I think I was five."

"Five?"

"It's a family business. My parents wanted me to get used to it. I'll admit, it was scary at first. I had nightmares for a while. But the more I watched my parents work, the more I came to realize it's an art. It's sacred, what we do. The dead are to be respected."

Thorn winced. What he and Sage were doing wasn't exactly respecting the dead.

Sage must have interpreted his expression. "It's not as if we're desecrating them," he said fairly, then quirked an eyebrow. "Not after Mr. Lichen, anyway."

"I apologized, didn't I?"

Sage made a humming noise and stared out the window. It was high on the wall, casting moonlight down onto the remains of their picnic. The little tiger was curled up within a mushroom cap.

"Thank you," Thorn said after a moment. "For helping me do this."

Sage looked at him. His eyes were pale and vivid, moss climbing over gravestones. Thorn had come to realize that Sage had his own scent, beneath the incense that crept into his clothes: something warm and clean like rosemary or lavender. When he stood or sat next to him, Thorn could smell it, and feel the heat of his body, pleasant after standing so long next to cold crystal.

"Thank you for showing me magic," Sage replied softly.

And then, somehow, they were crossing the small distance. The warmth of Sage's mouth on his was another reminder that Thorn was *alive,* that he was made up of so many parts, from the wild pumping of his heart to the buzzing tips of his fingers. He felt as if he had been spooled out into the universe only to come back to a body that was lighter and more extraordinary than the one before it.

Sage's lips tasted like sugar. Thorn ran his tongue over them and collected all the stray granules, and allowed Sage to do the same to him, as if they were sweet things to be savored. And then they were kissing in earnest, beneath the waning moonlight and an open display coffin.

When they pulled back a few minutes later, Thorn was out of breath and happy for it. He was dazed, drunk on the heat of Sage's mouth. The honey beer seemed flavorless and weak in comparison.

Sage watched him under dark lashes, fingers brushing back Thorn's pale hair. Thorn allowed himself to be touched and petted, distantly thinking that these same hands opened up the dead. But they were so attuned to living flesh, from the pulse at Thorn's neck to the soft underside of his jaw.

"I wish you would tell me who you really are," Sage whispered. "And why you're doing this."

Thorn's eyes shot open. Sage looked confused at his shock until he realized exactly what he'd said, slapping a hand over his mouth.

But it was too late. The magic began to seep out of the obsidian in his pocket, recognizing the cadence of a promised wish. Just as the thread of it had wound around the tiger figurine, it looped around Thorn's neck, tickling his throat with words. Thorn clenched his teeth and kept them trapped for as long as he could, eyes burning at the strain, at his inner plea of *No, please, stop.*

There was no fighting the magic. It wrenched his jaw open, and the words spilled out.

"My name is Rowan Briar," he said, his voice the monotone of one reciting information. "I come from a family of researchers who lived outside the city. They tested the properties of the stones until they realized the secret behind them. They discovered the magic that created them."

Sage knelt there, hands held up ineffectively between them, unsure how to make Thorn stop. He couldn't wrench his gaze away from Thorn's face, tight with grief and humiliation.

"They wanted to tell everyone," Thorn went on. "They wanted to spread the word. But the owners of the stone quarries didn't want the truth getting out. One of them hired a mercenary. He killed my parents."

A tear began to roll down his face, body shaking at the strain of trying to shut up. "They would've killed me too, but my mom helped me escape before they got into the lab. I ran to the city and hid, and I've been here ever since. I knew about the magic—I overheard them talking about it often enough—so I decided to test it out. I dug up my first body. I made my first wish.

"But wishes have properties, like anything else. You can't make a wish on yourself. I tried to wish to change my hair, so that it wouldn't stand out, but it didn't work. I wished to go back in time, to save my parents. That didn't work either. I wished for money, for food, for strength, and none of it came. So instead, I wished for the next body to be dug up, and that came true.

"I wanted—" His voice faltered, but the magic pressed the words on regardless. "I wanted to bring them back. My parents. But a single wish couldn't achieve that, so I needed more of them. A whole universe of wishes. I began to collect them, hoping I could get enough. And I'm still collecting. That's why I came here. Why I continue to come here."

The magic lifted from him, and Thorn took a deep, shuddering breath. The silence after his words was terrible. Sage was no longer looking at him, but rather at Thorn's pocket where the obsidian was hidden. After a moment, Sage opened his mouth.

"Thorn . . . Rowan . . ."

Thorn pushed himself to his feet. He was unsteady, his head spinning from the aftereffects of the magic. It was usually sweet, but now it tasted bitter and ashy.

"I'm sorry," Sage hurried to say. "I didn't mean—Thorn, wait!"

Thorn ran out of the funeral parlor, into the city cloaked in midnight. The air was thick from recent rainfall, the paved streets dark with water. He couldn't draw enough of that ozone-heavy air into his lungs, but he kept running, driven by a single stabbing thought: *Get away.*

Desperation grasped at him. He tripped and nearly fell to his knees. He sobbed in a breath, stumbling madly through the city and the night, shrinking away from jadelight and the sound of voices. If anyone saw him, they likely thought him drunk.

He was choked with memories. His mother's white hair in its usual braid, her dark eyes fixed on his. *Rowan, go!* Her strong hands pushing him out the window. The sound of glass breaking from within, beakers and cylinders and whatever else his father had thrown at their attacker. It wasn't enough. Arcs of blood, the thud of bodies. Thorn, cowering in the birch grove beyond the house, watching the first flames lick up the walls. Consuming his mother and father and all their work.

Leaving only him, and what remained of their voices in his mind, in the shapes of secrets and stones.

But not for long. Thorn finally reached the abandoned warehouse and made his familiar scramble through the broken planks. Up the creaking stairs, into the dusty, empty office that boasted merely a thin straw pallet on the floor, a cracked jade lantern, and a small barrel of rainwater that tasted of iron.

He fell to his knees, fumbling with the obsidian. He drew in sharp, rasping breaths, and it was hard to believe that just moments ago he'd been kissing Sage, warmth and sugar and the edge of possibility. There was none of that now—just cold ash on his tongue in the wake of the truth, and the weight of the impossible in his hands.

He held the obsidian before him. Hundreds of galaxies contained between his palms.

"I wish," he croaked, but he had to stop, to close his eyes tight and simply allow himself to shake under the thrall of wild despair. How cruel it seemed for it to walk hand in hand with hope. "I wish . . ."

He forced himself to breathe, to let the tears escape, to think only of his mother's dark eyes and his father's loud laugh, and the big and extraordinary way in which he had once been loved. The magic swirled against him, almost as if raising its head, almost as if taunting, *Yes?*

"I wish," he whispered, curled around the obsidian, his lips nearly brushing its glassy surface, "for my parents to be alive."

He waited. Despair and hope. Hope and despair. The magic swirled, as if thinking.

And then it sank back down into the rock, unused.

His universe had rejected him.

Thorn allowed the stillness to become its own living thing, a silence that was made for boys like him, with nothing and no one. His tears dried, and his mind was quiet. The moonlight crept across the floor through the window, and although it could have whispered all his secrets back at him, it, too, was silent.

His hands tightened around the obsidian. *Sage.* He had used one of the wishes, diminishing the power he'd been building for so many nights. If he collected more—if he tried again—

He eased back into motion, shedding the stillness, the silence, until he was running back out the door.

Thorn made sure to grab the shovel on his way out. The night was still heavy over Rastre, but dawn was a few hours off, and he didn't have much time to work.

He couldn't go back to the funeral parlor. He couldn't.

Even though a part of him—a traitorous, weak part—wanted to.

Instead, he took his familiar route to the graveyard, shovel slung over one shoulder and determination calcifying his heart.

Belief was stronger than wishes, and he believed that his family's death would not be in vain.

Trees blotted out the moonlight as he stole through the boundary of the cemetery. It was a verdant block within the city, a walkable path from the park. The citizens of Rastre didn't shy away from death; they didn't cart out their dead or burn them. They preferred to visit, to make outings of it. Thorn had watched families gather around tombstones and lay out offerings: flowers, candles, incense, coins, food. They would linger and sit on the grass above their late loved ones, sharing lunch and stories, their laughter like birds taking flight.

Thorn would never have that experience.

Gritting his teeth, he waded through the shrubbery and made it to the central plot. Grave markers stood in neat rows, occasionally interrupted by statues limned in moonlight. A carving of a girl with smooth marble limbs held a hand outstretched as if to tell him, *Go back, Thorn.*

He trudged into the forest of stone. His eyes swept the ground, looking for the telltale signs of a new grave: disturbed earth, the smell of restless soil and newly shed tears.

Dig it up, take your wish, and get out.

He didn't hear the rustling grass behind him. He didn't see the shadow rising up beside his.

A hand smothered his mouth before he could cry out. Another strong hand took hold of his arm and wrenched it up behind his back.

"Got you," said a voice in his ear, low and male and like the scraping of metal on metal. Thorn's eyes widened; it was a voice he associated with breaking glass and the crackling of fire, a voice woven with memories of blood and loss.

"They said there was a white-haired boy sneaking about the cemetery," the mercenary drawled. "I was about to give up, but now here you are at last."

Thorn couldn't breathe. His valor turned to terror.

But something else filled him. Not vengeance—what was that, really, but the expulsion of helplessness and anger? He wasn't helpless, and he wasn't angry. He was livid with loss, and brimming with power.

He didn't want more death, he wanted *life*. He wanted his parents alive.

And this man had taken that away from him.

Thorn swung the hand that still held his shovel and knocked the spade against the man's head. The mercenary grunted and staggered, loosening his grip enough for Thorn to tear free. Gasping for breath, he turned and finally looked at his parents' murderer: dressed in black, hair shorn close to his scalp, eyes tight with pain.

Thorn grabbed the obsidian in his pocket. "I wish—"

"What's going on here?"

Two members of the city guard were stalking over, weaving through the tombstones. Thorn cursed under his breath.

No time to make a wish. He turned to run, to hide, to do again what he'd been doing over and over for two years.

But before he got very far, the mercenary lunged and grabbed him again, and Thorn felt the sharp kiss of a knife at his throat.

How ironic, to die in a cemetery.

Before he could close his eyes against the inevitability that glinted along the blade's edge, he heard another voice, familiar and clear. It rose above the confused shouting of the city guards. It rose above the fear that he was about to die, and all his family's secrets with him.

Sage stood at the edge of the graveyard, chest heaving and eyes wide with horror. He called Thorn's name, and it was its own kind of magic.

"Thorn!" Sage called again.

The mercenary growled. The knife dug into Thorn's skin.

"I wish everyone knew the truth!" Sage shouted.

The night froze. Thorn's heart faltered. Everything turned fragile, the city as delicate as a lacework of sugar.

In his pocket, the universe of wishes swirled and lifted. The magic leaked out of the rock, up into the air, dancing and darting higher. And, like a firework, it blew apart and rained down over Rastre, sparks of glittering possibility.

Thorn heard twin gasps behind him from the guards. Even the mercenary's grip had grown slack. Thorn pushed himself away and ran to Sage, nearly collapsing into his open arms.

They watched as the guards touched their sides. There was wonder and uncertainty in their expressions. The mercenary's brow was furrowed, the tip of his knife red with Thorn's blood.

What exactly had been Sage's wish? There were mechanics to these things—there were rules. *I wish everyone knew the truth.* The truth Thorn had told him hours ago? The truth about magic?

He had his answer when the guards' eyes focused on the mercenary and hardened. They hurried forward and pinned him to the damp cemetery grass, wrestling the knife out of his grip. They claimed he was wanted for the murders of Dr. Ash Briar and Dr. Tansy Briar, and that one way or another, he would lead them to his employers.

Their words blended and lost shape in his mind. All he heard was *Justice, justice, justice.*

But the taste of it was not sweet. He was scraped out, hollow. Defeated.

Because the truth was out, his wishes were gone, and he was falling into the reality he'd refused to believe, even when he'd always known: his parents were never coming back. Not even wishes could raise the dead.

He didn't realize he was shaking until Sage wrapped him in his arms, and they swayed together. The little tiger padded from Sage's shoulder onto his. Thorn felt like a flame blown out, charred and tired, and the only thing he cared about was that the boy who held him smelled of lavender and life.

Thorn would have gladly stayed there all night, but there was a cough behind him and he had to draw back from Sage's embrace. A guard was looking at him strangely, as a dreamer woken abruptly from sleep. It was the wish; it had been sloppily crafted, and she likely had no idea why she was doing what she did. But the guard knew what had happened to him. He could see it in the pity on her face.

"Rowan Briar?"

His chest tightened. "Yes."

"Can you come with us, please?"

Sage held on to his wrist, a question and a promise.

Thorn met his gaze. "I'll find you," he said.

Sage nodded. Thorn turned to go, stopping with a muttered "ow" when the tiger bit his earlobe. He returned it to Sage and followed the guards and their prisoner out of the cemetery, looking over his shoulder at boy and figurine. Even from a distance he could read the trepidation on Sage's face. But Thorn believed that everything would be all right.

And after all, belief was stronger than wishes.

The tall, slender boy closed the door to the funeral parlor behind him, digging out his keys to lock up for the night. He didn't see the other boy across the street, leaning against the wall with his arms crossed.

"You know, you're really bad at making wishes."

Sage jumped and whirled around, dropping the keys with a clatter. His eyes widened when he saw Thorn.

"You're all right," he whispered. The little tiger poked its head out of his pocket.

"I said I'd find you."

Sage's mouth trembled, as if wanting to smile, but he didn't give in to the urge. His gray-green eyes looked Thorn up and down. Looking for signs of injury or worse. But there was only the cut on his neck made by the mercenary, and it was already healing.

"Well, it's been a while," Sage said. "You can't blame me for worrying."

Thorn ducked his head. He should have sent word to Sage somehow, but it had been a busy few days. Days of talking to the authorities, higher and higher up the chain of command until he was pulled into a meeting with the chief inquisitor, a severe woman who was now rounding up the stone quarry owners and questioning them for their involvement in his parents' deaths.

For their part in concealing the findings of the Briars' research.

Justice. It still felt like a hollow word. Strangely, he was happy for the pain of the cut on his neck, the bold red mark it made. It was physical proof that he had fought for this and won.

Sage wandered over to him, from the moonlit-drunk side of the street to Thorn's shadowed one. "And I'm *not* bad at making wishes."

"No?"

"Just take a look around."

Thorn had. All of today he'd wandered Rastre in a daze, hardly believing what he was seeing. *Magic.* It was everywhere. With Sage's third and final wish, he had unleashed this upon the city: the knowledge of what sat between a person's ribs, the swirling little galaxies of possibility. He'd seen a little girl channeling her power of heat, laughing with glee when her fingertips came alight with flames like birthday candles. He'd seen an elderly man glowing like a jade lantern. A harried mother accidentally frosting over the front of her house until icicles hung from the eaves. He'd seen . . . so much.

The result of his parents' work.

In this way, he thought, perhaps they were brought back after all. He saw them in people's smiles, in their wonder.

"And you?" Thorn asked. "What trick can you do?"

Sage took the tiger from his pocket and placed it on his shoulder, where it sat and swished its tail from side to side. "Life."

"Life?"

"My garden. My parents always thought it was odd that it bloomed through winter. I didn't think much of it—just thought I was good with plants, like how I was good with animals." He patted the little tiger's head. "I guess I was tapping into a bit of me I didn't understand." He looked up at Thorn through his lashes, his dimple returning with his smile. "Until now."

Thorn's heart beat. He was alive. The simple fact rushed through him, spectacular and surreal, like a word you say too many times until it's lost its meaning. But this, this was nothing *but* meaning, and he felt it from crown to toes.

Magic, he realized, took so many forms.

And when Sage leaned into him and their lips met, it was more powerful than any wish.

THE
SILK BLADE

NATALIE C. PARKER

The Bloom of Everdale is ready to choose a consort, and I have come to win his hand.

The Garden Palace is sculpted in the likeness of the summer star flower, its walls overlapping like petals as they curl and climb toward the center, where a thin spire of glass glitters in the sun. It is surrounded by a wide canal painted silver along the bottom to give the running water a perfect iridescent shimmer. Thin bridges arch elegantly over the canal, leading to one of the six gates that give entry to the palace, each one more delicately constructed than the last.

My invitation directs me to the Silk Bridge, and as I step onto the pedestrian pathway, I am amazed to discover that the name refers not only to the fine weave of jewel-toned pennants flying above my head but also to the bands beneath my feet. What at first glance I took to be narrow boards of wood are layers of silk pressed and bound into planks that extend the width of the bridge. For an instant, I forget my purpose here and stoop to run my fingers over the material. It is both soft and worn from years of foot traffic, while also as firm and strong as a plank of wood might be. It is a metaphor for our nation, and I am astonished at its quiet perfection, astonished to find it directly beneath my feet.

If I win the Bloom of Everdale, if he chooses me to be his consort, this bridge will be a part of my home. I will walk across silk boards, learn the layered corridors of the Garden Palace, even feel the kiss of sunlight through the glass spire daily if I choose. And I will bring my mother with me. If I win.

When I win.

Of all the warriors who answered the first call and endured weeks of trials and dozens of opponents, only three of us have been invited to compete before the Bloom. We are the finest, the strongest this nation has to offer, but only one of us is his perfect balance, the force to his precision, the protective wall to his perfect vulnerability. When this started, my mother rushed home with a flyer crushed in one fist and my sword clutched in the other. Her eyes were a little wild, her cheeks glowing as she exclaimed, "You will change the path of our family walks now and forever! Pack your things."

I'd answered the first call with a trembling kind of desperation, my mother's hopes always stirring in my heart. Now I don't feel desperate at all. After weeks of trials, dozens of opponents, and a lifetime of thin soup, I know I can win.

"Strength in the slight," I whisper in an attempt to release the swell of love that threatens to unsettle me.

"Grace in the might." The answering voice is both reverent and amused, like silk itself in my ears.

I raise my eyes, knowing my moment of admiration has exposed me as one who has never before tread so near the Garden Palace, to find a girl standing over me. And for a moment, I do not breathe.

Her eyes are a golden honey brown, barely darker than the sun-warmed tan of her skin. Her round cheeks perch above lips pressed into a lopsided smile. Only her top lip has been painted in a dark berry purple to signify she is unpaired, and I don't think I have ever been so grateful to see an unpainted lower lip. It is full and pale peach, and I immediately wonder what it would taste like between my teeth.

She is dressed like me, to boast the obvious strength of her body, as is traditional for those who follow the way of the sword. A bodice fits against her breasts and her belly, tight enough to cling to the muscles there, but not enough to restrict her movements. Ochre bands tied around her bare upper arms highlight the dip and valley of her biceps, and a skirt of flawless purple damask splits over each of her thighs, where four matching ochre bands sit above and below her knees.

With her standing over me, I forget my entire reason for being here.

"Are you lost?" she's asking, and I realize at once that she has been speaking to me for, well, I don't know how long.

"I am not lost," I say, feeling as though for the first time in my life I have found my way. "At least, not yet."

I rise slowly to my feet, noting the way my head spins. Whether it's from spending so long crouched on the ground with my hand pressed to the deceptive layers of silk or from my proximity to her, I cannot tell. Now that I'm standing, it's I who looks down and she who looks up with a squint of her golden-honey eyes that makes my mouth go dry.

"This must be your first time. Most people don't stop to bless the bridge." She says it all with an amused twist to her mouth. "Though I suppose they really should. It is a marvel. Perhaps even more so than the Winged Bridge or the Bridge of Whispers."

But not more marvelous than you.

I want to say something she'll remember. I want to make myself a landmark in her mind, but don't know how, and I settle on a request. "I think neither would compare to you. May I have your name, lady?"

Her lips part in surprise as she extends her hands to mine. "Arabeth Caswell. Rabi, if you like, lady."

My heart begins to pound in my ears. I know that name, and I wish to all the heavenly gardens that I did not. That name along with two others is written across the top of the invitation I hold: CHARLISH BLUETHORN, ARABETH CASWELL & WILLADOR MAYHEW. The names of the three warriors here to compete for the hand of the Bloom.

The reason for my visit smothers me in tight bands of vicious silk. "Willador Mayhew."

Understanding siphons the smile from her lips. Her eyes drift down my body, surely taking in the dull fabric of my own bodice, the ragged state of the hem of my skirt. I feel a familiar wash of fitful, stubborn pride as she studies me in a new light.

If she is like the others, she will take my dress as a reason to underestimate me. Usually, I encourage it, shifting my feet in a practiced gesture that makes me look smaller than I feel. Right now,

I don't know that anything could make me look smaller than I feel.

I see her take in my body and my performance, in the space of a few seconds. Then she drops my hands and says, "See you in the ring, Willador."

It doesn't matter that we were both crossing the Silk Bridge at the same moment; we are greeted and led to separate chambers, where we are to wait until the Bloom is ready to receive us.

I walk the halls in a quiet haze, all my earlier confidence drizzling from me like a sudden, unstoppable rain. My guide weaves through the corridors with the ease of someone who was raised inside them, but my eyes follow Rabi, who travels a few yards ahead, her steps measured and sure.

My chamber is the finest space I have ever inhabited, and I feel in sharp contrast to its dressings. The floors of marbled cream and icy white are smoothly polished, the furniture is carved so organically it bends around the room like thin blades of grass, and the ornamental filigree curling over the doors like tiny metallic flowers is so finely crafted I do not dare to touch it. At one end of the room, my ceremonial garments are displayed on a rack of polished obsidian. I stand in the center of all of it, a great dull stone, too unsure of myself to relax.

"Would you like a glass of water?" The question comes from the boy who led me here. He is too young to paint his lips, but old enough to have chosen the way of the flower. His dress is tied around his neck and shoulders, exposing the moon-pale skin there and falling down his slender figure like a layered water-fall. He perches atop shoes that elevate him from the ground by several inches, his toes peeking over the edge with a shimmery paint glazed over each nail.

"Yes, thank you," I say, because I at least know what to do with a glass of water.

The boy brings me a glass that is shaped like a hollow reed and contains not more than a sip of liquid, but the water is sweet and leaves my mouth with the lingering perfume of mint. I want more, but don't feel as though I should ask, so I pull in a deep breath, letting the mint open my lungs, and change into the clothing laid out for me. When I'm ready, I begin a familiar routine of stretches and strengthening poses to still my mind and prepare my body.

I have come here to win the Bloom. That is the only thought that should occupy my mind. Not the curve of a thigh between the slits of a skirt, not the pale peach of a bottom lip, certainly not the caress of an enthralling voice. I have not come here to feel these things; I have not come to pursue them. I have come in pursuit of balance.

My meditation slowly returns me to that place of ensured calm. I breathe in and out until time releases me, until I am the boulder at the bottom of a swift-running river, constant and unmoving as the world travels around me.

"Lady Mayhew." The boy's voice is tentative. "Lady Mayhew, it's time."

He gestures across the room to a door layered in delicate metalwork.

"Thank you," I say, rising from a deep squat that burns through my thighs and lower back.

I move to stand before the door, pushing my shoulders back, keeping my stance wide. And when it opens, the world before me is one I have only dreamed of.

The wide bowl of the Perennial Court is scooped from walls that are the perfect green of sepal leaves cupped around the base of a flower, while the glass ceiling is chiseled to allow light through in shattered rainbow prisms that flutter around the room like birds. At one end, the stairs of the dais unfold toward the main floor, the edges of each step curling into the next, fanning out at the bottom in a graceful semicircle. On the highest platform of the dais sits the throne blossom and upon it, the Bloom. But I am not ready to look upon him, and instead I let my gaze carry across the floor, which is covered in shimmering courtiers as colorful as any garden.

They have arranged themselves in wedges, leaving three paths between the doors of the contestants and the throne. My path was determined before these doors ever opened. No sooner has the thought occurred to me than I hear the herald announce the three of us in a voice both clear and deliciously soft. It fills the room like a song.

"Lord Bluethorn, Lady Caswell, and Lady Mayhew!"

I step into the court like the consort I intend to be, strong and bold and capable of commanding the attention of all who stand near. After enduring so many previous trials, being the center of all this focus does not unsettle me, but as I travel through the crowd, I become aware of the two figures moving down similar paths to my left.

My competition, I remind myself as I spot Rabi, her dark hair hoisted into a braided bun. It wasn't up when we met on the Silk Bridge. There it had been loose, hanging long enough to brush her shoulders and twist into soft curls by her jaw. If it weren't piled high now, I wouldn't be able to see her at all.

Which would be better. I shouldn't be concerned with her

hair. I should only be concerned with her skill.

Beyond her, Lord Bluethorn stands a head above the crowd of courtiers craning for a peek at him. If it had been he I'd met on the Silk Bridge, I wouldn't have been taken off guard. Charlish Bluethorn, who'd made himself a star in the early rounds by inviting five competitors to engage him at once and defeating them all, was a crowd favorite. I couldn't have avoided learning his face if I'd tried. But Rabi? She'd been a name on a piece of paper, a complete mystery until she'd found me whispering benedictions to the pressed silk of the bridge.

The crowd has left an open space near the dais, and as I approach the end, I have no choice but to look upon the Bloom of Everdale.

He sits lightly upon the throne blossom as though his limbs float on the air. His skin is a cool, earthy brown, the mark of the Astera region where the royal family keeps its roots, and his eyes are even darker, two deep wells. Diaphanous sleeves open around his shoulders like the thin wings of a moth, and around his waist is cinched a skirt, flowing and layered in the colors of the sunset. His upper lip is painted a pale frothy green, and the color is echoed in the delicate ties that hold his black hair in an artful tangle of loops and braids. He is the picture of grace, a flower in full bloom to the sun, open and glorious and beautiful in his vulnerability.

Six guards stand at perfect intervals around the throne, providing a stony backdrop to his radiance, and behind them the dais lofts once more. Three more steps lead to the Court of Roots, where the Bloom's mother sits to observe the proceedings. Like her son, she is a vision. Her brown skin is made darker by the pale-blue gossamer of her dress, her sky-and-stars hair woven into place with the thinnest threads of silver. On her right sits her own consort, whose story I learned when I was a small girl choosing the way of the sword. She once stood where I do now, and though she came from beginnings more secure than my own, an accident in her youth required the removal of her left leg from the knee down. She fights with and without the use of a molded limb, and I have long wished to see this woman who is grace in the might.

I stop halfway to the dais, where a podium has been placed to display a vase, inside of which stands a single summer star flower. From the corner of my eye, I note that both Rabi and Bluethorn stand before their own vases, each of us awaiting instructions.

The Bloom lets his eyes drift down the line. He is unhurried in his assessments, unconcerned by the number of courtiers waiting for the show to truly begin. Instead, he is contemplative, studious.

When he reaches me, I do my best not to look away. The consort is meant to balance the Bloom, not be subdued or intimidated or awed by his presence. If I am to take his hand, to win him, he should be just as awed by me.

I hold his eyes and tell myself what he sees before him. He sees a warrior who made it through the trials and all the way to his court. He sees a girl from the shallows, her edges rough from fighting for every scrap of food she's ever had. He sees someone who believes herself strong enough to be his balance in the world, to be the sword at his side, the blade to his bloom. I have no wealth or influence to offer him, but without speaking a single word, I promise him that what I do have will be all he needs.

The Bloom removes his eyes from me, and I feel the cool release like a cloud moving across the sun. He tilts his head in a movement so graceful I feel the power of our nation reflected in it.

"Begin," he says, his voice as light as nectar and just as sweet.

The three of us move as one, loosening the ties of our overskirts to let them fall away. We are left wearing only our singlets, the formfitting suits that hook over our shoulders, hug tight to our torsos, and cinch around each thigh to display our bodies and our strength.

I make the mistake of looking to my left, where Rabi stands in a deep-purple suit, her ochre bands like smears of spring pollen over her arms and legs. Again, my breath hitches in my throat, and I force myself to look at her head-on until my heartbeat returns to normal. If I can't look at her, I sure as hell can't fight her. And if I can't fight her, then I can't win.

And I came here to win.

A herald steps before the dais with a small paper in her hands. With great care, she raises her young voice. "Let these final games reveal the consort to our Bloom. In their strength our nation will find balance, and with balance we will endure and thrive." She pauses as the courtiers cheer their approval, tossing handfuls of fragrant petals into the air. "Lord Bluethorn will defend first!"

The crowd murmurs and rearranges itself in anticipation of the first fight. Rabi and I move into offensive positions while Bluethorn places himself between us and his podium. His goal is to protect; ours is to threaten. And while on the surface that makes allies of me and Rabi, I gain nothing if she is the one to successfully destroy Bluethorn's vase.

There are no weapons in this challenge. We have already demonstrated our skills with blades, arrows, and spears. Now we must show that when steel is not an option, we will become a shield. Here, our weapons are our bodies.

The herald moves to the lower step of the dais, positioning herself near the pendulum clock.

"Three pegs!" she announces, holding the bronze pendulum between her fingers. "Beginning now!" She releases the device, giving it momentum to travel in a slow circle, knocking down pegs to mark the passage of time.

Keeping Rabi in my peripheral vision, I circle wide, forcing Bluethorn to spread his attention between the two of us. Rabi moves in the opposite direction, using me as well as I'm using her, until we make a straight line, with Bluethorn between us.

He is tall, with muscles that bunch around his shoulders and thighs. His skin is the same pale cream as my own, marking us as descendants of the Lilia region, and it all but glows against the cerulean blue of his singlet. He holds his chin down, his face forward, as he tracks our movements from the corners of his eyes. His body is coiled and ready, everything about his defensive posture communicating sharp strength.

Rabi moves a second before I do, both of us racing toward the center. Swiveling, Bluethorn catches the vase up in one arm and spins it away from the podium just as Rabi delivers a precise kick. Her leg sweeps through the air the vase occupied a second before. The crowd gives a collective gasp, and there's a smattering of applause for the romantic nature of the rescue.

I move on instinct. Taking advantage of Rabi's need to recover and Bluethorn's cargo, I attack his weak side, forcing him to expose his back to me in an effort to shelter his summer star. He's off-balance when Rabi returns, driving him into my attacks with a series of pristine jabs. But Bluethorn delivers on his reputation by feinting toward me, then spinning around to aim a vicious kick at Rabi's chest.

She flies back, and I can't help the pinch of concern that worms its way through my chest as she hits the ground. There's no time to consider all the ways that feeling is troubling as Bluethorn rounds on me, forcing me back with his long-legged kicks.

Across the room, Rabi rolls onto her knees, one hand clutched to her chest. I drop to the floor, letting the momentum of Bluethorn's attacks carry him past me, and as soon as his back is turned, I drive my fist into his side. It's a solid hit, one he won't soon forget, but I'm on the wrong side of him and time is running out.

Before he can recover, I dig my knee into his thigh, forcing him to bend. I have him exactly where I need him to be, but before I can swing around to his other side, Rabi is there. She approaches in silence, and then the vase shatters against the thin side of her hand.

Water, glass, and a single flower pool at our feet. The pendulum knocks down its final peg. And a stony mask falls over Bluethorn's face. He hasn't lost. At least, not yet. Nothing will be decided until all three of us have defended, but he gained very little in this fight, and he knows it.

The courtiers issue delighted applause, and three young boys hurry out to sweep away the destroyed vase as the herald calls out, "Caswell will defend next!"

We take up our positions around Rabi's vase, this time with her assuming the point of defense. She shrugs as she settles into a crouch, and I understand instantly that she's hurt, though not deeply. Her eyes flick from me to Bluethorn, and I know she's thinking the same thing I am: Bluethorn will be out for blood.

I should use that to my advantage, but when I look at her, my desires travel in confusing ways. I want to protect her as much as I want to win.

You will change the path your family walks, I think. Outside the palace grounds, my mother waits for word in the Thorn Garden. She has been there since the earliest hours of the morning, afraid that arriving too late would mean a spot too far to be among the first to hear the news. Sometimes I think she's been waiting for this moment longer than I have. Winning will change everything for us, it will root the Mayhew line in the very bedrock of our nation.

"Three pegs!" the herald's voice calls. "Beginning now!"

Bluethorn moves instantly. He doesn't know or care what I will do, only that he makes the first attack. He aims low, forcing Rabi to dance away from his sweeping legs and put space between herself and the podium. Thinking the move afforded him an easy advantage, Bluethorn moves in to swipe the delicate vase from its perch. But Rabi is there. Her body arches in the air as she performs a tight flip that brings her legs slicing down against Bluethorn's arm.

It's an exquisite move, and the crowd loves her for it. They cry out and fling petals, filling the cavernous room with her name. "Caswell! Caswell! Caswell!"

Rabi hears them—there is no way she doesn't—but she is a wall of focused intensity. Her eyes remain locked on Bluethorn, but I can feel her tracking me as I circle around her side.

Bluethorn strikes again, this time with a punishing effort. Rabi dodges, deflects, and counters, matching Bluethorn's speed if not his force. The fight pulls them away from the podium, just far enough to give me an opening.

I take it, charging in, my eyes on Rabi's form.

Which is why Bluethorn takes me by surprise. His fist crashes into my jaw, neatly curtailing my approach. Rabi is on his heels, leaping high in the air to drive her own fist into his neck.

For the flash of a second, her eyes skip to mine, marking the blood now sliding down my chin, and I know—*I know*—her attack was a retaliation for me. It's over in a beat, there and gone, but it leaves me with a swollen feeling in my chest.

Bluethorn moves again, returning his attentions to Rabi. This time she swings low.

It's a mistake.

I see it the instant she does, though it's too late to change course, and now there is nothing standing between Bluethorn and Rabi's summer star.

I'm trapped on Rabi's other side, closer to the vase than I am to Bluethorn. There is only one option before me, and I'm startled to find that I do not want to take it.

You are here to win!

I drive my leg out in a low kick, nailing the podium dead center. As it flies across the room, the vase crashes to the floor. The summer star comes to rest at my feet, and I raise my eyes to find a wounded look in Rabi's. I destroyed her vase so that Bluethorn would not, but that is a look that will haunt me.

I tell myself that it won't matter when the Bloom chooses me and the line of my family is restored.

The crowd is cheering, but I do not hear the words. Instead, I move to my podium. I pause and bury my nose in the layered ice blue and lilac petals of the summer star flower, letting the lacy fragrance remind me of my purpose, then I turn to face my opponents.

"Mayhew defending!" The herald has to stretch to be

heard above the excited clamor of the courtiers. "Three pegs! Beginning . . . now!"

Once more, we initiate our violent dance. I take a wide stance, knowing that Rabi will bide her time, while Bluethorn will attack head-on.

I give neither of them the opportunity.

Pulling my vase into my arms, I kick the podium into Bluethorn's shins. He goes down but rolls with the impact, and he finds his feet as I turn to Rabi. I expect to find resentment in her honey-brown eyes, but what I find there instead is a message: *Get behind me.*

It is impossible that we know each other so well so quickly. Impossible that I know beyond the whisper of doubt that just as my desire is to protect her, her desire is to protect me. Days ago, I thought the impossible task before me was getting to this moment. Now I know the true challenge will be in getting out of it.

I curl my body around my vase and circle wide, putting Rabi between myself and Bluethorn. It's a temporary reprieve. Bluethorn drives forward, and the three of us trade a flurry of blows. I dance and weave, kick and sweep. My body absorbs fists and elbows and knees until I feel certain I have cracked a rib and more.

Then the herald's voice calls out, "Three pegs down!" and we stop.

The vase in my hands is unbroken, the flower unharmed. I retrieve my podium from where it landed and return it to its upright position, placing the precious vase on top. My ears ring and my heart pounds, and though I know the crowd now chants my name, I do not hear it.

The room quiets as the Bloom stands and carefully descends the dais on slippers elevated on spires of green glass to match the paint on his lip and the ties in his hair. He moves effortlessly, lighting before us as a butterfly graces a blossom.

All around, the room holds its breath, and I think I do, too, my lungs arrested on his glance, which is at once unafraid and approving. He extends a hand and presses two fingers beneath Bluethorn's chin.

"You fought with the might of many." The Bloom's voice is silk. It brushes over our sweat-soaked skin, our split lips, our bruises, and somehow it gives us strength.

He moves to Rabi, standing next to me, so close I can smell the salt of her skin. The Bloom lets his fingers flutter down her cheek. "You, with the bravery of legend," he says.

Then he is standing before me, and all I can smell is the heady perfume of the summer star. The Bloom's eyes are endless layers of brown, drawing into the perfect black points of his pupils, and when he smiles, I find the gray ring that encircles the outermost bit of brown. I could spend a lifetime studying all the ways the details of him come together to form this pristine person before me.

He raises both of his hands, cupping my jaw in cool palms. "But you, Lady Willador Mayhew, fought with pure devotion. You are my balance and consort, the sword to my bloom." He bends in, brushing his lips lightly over my own, and pulls away to the beautiful song of the crowd.

This is everything I have fought for. I should feel elated, relieved, elevated, and ready to assume my place next to the Bloom. My mother will never want for anything for the rest of her life. My family will forever walk a different path. I have everything I have ever needed in this moment and more.

My eyes stray from the glorious sight before me, searching

for Rabi, who is still by my side. She looks straight ahead, avoiding my eyes, but there is a tremble in her lip, and I know it is not because she wasn't chosen. Something has changed for both of us since crossing the Silk Bridge this morning.

I lift my eyes once more to the Bloom. We are locked inside tradition. This is my moment. It is my turn to accept this offer and ascend with him to the dais, where the court may accept me as the strength to his grace. Where I will spend the rest of my days at his side until it is our turn in the Court of Roots, when the child of the Bloom's line will once again choose a consort in this very room.

I open my mouth, my heart thrashing wildly against my ribs, unsure about what will happen next. Because the Bloom has chosen me.

But I do not choose him.

THE SCARLET WOMAN

A GEMMA DOYLE STORY | LIBBA BRAY

New York City - July 1897

The note, black ink upon pale paper, reads simply:

Your presence is required. The matter is urgent.

There is a time—three o'clock this very afternoon—and an address, a tearoom at the Lenox, a fashionable hotel on the east side. There is also an edict:

Trust no one. Come alone.

To be certain that the letter is indeed intended for me, I read the front of the envelope again. There is my name, inked neatly across its yellow-tinged expanse: *Miss Gemma Doyle*. And on the back, a wax seal bearing the unmistakable skull-and-sword insignia of the Rakshana.

Here at the Ashfield Residence for Women in New York City, I receive very little mail. Dutiful and infrequent letters from my often insufferably arrogant brother, Tom, back in London, where he is studying to be a physician when he is not trying to romance women far too good for him. An occasional postcard from whatever glamorous city my friend Felicity Worthington happens to be visiting, each one proclaiming her undying devotion to it, for Fee falls in and out of love with cities the way that some women change brooches. My other friend, Ann Bradshaw, has also managed a missive here and there, though her new life as a rising star on the stage leaves little time for letter writing. The bulk of my correspondence comes from my grandmama, who, in between complaining about various ailments, never misses an opportunity to remind me that, at nineteen, if I don't find a husband soon, I will become unmarriageable—though, she remarks, she isn't sure that I am marriageable at all. I am far too headstrong ("Why can't you simply smile and agree and be pleasant, Gemma?"), too freckled ("Why do you *never* remember your parasol?"), and, she fears, too educated ("Why must you *read* so very much? It's unseemly!").

In truth, there is only one man I'd wish to call husband.

But I won't think about that.

I sink down on my too-soft bed. The room's creaky corner window has been propped open with a stack of books to keep it from sliding down like a fainting dowager. The gritty city air barely moves the lace curtains; the jagged rooftops of Twenty-Eighth Street seem to undulate in the July heat. No one warned me about New York summers. I fan myself with the letter and stare at the envelope's broken wax seal. For some time now,

I've had no communication with that particular brotherhood. I've been free to attend classes and lectures at Barnard College, to read and study and try to forget the pain of the past. I have lived almost like a normal girl—*woman,* as my new friend Juliet would correct me with characteristic firmness: "We are not *girls* any longer, Gemma!" I should like to burn this letter and forget all about this meeting, but I know that I won't. Like a cat, I am insatiably curious. And, probably, like that cat, my curiosity will be the death of me one day.

I do not intend for that day to be today.

The maître d' of the Lenox Hotel escorts me past marble-topped tables occupied by ladies in puffy-sleeved dresses and giant decorative hats who sip tea and eat sponge cake whilst gossiping. It's as if I never left England: the accents are different but the affectations remain the same. Still, I tug at my practical navy dress and adjust my plain straw hat as I make my way past these elegant women and wish, for a moment, that I had something more suitable to wear. Funny how you can sneer at something and covet it at the same time. *Pay me no heed, puffy-sleeved ladies! For I am simply passing through in this sensible frock on my way to a clandestine meeting full of danger and intrigue, as one does!* Their eyes glance at me and back. And there it is: I am less interesting than their sponge cake. I should be offended if it didn't happen so often. As Felicity would say, "*Quelle tristesse,* Gemma!" I am convinced she speaks French solely to annoy me.

The maître d' and I come at last to a section set off by claret velvet drapes, and I am reminded of Felicity's tent in Spence

Academy's great room, where we often gathered to discuss our deepest secrets. Was it only two years ago? Seems ages. Behind the drapes there is but one table, and it is occupied by a man who rises, politely, at my arrival. He is tall and solidly built, his wavy blond hair brushed back from a patrician face and a long, straight nose that seems to peer down in judgment at his neat, slightly darker mustache. His eyes are a startling blue.

"Miss Doyle, I presume?"

"You have me at a disadvantage, sir. For I do not know your name, Mr. . . . ?"

"Dwight. Edwin Dwight."

He helps me into my seat and takes his own. The maître d' presents me with a menu, which Mr. Dwight waves away. "The lady will have what I'm having, George."

"*The lady* is accustomed to making her own decisions about tea," I say with a genteel smile. "I'll have the Ceylon, if you please, and the petits fours. Thank you."

"How do you know they serve petits fours?" the blue-eyed stranger asks once we are alone.

"It is a tearoom. They all serve petits fours."

He smirks. Drums his fingers. He wears the Rakshana's ring. "So, a Spence girl, eh? Fine manners, raised pinkies? And magic mayhem, of course." His bland American accent betrays no trace of place, but his air of polite condescension reeks of a certain breeding and elite schools.

"Mr. Dwight. I think it best if you tell me what this is all about," I snap. Despite the best intentions of the Spence Academy for Young Ladies, it did not succeed in making me much of one.

Mr. Dwight takes my impatience in stride. From his pocket

he retrieves a square of newspaper and slides it across the table. I unfold the newspaper, reading quickly whilst Mr. Dwight narrates the article to me—an annoying habit particular to certain arrogant men and my grandmama. Why ask me to read the bloody thing if you're only going to tell me what it says?

"His body was found near the Metropolitan Museum of Art. . . ."

The victim, twenty-one years old, was a clerk at a bank. Just as Mr. Dwight said, the man was found near the museum . . . with his heart removed. Inside the chest cavity was a feather and a scrap of pale paper inscribed with symbols and one sentence: *Think upon your sins.* According to the account, the murder was eerily similar to the murder of another man found three months prior.

"Did you read it, Miss Doyle?"

I manage a tight smile. "Yes. It's astonishing the things one learns at Barnard. I'm doing all of my own reading now. Soon I shall be able to lace my own boots!"

Mr. Dwight glowers. "See here, Miss Doyle. Both of those men were Rakshana. Two of our brotherhood have been murdered."

A flush warms my cheeks. "Forgive me, Mr. Dwight," I say, chastened, yet also angry. I am sorry for the loss of these men, but I do not care for Mr. Dwight and the organization he represents.

Mr. Dwight leans forward, lowers his voice. "Someone is hunting us."

"But why?"

Mr. Dwight twists the ends of his mustache. I can tell he's considering just how much to tell me. "We have reason to believe that these men were sacrifices. Someone here in the city is using sinister arts in order to enter the realms."

"What makes you say that?"

"Rumors. We have ears everywhere, Miss Doyle," he says rather smugly, a little power play to remind me that I am just one stupid girl with a few friends at her side and he part of a vast, shadowy organization. What I want to say is, *I do hope that you also have* brains *everywhere, Mr. Dwight.* But if I did, I feel certain that my former headmistress, Mrs. Nightwing, would reach across the ocean and give me a deserved slap for the breach of etiquette. "These men were most likely offered to the Winterlands."

At that, I go cold inside. "But Circe is dead. I saw her pass into the next world with the Three. She couldn't be—"

"Not Circe."

"Then who?"

"We've been hearing reports. Of a new Order trying to come into existence here in the city."

"A . . . *new* Order?"

He smirks. "Did you imagine yourself the chosen one, Miss Doyle? All starry-eyed about your importance? There are others who have heard of the realms and the power within them. Others who would seek out the runes and try to steal that power for themselves. Others whose mothers or aunts might have told them the tales."

"I've never encountered anyone of the sort. I would know."

"Would you?" Mr. Dwight holds my gaze until I am forced to look away. "Tell me, Miss Doyle: When did you last visit the realms?"

The question slips under my skin, pricks at my nerves.

"Almost a year, Miss Doyle. You've not been back for eleven long months."

My cheeks warm again. I busy myself rearranging the silver on the table, wishing I had my tea to stir. "I've had my studies to tend to. And it was time to allow the realms to heal themselves and let the creatures there work together. Surely as an American you can appreciate democratic ideals, Mr. Dwight."

"Democratic ideals?" Mr. Dwight laughs. "That's what we let the common folk believe. So they'll vote for whomever and whatever we want them to."

It is decided: I do not like Mr. Dwight and his shiny forehead and his oily manners. Not one bit.

"What did you imagine, Miss Doyle? That after so many years and so much fighting, democracy would spring up overnight in the realms, with a charter drawn between all the warring creatures there?" He shakes his head and chuckles, and I imagine jabbing the point of my parasol down on Mr. Dwight's expensive shoe. If I had remembered to bring a parasol. "The Winterlands still exist, Miss Doyle. And we know little of what else is there, what foul monsters populate its icy wilderness. What has become of the Tree of All Souls."

"You're being deliberately cruel!"

"No, Miss Doyle. I'm being brutally honest out of necessity. Even democracies require oversight. Checks and balances. *You* are to be one of the checks on that delicate balance."

The last time I visited the realms, things had been going rather well, I thought. The centaurs, the forest folk, the Hajin, and others were working together to rebuild the land, share the power, and guide souls across the river. But that world, which had brought me so many times of great happiness, had also brought me great loss. Trailing my fingers across the silver arch where I had visited with my mother's spirit, walking through fields of achingly beautiful flowers along the river where once we girls had ruled as queens, I thought of Pip. Of Miss Moore. Of Kartik. It was so much easier to lose myself in a philosophy lecture at Barnard or in a game of badminton with Juliet or even in a visit to Samuel at the morgue. Have I shirked my responsibilities, my duties, in order to avoid the pain of my memories?

"I'm afraid I don't understand what any of this means, Mr. Dwight." I am angry—at him and at myself. I'm also famished. Why has no one brought my tea yet?

"A month ago, we sent one of our brotherhood to find these women. This *coven.*" He spits the word, and I can only think of Miss Moore telling us girls that women with power are always to be feared.

"And did he?"

"He believed so. He sent two messages. The first was that he thought he had found them and would send word soon. The second arrived a week ago. It stated that these women were far more dangerous than we had surmised. That they were 'playing with fire' and that he feared for his life and his soul and no longer trusted his mind. The third and final message came to us two days ago." He slides over a scrap of paper. There are drawings of symbols: Birds. A jackal. A scale with a feather in one dish and a human heart in the other.

"Hieroglyphics," Mr. Dwight says as I peer at it, for, apparently, I cannot be trusted to come to any conclusions on my own; he must narrate it *all* for me. At the bottom is scrawled a strange message: *They have shown me the way. It is beautiful beyond measure. I am with them now until the end.*

"What does it mean?"

"Clearly, they've done something to our agent. Enchanted or

61

bewitched him by some occult means. This is what comes of allowing women to run things. Go on. Turn it over."

I don't like being commanded to do anything. But again, my curiosity wins out. On the back is a drawing that chills me through and through: an enormous ash tree and, within it, a young, handsome man with dark curls. His eyes are closed, long lashes resting against his cheeks as if he were a sleeping prince in a fairy tale. I feel suddenly faint, as if all the air has left the room.

"The Tree of All Souls . . . ," I whisper.

"Yes, Miss Doyle. So you can see the urgency of this mission." Mr. Dwight speaks through his teeth. All pretense of gentlemanly behavior is gone. "And that is why you will accompany me to the Rakshana. And then, Miss Doyle, you will take us into the realms, where we will assert ourselves once and for all to ensure the safety and security of that world."

"I do not take orders, from you or anyone, Mr. Dwight," I say, drawing in gulps of steadying breath. "I've had a very unfortunate association with your little club. You tried to have me killed—more than once, you might remember. That rather soured me on our ever being friends."

Mr. Dwight gives me that same condescending smile. I don't tell him that it makes him look as if he's eaten too much cheese and has a case of bad wind. Though I really want to do so.

"I thought you might say that, Miss Doyle. I've taken the necessary precautions." He grabs hold of my wrist tightly. "Don't make a scene," he says to me in a low, chilling voice before calling out, "Assistance, please! My companion is ill!"

With his other hand, he signals urgently to the maître d' now making his way toward us. A dagger glints beneath a napkin draped over the maître d's arm. I realize at once that he is also Rakshana. No wonder I never got my tea. Everyone is staring at us now.

Mr. Dwight tightens his hold on my wrist. Instead of fighting, I lean in close and whisper, "You're not the only one who took precautions, Mr. Dwight."

"Gemma, *daaarrrling*! There you are!"

Ann's voice rings out over the tearoom. Every head turns to take in the sight of one of the theater's rising stars threading her way toward us past the tables of curious gawkers and the baffled maître d'. Even Mr. Dwight is confused. He loosens his grip and I yank my hand away, out of his reach, and stand, arms open to receive Ann.

"Dear Miss Bradshaw! What a delightful surprise. And how well you look!"

"Oh, but, Miss Doyle, you are looking rather peaked! Did I not just hear that you are unwell?"

"I'm afraid it's true, Miss Bradshaw. I believe I should return to my residence at once."

Ann pats my hand. "Indeed you must. How fortunate that I've a hansom waiting at the curb. This way, if you please, dear Miss Doyle."

"You are most kind, Miss Bradshaw. Mr. Dwight, thank you for such an illuminating conversation," I say, and deposit the note he showed me into my purse, closing the strings tightly. "I'll look into the matter we discussed and send word. I'm so sorry we shan't be seeing each other again for such a long, long, *long* time."

All Mr. Dwight can do is stand at attention, like a gentleman, and allow me to leave. Arm in arm, Ann and I stroll from the restaurant, leaving him furious and utterly at a loss, which pleases me no end.

"What was that all about?" Ann asks as we hurry down the street, still arm in arm.

I chance a look behind me. No one follows. "Someone's mucking about in the realms."

"Isn't someone always?" Ann says matter-of-factly.

I look to the empty curb. "Where's the hansom?"

"I'm not paying for a hansom! Not on an actress's wages."

I tell Ann about my conversation with the overly shiny Mr. Dwight as we walk along crowded New York streets abustle with activity that puts me in mind of the markets of Bombay, and for a moment I am homesick for India and the happy family I once had there—rather, the happy family I thought I had—and a life uncomplicated by magic and responsibility. Two boys race around us like floodwater toward a man selling ice cream from a cart. The ghastly heat has everyone lined up for it.

"Do you think he's telling the truth?" Ann asks once I've finished my tale. "The Rakshana are always looking for a way to take the power away from us. And it would be easy for him to add the bit about the Tree of All Souls in order to pull you in. After all, you've no idea who drew those hieroglyphics."

"A fair point. The only certainty is that two of the Rakshana have been murdered. By the way, you were marvelous in there. Truly."

"It's good for you that our company happens to be playing New York this month. And that I received your note in time."

"Oh, Ann! I have missed you!" I clasp her hands in mine, not caring if it's unseemly to do so on the street. At least in New York, unlike London, people frown less at such exuberance.

Ann gives me a shy half smile. "You really do look well. New York suits you."

"You look radiant!" I say, and she blushes. I know that Ann does not consider herself a beauty. In truth, many would consider her plain. But when she sings, she commands a stage, and there is no one more beautiful. Even so, there's a pinkness to her cheeks that is new and most becoming. She walks taller. Prouder. No longer looking down at the ground, undeserving. "You look . . . happy," I add.

"I am." She breaks into an elated smile. "Mr. Smalls has asked me to marry him. This month. Whilst we're in New York. Gemma, I'm engaged!" She removes her glove to show me the ring wrapped around her fourth finger—a golden snake much like our Queen Victoria's engagement ring, with a tiny garnet for an eye.

"Oh, Ann. It's lovely!"

"Will you be my maid of honor, Gemma?"

"Of course." I laugh. "Felicity will be green with envy, wherever she is. Paris. Rome. I can't remember. You know Fee—she bores easily."

"She's here. In New York. She arrived Tuesday." Immediately, Ann's face betrays her mistake. She's a good actress but not enough to fool me. "Oh. Oh dear. I—I'm sure she meant to pay a call, Gemma. . . ."

And just like that, my chilling conversation with Mr. Dwight and my excitement over seeing Ann vanish like a magic trick, only to be replaced by a familiar irritation. *Bloody Fee.*

"Where is she?" I demand.

~

Of course, Felicity Worthington would take rooms at the venerated Fifth Avenue Hotel on Madison Square. Only a hotel dubbed "the

Buckingham Palace of New York" would do for our Fee. When we arrive, she is finishing up with a milliner, making final choices from an array of hats, each one lovelier and more ornate than the last.

"Ah! You're here!" Fee says, as if she's been expecting us all along. She has the audacity to be even more beautiful than the last time I saw her. She is dressed in the latest Parisian fashion, her blond hair, lightened by the sun, heaped upon her head in Gibson Girl voluptuousness. "Which do you think—the burgundy velvet or the deep green ostrich-plumed with veil?"

"They're both very pretty," Ann says at the same time that I snap, "Why not wear them both at once? Be bold!"

Fee's eyes flash. "I believe I *shall* have both. What an excellent idea, Miss Doyle. Thank you, Miss Forman," she says to the milliner, who, sensing storminess in the air, seems quite happy to take her leave.

The suite is enormous. I think of my own modest room at the Ashfield. It would fit inside this suite twice over. I glance about at the half dozen flower arrangements. "Were you planning a funeral as well, Felicity? Is that why you need the proper hat?" I say, removing my gloves and dropping them beside a vase that I'm certain is more expensive than my tuition.

"I meant to pay a call, Gemma. Honestly, I did. But none of my hats were suitable. My favorite blew off my head whilst I was boating across the Rhine. It was a tragedy. I tell you, a good hatpin is worth everything," Felicity says blithely. She bites into a chocolate, makes a face, and returns its half-eaten carcass to the box. "Marzipan. *Je déteste le massepain!*"

I exhale loudly. "Must you speak French?"

"*Oui. Je dois.*"

"I adore marzipan," Ann says, playing peacekeeper.

Felicity offers her the box and the half-eaten one.

Ann's lip curls in distaste. She picks around the mangled chocolate and takes a fresh one.

"We are not here to discuss hats and sweets," I say, dropping onto a fat, tufted ottoman. "It seems there's a crop of women here in New York who want to become a new Order and rule the realms, if Mr. Dwight is to be believed."

"Who is Mr. Dwight?"

"He's an agent of the Rakshana," Ann says around a mouthful of chocolate.

Felicity looks to Ann, then to me, clearly upset that she is not in the know.

I smile. "If you'd bothered to pay a call, perhaps you'd know more."

"The very nerve of those ladies! Well, they can't be the Order. *We* are the Order," Felicity sniffs, ignoring my jibe. It is such a Felicity Worthington answer, elitist and yet slightly funny.

"*Is* it a coven, do you think? Witchcraft and blood rituals?" Ann asks. In addition to her beloved schoolgirl melodramas, she's begun indulging her thirst for macabre tales by reading penny dreadfuls.

"I'm sure it's not a coven," I say. "I'm not even sure it exists at all."

"It *could* be a coven. You don't know everything," Ann mutters.

"What if this is another of the Rakshana's attempts to wrest control of the realms from us and have it all—as if they don't already have gentlemen's clubs and cigars and brandy and *the vote*!" Fee protests.

"That's what *I* said!" Ann asserts once more, till I fear it shall become her patented line, like Lady Macbeth: *All the perfumes of Arabia* . . .

With reluctance, I put aside my peevishness with Felicity for not calling on me as soon as she arrived and tell her of my meeting with Mr. Dwight. When I've finished, Fee claps her hands, eyes alight. "At last! A proper adventure!"

"Two dead men and a missing Rakshana agent isn't an 'adventure,' Fee. It's trouble."

"Trouble is always an adventure. I say, Gemma, you've become a true bore now that you're a university student!"

"Miss Worthington, are we certain that your presence here in New York isn't because you've been run out of every other city in the world for being a nuisance?"

"Now that *would* be an adventure!"

"You could have let me know you were here," I bark. I'd meant to keep it inside but the cork has come loose.

Felicity glares. "I was choosing a *hat*!"

"Ladies, please," Ann pleads, and it's hard to know if she's exasperated with us or jealous of the way Fee and I can fall into argument so easily, our strange little dance of friendship that leaves her on the outside.

"I suppose you've made all new friends here in New York," Felicity says whilst fluffing her skirt to show that she doesn't care, when, in fact, she does. It is tempting to say, *Why, yes, I've made simply heaps of new friends! Why, I scarcely remembered your name.* But that would be a lie. I've made precisely two friends in the time I've been in New York: Juliet Stevens, a suffragette who arrived at Barnard last year and lives on my floor in the Ashfield Residence. And Samuel Henson, who works at the morgue and offers occasional instruction in vivisection at Barnard.

"No one like the two of you," I say.

"Because there is no one like us," Fee asserts.

"Thank heavens for that," I snipe.

And then, for no reason I can name, we are immediately convulsed in laughter. We come together in one fierce embrace, and just like that, it's as if I've been wandering for ages and have finally seen the light of home.

"What do you make of these symbols?" Felicity asks, looking over the note I took from Mr. Dwight. "Egyptian?"

"Some of them seem to be, yes. Not all." I trace the outline of the Tree of All Souls.

"It could be a forgery," Ann says.

"What if it's not? What if . . . What if he's in trouble?" I say.

"Or someone wants you to believe that he is," Ann says gently.

"There is a way to find out," Fee says. "We could go in."

"Not yet," I say. How can I tell my friends I've become afraid to enter that world? That when I think of it, my palms sweat and my heart races so desperately that I fear I am dying? What I feel when I think of going back is pure, terrifying panic. "There was something about that note that jarred my memory. Do you remember Wilhelmina Wyatt's book on secret societies? Let's see if Miss Wyatt's book can shed some light on any 'coven' that might be using these symbols."

"But we don't have that book with us," Ann says.

"True. But the New York Public Library might."

Felicity crumples onto the chaise in dramatic fashion. "No. Please not that old fossil, the library, Gemma."

"No need for melodrama, Fee. Ann is the actress, not you.

69

Cheer up! Perhaps they'll have a book on hats," I say, grabbing my purse and gloves. "Let's go."

"I've just remembered that I sometimes hate you, Gemma," Felicity grumbles, and I can't help but laugh, completely overjoyed to see her again.

The New York Public Library is anything but a fossil. It is a living, vibrant thing, like being inside some time-traveling ship that is also a sea creature. A helpful librarian directs us to the proper room, and after perusing the card catalog, we find what we're looking for. Except that Miss Wyatt's book isn't on the shelf where it's supposed to be.

"Excuse me," I whisper, troubling the librarian again. "I can't seem to find this book."

She sorts through a stack of library cards and selects one, tapping it with her finger. "It's out."

"Out?" Who could possibly want to read such an obscure title?

She smiles, raises an eyebrow. "Yes. Borrowed. That's how the library functions. You're in luck, though. Looks as if it's due tomorrow. Come back then. I'll set it aside for you."

"But who borrowed it?" I blurt out.

She stops smiling. "I'm afraid that's not allowed. We protect the privacy of our patrons. I'm sure you would want the same. Come back tomorrow."

The next morning, bright and early when the library opens, Felicity, Ann, and I are there, seated at the table nearest the circulation desk, waiting to see just who will be returning Miss Wilhelmina Wyatt's exposé on secret societies, which the now-wary librarian has promised to hand over to us straightaway. "My. It must be very important," she says quietly, giving us a narrow-eyed once-over as she stamps cards with the date.

"Very," I whisper. "Why, our Kappa Kappa Gamma garden party will be simply *ruined* without it."

"I must leave for the theater by six o'clock," Ann reminds us as we wait.

"This is so terribly dull," Felicity complains in a loud whisper.

"It's only been twenty minutes, Felicity," I singsong under my breath.

"There is nothing to do here!"

I glance pointedly at the beautiful room whose shelves teem with books on every subject under the sun. "I'm sure they have a book on Parisian fashion or poisoning your enemies. Perhaps there's even one on both."

"You only pretend to be nice," Felicity sniffs. "No one knows your wicked heart like I do."

"That may be the truest thing you've ever said."

I select *Middlemarch* by George Eliot, but I can scarcely pay attention to its prose. I keep glancing at the desk in hopes of seeing our mystery reader. The hours tick by. The room is hot and still. Drowsiness sets in. My eyelids flutter. And then I am dreaming of the realms and the Tree of All Souls. That bargain of peace. That terrible sacrifice. I hear the gate to the Winterlands asking its eternal question: *What is your heart's desire?*

I snap awake, heart pounding. "What time is it?"

"Half past four," Ann says with a yawn. "They'll be closing soon."

"Thank heavens," Felicity grumbles.

"What if the borrower doesn't return it after all of this?" Ann asks.

"We murder Gemma and you and I go to Delmonico's for dinner," Felicity says.

And then, suddenly, a woman sweeps through on her way to the desk. She walks with quiet confidence. Her black hair is pinned beneath a pale yellow straw hat adorned with feathers, which pairs well with her bold black-and-white striped dress. Draped across her arm is a red cloak. Her beauty could best be described as handsome—there's a sharp, nearly masculine quality to her face and manner. Felicity sits up straight and does her best to look disinterested, though, from her frequent sideways glances, she most decidedly is.

"I should like to renew this book," the woman says softly to the librarian, setting the book on the desk. Her accent is hard for me to place—faintly British but not quite.

The librarian gestures to me. "I'm afraid this woman has been waiting for it all day, miss."

The dark-haired woman whips around. Her brown eyes widen and her mouth opens in shocked surprise. Without another word, she hurries from the room. Felicity, Ann, and I give chase. From behind me, I hear the librarian breaking the hush of the room: "Miss Doyle! Don't you want the book?"

The woman in the yellow hat scurries down the marble staircase. She is quick. *Blast!*

"Please don't force me to chase you in this hideous corset. I can . . . scarcely . . . breathe," I plead from the top of the staircase.

To my surprise, she turns to face me, allowing us time to descend. "Who are you with? Are you one of them? Where is my sister?" she demands. There is both fury and fear in her tone.

"I'm sorry. I—I don't know what you mean," I say.

"Where is my sister?"

"Your . . . your sister?"

"Yes! Where are you keeping Noor? *Noor Hassan!*"

"I'm afraid I don't know what you mean. My name is Gemma Doyle—"

Her eyes widen further at this. She gasps, and then something hard, hidden by the red cloak, pokes into my side. "If you scream or run, I will shoot. Now. Come with me."

It has been some time since I've had guns or knives drawn on me. In the past twenty-four hours, I've been threatened twice. But where Mr. Dwight and his Rakshana failed, Miss Hassan, if that is indeed her name, is winning. She marches us onto an omnibus and all the way to Central Park, where she leads us to the reservoir beneath Belvedere Castle. It would be hard for her to kill us here amongst so many people. But I must also consider that Miss Hassan doesn't care if she has an audience. The end of the pistol peeks out from under the cloak.

"*Can* you shoot it?" Fee asks with a gleam in her eye.

"Yes, I can," Miss Hassan answers.

"Before you shoot us," I entreat, "could you at least tell us who you are?"

"Miss Sameera Hassan."

Felicity introduces herself, giving her full name in the most excruciatingly Kensington debutante tone she can muster. Even with a loaded pistol pointed at her, Fee is a snob, through and through.

"I would say it's good to meet you, Miss Hassan, but the pistol makes that rather difficult. Could you please tell us what all of this is about?" I say.

Sameera at last lowers the pistol. She retrieves a photograph from her purse and hands it to me. It is a picture of a beautiful woman. Her face is longer and thinner than Sameera's, but the deep brown eyes and thick black brows are the same. "My sister, Noor," she says, a new tenderness in her voice. "She came here to work at the Metropolitan Museum of Art."

"To work?" Felicity says, as if the idea of a woman with a profession is as fantastical as the Loch Ness monster.

"Not all of us are free to visit the shops of Paris on a moment's whim, Fee."

"That would explain your dress," Felicity grouses.

"Forgive us. We've not seen each other in some time," I say to Sameera in apology.

Sameera's brows rise. "And you're *friends*?"

"We're very close. Like sisters. But more like the Borgias than the March girls." Fee gives a coquettish smile. She's *flirting*. We're talking of murder and dangerous magic with a pistol-toting stranger, and Fee is flirting. *Ye goddesses.*

"*Little Women*! Why, Fee! You've been reading! This *is* a surprise."

"Don't be ridiculous, Gemma. Someone else read it for me. I hear it's very sad at the end. I don't enjoy sadness. It's pathetic."

Sameera regards us warily. "Shall I continue? Or is there to be further tiresome arguing?"

I blush. "Please. Do go on."

"Noor attended Vassar, where she studied antiquities and ancient languages. Education is very important to my family. My father is a professor who wanted his daughters to be as educated as any man."

"Your father is quite extraordinary," I say, thinking of how Tom and Grandmama balked at my coming to New York to study.

She nods, pleased. "Yes. My family is quite . . . *was* quite wonderful before all of this."

I know what it is to watch your family fall apart before your eyes. In this matter of the heart, Miss Hassan and I are not such strangers after all.

"Noor was occupied with artifacts discovered in a recent archaeological dig. There were funerary amulets. Scrolls of hieroglyphics. Daggers and ceremonial objects. But she also found some very strange artifacts she'd not encountered before. Artifacts that seemed to be tied to some sort of afterlife or underworld ruled by a powerful tribe of sorceresses who had the gift of traveling back and forth between that world and ours. Women who could possess and wield its phenomenal magic."

Beside me, Ann gasps.

"Do you need a handkerchief for that sneeze, Miss Bradshaw?" I say with intent.

"No. Thank you," Ann says, catching my warning. Beside her, Fee's eyes find mine and look quickly away again.

"Go on," I say to Sameera.

"This was an extraordinary find, and Noor was consumed with it. She imagined an important exhibition dedicated to these powerful women who had been erased from the historical record. She talked of her work to the exclusion of all else. She began to translate a papyrus of magical rituals and spells. And there was an amulet found. Noor was familiar with amulets, of course— they offer protection, both to the living and the dead. But this was one she'd not seen before. It wasn't Egyptian. In fact, it seemed to have no known origin and could be found among many cultures—from the ancient Celts to the Mesopotamians. She sent me a drawing in one of her letters. Here."

Miss Hassan riffles through her purse. If there were a time for me to charge her for the pistol, this would be it. But again, I am the curious cat. She shows us the drawing. The symbol is clearly that of the crescent moon. The paper shakes in my hand and I hope that Sameera doesn't notice.

"These priestesses called themselves the Order." She stares into my eyes. I force myself not to break.

"Interesting," I manage.

At last, Sameera looks out at the ducks floating peacefully upon the reservoir. "Noor gave a small lecture about her findings at the museum in the hopes of raising interest. It seems the museum was not quite as consumed with the importance of these women as Noor. Afterward, she was approached by a woman who *was* very impressed with Noor's findings regarding the magical rituals and spells in the papyrus. She wanted to fund Noor's work. The woman called herself Sekhmet."

"Sekhmet . . . ," I repeat, for the name rings a bell.

"Sekhmet was the Egyptian goddess of destruction and war. At first I thought it an irritating affectation, some wealthy American woman fancying herself an Egyptian goddess. You can find bored socialites like that hosting salons and thinking themselves clever."

"We are not American. We are British," Fee feels it necessary to explain.

Sameera turns her steely gaze on Felicity. "I hope you weren't expecting a medal for it. My country is occupied by the British."

She gives a rueful snort. "The British! Always looking for another world to conquer and rule. Another puzzle piece to place into their never-ending empire."

I think of the realms. Everyone wants to rule that world, including us. It gives me pause, like a tiny bit of grit in my shoe rubbing up a blister. The realms should be self-governed, and yet, as a woman, I can't help but think that our sex so seldom rules anything. Why should the Order have to give up this power? It is an uneasy question with no answer. I can see that Felicity is about to say something we will all regret.

"And did your sister go to be with this woman, this Sekhmet?" I say quickly.

"Yes. Noor referred to herself as Bastet, saying that she and Sekhmet were two sides of the same person, and that they had grown as close as sisters." Sameera pauses, the hurt of this evident in her downturned mouth, fighting a cry. Her voice fades to a thin semblance of itself. "But *I* am Noor's sister, and I will not stop until I find her."

"Of course," I say.

Sameera regains her composure. "In the beginning, Noor sent us two letters a week. She loved her work, but she was homesick for the warm sun, our family. It wasn't long after she met her new friends that her letters became infrequent—two letters a month. Then only one, which was addressed only to me. It was strange. The writing was all over the page, as if she were doing some sort of calculations. Her own hieroglyphics. I could feel the madness in it. Her fear. She said something about these women and blood sacrifices and conjuring demons. Of reckless magic. She also mentioned *A History of Secret Societies* by Wilhelmina Wyatt.

That was why I sought it at the library when I arrived."

A man selling popcorn approaches us, tips his hat. He gives us his full introduction, though it should be clear to all that we are engaged in deep conversation and do not wish to be interrupted.

"No, thank you," I say, and wave him on, and he scowls at us and mutters under his breath.

"After that cryptic letter, there was nothing for ages," Sameera continues. "My parents wrote to the Metropolitan Museum. They told us that Noor had left months before and taken artifacts with her. My parents were beside themselves with worry and disappointment And then, suddenly, a month ago, a postcard arrived."

Sameera produces a postcard of Cleopatra's Needle; from our spot near the reservoir, we can see its sharp stone point. The obelisk's twin sister lives in London. On the postcard's other side is a brief note: *They have shown me the way. It is beautiful beyond measure. I am with them now until the end.*

A cold chill runs through me. It is word for word what the missing Rakshana agent wrote to his brothers. "And this is from her? You're sure?"

"That is her handwriting," Sameera says. "I've come to retrace her steps. And to find this woman who calls herself Sekhmet. She's the key."

"Do you know anything about them?" Ann asks.

"I know that they wear red cloaks."

I think of the red capes we wore to chapel at Spence. Little Red Riding Hoods, all of us. The world one Big Bad Wolf, ready to eat us down to bones.

"Like yours?" Ann nods at the cloak draped across Sameera's arm.

"I had this one made in the hopes that I might draw their attention somehow. Noor told me the scarlet capes were a way of recognizing each other."

"Like a fraternity?" I ask. There are fraternities at Barnard, with names like Chi Omega and Kappa Kappa Gamma. *Why aren't they called sororities?* Juliet often harrumphs when we see the sisterhoods traipsing about campus, singing sentimental songs or organizing poetry readings. The sight of those laughing girls always leaves me with a wistful feeling. I am torn between wanting to be asked to join their number and wanting nothing to do with any of it. I wonder if I will always have a foot in and out of every world, never standing in any one for long.

"The red cloaks are also a reference to the goddess Sekhmet," Sameera says. "She is known as the Scarlet Woman."

"I rather like the sound of that," Felicity jokes. When she doesn't get the desired response, she turns defensive. "Are you saying that these women, this new Order, are trying to conjure Sekhmet? But she's a mythical goddess. She doesn't exist."

Sameera's eyes narrow. "Does your Christian god exist? Do you believe there's a white-bearded man in the sky judging your sins?"

I am reminded of Miss Moore, how often she challenged us.

How often we needed to be challenged in our beliefs.

"Sekhmet is not the point. Not entirely," Sameera says. "The point is that somewhere in this city there's a secret society of women cobbling together different belief systems and playing with dangerous magic. They are appealing to forces they don't understand, forces they can't begin to control. I don't know about gods and goddesses, Miss Worthington, but magic is real. Magic exists. Both good and bad."

"We understand that. More than most," I say. "Did your sister ever tell you this woman's real name?"

Sameera shakes her head. Her eyes fill with tears again. "But she sent me this." From her hat, Sameera removes a beautiful pin, silver filigree with engraved initials: E.S. "And I feel that the letter itself is a clue. Here." She takes it out again, turns it over. The other side is an advert for a charity ball hosted by a women's club. "These women have my sister. And I will stop at nothing to get her back. Nothing. But I have heard your name before, Miss Doyle," she says coolly. "In Noor's last letter, your name was written along the side. *Find Gemma Doyle.* And now, it seems, *you* have found *me.* I can't help but wonder why."

The pistol is raised once more. Before I can say another word, a whistle, shrill and insistent, breaks the peace of the park. People scurry past us toward Cleopatra's Needle, where a policeman blows for all he's worth. A crowd is gathering, craning their heads to see, asking questions—*What is it? What has happened?*— whilst the policeman pleads with them to stand back.

Fee breaks into a devilish grin. "Come on, then," she says, running toward the others, pistol at her back be damned. But instead of shooting us, Sameera hurries after Felicity, and Ann and I follow suit.

"What is it?" I ask breathlessly of a man nearby.

"It's a dead man, miss. You shouldn't look. It's not for women's eyes."

Felicity scoffs. "We'll be the judge of that."

People shout and shriek, turn away. Others jockey for the chance to see. Policemen on horseback trot toward the lone officer, who has his arms outstretched, trying to keep order. A man near the front of the crowd breaks away, pale and sweating. "He's torn open. His heart is missing! Animals! Animals!" The information is repeated, carried through the crowd.

We push through the scrum so that we can see for ourselves. The dead man's chest has been sliced down the middle, his internal organs ripped out. His mouth is open. So are his eyes. They look up toward the cloudless sky. They are a startling and familiar blue. The dead man is none other than my recent tea date, Edwin Dwight. I turn to say something to the others.

And that's when I see that Sameera Hassan has vanished.

"I met with him only yesterday," I say to Ann and Felicity as we leave the park, which has drawn a crowd of onlookers eager to be a part of New York's latest crime. Could the murderer be here among them? I see no red cloaks.

"We've been back together less than a full day, and already things have taken a dreadful turn. I'd hoped we could do something ordinary, like eat cake," Ann says. She stops me with a hand on my arm. "Gemma. Are we going into the realms again?"

My heartbeat quickens with panic. *I can't. I can't.*

"Funny, once I couldn't wait to go into the realms. But now . . . without Pip . . . now . . . ," Felicity says out of the blue, a rare moment of doubt. She trails off, but she doesn't need to finish for me to understand what she means: everything is different. Once, we had a need for that world's magic. But our lives have moved on and become so busy—mine with school, Fee's with travel, and Ann's with both the theater and Charlie Smalls—that we've felt less of its pull. We are no longer schoolgirls. We are young women, making our way in a world that seems at best to tolerate us, and then only if we behave according to rules we had no part in making.

All the adrenaline of the past two days and from this latest attack of panic leaves me at once. I feel faint. I stumble, and Felicity and Ann right me.

"This time it isn't acting. We really do need to see you home," Ann announces just before she makes Felicity secure us a carriage.

When I return to the Ashfield, there's a note from Juliet pinned to my door.

Gemma, where are you? Marian Tortham is wearing the most appalling dress. I'll tell you all about it over dinner. Eight o'clock downstairs?
Fondly, Juliet

Alone in my room once more, I lie down, exhausted and drained. Sleep overtakes me.

In my dream, I stand again at the gate between the Borderlands and the Winterlands. The cold bites at my skin, excites my blood. The beating heart encased in bone thumps louder and louder, till it is like distant war drums getting closer. The gate asks me its age-old question: *What is your heart's desire?*

"You know what it is," I answer, my voice as bitter as the wind coming off that vast, desolate place.

The heart exhales, a small sigh that could be satisfaction or regret—which, I cannot say. I step across the threshold into that forbidden land, running through smoke until I am before the Tree of All Souls. I see through the bark into the tree's womb. He sleeps within it, curled upon himself, naked. The heart inside the

Winterlands gate beats a steady rhythm, gaining speed like war drums. The tree is *moving*. Its limbs unfurl, pushing out, racing along the ground, reaching for me. I cannot lift my feet. I cannot do anything but stare at him. His head turns toward me. His eyes snap open. They are cold and dark and fathomless.

I jolt awake to Juliet banging on my door. The light outside my window has faded to a purplish gold. Dusk is well under way. Night comes soon. When I open my door, Juliet stands outside with her impish, freckled face and gap-toothed smile. She holds what looks like a hatbox. Her smile fades. "Gemma! Are you ill? You look just awful."

"Thank you, Juliet."

"Oh, isn't that just like me? I'm sorry, pet. I didn't mean it like that."

I like Juliet. She's a cheerful soul from Poughkeepsie. "No one wants to be from Poughkeepsie," she often says in her flat American accent.

"I've had . . . unexpected visitors," I say. It isn't quite a lie. "Friends of the family."

"Say no more! My brother and his wife were here, and I thought if I had to take one more stroll down Broadway, listening to them prattle on about New York being a modern Sodom and Gomorrah and asking when will I come to my senses and go back home, I'd lose my mind!"

"What's that?" I ask, nodding at the box.

"Oh. Someone delivered this for you. I brought it up." She frowns. "But it isn't your birthday. That was June, wasn't it?"

"Yes," I say, pleased that she remembered.

"Well. Whatever it is, it looks fancy. Beautiful red bow. Or, no, what would Professor Lyttles call it if we were painting? Ruby? Crimson?" She snaps her fingers. "Scarlet! Like Hester Prynne's mark of shame!"

"Scarlet . . . ," I say. Already my fingers are at work untying the ribbon. My pulse beats faster, like the drums of my dream. I lift the top from the box and fall back, a hand to my mouth as my stomach lurches.

"Gemma? Gemma!" Juliet races to my side. "Merciful heavens! What on earth?"

Inside the box, nestled in a bed of silk, is a human heart. There is a note stabbed to it with an initialed hatpin. Gingerly, I remove it and read: *Greetings from the Order of the Scarlet Woman. Sekhmet.* The hatpin is engraved with initials: E.S.

I turn to Juliet, wild-eyed. "Did you see who left this?"

Juliet nods, frightened. "I might have? Not her face, really, but there was a woman just leaving as I came into the lobby. She wore a red cloak, same color as the ribbon on the box. And she had on a pendant just like the one you wear, Gemma. The funny little moon with the eye—say! Where are you going? Gemma? *Gemma!*"

I stagger along the hallway of the Ashfield and down the staircase, hoping against hope that the woman who delivered this bloody muscle of a gift is nearby, watching, waiting for me. Still dazed, I race out into the street. A carriage nearly runs me over. The coachman jolts the reins at the last minute. "Watch where you're going! You wanna get killed?"

My eyes are wide and wild. Where is she? The street is alive with strolling couples. Women in white dresses, brown silk. Businessmen in black bowler hats. Chimney sweeps in gray finishing up a day's work, ready for the cheer of a good pint. *Where. Is. She?*

It is not something I see but something I feel, like an invisible thread pulling my attention. Someone *is* watching me. I sense it. Slowly, I turn my head to the right, where the crowd parts just enough to expose a flash of bright color. There's a cloaked and hooded figure at the end of the block, standing perfectly still in the storm, facing my direction. And then, quick as a snake, she turns and races around the corner out of sight, trailing a blood-red swish of fabric in her wake.

CRISTAL

Y
CENIZA

ANNA-MARIE MCLEMORE

It was, of course, my aunt's idea; my mothers never would have suggested it. In fact, when my tía put forth the possibility, my mothers' exclamations of "No" were as clipped and identical as two branches snapping at once.

"It's too dangerous," my mother Lydia said.

"Do you have a better plan?" my tía asked, knowing neither of them did.

The thought had come to my tía the night we first heard about the ball. The kingdom that bordered ours would hold a great dance in honor of their prince's coming of age. The king and queen would throw wide the palace doors, including to all young women who made the journey.

It was, apparently, never too early to have their son think

of marriage.

Girls in our village spoke of all this as though it were some grand fairy tale, all jeweled gowns and candlelight. Something that had happened a hundred years ago, or a thousand miles away. Rather than a thing that would take place within days, in a land whose fields and forests ran up against ours.

I believed so little in los cuentos de hadas that any mention of such fairy tales left the taste of ashes on my tongue. Of course they did. Lately, las cenizas were far more familiar to me, to all of us, than magic.

But I had to have faith in my tía's plan. Such a grand ball, one showing off a prince to a kingdom, would be full of girls who wanted to catch his eye, or whose families prodded them into trying.

One more girl could go unnoticed. One more could slip into the palace, and near the king and queen.

Despite the stories I'd heard of half the land having blue eyes, I knew there were girls like me in that kingdom. Brown-skinned girls with eyes as dark as our hair.

The question was if I could act as one of them.

"You're talking about sending her off to a foreign kingdom," my mother Lydia said to my tía. "A land we've never even been to."

"You would be sending her to the palace," my tía said. "Not into the woods with the wolves."

"Los palacios have their own wolves," my mother Alicia said. "Plenty of dangers disguise themselves in fine clothes."

"La corrección will reach this village any day," my tía said. "That's the greater danger if you ask me."

Any touch of color drained from all of us at once.

My mother Lydia and my tía so closely resembled each

other, their skin such identical shades of brown, it seemed as though one woman was watching her health drain in a looking-glass image of herself.

La corrección.

All it took was the mention of it, and we quieted. Even my tía, as though the word had weighted her tongue.

La corrección had begun in la ciudad, with an order that all men who lived together "en pecado" and all women who lived together "in sin" be taken from their houses and matched, respectively, with suitable wives and husbands.

La nobleza had the silver and copper to pay the king's officers, and that meant being matched with men or women of their choosing, and being allowed to live close enough to carry on their midnight visits. We heard stories of wealthy couples setting up neighboring households and switching beds at night to be with their true lovers.

But us, los campesinos, what did we have to pay them with? How much corn would it have taken? How many trees' worth of lemons and fields' worth of pumpkins would have kept our family together?

"If you do nothing, she'll be taken from you," my tía said.

The words were a shock of cold water.

"You'll each be given to men who'll call themselves your husbands," she said.

The chill spread through me.

"We'll be lucky to see you for Nochebuena," she went on. "Is that what you want?"

"I'll do it," I said, blurting it out.

They all looked to me, startled by the sound of my voice. I usually listened more than I spoke.

I took my mothers' hands, my mother Lydia's right and my mother Alicia's left.

"Let me try," I said.

"If you fail . . . ," my mother Alicia said, worry passing over her face.

"She won't," my tía said.

I looked to my tía, and then to my mothers. "I won't."

Within a day, my mothers and aunt had sold what little jewelry they had—an emerald ring, the ruby from an earring that had long ago lost its mate—to buy me las zapatillas de cristal. Glass slippers with enough enchantment to sweep me from our land and into another. It would be, las brujas told us, as though the mist was carrying me there.

My mothers combed rosewater into my hair. My tía dotted color onto my lips and cheeks. They put me in the best dress they had, red satin as deep as our blood. Then they and my tía took me out into the night.

My tía set las zapatillas de cristal on the evening-cool ground. The glass sparkled like cut jewels, drinking in the moon, reflecting back each wink of the stars.

"Now, mija," my aunt said.

I lifted the deep red of the skirt and stepped into las zapatillas. Even through my stockings, the glass chilled my feet.

As soon as my weight settled into the glass, as soon as I was as still as las brujas told me I would need to be, the mist came. It whirled around me, the slippers brightening like crystal catching candlelight.

My mothers held hands, their faces pinched with trying not to cry.

89

"Come back to us," my mother Alicia said.

"Lo prometo," I said, just as the mist thickened so much I couldn't see them or my tía.

La niebla grew so solid I couldn't even see the night through it. I could barely feel it, the slippers' magic sweeping me over fields and woods and water. But when the mist finally cleared, I stood in a palace garden. Hedges shaped like swirling walls curved around me. Roses sweetened the air, damp with rain or dew.

I took a deep breath and walked the smoothed dirt of the garden path.

I paused before the stone steps that led up to the doors. The palace loomed over me in curls of granite and marble. Every buttress declared how far out of my depth I had waded. Every limestone scroll of acanthus leaves and layered flowers reminded me I was a stranger here. Even the warm spill of the garden lamps, splashing gold onto the sculpted hedges, seemed to whisper it.

Yes, there were other brown-skinned women here. But as they took their promenades toward the ballroom, the distance between them and me seemed as vast as from here to my home. Their postures were so regal they seemed to float, borne along on columns of brocade. They had gathered their hair into elegant sweeps, or left it loose and adorned it with jewels that grabbed the light out of the air.

My mothers had set mine in tidy curls, but among these women, even my carefully combed hair felt hopelessly out of fashion.

I pressed my hands to my stomach, palms against the satin. I took as much of a breath as the corset would let me.

I lifted my skirt enough to climb the stone steps and gave the smallest of curtsies to the men at the door.

One smirked.

My cheeks flared.

This was probably a kingdom where proper ladies did not curtsy to men standing sentry. I hadn't even entered the ballroom, and already I'd made a mistake.

But the man's smirk became an amused smile.

Maybe they would take me for some foreign princess, unfamiliar with the customs of this land.

I raised myself to full height, and the men opened the doors.

The grand hall unfurled before me. The dip of the staircase and the whorled gold of the banisters opened onto a floor of swirling gowns and satin waistcoats. Floral perfume sweetened the air. Couples as posed as garden statues spun across the inlaid floor, dancing to the thin rhythm of soft music.

With a pinch of recognition, I noticed the familiar lemons in the silver bowls. They were the smooth-rinded variety my village harvested in winter and sent off to wealthier kingdoms.

That particular shade of yellow, how it was the brightest color in the room, tipped me toward the horror of realizing something else.

The gowns and tunics before me had all been cast in dove grays and blush pinks, pale golds and soft ivories. The brightest skirts had been stitched in cream mint, or the demure blue of the most delicate birds' eggs.

And here I was, in a gown as deep red as my painted lips.

Back home, red was a favored color, alongside black. The dresses of any party or wedding seemed a sea of rubies and ravens' feathers. But here, I looked as strange as a drop of blood in a bowl of sweets.

Their Majesties themselves wore colors as subtle as the fondant on the cakes. The queen, her hair done up in a whirl of white, sat on her gilded throne in a gown of pale rose. The king, on his nearly matching throne, had donned a coat as silver as his hair.

I set my hands on the bodice of my dress and breathed.

All I had to do was beg an audience with them. Surely they would consider allowing a place in their kingdom for families torn to pieces by la corrección; they must understand our hearts a little. Their son, the prince, had been christened a princess at birth, but when he declared himself as the young man he was, his mother had taken on the task of choosing him a boy's name with all the reverence of planning a mass. This very ball was meant to celebrate not only his age but his introduction to the kingdom with his true name.

I raised my skirt enough to mind my feet, careful of las zapatillas de cristal.

On the last stair, I eased my weight down slowly, as though too heavy a step might crack the glass.

When I lifted my eyes, they found a gold waistcoat, the color of candle glow cast on snow.

A young man with hair as dark as his eyes offered his hand.

"I'm sorry," I said, stalling. "I don't know these dances."

"If you don't mind letting me lead," he said, "I think you'll find them easier than they look."

My eyes drifted to the king and queen.

What good would it do to offend this young man? By the way he was dressed, he was probably the son of some favored noble family. Maybe by dancing with him, I could even make myself seem less a girl who came wrongly dressed and more a mysterious stranger. Someone who belonged here.

Someone the guards would not throw out before I'd said my piece.

I held my skirt and curtsied to the young man. I stepped close enough for him to take my waist, and he swept my red skirt into the whirl of cream and pale blue.

He smelled so much like my mothers' campanillas—the vines, not the flowers—that I had to try not to shut my eyes and fall into the scent. His lead kept me from colliding with the other girls. He took the cue of my body when I wanted to widen the distance between us, adjusting the frame of his arms, and when I drew in, each time pretending it was accidental.

For the first turns of the music, I worried that las zapatillas would crack under our steps. But the glass felt light on my feet, and strong as diamonds.

I opened my eyes just as we swept by another couple. They brushed so near that I startled, the bodice of my dress falling against the young man's chest.

"I'm sorry," I said, instinctively looking to see if the red fabric had somehow left a stain on the pale gold.

For the first time, the contour of his chest struck me, the shape beneath the heavy embroidery.

"You're worrying me," he said.

My eyes leapt up to his face.

He glanced down at his front. "Have I spilled something on myself?"

"No." I lowered my head. "I'm sorry. I didn't mean to stare."

His laugh was small but good-natured. "I'm used to it."

The heat in my cheeks rose to my forehead.

His smile stayed. "Whatever it is you're wondering, you can ask me."

I tried not to look at his chest. "You don't bind yourself?"

"Only if I'm riding," he said. "And then only because it hurts if I don't." He winced, and I imagined the pain of riding out with my breasts free, the soreness afterward.

"Is that the way here? For"—I stumbled as I tried to finish the thought—"everyone like you?"

He laughed again. "There is no one way for everyone like me. Some of us bind; some of us don't. Some wear one kind of clothing; some, all kinds."

Envy fluttered through me. I couldn't imagine growing up in a kingdom where a single person would be allowed to wear a dress one day and trousers the next, where a boy like the one before me could let the shape of his chest show and still be acknowledged as the boy he was.

I drew myself back to the present moment.

"And you?" I asked, grasping at the easiest change of subject.

"I mostly wear the clothes my father wore at my age," the young man said.

"Was this his?" I traced my fingers over his sleeve. I tried to make the gesture airy and flirtatious, like those of the women around me, but I only felt ridiculous.

The young man nodded once. "From one of the first balls he attended."

As though to save me from my own attempts at charm, a tall figure in pale blue stopped alongside the young man.

"Your Highness," he said, "Her Majesty wishes a word."

"Forgive me." My dancing partner—His Highness?—kissed my hand. It was quick and light enough that it seemed more out of custom, a habit of politeness, than any kind of overture.

But I stood, silenced by that press of his mouth to the back of my hand.

I had been dancing with *His Highness*?

This was a kingdom where His Highness could choose not to bind his chest?

I could almost imagine my tía pinching my arm, telling me not to show myself as una campesina. If I wanted to be believed as a girl who belonged here, I needed to stop gawking at everything. I needed to stop gazing upward at the blue-painted ceiling set with gold stars. I needed to stop staring like a girl who had never seen a handsome young man before, and worse, a country girl who didn't recognize the royal cloth of the prince's coat.

And if I was going to gather myself enough to beg an audience with Their Majesties, I needed air.

I set myself toward the garden doors. The pinprick nervousness of having been so close to the prince lingered.

It mixed with the terror of holding my family's fate.

The air through the open doors washed the heat from my face. It brought the kiss of night flowers and the clean smell of the moon.

"I suppose there's no accounting for taste," came a voice as tart as a green apple.

My pride rose to meet her tone. It broke through the brittle shell of fear between my dress and my skin.

"Do you mean *my* taste," I asked, glancing first down at my dress, then into the ballroom, "or his?"

A woman, younger than my mothers but not by much, stepped

into the light of a garden lamp. The yellow of her hair matched the shade of her gown.

She surveyed my gown, and suddenly it felt pieced together from scraps of ribbon.

"You're one of these country people fleeing into our kingdom, aren't you," she asked. It was worded as a question without being spoken as one.

I lifted my chin, meeting her eyes.

"Oh, calm yourself." She let out a tinkling laugh as she set a wineglass to her lips. "I have a proposition I think you'll like."

I didn't reply.

She seemed undeterred.

"The first thing you should know is that the true currency of court is not money, but favors." She took another sip of wine. "And I would call in a few I'm owed to ensure your family's lawful place in this kingdom. That is, should you decide to do a favor for me."

My throat tightened. "What would you want from a country person?"

I wanted my voice to match hers, as brisk and sour as an underripe plum.

"The prince seems taken with you," she says.

I bristled at how wrong she was. The prince had chosen to dance with a girl who seemed ill at ease. He had been kind, not interested.

"All you need do is dance once more with him," she said, "let him say whatever ridiculous things boys his age come up with, and then"—she waved a ring-jeweled hand—"let's say at midnight, when everyone is still here to witness it, flee from him, and the palace, and never see him again."

I should have been flattered that she was so threatened by

a single dance that she couldn't wait to be rid of me. Did they believe such cuentos de hadas in this kingdom? Stories of princes gazing across ballrooms and falling, instantly, in love?

Maybe it was something smaller and sharper than that.

Maybe this woman simply couldn't stand having her kingdom's prince near a girl like me.

It was a tiny mirroring of la corrección.

As tolerant as la nobleza seemed to be of a prince who had once endured a wrong name and now had a true one, a prince who did not bind his chest under his shirt, maybe that was all it was beneath the polite posturing. Tolerance. A begrudging acceptance. They probably considered him unusual enough (and they probably would have used a word like that too—*unusual,* said with a mild sneer). It would be too much for them to see the prince also show interest in a brown-skinned girl who did not know better than to wear a red gown.

What this noblewoman asked was not meant to dissuade him from wanting me. It had little to do with me, and more with what I was.

What this noblewoman asked was meant to show the prince that girls like me were inconstant, deceitful, cruel even.

And it was meant to cure him of any interest in us.

"But how would any of that help you?" I asked. There must have been more than her wanting to give the prince a morality lesson.

"I don't see how that's your business," she said.

"It is if I'm putting my family's survival in your hands," I said.

Something glinted within her, like the edges of the jewels at her neck.

Respect, in some small measure.

She inclined her head toward the glow of the ball.

"My daughter"—she gestured a delicate hand toward a girl in an ice-white gown—"she would make a fine princess, don't you agree?"

The girl had the willfully bored look of so many noble daughters. She was sighing and glancing around, as though waiting for some signal that would allow her to leave.

"And how would this help her?" I asked. "Even if I'm gone, I'm sure there are dozens of other girls waiting."

"A little heartbreak at just the right moment can be good for a man," the woman said. "It can bring on an instinct to settle down. And if I know the moment that instinct is to come, how much better for me and my daughter? While so many other girls who would love to be princesses are standing around being sour about you, my daughter will be patient, and ready."

A small protest bucked within me. Not so much the thought of being used by la nobleza; la corrección was proof that the nobility of my kingdom used its own just as thoughtlessly.

It came more from the idea of leaving this cut on the prince's heart. Not because I owed him anything. But because he seemed the kind of prince who would never let la corrección stand in his own kingdom.

My hesitation sank beneath all I would gain. Safety for my family, without ever having to approach the king and queen. Because who knew if that would come to anything anyway? I could so easily err in my speech and ruin the only chance my family had.

No. This was the way of the world, how things came to be. Not by kneeling before sovereigns, but by small bargains made, with those who wanted what little I had to give.

"And what assurance do I have that you'll keep your word?" I asked.

"A very simple one," the noblewoman said. She did not seem insulted. "I need you to remain vanished forever. Never approach the palace or the prince again. If I should fail my side of the bargain, you wield the threat of reappearing. And should you reappear . . ." She inclined her head.

I caught the edge of the threat, like knocking my hip on the corner of a table.

On her way back toward the doors, the woman eyed the glittering glass on my feet. "Lovely shoes."

Later, when the prince approached me again, my guilt was weighing down las zapatillas de cristal. But I let my skirts sweep over it as he drew me into his arms.

And I trod it down when, at the clock's twelve chimes of midnight, I slipped from our dance and dashed from the ball.

I sprinted for the garden doors, the thought of my family humming in my chest. Yes, we would live as strangers in this kingdom, but we would live, together, free from la corrección. I would bring the news home, and it would burn bright enough to keep the shame of my own cowardice off my skin.

It blazed enough to lessen the sound of the prince calling after me.

I made my heart as solid as the glass on my feet, so I would not hear him.

It would be better this way, whether the prince knew it or not. He needed to glance less at girls like me. How much better would the noblewoman's pale daughter, in her pristine gown, look on a prince's arm?

All I had to do was get far enough into the garden that I wouldn't be seen. I couldn't risk anyone watching me stand in las zapatillas de cristal, a swirling mist enveloping me. They might pull me from it before the magic could carry me off. Where I came from, we revered las brujas, but so many lands considered *witch* a condemning word, and I did not know if this was one of them.

The outside lamps gilded my skin and turned my dress to deep amber. They lit the bursts of roses and neat lines of bulb flowers.

But they did little to show the way out of the maze of hedges. Each tunnel of green looked the same as the one before.

My next step caught on a root, and I felt a sharp giving-out beneath me. It came with the sound of splintering glass. I fell forward to my knees, fine dirt paling the red of my skirt.

I twisted to inspect las zapatillas de cristal.

One of the heels had broken off, leaving a clear, jagged knife behind. The other had a deep crack through the arch that might break the slipper in two if I put more weight on it.

I slid out of las zapatillas de cristal. I chose a path and kept on in my stockings, the broken slippers in my hands.

The leaves flew by. Branches brushed my shoulder and scratched my arms.

I took the dark bend of a corner, and the sight of tulle and satin halted me.

At first, the scene before me gave the effect of a lovely and enormous dessert, an adorned cream puff. A frosted cake set in a nest of fairy floss. It was as though the confections from the ball had come to life and gone out to roam the gardens.

My eyes adjusted to the faint light.

A white gown.

A skirt the color and texture of a storm cloud.

A head of blond.

A braid of brown.

The noblewoman's daughter, the one she wanted to throw into the prince's arms.

She was in the cool darkness of the hedges, kissing a dark-haired girl in a dove-gray gown.

I stilled my breath so they wouldn't hear me.

The way they kissed was so gentle and so fierce that I lifted my fingers to my own lips.

As I stood in the tulip-scented air, I thought of my mothers at this age, the age of these girls, the age I was now. How my mothers, too, had once hidden in the shadows of leaves. Yes, those leaves had trembled from ahuehuete trees and not from hedgerows, but in this light, they were closer to these girls than I ever would have noticed in daylight.

The thought opened into another, of all those who could meet only at night.

Of all the families la corrección rended like worn fabric.

Of the villages where families like ours resisted, their homes burned down to ashes.

I couldn't usher my own family into the safety of this kingdom's borders and think nothing for those left after us.

The deepening of the girls' kiss thickened the guilt in me, until it grew into a current and became something else.

Resolve.

Nerve.

Will.

Las zapatillas de cristal knew my heart better than I did. They had stopped me from fleeing back into their mist.

They had brought me to the palace gardens, and now they would make me carry myself the rest of the way.

I left the enchanted glass beneath one of the hedges.

In my dirt-dusted stockings, I wound back through the hedge tunnels, back past the bulb beds, into the flow of light from the ballroom.

I lifted my skirt so I could dash up the stairs.

I burst through the garden doors.

The ball quieted.

The prince stared at me, looking as breathless as I felt. His gaze pinned me where I stood.

Seeing that kiss in the garden made my lips hot with wanting to be against his, to know what it might feel like. But I folded that thought into the bodice of my dress.

I walked to Their Majesties' thrones, the crowd's surprise opening a path for me. The king and queen were on their feet, talking to guards, who, for all I knew, were moments from being dispatched to look for me.

I curtsied as though they were seated to receive an audience. I dropped into a bow so low it set my knees against the marble floor. My skirt billowed around me like the cap of a milk mushroom.

"Your Majesties." I lowered my head, both in respect, and so, whatever their expressions, they would not unnerve me. "I come here from a land that is being torn apart by what men in power think we should and should not be." My heart beat in my neck like a moth in a jar. "My mothers live in fear of me being taken from them, and them being taken from each other. Our friends face the choice of losing their lovers or their lives."

My skirt settled to the floor.

"We beg your help," I said.

We. The word came out of me, slipping in place of any *I.*

"We beg you to open your kingdom to us." I took a few breaths to get the air I would usually get from one. "We are hard workers. We keep at our crafts and our fields as though tending to our own bodies. Everyone like us, we will bring more to your kingdom than we will take from it."

I meant it as truly as my own name. I would have staked my life on the trueness of those I came from, people la nobleza saw to be nothing more than nuisance.

I could feel the noblewoman's glare, and the glare of so many others, on my back. They mixed with the puzzled interest of the rest.

Enough silence passed that my own curiosity lifted my chin.

The king and queen were looking not at me but at each other. The consideration on their faces seemed like a silent conversation between them.

I held my breath until the queen moved her attention to me.

"There will come a day when all such decisions will fall to our son." She cast her eyes to the prince. "And it's never too early to see how well he takes them in hand."

The stares of the ballroom met at the young man in the gold waistcoat.

Panic took hold of his expression for only a second before he regained the composure of a prince.

"I think we must ask the opinion of everyone here," he said.

Confusion crossed his parents' faces.

Rage-tinted frustration bubbled up in me. Was this the way of this kingdom? Kings and queens passed the burden to princes, and princes passed it on to la nobleza?

"If it were your own mothers," the prince said to everyone in the ballroom, "your own fathers, your own siblings, your own children, if you would have a kingdom bar their doors to your own in their hour of need"—he seemed to eye each of them at once—"then please"—he gestured as though to offer the floor—"let us hear your objections."

My breath caught.

His words were as neatly forged as the gold of a crown.

The guests, with their damask and wine, stood silent.

The pride on the king and queen's faces brightened the glow in the hall.

The prince looked to me.

Go, he mouthed without sound.

Thank you, I said just as silently.

Relief and sadness crowded my heart. I had done what I thought myself too small to dare. But to this young man I had danced with, this young man who had stirred in me the slightest measure of how my mother Alicia looked at my mother Lydia, I would never again be seen as anything but la campesina. I was nothing more than the simple country girl who had snuck into the palace for an audience with his mother and father.

He would never know me, and I would never know him, beyond tonight.

I shored up the crack in my heart. I let myself sink into the knowledge that I would forever be grateful to the prince, from this moment and into the years after he was crowned in his father's place.

Guards led me to the stable. Grooms lent me boots for riding.

They showed me to a mare who let me approach her in a way that spoke of her tameness, but who breathed in a way that signaled how ready she was to run.

A pair of heavily gloved hands helped me up into the embossed saddle.

I looked to the groom to say my thanks.

A familiar face caught me, along with the green smell of campanilla vines.

He wore the plain trousers and tunic of a rider, his chest bound underneath.

The prince set a hand on the mare's haunch. She turned her head as though greeting him.

His eyes shone in the dark.

"If you'll let me go with you . . . ," he said.

The glint to him was different than by the ballroom's candle-light. Here, in the blue dark, it was more pain than mischief.

"I know it's your home." He cleared his throat, as though the words came hard. "But they're my family too. All those like us, we belong to each other."

My own throat clenched.

I lifted his hand to my mouth, pressing my lips to his fingers, the closest to a yes I could manage.

He understood, giving me a slight nod as he pulled himself onto a gray stallion.

And we rode out into the dark, toward everyone we called our own.

LIBERIA

KWAME MBALIA

If I could do one thing over—if I had one opportunity to correct a mistake or right a wrong or fix a problem—I would ask Nana Gbemi if fufu should be pinched off or twisted off. She'd taught me the recipe on my seventeenth birthday. The best going-away/birthday gift I'd ever received, since she holds on to recipes like she used to hold on to my ears when I got in trouble.

"Kweku?" A gentle clap on the shoulder accompanied the question. "You all right?"

I shook myself out of my memories. The ship's ancient lift groaned to a halt at the Science and Research module. This was my stop. I smiled wearily at the older boy staring at me with concern.

"Tired, Tomas. Tired. Reran those numbers for the colony

food budget. Took way too long." A yawn split my words as if to punctuate my point. "Need to check on the babies before I crash—if I can get in my office. The door's been acting up."

Tomas flashed his trademark grin—all gold teeth and dimples framed by a smooth brown face. He gestured at the lift. "Good luck, bro. This whole ship's been acting up. I'd help, but Hustlin' Harry wants another run-through on the drop-ship landing."

Harold Bolaji, our leader and mentor, and the ship's captain, earned his nickname when he famously worked three straight shifts trying to retrofit the ship's filtration system with "improved adsorption purifiers." Rumor has it he hated the lingering odors after the cafeteria's Fish Frydays.

"Again?" I asked.

Tomas nodded. "He wants to be absolutely certain the 'process proceeds propitiously,' or whatever he says."

"I guess. Don't pull an all-nighter—we need you for loading tomorrow."

"If Harry doesn't want to do another inventory count, sure. Otherwise—" He shrugged, the universal sign for *Harry's going to be Harry,* then changed topics. "How's Nana?"

I tensed. At first, I thought he meant my grandmother, but then my shoulders relaxed. No one knew how the unofficial name for my project first came about. One day it slipped into a conversation, it felt right, and so it stayed.

"Fine. Should be ready once we touch down."

"Glad to hear it. I—"

"Tomas, Harry." The hail came through fuzzy and distorted on the general line. Tomas sighed and fiddled with the old comm system clipped to his belt. I snorted, and the older boy glared at me as he played with the dials. Eventually he got the system working and cleared his throat.

"Tomas here."

"Run-through's in ten. You see Kweku?"

Tomas glanced up at me. "Not since this morning."

I mouthed *Thank you,* and he rolled his eyes.

"Well, if you do, tell him I need those numbers run again—they're too high. And tell him to come to the run-through once he's done."

I pinched the bridge of my nose.

"Roger. Tomas out." A frown crossed his face as he disconnected. Tomas patted his pocket, then reached in and pulled out a thin, twisted piece of metal. "Here."

"What's this?"

"Your door isn't the only one acting up. Francis and I had to break into our room a few days ago. Papi taught me how to make these when I was little. 'Papi's Last Resort,' he called them."

I took the lockpick and grinned. Tomas's grandfather was nothing if not a scourge on the elderly community he stayed in. The thought of the tiny old man clothed in nothing but a too-short bathrobe playing cat burglar pulled a chuckle from me. Tomas grinned. No doubt the same image played in his mind, but too quickly my grin faded and I sighed.

"He would've loved the colony. My nana too. The real Nana," I added for clarification. I fiddled with the lockpick. "Do you ever—"

"Wish we could've brought them along?" he finished for me. "All the time. Every single day. But their bodies couldn't handle the strain. Neither could our parents'. Ours barely can. You know that. And they knew that even while they helped us build and grow the things the colony needs."

"Yeah," I said, my thoughts a thousand light-years behind us. "Yeah, I know."

The thought of those we'd left behind put a somber mood on the conversation, and so it ended. I got off the lift, each of us departing to handle our respective tasks. Overwhelming tasks to be sure, but these days if it wasn't overwhelming it wasn't important.

"Authorize," I said as I entered the outer room of my laboratory. The dry automated voice of the ship's virtual assistant filled the room as I quickly stripped out of my uniform and into a clean pair of scrubs.

"Kweku Aboah, age seventeen, ship's acting research officer, *Liberia,* Black Star Line. Authorization complete. Welcome back, Kweku."

Liberia.

The first and greatest colony ship, the sweet chariot that swung low and carried us home, the mule that pulled us to our proverbial forty acres.

Liberia.

It was still surreal, even now, seventy-five years after the first wave of settlers arrived in the Colonies. Yet this would be the last voyage this ship would make before being retired, carrying the youngest generation possible, the teenagers who would grow to be the scientists, the doctors, the engineers, to push the Colonies into the future.

Liberia.

I smiled. The name was fitting.

The outer door shut, and the sterilization process began.

Several minutes later the inner door hissed open, and I stepped into a different world.

Sweet, rich, earthy scents pulled me deeper into the laboratory, past hanging vines of kudzu creeping up the walls, around the obstacle course of floating herb pots humming waist-high off the floor, and through fingerlike tendrils of bean plants dangling from the ceiling. But it was the bed of earth stretching across the floor that called to me.

Rows and rows of chest-high cassava plants lined the laboratory, their stems standing rigid and tall. Broad green leaves twice the size of my hand stretched to the artificial ceiling light and rustled beneath the recirculating air. I held out my hand to brush against them and inhaled.

In the far corner, more than twice as tall as the others, stood a single cassava plant. Deep green leaves the size of my arm fluttered in the manufactured breeze, and the thick stem dropped ramrod straight to a wide patch of soil all its own. Beneath it spread a tuber-and-root system that arched out of the soil like leaping dolphins frozen in time.

"Nice to see you again, Nana," I murmured.

It was magnificent and by far my favorite place on the ship, though I needed to do one thing before working in my sanctuary.

"Secure," I called out.

"Outer door locked. Inner door locked. Laboratory secured." The voice came from a speaker somewhere off to my right, though it was probably covered in kudzu now. I nodded—as if the AI could see me—and then slipped off my thin, gauzy gardening slippers. My toes stretched and wiggled, as if knowing what came next and too eager to remain still, and I stepped forward into the loamy earth.

My feet sank into the cool soil, and with one deep breath all of the day's stress and confusion leached out of me, as if the garden needed it for nourishment, when in fact I needed it for my sanity.

"Skip to next recording," I said after several seconds of restorative breathing.

"Current recording not complete—would you like to finish?"

I must have paused it during the last whole ship power interruption. "Yes," I answered before dropping to my knees to examine the leaves of a stunted plant below me.

"Playing."

The voice stopped, then a popping, crackling, hissing sound filled the lab as I began to weed. It carried on for several seconds before another voice, a woman's voice, loud and deeply accented, started speaking.

"Look here. If you don't lissen to one thang else, you lissen to this: Ain't no village without the harvest. And ain't no harvest without the village. You understand? You can't do this thang by yo'self."

I listened to Nana Gbemi's words as I moved down the rows of cassava plants, pushing fertilizing beads down to the tubers and pruning wilting leaves.

"Yo' bent back is all you can control. Can't control the sun. Can't control the rain. Can't control any of that 'cept for yo' fingers and yo' back. Work, and work hard, and know that when the time comes help will arrive. Why—"

Two loud beeps cut through the recording.

"Kweku, it's Jen." The ship's pilot sounded apologetic. "Harry's looking for those revised food budget numbers."

I closed my eyes. "Yep, I'm on it, Jen. Thanks for checking, though. Tell Harry I'll bring them up in the morning."

"You might want to bring them up tonight." Her voice dropped to just above a whisper. "He's been hovering around me for the last half hour during run-throughs, and I can't take much more."

"Why doesn't he—" I began, then inhaled and counted to five. "You know what, never mind. I'm on my way."

"Thanks, Kweku. And I'm sorry." Jen signed off, and I sighed, staring at my dirt-covered hands. After some time I brushed them off on my scrubs and headed back out to the office.

"*Liberia,* rerun Resource Analysis on current projected yields," I said.

"Existing parameters found. Would you like to revise them?"

I stared at the garden that took up most of the space in my lab—an acre's worth of crops stuffed into what once was the lower level of *Liberia*'s holds, now repurposed as the Science and Research module. I stared at the young plants propagated from Nana, the giant cassava cared for by dozens of others in preparation for this moment. I imagined Nana Gbemi showing me how to harvest the tubers without damaging the roots, with my mother crying softly in the corner when we found out I was selected for the journey. I imagined the thousands of faces gathering at the landing site on the colony. Eager, hopeful faces.

"Existing parameters," I said. I couldn't justify lowering the colony's requirements. I just couldn't.

I stripped and put back on my uniform and removed most of the dirt from beneath my fingernails. Every movement seemed to require three times as much energy, and I grabbed a coffee cube from my stores. Any help right now was appreciated.

"Analysis run. Verbal or hard-copy report?"

"Hard-copy."

"File transcribed."

A small disk popped out of a slot on my desk and I tucked it into my pocket before heading up to see the boss.

The lift shuddered its way up to the command deck. I gripped the railing tight as the lights flickered and the ancient system groaned past each floor. *Someone should really take a look at this thing,* I thought, resolving to mention it to Sirah. Then the doors opened, and I immediately forgot about it.

Everyone stood or sat around the various instrument panels in *Liberia*'s center of operations. The equipment, like everything else, was outdated, but it gleamed like fresh polish. Jen, a tiny caramel-skinned black girl with freckles dotting each cheek, took great care of her domain. We'd been in the same orbital piloting class when we found out we'd miss the rest of school to train for operating *Liberia,* and the fierce determination she constantly wore on her face powered me through our exercises too. Now she just looked irritated at the impromptu gathering cramping her workspace.

"We have to do better," Harry said as he stomped around the pilot console, carving a path through the gathered personnel like rapids through a canyon.

I slipped into a space against a panel next to Francis and Tomas. Tomas scrunched up his nose and leaned into his boyfriend's chest and away from me.

"You smell like the business end of one of those old plows."

I tilted my head. "Weird . . . I *am* really close to a horse's ass right now."

Francis snorted back a laugh, and Tomas straightened up and glared at him. "Oh, that's funny to you?" Tomas said. But Francis pulled him back close, and I chuckled at the two of them. Harry heard the disturbance and squeezed his way back toward us.

"Kweku," he barked. "Where were you?"

"Uh-oh, here we go," Tomas murmured.

Tall and thin with black skin that glittered like the star-filled space we traveled through, Harry was the oldest of us all. Our fearless eighteen-year-old captain wore his full harness and carried his helmet beneath his arm. He chewed gum as if it single-handedly kept him alive. He blew a bubble—defeating the fierce image he tried to cultivate—and folded his arms.

I held up the disk. "You wanted to see the numbers?"

"No, I wanted to see those five hours ago—I wanted to see you here ten minutes ago. You missed the drop-ship run-through. Again."

"Well, I have the numbers, Harry, and"—a huge yawn slipped out between my words—"besides, everyone's exhausted. We need to sleep."

"Sleep?" He looked incredulous at the thought. "Sleep? You can sleep when we land. Until then everything has to run smoothly."

"What about your crew, Harry?" I said. "Don't we have to run smoothly?" I saw Tomas shaking his head, but I couldn't help myself. "We can't keep going at this pace."

Harry glared at me, silently chomping on his gum, and I sighed. This wasn't what I wanted.

"Look—" I began, but an alarm chimed a warning and Jen cut me off.

"Tremor coming up."

That got everyone's attention. A fluctuation in the jump lanes we cruised along could turn a million-ton colony ship like ours into shimmering space dust. Impressive quantities of space dust, but space dust nonetheless.

"Okay," Harry said, "everyone strap up and strap in. This isn't a drill. I want you all secured in five minutes." His eyes found mine, and he motioned for the disk. "Give it here—I'll run it while we wait."

I handed the data over and turned to head toward my post—I was backing up Jen and Francis, so luckily I didn't have far to go, just had to slip into my overharness. Before I could strap in, however, Harry's voice stopped me.

"Kweku."

I turned and raised my eyebrows. The older boy held his helmet just above his head, his jaw clenched as his eyes bore into mine.

"We're all in this together—we've got to be a team."

I forced out a thin smile. "I know, boss. I know."

We navigated the tremor without trouble. As *Liberia* skirted the gravitational distortion, Jen, with Francis beside her as copilot, monitored the readouts like a hawk, making minute adjustments until she rang the all-clear alert. I was on the lift, mashing the buttons, before the siren had finished ringing.

Back inside my lab I bypassed my small cot in the corner—it took some doing; I was incredibly tired. But the garden called to me. It sang to me of sustenance for the body and soul, of a future of new beginnings, of a chance to spread fresh roots in greener pastures.

The giant cassava cultivar waved at me as I walked toward it over the soil, barefoot once more. A breeze from the recirculation pumps ruffled its leaves, but I imagined it was greeting me after an elongated absence. Silly, perhaps, but comforting.

"Play," I said. After a few seconds, Nana Gbemi's cackle filled the lab, and I began to walk up and down the rows of cassava, misting the leaves as I went.

"Why, I remember I thought I was all alone. That nobody cared if the harvest lived or died. It was just me and the dirt and the scrawny plants strugglin' just to make it. I thought I'd never be able to care for all them. But I was thinkin' 'bout it all wrong. 'Cause when the time comes, just when you think you ain't able to carry on, help comes along from the last place you was expectin'."

The system cut off as the lab door chimed, and I groaned at another interruption, then frowned at the entrance. My lab didn't really get visitors. Tomas's joking aside, there *was* an earthy, pungent aroma down here that took some getting used to.

"Who is it?" I called as I set down the mister.

"Harry. We need to talk."

Damn. What now? But I wiped as much dirt off my scrubs as I could and moved to the front to let him in. Harry stepped inside, still wearing his harness and chewing his gum, and a familiar expression, complex and fleeting, swept across his face. Disappointment mixed with apprehension and discomfort. He didn't like my lab, didn't think it was a necessity. He glanced down, and too late I realized I hadn't put my shoes back on, let alone brushed the dirt off my feet, and I flushed with anger at my embarrassment.

"Yes?" My tone was curt, and his eyes narrowed. He held up the disk.

"Care to explain this?"

"What? Did the data not transfer over right?" Confusion replaced anger. "I can run them again for you real quick."

"No, they transferred over fine. They're too high. Still."

I stared at him. "Too high? They're too conservative if anything. I've run these projections a dozen times, and they're all saying the same thing: We need these plants, Harry; the colony is depending on these seedlings to help generate a new farming system. If we're off by even a little, we risk jeopardizing the nutritional—"

"You really think we need all of this"—he waved a hand at the garden behind me—"to come down with us?"

Damn it, why couldn't he see? "Absolutely. Failures in the transplant process—"

"And this . . . cultivar? You need a dedicated support pod just for a large plant?"

"It isn't just a large plant," I said, growing angry again. "The cultivar is the ancestor of all of these plants. If we experience any sort of yield loss, her survival is critical in—"

"'Her'?" he interrupted, and I closed my eyes, fighting off another wave of exhaustion. "Kweku, your personification of these . . . these plants, was amusing at first, but it's quickly growing old. We can't take all of this with us."

"Harry—"

"No. Find a way to cut it. End of story. And go see Jen—we need a full run-through with all reserves." He glanced at my feet one more time, then shook his head and left. I stood there as the door slid shut behind him, trying to suppress an overwhelming urge to shout, scream, swear, kick something, and pull my hair out. The frustration spread from a tight ball of anger in my stomach. I counted to ten before I walked stiffly back to the garden. The cultivar—no, Nana—stood there, her leaves still, even as the recirculator chugged along.

The second tremor caught us all by surprise.

We were minutes from approaching the exit window to drop into the system for the Colonies. I was standing in the back of the command deck, staying out of the way as Jen and Francis ran through checklists and whispered instructions and murmured confirmations. They were surrounded by printouts and barely focusing on the console's readouts. Ironic, really. We'd been preparing and double-checking and readying ourselves for anticipated disaster so much that when it actually showed up we didn't recognize it.

There really was no need for me to be there. Those two could handle any situation. I was just beginning to announce I was heading back to my lab when *Liberia* slammed into the tremor and reality twisted inside out.

The distortion picked up the room and shook it, turning everyone on their heads and sending objects whizzing by at breakneck speeds. The floor was the wall, and the wall was a mess of broken displays flashing pixelated streaks of red, green, and blue lightning.

Sirens wailed. I could hear them through the muffled helmet that had snapped out and over my head during the impact. Vital signs flashed green in my display, so I stood, waited for the wobble in my knees to steady, then hailed the emergency frequency.

"Everyone all right?" I asked. While I waited for a response, I checked on Francis and Jen. Both seemed fine, though Francis had a yellow warning flashing on his display—he had a gash below his eye, which his suit was working on patching up. Still, he flashed me a thumbs-up and began sorting through his readouts.

"Okay, I think," someone responded before coughing.

"Tomas?"

"No, Ty."

"Sirah here. Tomas is with me in Medical. He's fine, but his comms are damaged."

"Okay, thanks, Sirah." I cleared my throat and fidgeted as others began to check in. Jen moved next to Francis, looked over his numbers, crawled over to the only functional console on the former wall, now the floor. I flashed her the okay sign and waited for someone else to take over.

"Harry here. What's the status?"

"Running diagnostics now," Jen said, "but it looks like that tremor triggered a premature separation." She tapped a few commands and then shook her head. "Yep, the entire Research module is partially disengaged. Holding steady for now, but no telling if it'll hold through reentry."

"Research?" My voice sounded faint in my ears. The lab. "Air loss?"

A pause, then, "Can't tell. Seals are still holding, it seems."

Please, God.

"Okay," I said, thinking fast. "Okay. I'm heading to prep for harvest and storage. Sirah, tell Tomas to ready the containment pod for Nana, and—"

"Wait," Harry broke in. "Kweku, we need all hands up here. There isn't time."

"Jen and Francis have it covered, Harry, and I need to assess the damage."

"No, I need you to assist them while we start reentry. We don't have time—"

"They've got it handled, Harry."

"Kweku, the time—"

"Make. Time."

Jen's helmet whipped around as she stared at me. My voice was tight and my fists were clenched, so I took a deep, shuddering breath and forced some calm into my words. "Please, Harry, make time. This whole venture is a failure if we don't rescue the harvest."

Silence stretched on the line, then Harry sighed.

"No unnecessary risks, hear me? We need you."

I exhaled as well. "Roger." I commed Jen directly. "Jen, I'm heading down. Tell Tomas through Sirah that Francis is here and has a head injury, but he's okay."

"Got it," she answered. Then, "And be careful."

The lift was a disaster. A ladder system connected all of the modules in case of emergencies, so I squeezed through the narrow trapdoor and started the climb down, hand over hand, my breath echoing in the confines of my helmet.

Each floor I passed had bright-red emergency lights flashing above the entry hatch. I glanced in a few of the windows, trying to determine the extent of the damage, but darkness and impatience prevented me from seeing much. After a while I stopped checking and just continued down. My hands were beginning to ache, and a knot formed at the base of my neck from the position I was holding it in, trying to watch my footing. I stopped once to rest, but the panicky need to verify that everything was okay quickly swamped me, and I continued on. No more breaks.

Down and down and down some more. Dark and dark and darker. I planned as I descended. Talking out loud reassured me.

"Bag and seal the herbs. Separate by soil pH, and send them on. Have the tractor start pulling and boxing the cassavas, then move to the beans. Once the pod gets here, we can load up Nana and go."

On and on, again and again, I ran through the steps as I climbed down farther and farther, and after a few repetitions I started numbering them. I was on repetition 217 when the connection hatch for the Research module came into view at the bottom of the ladder. A flashing red warning brought me to a sudden halt.

Breach.

"No no no no no no," I whispered as I swung into the module, activated my grav boots, then sprinted down the hall, hurdling toppled furniture and ducking dislodged paneling. "Please be just the hallway, please be just the hallway, please—"

A bright-red light blinked on and off above the door to my lab, and I swallowed the sudden lump of fear. The outer doors were partially ajar. I keyed the entry code, but nothing happened. I entered it again. Still nothing.

"Let me in," I shouted at the door, but that didn't work, nor did slamming my fist into it. My chest heaved in the tight harness, and I glanced about wildly, looking for anything that could help. I ran back to where some ceiling panels had come loose and wrenched off a rectangular piece the length of my arm. I shoved it into the cracked door, threw my shoulder against it over and over, and finally somehow managed to slide it open far enough that I could squeeze inside if I crawled.

Inside my office I stood up and surveyed the damage. My books and papers were everywhere. The inner door to the lab was closed, and the wall light faded in and out, so there was still power of some sort. I connected to the console and took a deep breath.

"Authorize."

The console remained quiet.

"*Liberia,* authorize."

My breathing echoed in my helmet, and it sounded shallow and panicky, which annoyed me, and why wasn't the damn ship responding? It had power!

"Authorize?"

"Auth-o-rize."

"Authorize! Please!"

My office chair lay overturned beneath a bookshelf and the desk. I pulled it free and was preparing to hurl it at the inner door when a gleam caught my attention. Partially buried beneath the debris of my office lay the twisted metal bangle Tomas had given me.

"Papi's Last Resort," I mumbled. I set the chair down, picked up the lockpick, and slid it into the door release in the top right corner. My shoulders sagged with relief when a loud click sounded and the seals disengaged. Papi was going to get a case of his favorite bourbon after this was all over. I chuckled at the thought of his face when he opened it, then headed into the lab.

The smile froze on my face, then melted into horror at the sight of mangled plants strewn about.

"No."

Snarls of kudzu lay everywhere, as if the curtain of creeping vine had been snatched aside by some angry hand.

"No no no," I said.

The hover-pots lay in piles—in corners, half buried in mounds of soil—cracked and broken shards sprinkling the floor. Tufts of herbs could be seen here and there, but very little was salvageable.

"Sweet God, no."

Broken cassava stems poked out everywhere I looked, like small groups of bristling stakes warning me away from what I needed to collect. What we needed to survive. Fresh green stems sported white gashes that were rapidly browning.

The air, I realized. There was a leak somewhere, and soon the harvest would be worthless.

"Nana?" I don't know why I called out to the large cultivar as if she could answer me. Darkness shrouded her corner, though I could make out bits of her form, and I shook my head, the corners of my eyes burning.

"Nana, don't play with me. Don't play!"

Something hissed and popped, causing me to jump a yard in the air and come down clutching at my heart. My suit's audio system had activated. I was about to turn it off, but the thought of scrabbling around in the dark by myself with only the dying plants and my breathing to keep me company—no, I decided to let it play.

"So, look," Nana Gbemi's voice said into the darkness. "Just 'cause it feel like you been workin' all your life, and it keep pilin' up and don't look like there's an end in sight—don't think you alone now. Hear me? You ain't alone. Ha! You ain't never been alone, you ain't never gon' be alone."

I got on my hands and knees and started working. The cassavas were the most important—everything else could be started from seed if we landed. When we landed. For now, I just had to bag and seal the tubers off from the atmosphere.

"You gon' face a whole heap of mess." Nana Gbemi laughed. "If you only knew. Every time you climb one heap, you gon' stumble into another one. Probably bigger too."

Somebody paged me, and I answered automatically. I didn't know who it was, but somehow I communicated the emergency. All thought, all concern and sorrow and fear, had been shoved into my own personal lockbox. The only thing that mattered was saving the harvest.

A flashing icon interrupted the recording, and INCOMING blinked on my display in bright-red letters.

"Kweku here," I answered.

"Kweku, it's Harry. Status?"

"Uh, it's bad down here, Harry—there's a breach in the lab. I'm trying to save what I can now. Any help you can send would be a blessing."

Silence stretched on the line. I continued to sift through dirt, snagging cassava tubers—two, sometimes three, at a time—and stuffing them into the protective transport bags.

"Jen says we've got an hour before we need to force the separation. I really need you to come back so we can go over the emergency landing proto—"

"I know the protocol, Harry. We all do. What I need is time and help."

"Jesus, Kweku, this is no time to pull stunts." Harry sounded tired, and part of me felt sorry for him. But the other part of me continued to rescue as many plants as possible, knowing it might mean the difference between a successful harvest and slow starvation.

"Harry, just give me time, and make sure Tomas has that pod ready to go. In fact, send him with it—I'm going to need it soon."

"No."

The word echoed softly in my ears, so softly I thought I misheard it.

"What?"

"I can't jeopardize the safety of the crew for the garden you've got down there."

"Harry," I said through gritted teeth. "We're jeopardizing the survival of the colony if we don't grab as many—"

"You don't know that. I'm—"

"I ran the numbers, Harry. I do know that."

We were talking over each other now, comm etiquette clearly forgotten. Lights started winking on at the bottom of the comm feed—the others were joining the line, though no one else had spoken up yet. Tomas. Jen. Sirah. Even Francis was there.

"Those numbers weren't verified, and this isn't a discussion."

"I ran the numbers, Harry. They're verified." I didn't have time for this—I dropped back to my hands and knees and moved quicker. A line of transport bags was scattered behind me, yet I wasn't even a quarter of the way into the lab.

"Kweku, cut the losses, grab what you can, and come back up. That's an order."

"I still need to grab the cultivar, and there's a bunch of tubers still—"

"That's an order!"

"This isn't—"

"Leave the cultivar and that garden, and come on!"

"Give me forty-five minutes, Harry. Jen can buy me forty-five minutes. Send the pod down."

"Leave it, and let's go. We're wasting time."

"Thirty minutes." My arms were getting tired, and I shook them out. "Gimme thirty minutes and the pod, and I'll be up."

"Damn it, Kweku, leave—"

"I'm not leaving her behind, Harry!" I shouted into my helmet. *"I'm not. Leaving her!"*

Nobody spoke.

I squeezed my eyes shut. "I'm not leaving our shot at survival. This is . . . This is all we've got. All I've got. I can't leave another piece of us behind, Harry. Not one more piece. I can't do it. I can't do it and think we can survive. We need this food. I know you don't believe the numbers or the projections or the estimates. I know you think this is a silly project, but it's more than just a project, Harry. It's all of them. All of them that couldn't make it with us. My mother and your mother and grandmother and grandfather and . . . every single one. They all worked on this, kept her alive, just so she—and they—could make it home."

My chin sagged to my chest, my breath fogging up the display.

"I know you don't believe in that ancestral nonsense," I went on. "Just . . . believe in me. Trust me. Give me the thirty minutes and the pod. Please. I'm begging you."

He didn't answer.

"C'mon, Harry, thirty minutes and the pod. Thirty minutes. That's all I—just thirty minutes. *Thirty minutes! Please!*"

Tears burned down my face as I continued to scrape in the cold dirt. There were too many. Too many were going to be left behind, too many weren't going to see the future, but if I could just take what I had and rescue Nana, maybe we could press on.

Maybe.

"Harry." Jen's voice broke into the silence. "We can dump the fuel reserves the Research module carried. That should help Kweku get her. . . . That should be enough."

"Pod's up," Tomas added. "Ready to run it down."

A few more heart-wrenching seconds passed before Harry sighed. "Fine. Thirty minutes, then you're all back up here and strapped in. Got me?"

"Roger, Harry," I whispered. "Roger." And I resumed digging, trying to bring as much of my old home with me to my new one.

"It ain't gon' be easy. Never is and never will be. But harvest time come 'round, you gon' see your family show up right beside you, singing and working until that whole field is stripped to the bare. Hear me?"

Nana Gbemi laughed her harsh cackle in my ears as we all watched the Research module—and a third of the cassava harvest—tumble away slowly into space. The cultivar pod sat strapped next to me, taking up the rest of the row, and I draped an arm over it as I yawned and settled in to nap during the eight-hour reentry. The last thing I heard were the adults of my family, my uncles and aunts and my older brothers, who just missed the cutoff—generations of farmers who'd put their all into ensuring our future, guaranteeing that the chain linking us all remained unbroken—and I smiled as I recognized each voice.

"Now how do I turn this durned thing off? What? Oh, I see it—well . . . this is Gbemisola Aboah, signing off."

"Transcribed by Ahmed Aboah, signing off."

"Digitized by Mama D, signing off."

"Reedited by Ammar Aboah, signing off."

"Transferred and uploaded by Baba Ahmed ibn Ammar, signing off."

"Cleaned and audio reimaged by Sister Afo, signing off."

"Downloaded to the colony ship *Liberia* by Anja Aboah, signing off."

"Packaged and beamed to Colony 031, New Africa, by Kweku Aboah. Signing off."

ROYAL
AFFAIR

V. E. SCHWAB

Set in the world of Shades of Magic, this story
reveals the beautiful beginnings and tragic end of the affair
between Rhy Maresh and Alucard Emery, long before the
events of the series unfolded.

I

Alucard Emery stood at the prow of the *Night Spire,* watching
the river turn red.

To normal eyes, the water below glowed with a steady light,
but he could see the threads that twined and tangled beneath the
surface, ribbons of power slowly darkening from pink to red,
like blood dissolving in a stream.

His chest tightened at the sight of it, every moment's progress carrying the ship farther up the Isle.

Toward London.

Toward home.

But of course, it hadn't been *his* home in years.

There was an old saints' tale—he couldn't remember the words—about the dangers of getting lost trying to find what had been, and wasn't anymore.

The past was like a heavy wind, best kept firmly at one's back.

Speaking of one's back—

"If you're planning on stabbing me . . ."

"You'd already be dead," answered Lila Bard.

She had a thief's tread, steps swallowed by the shallow sounds of the ship. But he knew when she was there. He could feel her power, could see the silver threads of her magic dancing at the edges of his sight.

His white cat, Esa, trailed in her wake. Bard hated the cat, and it seemed to hate her back, and yet it followed her around the ship, its violet eyes watchful.

Bard ignored the cat and leaned her elbows on the rail, looking down at the reddening water.

"Don't worry, Captain," she said, misreading his concern. "I'm sure you'll hold your own."

She was talking about the tournament. Their reason for returning, or at least their excuse. The Essen Tasch—the greatest competition in the three empires.

He held out a hand, as if to cup the misty air. His lips moved: the soft, almost soundless ushering of magic. A tendril of water drew up, gathered in his palm. His fingers twitched, and the water hardened into ice.

The Essen Tasch—a place where power mattered more than title, more than name, more than anything. A place where futures were made, and pasts erased.

Even now, his heart beat too hard in protest, a warning to turn the ship, to go back out to sea, where the deck felt steadier than any land beneath his feet.

Perhaps he was making a mistake.

Perhaps three years was too long, and not long enough.

Perhaps—

Bard cleared her throat.

She turned, putting her back to the river as she folded her arms. "It's funny, though," she said, almost absently. "I've never seen you flinch in the face of a fight. Four months on this ship, and I've never seen you so much as nervous. Makes me wonder what else we might be sailing toward."

Delilah Bard had always been too sharp.

Alucard let the ice melt between his fingers. "London and I did not part on good terms."

Bard's smile flashed. "I didn't know a city could fall out with a man."

"It can," he said, "when a man falls out with its prince."

Three years ago.

They stumbled down the narrow hall, fingers tangled in each other's clothes.

The prince pressed Alucard back into the nearest wall, and he winced as the unhewn stone dug between his shoulders. The secret passage was rough, unfinished, so unlike the polished marble that lined the rest of the palace, the parts always on display.

Alucard pushed off the wall, drawing the prince farther down the corridor. A few small lanterns lined the passageway, each burning with a low, enchanted light that was just enough to see by.

And he could see.

He could see the shape of the corridor, and the place it split, each branch leading to a different room. And he could see the door at the end of one passage, embossed with the royal seal, and the letter *R* inside. And he could see Prince Rhy Maresh, his edges laced with gold. It ringed his fingers and trimmed his cuffs; it dusted his lips, and rested in a narrow band against his temples, and shone, like molten metal, around the pupils of his eyes.

He had watched Rhy grow from boy to youth, and youth to royal, had always felt a certain warmth toward the prince, but four years was a chasm between children. And yet, in the last year or two, it had begun to close. And this past spring, at a saint's day feast, when the prince's eyes met his across the room, the gold in them had spread like blush on summer fruit. And when the prince came toward him, full of pleasantries, his voice was deeper, lush and smooth. And when the prince's hand had come to rest on his arm under the pretense of a laugh, a sudden need for steadying, his grip was firm, an unspoken question— almost an order—in the touch.

And when the prince kissed him in a shadowed corner of the hall that night, there was such hunger in his lips, his racing heart, but Alucard was the one left out of breath. Where was the boy he'd teased growing up, the powerless prince? Rhy, seventeen, and Alucard, almost twenty-one, and yet he was the one who felt unsteady, thrown by the passion in the other boy's kiss.

"Are you sure?" he asked when he could speak again.

"Are you certain?" he asked with every stolen breath.

"Do you want this?" he asked, again and again, until Rhy broke away, exasperated.

"Am I not making that clear?"

"You're young," he said, as if it were an answer.

"Nokil Maresh took the throne when he was my age," Rhy shot back. "I am old enough to rule the empire, and old enough to wed."

"Are you proposing, then?" asked Alucard, but the prince only laughed, and dragged him down into the bed.

And so began a courtship in dark corners.

An affair of stolen looks and knowing smiles, of fingers tangled out of sight, of kisses along collars, and hands pressed over mouths to stifle sounds of pleasure.

They found the door, their progress halted only by Alucard's teeth along the prince's shoulder, and Rhy's hands questing beneath his shirt.

Alucard felt blindly behind him for the handle, and it gave, just as Rhy pressed flush against him. They gasped, crashing backward into the prince's room. Alucard laughed, too loud, and Rhy pressed a hand over his mouth. He smiled into the touch, gold rings grazing his lips.

Around them, the royal chamber was a thing of beauty. Dark wood furnishings, threaded with gold, and gossamer gathered into a sunset on the ceiling, and silk curtains, spilling down the wall around his massive bed.

Like the prince, it was immaculately groomed.

And like the prince, he could not wait to cast it into disarray. To knock the furniture askew and sweep the pillows from the bed.

He hooked his finger in the prince's crown.

"Your Highness," he said, casting the band of gold onto the nearest divan.

"How impertinent," said Rhy, kissing his way down Alucard's jaw, leaving a trail of gold dust in his wake.

They stumbled toward the bed, wrestling with the clothes between them.

"Too many buttons," growled Alucard, tearing one off with his teeth.

Rhy let out a gasp of mock horror. "Those are very expensive," he said as Alucard spat it like a seed into the dark.

They reached the bed, and Rhy leaned back, fingers sliding over the sheets. His shirt hung open, exposing a stretch of smooth, dark skin from collar to waist.

Alucard marveled at the prince.

He could see the threads in everything. The filaments of magic that wound through the room, enchanting the lanterns, protecting the windows and doors—spells laced into the palace after the prince's abduction years before. He could see his own magic, lines of light that wove over his skin. But around Rhy Maresh, there were none.

No natural magic, no threads of power.

Nothing, and yet he was powerfully handsome, powerfully charming, powerfully witty, powerfully sharp, powerfully kind. He was—

Impatient, thought Alucard, and the prince pulled him down into the bed.

Just then, someone pounded on the door.

"Send them away," said Alucard, breathless, but then the knocking ceased, and Rhy must have known what was coming because the prince dragged Alucard close and, instead of kissing him, pushed him roughly into the mountainous curtains beside the bed.

Alucard gasped, and nearly spat out a curse, when the door swung open and Kell walked in.

Kell, the prince's older brother.

The king's adopted son.

And a royal pain in the ass.

"You look flushed," he said, his tone flat as wood and just as humorless.

Even through the curtains, Alucard could see the shine of Kell's magic, silver as starlight and bright as a forge.

Alucard Emery was one of the most promising magicians in the empire. He could already wield earth and air, was learning water, too. He would become a triad, one of the few people who could control not one element, or even two, but *three*.

He had spent the last decade learning to wield his power.

And Kell made him look like a child fumbling in the dark. All because he was *Antari,* born with magic in his blood. It came to him as naturally as breathing.

Alucard hated him for it, though in truth he would have hated him a great deal less if he weren't also such a *bastard*.

Rhy cleared his throat. "I was dreaming," he said.

Alucard could hear the smile in his voice. He held his breath, felt the silk shift a little. The next thing he felt was Kell's power, forcing him bodily out of the curtains.

"Well," said Kell, crossing his arms. "I must be dreaming too."

Alucard straightened, brushing off his hands. "I didn't realize I was in *your* dreams, Kell."

"Only my nightmares," said the prince, raising a copper brow. But it was the eyes beneath that unnerved Alucard.

One blue, the other black.

He turned to Rhy. "The king sent me to fetch you."

Alucard snorted, and Kell rounded on him.

"Do you have something to say, Emery?"

"I'm just marveling. Is it some spell that compels you, or did you choose to be an errand boy?"

Kell glowered, but Rhy spoke first.

"Tell him I was asleep."

"I will do no such thing."

Rhy furrowed his brow and drew his mouth into a pout, and even though it was a farce, Alucard found himself impacted, wanted to wipe the lines from the prince's face, to kiss away the crease between his eyes, to make him smile. It was a kind of power, he thought, even if it was not magic.

"Come on, Kell," said Rhy.

"Yes, come on," said Alucard. "Prove you're not a little—"

"You forget your place."

"Not at all," said Alucard. "It is, of course, beneath your brother."

His face cracked sideways.

Pain, swift and bright, bloomed on his skin. Kell hadn't moved, but the air had moved, like a palm, against his cheek.

His own power rose, like heat. The floorboards groaned, the air began to churn, but Alucard only touched his face.

"You will regret that," he said. "It is a crime to strike a noble."

136

"The king is downstairs, waiting for his son. You could go down and plead your case. But then, he might want to know what you were doing in his *bed*."

Rhy laughed, but there was not much humor in it. The breath escaped like steam, simply seeking a release. "I'll be right down, Kell. I promise."

Kell didn't move. "I'll wait," he said, flicking his fingers. The discarded crown flung itself back into Rhy's hands. "And you better change your shirt."

Rhy looked down. "Why?"

He turned away. "You're missing a button."

The royal palace was traced with spells.

Some were there to keep things out, and others to keep things in, and a few to simply keep the massive structure looking its best. Alucard could see the threads of all of them, and thus could find the seams, the places where they did not reach.

He slipped out of the palace and onto the street.

The Night Market rose to one side, tents spilling golden light into the street, the air filled with meat, and song, and scented smoke, but Alucard turned the other way, and walked past the palace grounds and onto the bridge.

He paused near the center and looked down at the crimson light of the river, a thousand threads running like silken fish beneath the surface. He smiled and held one hand over the side, the water rising to meet his fingers. It was then he caught sight of the gold streaked along his wristbone, remembered the touch of Rhy's lips against his skin.

He cupped the water, rinsing the gold dust from his hands, his throat, his face, washing away the last traces of the prince before he went home.

II

The Emery estate sat just above the northern banks.

Alucard passed through the open gates and looked up in time to see a shadow sitting on the steps. His heart seized, but it was too small to be Berras. Gold hair trying to escape its braid, a dress bunched around her knees, his little sister, Anisa, sat at the bottom of the stairs, scowling at the courtyard floor.

He thought she must be angry, or hurt, but as Alucard drew close, he saw she was concentrating. Her magic danced around her in strands of vivid blue, and she bit her bottom lip as she squinted at the ground between her shoes, coaxing the dust into tiny sandstorms at her feet.

Alucard sank down beside her on the step.

"You've been practicing." He brought a hand to rest on his sister's hair. "What are you doing out here?"

"Father isn't well," she said. "And Berras is in a mood."

Their father hadn't been well in years, and their brother, it seemed, was always in a mood. He held out his hand, and the wind whipped beneath his palm, twisting itself into a small cyclone.

Anisa stretched out her hand, and he guided the curl of wind beneath her palm.

The cyclone held a moment, wobbling slightly, and Anisa let out a small, delighted laugh.

But it trailed off as footsteps sounded at their back.

The cyclone fell apart as Alucard turned and saw a shadow in the open doorway.

Berras.

They say that blood binds tightest, that family matters most. But if Alucard felt anything for his brother, it wasn't love but fear.

Berras Emery was not powerful. His magic hung wisp-thin around him, rose and fell in brittle filaments. But what Berras lacked in magic, he made up for in temper. In muscle and bone, in hands on skin, brutal and inelegant.

"Go inside, Anisa," he said.

She opened her mouth, as if to argue, but Alucard touched her arm. "Go on," he said. "And I'll tell you a story before bed."

Anisa rose and ran inside.

He would have gone with her, but Berras blocked his way.

He had their mother's coloring, the dark hair, the storm-blue eyes, but in every other way he was their father's echo. The set of his jaw, the way he flexed his hands, the judgment in his voice.

"Where have you been?" he demanded.

"Out for a walk," said Alucard, feigning levity. "It's a lovely night."

"Don't lie to me."

"It's not a lie. Look up—you can see the weather for yourself."

"And did the weather leave that gold streak along your jaw?" *Sanct.*

Alucard fought the urge to reach up and wipe away the kiss.

"You caught me," he said, forcing a smile. "I went down to the Blessed Waters. I know, not an establishment fitting my station, but the women there know their way around a bottle and a body."

"You came from the palace."

"No, I—"

Berras punched him hard in the stomach. The wind rushed out of his lungs.

"I told you not to lie."

Alucard resisted the urge to reach for magic.

It would only make things worse.

"I will not let you ruin our name."

"Oh, I assure you," growled Alucard, "I haven't ruined it at all. The prince uses it *quite fondly*."

Berras slammed him into the doorframe, one hand wrapped around his throat.

"You are an Emery, not a whore. Whatever passed between you, it is done, little brother. It must be. There is no future in it."

He let go then, and Alucard slumped, dragging air back into his lungs. He brought a hand to his throat.

Berras was right.

A prince could do as he pleased, indulge in lovers, feast on anyone who caught his fancy, but in the end they were both nobles, and nobles needed heirs.

In the end, it was nothing but a dalliance.

A flirtation that had run its course.

"Do you understand?" demanded his brother.

Alucard closed his eyes. "I do."

"Good," sneered Berras. Alucard exhaled, hoping he was done. And then Berras added, "Prove it."

III

The carriage jostled as it went over the bridge.

Alucard kept his gaze on the window, the Isle glowing red beyond. It was that or be forced to look at Berras on the opposite bench. He was dressed, like Alucard, all in white, the Emery colors picked out in the blue trim of his coat, the silver buttons running down his tunic. Alucard wore a blue-and-silver scarf at his throat, to hide the bruising left by his brother's hand.

The carriage pulled up in front of the palace.

A servant drew open the door, and Berras nodded for Alucard to step out first.

He didn't move.

If he stayed in the carriage, if he didn't go in, he wouldn't have to—

"Out," ordered Berras.

Alucard rose and climbed down. Berras followed, a silver walking stick in one hand. He held it not by the carved bird handle but by the staff, like a weapon.

A dozen carriages circled before the palace steps, the arriving guests all dressed in white, like priests. A tradition of the Summer Feast.

They were ushered inside, to the Grand Hall, a three-story ballroom of polished wood and shimmering crystal, a domed glass ceiling, and balconies that ran in filigreed bands beneath.

The terrace doors had been flung open to let in the summer air, and in the center of the hall, candied fruit spilled over banquet tables, gold platters piled high with meats. Summer wine poured from fountains and glittered on every passing tray.

Berras handed Alucard a drink.

"Smile, Brother. It is a party, after all."

Alucard's fingers tightened on the glass. Inside, frost spread across the surface of the summer wine.

He drank it in one freezing gulp and searched the room for Rhy.

The king and queen stood at the center of the hall, making pleasantries, but the prince was not with them. He scanned the hall and caught sight of Kell up on one of the balconies, perched like a crow. He searched the staircases, the dancing forms, but there was no sign of the prince, and Alucard held his breath and hoped Rhy had taken ill, hoped—

But Rhy Maresh had never missed a party.

Or a chance to make an entrance.

He arrived on the stairs in a crisp white suit and cloak, dripping gold. It lined the inside of his cloak and collar; it covered every clasp and trim. It hung from his ears, and painted his lips, and shone in his eyes.

He was dazzling.

And, for a brief, wonderful moment, Alucard forgot why he was there, forgot everything except the prince on the stairs.

And then Berras's walking stick dug into his back, and he remembered.

"Put an end to it," he said, "or I will."

Alucard forced himself to move, and the silver cane fell away.

He should have felt lighter then.

Instead he just felt sick.

Alucard crossed the room toward Rhy. And Rhy, unknowing, came to meet him.

"Your Highness," he said stiffly.

And Rhy must have thought it was a game, because he smiled and answered, "Master Emery, how fortunate we are to have you at the Summer Feast. Tell me . . ." The prince leaned in, as if he could not hear over the swell of the party. "Have you tasted anything sweet?"

This was the part where Alucard smiled. This was the part where he found some excuse to touch the prince, to fix a curl that had escaped his crown, to make a joke, simply so he could brush a hand, a sleeve, a shoulder.

But instead he frowned, forcing all emotion from his voice.

"I fear I have no appetite tonight."

"Oh?" The prince thought it still a game. He reached out and touched his arm. "I'm sure we could find something."

Alucard withdrew from the prince's touch.

"Your Highness," he said curtly. "I think you mistake my friendship for something fonder." He did not raise his voice, nor did he whisper. The nearest heads turned, and Rhy faltered, the humor bleeding from his face.

"Friends?" he said softly. "Is that all we are?"

"You are a spoiled child," he said under his breath. Alucard closed the final space between them. "What else could I want from you?"

He hated the words, even as he forced them out. Hated the open shock in Rhy's face, the moment before it snapped shut, before his features hardened into a mask of royal composure.

"Well, then, Master Emery," he said stiffly, "may we both find better company."

The prince turned and walked away, and Alucard felt

suddenly, horribly tired. He found Berras on the terrace, looking out over London.

"It's done," he said. "Let's go."

Berras raised a brow. "The feast has just begun."

Have you tasted anything?

Alucard swallowed hard.

"I'm not hungry," he said. "Do not make me stay."

Berras straightened, twirling his silver cane. "Very well, little brother. Let's go home."

Berras poured himself a drink.

"I'm going to bed," said Alucard, climbing the stairs. Anisa's room was dark. His father's, too. He locked his door, crossed his room, and threw open the balcony doors, desperate for the air, only to be met with the palace, its steepled spine rising over the river. He gripped the rail until his fingers ached.

What had he done?

Every time he closed his eyes, he saw the prince's face. Not the mask, but the one he'd seen beneath, the pain as bright as the gold in his eyes.

Bile rose in his throat, and he swallowed and told himself it was better this way.

But it didn't *feel* better.

It felt like a dull blade between his ribs. Like smoke in his lungs. He felt like a coward. A fool.

If only Rhy knew the truth.

If only Alucard had *told* him.

He should have told him, could have told him, found a way

to say, *It isn't you,* to say, *It isn't fair,* to say, *My brother is a monster, my father is cruel,* to say, *I want you, but I am afraid.*

To say, *We cannot all be princes.*

Alucard looked down, over the rail to the top of the garden wall below. He'd climbed out this way a hundred times, when he was young, when doors were dangerous, and he needed to escape.

Now he swung his leg over the rail.

He had to say *something* to the prince.

IV

Alucard knew the ins and outs of the palace.

Rhy had shown him the way. He knew that if he followed this path up the stairs and across the second floor, then—

He slowed, then stopped.

The passage lanterns all shone with a soft gold light. But the hall was filling with a silver glow. The unmistakable shine of *Antari* magic.

He swore under his breath as the voice rose at his back.

"I knew you were stupid, Emery, but I didn't think you were mad, too."

Alucard turned, and faced Kell.

"I need to see Rhy."

"You've seen him," he said, a cold anger in his voice.

"I didn't want to—"

"Leave."

"I *can't*," pressed Alucard, "not until—"

"Leave," warned Kell again, "or I will make you."

Alucard shook his head, muttering a soft prayer under his

breath. It might have sounded like a curse, if you couldn't see the magic gathering around his hands, the threads brightening with every word.

Kell took a single step forward before the wind slammed into him.

He threw up his arms against the sudden gale, but his boots slipped and slid over the floor until his back hit the wall. Before he could recover, Alucard pulled on the earth and stone to every side. Not enough to bring the passage down on top of them, just enough to make a barricade, bars of dirt and rock drawing lines across the narrow hall.

Kell looked more annoyed than overwhelmed.

He reached out, and the wind died, and the bars crumbled back into earth.

"Are you done?" he asked dryly, and Alucard was about to answer when all the air left his lungs, and his body buckled against the floor. It felt like he was being crushed beneath a massive weight.

This wasn't wind magic. Wasn't earth, or water.

No, his body screamed, this was *bone*.

A forbidden element, even for *Antari*.

"That's"—Alucard fought to fill his lungs—"illegal."

"So is breaking into the palace." Kell drew a dagger from his belt, the edge glinting in the dark. He drew the blade across his skin, blood welling, crimson shot through with silver only he could see. It poured from the shallow cut.

Alucard's body screamed in protest as he tried to rise, to move at all.

Kell touched the blood, then Alucard's forehead.

146

"You know," he said, "I could kill you just for trespassing."

He felt the drop of blood run like a tear between his eyes, down his nose.

Two words, and the *Antari* could turn him to ash. To ice. To stone.

"You wouldn't," he hissed.

Kell drew a mark on his forehead.

"As Tascen," he said, and the air lodged in Alucard's chest, the world rocking violently sideways.

And then he was kneeling on the grass, the night sky wide and dark, clouds blushing with the reflected light of the Isle river.

They were in the palace orchard, between two rows of trees.

Alucard shuddered, relieved to find that he could move again. He staggered to his feet.

"Go home," said Kell, already turning away.

"I have to see him. I have to explain—"

Kell stopped. "Do you care for my brother?"

"Yes!" hissed Alucard, exasperated.

"Then save your sweet nothings, and say them in daylight." Kell turned back, his gaze piercing, even in the dark. "If he is nothing but a prize, a way to pass the time, then leave, and stay away.

"But if it is love," he added, "then come back, and make your feelings known in the presence of the king. Court him in the proper way."

Alucard shook his head. "It's not that simple."

"It is now," said Kell, drawing a symbol on the nearest tree. *"As Tascen,"* he muttered, and then the world simply parted, and he was gone, leaving Alucard alone in the dark.

He sank back to the ground, his head in his hands.

If it is love.

But it wasn't. It couldn't be.

Alucard could not afford to fall in love.

And so he'd told himself he wouldn't. Told himself it was like summer fruit, savored in season but hardly mourned in winter. Told himself it would be nothing but a fun affair, a way to pass the warmest months.

He'd told himself every time he left Rhy's bed.

Every time he felt his pulse quicken at the prince's touch.

Every time he blushed at the prince's smile.

He'd told himself—as if his heart would listen.

That traitorous heart, now thudding in his chest, beating out the answer like a drum.

Because, of course, it was love.

He was in love with the prince of Arnes.

And he would have to tell him. And the king and queen. And then, somehow, he would have to tell his family. But what could they do, if the Crown approved? Perhaps it would be enough. Perhaps he would be free.

Alucard fell back against the grass and sighed. He closed his eyes, whispering the truth to the trees in the orchard, testing it on his tongue.

He thought of staying there, waiting for dawn, but his clothes were rumpled, the shoulder of his coat torn, his hair a wild mess of curls.

He could not stand before the king like this.

What a shabby suitor he would make.

A *suitor.* The thought of declaring himself left Alucard breathless and dizzy, his confidence flagging in the dark. But he closed his eyes and thought of Rhy, summoned the prince as if he were a piece of magic.

Those gold eyes lit his way across the river.

That warm voice carried him home.

He was in love.

The knowledge hung like a chain around his neck. And yet there was a warmth to the weight, like armor in the sun.

He was in love.

He scaled the wall of the estate, swung his leg up onto his balcony, the words beating in his chest.

He was in love, and in the morning he would say it.

In the morning—

The blow came out of nowhere.

He stumbled, his vision going in and out, taking his attacker with it. Berras flickered, then resolved.

"I warned you, little brother."

He swung again.

"Wait," said Alucard, throwing out his hands. He knew he couldn't stop his brother with words, or fists, but he had earth, he had wind.

The air wrapped like rope around Berras's wrist, holding it at bay. But what his brother lacked in power, he made up for in brute force. He tore his hand free. Alucard stumbled back, but not fast enough.

Berras slammed his forehead into Alucard's.

He reeled, blood in his eyes and a high ringing in his ears.

"Stop!"

A flash of blond hair, magic rising like steam as Anisa surged into the room, but she was too young to fight with magic, too young to shape the wind into more than a gust, as effective as open palms shoving at a wall.

Berras turned and struck her once, across the jaw. Anisa stumbled back, as much in shock as in pain, and Alucard summoned enough wind to push her back into the hall, then forced the door shut between them.

She pounded on the wood, her small voice pleading, "Don't hurt him, don't hurt him," as thin as a breeze, and just as useless.

Berras turned and kicked Alucard in the chest, slamming him backward.

He hit the wall with a sickening crunch, pain exploding through his shoulder and side. He staggered, trying to summon magic. The floorboards groaned, and the air churned, but before he could make sense or shape of it, a voice cleared its throat in the dark.

His father sat on the edge of the bed, fingers curled around his iron cane. When he spoke, his voice had all the warmth of stone. "What a disappointment you are."

"Father," gasped Alucard, pain lancing every breath. "Please, let me explain."

He tried to twist free, but Berras wrenched his ruined shoulder until the world went white. He screamed, in pain and rage, and the whole house trembled.

"I thought you could be bent," said his father, lifting his iron cane. "Clearly, you must be broken."

The last thing he saw was the metal slicing through the air, before everything went black.

V

When Alucard was nine, he fell from the garden wall.

The next day it felt as if he'd bruised every bone in his body, though none of them were broken.

This was worse.

So much worse.

He woke on the floor, dizzy and sick. He pressed a palm to his temple, or tried, but pain screamed through his arm and across his ribs. He rolled onto his side, and retched, tried to rise, but the floor rocked under his feet, swaying violently. Tried to walk, only to find a steel cuff around his ankle, a chain running to a pole in the wall.

The world was still moving.

It swayed with a rhythmic motion, and Alucard realized the floor wasn't solid at all.

He was on a ship.

Footsteps sounded overhead, several pairs, and someone was whistling. Alucard screamed until the boots sounded on the stairs, and a man's face appeared in the hull.

"Oh, look who's awake."

"Let me go," demanded Alucard. "I'm a son of the House of Emery."

"Maybe back in London," said the man. "But you're a ways from London now."

The words sank through him.

"Where are we? Where are you taking me?"

The captain shifted his weight.

"They paid me to break you in, thicken up that skin, but I think I'd rather sell you off at Sasenroche. See what a noble's blood is worth."

Alucard strained against the chain. "Let me go—I'll pay you more."

"You've got nothing on you. I checked."

"Once you take me back to London—"

The captain barked a laugh. "Right away, sir," he said, disappearing up the stairs.

Alucard wrenched on the chain until his body screamed, until he sank, exhausted, to his hands and knees.

He should have stayed in the palace courtyard.

Should have shed the blasted coat and waited on the steps until the sun broke over the city and the doors of the Rose Hall opened.

Alucard sat back on his heels and looked around.

He could lean on the walls of the ship, could peel the wood apart, but to what end? He did not want to sink, did not want to drown.

He tried to focus on the water against the hull, tried to draw it from the mist, the humid air, until he had a handful. He guided the water through the manacle's keyhole and then froze it, hoping to force the pins apart, the lock open. But it did not work. He tried again, and again, and he was still trying when the shouts went up, overhead, still trying when the deck filled with racing steps, when he heard steel on steel, and screams, and the whole ship rocked with a sudden force, and a body came tumbling down the stairs and landed on the floor a few feet away.

It was the captain.

His eyes were empty, a bloody line across his throat.

Boots sounded on the steps, and a woman came into sight,

lanky and dark-skinned and smiling.

"What have we here?" she mused, taking him in.

Alucard had never seen a pirate, but he was sure that was what she was. It was in the way she moved, the clothes that draped around her wiry form, the absence of light in the air around her. No magic. But she clearly knew how to use a blade.

If she knew he was a noble, would she ransom him back? Or slit his throat and leave him by the captain?

Alucard had to think, and fast. He had always been a decent liar. Most nobles learned the skill, along with flattery and politics. He rose to his feet, did his broken best to mirror her, to shed the polish of his accent, the perfect posture of his youth.

It was easy, with how much he hurt.

"Care to help a fellow wanderer?"

She cocked a brow. "Depends. What are you doing chained like a pup?"

"Bad luck," he said, "worse friends."

She knelt over the captain's body, fished about until she found the key. She tossed it to him, and he undid the manacle with shaking hands. She had already left.

Above, the deck was littered with bodies.

A handful of pirates kicked them over, freeing weapons and silver and whatever else caught their eye. Alucard looked past the bloody scene to the open sea.

He squinted into the distance, but there was no sign of land.

"How far are we," he asked, "from London?"

But the pirate only laughed and clapped a hand on his back. His vision went white with pain. When it cleared, the pirate was swinging her leg over the rail. Beyond a set of wooden planks, another ship waited, pitch-black against the pale blue tide.

"Welcome to the *Moonless*," she said proudly. "Seven years at sea, and never been caught."

Three days later, the *Moonless* was caught.

It pulled up alongside an empty vessel, an easy mark, only to find the ship swarming with soldiers. It was bait, dangled in the open waters, waiting for a catch.

Alucard was no pirate then.

He dropped the act. He tried to explain, to tell the soldiers who he was. But either they didn't believe him or they didn't care.

He was taken to Hasinar. It was a floating prison, an island off the southern coast, the kind of place where people went in and bodies came out.

He told them that he belonged to a noble house, told them that the Crown would have their heads.

He did not know if that was true, but he said it anyway.

He would have told them anything to get off that blasted rock.

When they didn't listen, he fought.

He fought until they pinned his broken arm against his back, fought until they forced the steel cuff around his throat, its surface etched with spells, and his magic dropped like a stone in the sea.

At last, Alucard lay in the darkened cell and thought of home, of Rhy, not the pain in his eyes at the Summer Feast but the way he smiled in bed, the way he hummed when he was falling asleep, ringed fingers running through his hair.

VI

In the end, an emissary came.

Days or weeks, he didn't know, but the cell door eventually scraped open, and he was led out into a leaden day, loaded onto a boat, and ferried back to London. The red light of the river should have been a welcome beacon, but it was not. His brother met him at the docks, and when Berras's arms closed around him, his bones, still healing, screamed in protest, but he did not.

Their father, he learned, was dead.

And he knew he should have felt more than relief.

But he didn't.

Alucard was ushered home, past Anisa's desperate hugs, her worried clinging, and dressed in the rich blue and bright silver of the Emery line, the cloth cut to hide the ruins of his wrists, the bruises that blossomed at his throat. He was made to look the part of a noble and then marched to the royal palace, to the Rose Hall, to face the king and queen, his heart pounding with every forward step, hoping and dreading that the prince would be there.

But as he stepped through, he saw that the place beside the thrones was empty.

Only Kell waited at the open door, those two-tone eyes hard and unblinking. Alucard grabbed Kell's arm, and the *Antari* looked at him with such bald loathing, it nearly burned his hand. But he did not withdraw.

"I must see him."

"Oh, you must?" sneered Kell. "You are owed *nothing*." That black eye, unreadable, but the blue glowed with anger. "Twice

155

you broke my brother's heart. You will not have another chance. Get on your ship and sail away. You are not welcome here."

"This is my home," snapped Alucard.

"It was. You burned it down."

Then Berras's hand, heavier than any chain on his shoulder, as he was led forward like a reckless child. As he dropped to one knee before the king and queen.

"We are sorry to hear about your father," said Queen Emira.

Then you did not know him well enough, thought Alucard.

"You have had a trying month," said King Maxim. "You have made mistakes, and you have paid for them. And we hope that you have learned."

"I have, Your Majesty," said Alucard, and it was true. He had learned that blood was crueler than water. Had learned the value of his own freedom. Learned that pain was a thing to be endured, and love was not worth the cost.

"Very well," said the king, and he was pardoned.

It was, he knew, a kindness granted only by his birth, a mercy bought and paid for by his family name.

And so, he was forgiven.

Forgiven, but not free.

King Maxim's voice rang low through the hall. "Your brother says you long to sail," announced the king, "and so you sail for me."

What is the difference between a pirate and a privateer?

The approval of a king.

The ship, he learned, was waiting at the docks.

It was a gift, and a dismissal.

From the palace.

From London.

Alucard felt numb as Berras marched him down the marble steps, past the tents of the market that wouldn't open until dark, when he was already gone, toward the docks.

The ship stood proud, a gleaming midnight vessel, its name painted silver along the polished wood.

The *Night Spire*.

Alucard approached the ramp, feeling less like the captain of a ship and more like a prisoner, sentenced to a floating cell.

He heard the footsteps crashing down the dock and spun, hoping, hoping, hoping—but it was Anisa, the light of her magic trailing in the air like sparks.

Berras reached to catch her arm, but she was too quick, around him in an instant, burying her face against Alucard's front.

"Do you have to go?" she whimpered.

He lifted her chin. "Nis," he said, managing a smile. "It is a mission from the king himself. It is an honor. You wouldn't want me to refuse."

Tears streamed down his sister's face, but she shook her head, and he hugged her close, only to be met by a soft squeak, a mew from somewhere beneath her cloak.

She opened it, revealing the small white kitten. "Her name's Esa. A cat is good luck aboard a ship," she said, pressing the kitten into his arms, "and she will keep you safe."

Esa buried herself against his chest, a second, softly beating heart.

And then Berras took her arm, and for once he was grateful as his brother held his sister back. He turned, the kitten clutched safe against his collar, and boarded the ship.

His ship.

As the *Spire* drew out of the berth, Alucard looked up one last time, craning his head toward the royal palace. He searched the upper windows, the rooms he knew so well, hoping to glimpse a shadow there, to find some promise of the prince.

But the curtains were all drawn.

And so Alucard turned and took the ship's wheel, and when the *Night Spire* sailed out of London, he kept his back to the city and his gaze ahead, until the red light of the river was gone.

Three years at sea.

It was long enough for wounds to heal and scars to form, silver and smooth. Long enough to change the map of one's skin, to transform a proud noble into a shrewd captain. Long enough to hone one's magic, and bury one's heart behind charm and wit.

And long enough, he hoped, to weather *this*.

The wind picked up, the *Night Spire* rocking in the sudden breeze.

Bard said nothing, and Alucard was grateful for the silence, his attention focused on the place where the river met the sky. The place where nothing became a distant shimmer of light. Not magic, but glass and stone and gold, catching the sun.

The first glimmers of the royal palace.

Alucard steadied himself at the rail as London drew close, closer than it had in a thousand days, for he had counted every one.

Had dreamed of, and dreaded, this moment.

But he kept his hands on the wheel, the ship pointed toward the palace. He was done sailing away from his life.

It was time to go home.

THE
TAKEBACK
TANGO

REBECCA ROANHORSE

I dropped into the Imperium airspace, my engines running hot. My little ship rattled and hummed underneath me and, not for the first time, I wondered how long the *My Heart Will Go On* would hold together. There was nothing inherently wrong with her except that I'd put her together from pieces I found in a scrapyard. And she was doing her best, just like me.

"Hold it together, Sis," I murmured as I checked my scanners. Yep, yep, all good. Nothing worse than a little too much heat coming out of hyperspace. My ship would be fine. Me, on the other hand, I wasn't so sure. Just because I couldn't see any hostiles didn't mean they weren't out there hiding.

I flipped on my internal comm. "Talk to me, Evie. What have I got?"

The old communications device sent static back along the line, and I asked again, "Evie, you there?"

"Affirmative," a voice said, resolving out of the static. The voice was female, friendly, and entirely not human. My Evolutionary Vocalization Unit, a.k.a. Evie. "Here as always, Vi. How can I help you?"

I grinned. Evie may have just been an AI unit in my ship, but she was my go-to girl and my best friend. She had gotten me out of more close calls than I could remember and was always a steady voice in my ear, whether she was reading the schematics of a space station to find me an escape route out of a tricky situation or jamming hostile frequencies to gain me the few extra moments I needed to pull off a job. I owed that AI my life a dozen times over.

"Any hostiles?"

"Negative. And I've secured the required landing clearance to get you to the Imperium capital for the big party."

"Sweet, Evie. Thanks millions." The "big party" was the Imperium's semi-annual Treasures of the Empire gala, where the elite of the galaxy gathered at the Museum of the Conquered to gloat over the wealth stolen from smaller, more vulnerable planets. It never failed to draw a crowd—and its share of enterprising thieves. Of which I was one. Sorta.

As if the Imperium isn't the biggest thief of all, I thought bitterly.

And that fact made this job different. Normally, I was what they call a cat burglar, light of touch and quick on the in and out. Most people didn't even know I had robbed them until I was three systems away, drinking a fruity daiquiri on some beach planet. I know not everyone approves of a criminal life, but the

Imperium didn't leave people much choice these days. We did what it took to survive, and this was what it took for me: Evie identifying and acquiring wealthy targets and me relieving them of their unearned wealth to redistribute to . . . well, myself. Not exactly Robin Hood—more like just robbing.

But this job was different. Stealing from the Museum of the Conquered was personal.

"Very personal," I said, rubbing the glass-vial pendant around my neck. The vial was filled with red dirt, a memory of my home planet. The only thing I had left. Once I had had a family, brothers and sisters and cousins, but the Imperium had taken them all. Razed the planet for its natural resources and enslaved the people to work the mines and pipelines and space elevators. And those who had rebelled had simply been killed, like weeds that needed pruning to allow the Imperium to flourish.

But the Imperium hadn't stopped with enslaving humans and extracting natural resources. They'd raided the sacred places of my people, taking the carvings and masks that had been our connection to our gods and our place in the galaxy and put them in their museums as a display of their dominance. There was never a thought of what those sacred items meant to us, the handful of survivors of their genocide. How their loss cut us off from both our past and our future. It was a violation that ripped our souls apart and cast them adrift in the vastness of space, both physically and spiritually.

They had come to my home planet fifteen years ago. I had been a baby, lucky to be sold to passing traders rather than killed outright. Traders who turned out to be pirates and happily made me one of them. They were my family for a while, and I loved them. Zinny with his goofy smile and bad jokes, Chrys who always shared their desserts with me, and our surrogate mom, Lantana. They gave me a name like theirs in memory of the flowers that grew on humanity's legendary home planet, because I couldn't remember my first name, the one my parents had given me. But the Imperium took my pirate family, too, in a raid on Primus. Everyone died but me, who'd had the luck (or un-luck) of being on a run to buy much-needed fuel. They'd been sitting ducks without it. And dead ducks in the end.

So now at the ripe old age of sixteen, give or take a few months, it was just me again. A me that ached for both my lost families, but mostly for justice. I wanted—no, I *needed* to take back something of what the Imperium had taken from me. Reclaiming the sacred objects of my home planet felt like a step toward that.

"Ready to break orbit and enter the atmosphere over the capital, Vi," Evie said, her voice smooth and reassuring, like it always was.

I nodded, although there was no one there to see me. "Lead me in, Evie," I said into the comm, and she did.

I could see the massive capital city splayed out below me, and for a moment I was awestruck. Gleaming metal structures, buildings that touched the clouds, millions and millions of kilometers of roads and airways and . . . civilization. Or what passed for civilization, since surely nothing civilized could build itself on the backs of so many of my people murdered. All those citizens of the Imperium down there, profiting off my dead planet without a care. Maybe those sacred objects weren't much to them—another exotic artifact from off-world savages to be admired in a museum between fancy cocktails and a catered dinner—but they were everything to me.

"Landing in three minutes, Vi," Evie said.

"Let's do it, Evie," I said, flipping on the autopilot. "Time to take back what's ours."

Sneaking into the Museum of the Conquered was easier than expected: I walked in the front door.

"They really are that arrogant," I murmured to Evie through my well-hidden comm device. It was a portable that kept me connected to the AI in the ship. That way Evie and her big brain could keep working for me while I was on foot, reading the blueprints and security cams of the museum.

"Yes," Evie agreed, "but some credit must go to the very convincing paperwork that supports your invitation, Princess Amaryllis."

I snorted. The princess thing I'd done on a whim. People of the Imperium often assigned royal titles to themselves when claiming ancestry from conquered planets. After all, no one wanted to admit that their great-great-grandfather was at best a promiscuous scoundrel, at worst something far different; better to say your grandmother was a princess of a long-lost kingdom, even if the other branch of your ancestry was the reason the kingdom was lost to begin with.

I'd traded my preferred trousers and pilot's jacket for more formal attire that befit a princess, albeit one from an obscure planet that hopefully no one in attendance had heard of. My long dark hair was pulled back from my brown face and twisted in an elaborate series of braids that Evie had determined were all the fashion in the capital. Blooms of violets I'd traded with a hothouse gardener I knew from my pirate days were woven into my locks—my own touch, and a perfect color match for my deep purple gown. I'd kept my boots on in case I needed to run and hoped the length of the dress would cover them. If not, I'd play off my unusual footwear as a teenage peccadillo.

"Do not become overconfident," Evie warned. "Security will be abundant, and you are not clear of impediments yet. As you know, the gala is a target for thieves, and the Imperium has taken precautions."

"I'm counting on that fact to cover my escape," I said. I had already sent out half a dozen false calls to notorious pirates I knew from my old days, purposefully increasing the interstellar chatter to cover any trail Evie and I might accidentally leave.

I passed a couple holding long-stemmed glasses full of golden liquid; they smiled indulgently at me. Probably thought I was someone's daughter at my first dress ball or something. I smiled back, showing teeth. Suckers. Little did they know.

"Which way?" I asked Evie once I'd cleared the foyer.

"The exhibit hall of artifacts is forty paces straight ahead and to your right. Then another fourteen paces before another right. Once there you will have to pass through security once again. That should place you directly in front of the sacred objects you seek."

"Cheers, Evie."

"My pleasure."

I tapped off the comm in my ear and made my way down the

hallway, counting my steps and exchanging bland but appropriate smiles with passing strangers. I took the right turn Evie had instructed me to, and then, after fourteen paces, the second right.

"Invitation, miss?" a tall, bulky man in a dark uniform asked me.

"Of course." I handed over the card with its fake information chip to the security guard, who ran it through a handheld device.

He frowned, brows creasing on a face a good half meter above my own.

My heart rate jumped. Nothing could go wrong now. I was so close. "Is there a problem?" I asked airily, hoping I sounded properly rich, annoyed, and innocent at the same time.

"My apologies, but . . ."

I held my breath. "Yes?"

"I referred to you as miss, when your proper title is princess."

I stifled a groan. Oh, stars. I'd almost had a heart attack for nothing. "It's fine, really," I said. I let a small smile spread across my face. "Just don't let it happen again."

"Of course not."

And then I was breezing through security, trying desperately to force my heart rate back to normal.

I wandered through the artifact exhibit holding back tears. Everywhere I looked were the treasures of a whole civilization—my civilization.

The first hall was full of jewels, some raw from mines and some exquisitely shaped by artisans into bracelets, necklaces, and earrings. The wealth of generations.

The next hall was labeled ARCHAEOLOGICAL ARTIFACTS.

Walking through it made my stomach roil uncomfortably. Here, the items were encased in glass with a tiny holographic plaque that described them in insultingly simple terms.

MASK. CEREMONIAL ITEM. RECOVERED AT MOUNTAIN 32B.
IMPERIUM YEAR 1598.

RATTLE. CEREMONIAL ITEM. RECOVERED AT MOUNTAIN 32B.
IMPERIUM YEAR 1598.

CHILD'S SKULL. FUNERARY OBJECT. RECOVERED AT VALLEY 12.
IMPERIUM YEAR 1599.

That last one made me gag. A human skull? What was it doing in a museum? Why had they taken it off-planet to begin with? My wave of nausea gave way to rage. I would return all these items to what was left of my people, if I had to spend the rest of my life searching the galaxy for them.

"Amazing, isn't it?" a voice asked. A boy stood behind me, his expression mildly curious.

"Amazing? It's barbaric," I growled without thinking.

"Is it?" he asked, looking at me through long black lashes. He passed a hand across his golden hair, pushing his already impeccably coiffed bangs back into place. He wore a long coat of bright blue that matched his eyes, and a solid ruby sparkled on his middle finger. I startled. That ring was worth more than the *My Heart Will Go On.*

"And you are . . . ?" he asked.

"Princess Amaryllis," I supplied haughtily. Inside, I was kicking myself. Why had I said anything to this boy? He was clearly Imperium born and bred. Would a princess really call the Imperium barbaric?

His smile was small and thin. "A princess? Never met one of those before."

I narrowed my eyes. "That ring and that jacket say otherwise."

He fingered his lapel as if noticing it for the first time. "Do they?" He shrugged broad shoulders. "Well, nice to meet you, Princess. Do enjoy the barbaric exhibit."

And then he was taking his smile and his ruby ring with him as he moved on to the next exhibit.

I frowned. Thought to shout out to him, say something more. But what? I should be glad he was gone and I was spared whatever that interaction would have been. It was one thing to pretend to be a princess for a security guard and a few random moments of intrusive questioning, but if the stranger had asked me more about my supposed kingdom, I wasn't sure what I would have said. Still, there was something about him. Something that seemed familiar. But how many blond-haired, blue-eyed Imperium rich kids did I know? Thankfully, none.

"Focus on the mission," I muttered.

The lights blinked above me, a sign that the exhibit was closing. I scanned the room, gaze roving over tables, stands, and glass boxes. And there, in the far corner, exactly where Evie said it would be: an air vent.

I did another circuit to make sure the room was empty, nodded at a few stragglers who were wandering out, and then made my way back to the vent. I slid on my gloves, checked the antigravity booster on my boots, and took a deep breath.

In one leap I was even with the vent. Two breaths and I'd

used my screwdriver to remove the vent, three breaths and I'd slid my body inside. Four and the vent was back on, and all I had to do was wait.

∾

I may have dozed a bit, because when I opened my eyes, the exhibit was dark, all the lights off except the security grid on the floor and the floodlights over the exhibits. Satisfied I was alone, I clicked my comm back on.

"You there, Evie?"

"Affirmative, Vi."

"Can you disable security on the glass boxes in the exhibit room I'm in?"

"Processing. Please stand by. . . ."

While Evie did her job, I got ready to do mine. I slipped my tools from the secret pocket in my ball-gown sleeve. Basics of the profession: a multifaceted lockpick in case Evie couldn't disable the lock, a pair of printless sensory gloves, vibro pliers, my trusty screwdriver that had gotten me into the vent, and a lot of nerve.

"Evie?"

"Negative, Vi. The lock system is not attached to the network. I'm afraid you're on your own."

"Got it." I carefully removed the vent, wiggled my body out of the small space, and dropped into an unlit square on the floor. I froze, waiting for a security wail telling me I'd picked the wrong place to drop, but the only sound was the low hum of the system still in place. Exactly how I wanted it. I would be in and out before they even knew they'd been robbed.

I slid the lockpick into my hand, ready to get to work.

"Ho, what have we here?" A voice, just to my left.

I spun, holding the pick out as a weapon, expecting to see the burly security guard. But it was the boy from before, the Imperium snot.

"What are you doing here?" I whispered harshly, brandishing the pick. I wasn't much for violence, but I'd protect myself if I had to.

The boy lifted his hands in the universal sign of innocence. In one hand was a crowbar. "Came back for a little smash-and-grab myself. Didn't expect to find company."

"You're a thief?" I asked in disbelief.

"I prefer 'artifacts liberator.'"

My eyes rolled all the way to Primus and back. What were the chances? I narrowed my eyes in suspicion. "Wait, are you making fun of me?"

"I don't even know you."

Right, but something was off. "But your hair. Your eyes. That damn ring. You're Imperium. I'd bet my best lockpicks on it."

"Then you'd lose your lockpicks. This is a disguise. Heard of them? Hair's a dye job; eyes are contacts. Even my pale complexion is a temporary color job."

"So you look like me?" I scoffed. Sure, he could be as brown-skinned and black-haired as me, but I couldn't see it.

"Cousins, for sure." He winked, but then got serious. "I was raised in an Imperium household, but not by choice. I'm an orphan, picked up as a baby from my home planet and adopted. So now I do a little liberating in my free time."

My heartbeat sped up. He *was* like me. Well, a little like me. But still . . .

"How do I know you're not lying?"

He made a show of looking around the room. "We could wait and ask the guard, who should be coming through here on his rounds in about four minutes, or we could just agree we're on the same side for now and get this done." He swung his crowbar. "Your call."

"What were you going to do with that?" I asked, using my lips to point at the heavy bar.

"Like I said, smash and grab. Not all of us are dainty lockpickers, Princess."

"You break the glass, you'll have guards down on us faster than four minutes."

"Three minutes and thirty-five seconds now."

I could see his point. And if he was telling the truth and his goal was the same as mine, I'd take the help.

"I'll open the glass boxes. You look out."

"Three minutes and twenty seconds."

"I'll get it done," I growled, "if you let me work."

He raised innocent hands as he took a step back . . . and right into a security square. The alarm screamed immediately, an eardrum-shattering screech.

"Whoops!" he said, laughing. Laughing.

A danger freak. I'd known them when I lived with the pirates. People who got off on the adrenaline of the job, the more dangerous the better. But I was not going to lose my chance. After the exhibit was over, the artifacts would go back in the vault, and I had no idea how long it would be until they were on display to the public again.

"Get to breaking, then, Cuz," I said.

"As you wish." He stepped up, took a practice swing, and

then *smash!* The glass box holding the rattle shattered.

I reached in with my gloves and gingerly slid the artifact out between the shards.

Two steps and he was at the next box, and *smash!* And again, until he'd broken all the boxes. I removed each artifact and placed them safely in my bag, hit the button to inflate the protective lining, and hefted it over my shoulder.

Shouting in the hallway, and I knew we were out of time.

"You got a way out, Princess?" he asked.

I looked pointedly at the vent.

"Oh." His face fell. I saw it, too. No way was he shinnying up and out of that vent with those broad shoulders and no anti-gravity boots.

"No worries," he said with another outrageous smile. "You go. I'll distract them."

"But you'll get caught!"

"Don't worry about me. I've been in worse situations."

I wanted to ask what, but it was too late. I could see figures coming our way. I had to go while I still could.

"Great meeting you, Cuz!" he said, swinging his crowbar. "Take care now." And then he was running down the hall away from me, smashing jewel cases and everything else he could reach.

I didn't waste the opportunity. In less than ten seconds I was up and out of the exhibit, belly-crawling through the vent, and on my way back to my ship.

"Evie?" I asked, hitting my comm.

"How can I help you, Vi?"

"Did he make it? That boy?"

"Your request is unclear."

I sighed. "Are there any new records of detainment coming in from the Imperium security force?"

A second where Evie was working and then, "Affirmative. A young man has been detained. Would you like his statistics?"

"No," I said quickly. The less I knew, the better. "But could you hold on to them? Store them in your memory? In case I want them another time?"

"Affirmative."

I dropped out of the ventilation system on the far side of the museum. I looked around, but all the ruckus was far from me, on the other side of the grounds. I made it back to *My Heart Will Go On* without incident, fired up my engines, and left Imperium airspace.

But a little piece of me—maybe the part that wondered if he was some relation to me, if I'd found not just some*thing* of my home planet but some*one*—stayed behind, wondering if I'd done the right thing.

"This seat taken?"

I looked up from my very delicious daiquiri to find a stranger blocking my sun. Black hair long and loose in waves, brown skin, dark eyes, and some very nice, well-muscled shoulders.

"Depends," I asked, appraising him through my sunglasses. "Who are you?"

"Well, the much more interesting question is who you are, Violet."

I looked around for possible backup, someone to scream *help* at should I need it, but this close to sunset I had the beach to myself. And I'd left my comm back on the ship, sure I didn't need Evie for a few hours of relaxation by the ocean. This resort town far away from the heart of the Imperium was known as a safe place, low crime because a lot of criminals liked the spot and professional courtesy kept things respectful. Even thieves needed a break now and then.

"You know my name."

"I know a lot of things about you."

"Seems you have me at a disadvantage," I said coolly. I took another sip of my drink. The metal straw would make a good weapon in an emergency. He must have caught my look because he laughed, a very familiar laugh, and stepped back, raising his hands in innocence.

"Don't get violent on me, Cuz," he said. "I just wondered if you got those artifacts back to the people they should be with or not."

Ah . . . it was six months and a very good disguise later, but now I saw it. The laugh, the raised hands. My mysterious accomplice from the museum heist.

"Sorry, never caught your name."

"Does it matter?" he asked, dropping into the seat next to me.

"I like the hair. I was never a fan of blondes."

"Told you."

"How'd you find me?"

"It took me a bit," he admitted. "But the purple dress, the flowers in your hair, the planet the artifacts you lifted came from, and a friend who has a connection to some pirates of questionable morals. It all came together." He winked. "I got skills."

"I see you are still annoying."

He tapped his hands against his stomach. "Listen, do you want to do this or not?"

I frowned. "Do what, exactly? Why are you here again?"

His grin was big and confident. "Imperium's throwing a birthday party. Heard the empress herself is going to be there, wearing the crown jewels, the ones they usually keep under lock and key. Seemed like the kind of job a princess might be interested in."

He cocked an eyebrow at me.

I took another sip, stalling. I worked alone. Well, me and Evie. I didn't need a partner. But . . . maybe I wanted one.

"What's your name?" I asked again.

"My friends call me Trevan, but it's an Imperium name and I always hated it. My partner can call me . . . Valerian." He flushed, looking at me with hesitant eyes. He'd picked a flower name for himself, something natural, a reminder of the land.

But I wasn't ready to accept his story quite yet. "First tell me how you got out of the museum."

"I didn't. I was arrested. But they couldn't find the artifacts, so they couldn't hold me for theft. Just criminal mischief for breaking the glass. I did four months in minimum security on a prison planet, and here I am."

He'd done time for me. I was touched.

"What do you say? Partner?"

I sighed. Did I truly want this? Another person to potentially lose, someone to be responsible for? Someone to keep me from being so alone.

"You'll have to meet Evie. And she has to like you."

"I can do that."

"And I'm the captain of the *My Heart Will Go On,* so whatever happens on my ship, I'm in charge."

"Still not a problem."

He leaned over and took a sip from my drink.

So annoyingly rude. I had to laugh.

"Sure, Val," I said, decision made. "Let's go take back some pretty rocks from the empress. But listen, you are *going* to have to learn to pick a lock."

He stood, held out a hand, and pulled me to my feet. Somehow he'd commandeered my drink for himself. Thief!

"Or maybe you will come to appreciate the benefits of a quick smash-and-grab. Hey! Val and Vi." He nudged my shoulder. "I like it."

"Or Vi and Val." I let the names sit on my lips. "It has potential," I admitted.

Another grin as he finished my daiquiri. "You bet it does."

DREAM

AND

DARE

NIC STONE

The sun plays coy on the morning that Dream takes to the woods. And she's encouraged: the way it peeks above the horizon—like she peeks around corners to make sure the coast is clear—almost feels like an act of solidarity.

It's early winter, and the cool air bites at the tip of her nose as she creeps through the shadows along unlit alleyways she'd typically avoid . . . not that anything *bad* ever happens in the town where Dream has spent every day of her short sixteen years. She keeps to brightly lit places out here for the same reason she keeps to them at home: Dream is afraid of the dark.

But she can't let that stop her now. The big iron gates to the city loom, open as always, and the varied treetops of the forest— some pine, some oak, some she can't readily identify despite the number of times she's climbed them—poke into the sky beyond.

It gives her the burst of resolve she needs.

This isn't a decision she made lightly, this vanishing just before dawn, very much on a mission. Though she certainly didn't give proper thought to the low temperature. As numbness spreads beyond her extremities and up into her ankles and palms, a wave of doubt crashes over Dream. She stops and looks over her shoulder at the peaks of the red-shingled roofs she's left behind. Within one of those dwellings are Mother and Father and her mother's father and her father's mother, all surely on the verge of waking to find her gone. Dream can almost hear the tongue-lashing she'd receive from the older women at the sight of her poorly covered arms. (Though *they'd* been the ones to order the froufrou dresses with thin chiffon sleeves.)

She's tempted to turn back. Slip into her warm bed as though she never left. Choose one of the "suitors" her parents have been parading before her over the past few months, and settle into the life they'd prefer for her. It's not like it'd be a *bad* life. The men, though not much older than her, have all been perfectly chivalrous fellows who doted on her and would certainly give her anything she wanted. Doesn't hurt that they were all really cute, too. . . .

She sighs and shakes her head as that *thing,* that feeling she's had lately, tugs her in the opposite direction. Dream has yet to figure out adequate words for it, but it's like a drumbeat thumping within her veins and setting her blood on fire: there's a monster in these woods. (Everyone knows that much.) And it needs Dream. She can feel it.

As if in confirmation, the moment Dream crosses the threshold between open field and trees, a rogue gust of warmth

177

presses through her skin down into the marrow of her bones.

She's not cold anymore. Quite the opposite now. After a quick look around to make sure she's alone, Dream exhales and lets her head fall back. It's been over two years since she last set foot in these woods (nothing like an overprotective mother to kill her fun). But now the trees loom large around and above her, and Dream feels better than she has in weeks. "Man, is it good to be back," she whispers into the breeze.

Everyone in town thinks Dream is strange. She knows that for sure. They always have. When she was small, she was *that bizarre one who thinks she's some sort of lady knight—as if such a thing could exist,* and now she's *that one who talks to the trees.* (She got caught *one* time, five years ago, and hasn't been able to live it down.) It's always driven Mother bonkers that Dream insisted on wearing her prettiest dresses but returned home—daily—with them covered in smudges, the chiffon snagged, and/or holes in the lace.

(As a *riiiiip* rings through the air, Dream turns to see that her hem has snagged on a gnarly exposed tree root. She smiles. "Ha!")

Even so, Mother has yet to stop replenishing Dream's *dreamy* wardrobe. As a child, Dream was never permitted to wear the leather trousers that were more suited to her rambunctious style of play, so she got used to running/jumping/climbing/tumbling while draped in layers of tulle and chiffon. And Dream *likes* the dresses. They feel good on her long, lithe limbs and accent her heart-shaped face. In fact, this has been her saving grace: her "overt femininity." (*God,* does she hate that word. It's so . . . limiting. As evidenced by the way that Mother side-eyes Dream for "being so rough-and-tumble while wearing such *feminine* garments." It annoys Dream to no end.)

And that is why she's in these woods. Well . . . partially why, at least. Four days ago, some new suitor and his parents came to call. (Stunning jawline and gorgeous deep brown skin on this one, but his eyebrows were even more manicured than hers. Definitely a deal breaker.) And the moment Dream entered the room in her shimmery indigo gown, the boy's mother burst into applause. "Aha!" she said, ecstatic. "Now, *that* is a true lady. Poised and well-postured." She pulled her own shoulders back. "Nothing like that . . . *person* we encountered last week. Would you believe the young lady greeted us wearing *trousers*? And had *grit* beneath *untrimmed* fingernails? Her father said something about a metalworking hobby, but we didn't even bother to sit down. You'd think that after what happened to that so-called princess, these girls would know better—"

"Ah." And Dream got up and left the room without another word.

Ever since then, *said* princess—"so-called" be damned—has been at the center of Dream's every thought. Dare was this princess's name. . . .

"*Is* her name," Dream corrects under her breath.

As of this morning, Princess Dare has been missing for two and a half years. She vanished a fortnight after her fourteenth birthday, and the search for her was abandoned after mere days. Disdain ran deep for the "princess" who dressed like a boy yet outright refused to court one.

Dream scowls as she forges deeper into the woods and the hem of her voluminous skirts gets heavy with grime. It bothers Dream that Dare's memory only survives in their pitiful principality because Dare's disappearance was the closest thing to a scandal any of the townspeople had ever seen. Most presumed Dare ran away under the cloak of darkness (*and good riddance, the royal family must be so* relieved, *can you even imagine?*). But there were some who believed a fearsome monster had snatched and eaten her in the dead of night (*even so, good riddance, at least she didn't suffer much*).

The latter isn't entirely unfounded because there truly *is* a monster. It took up residence in the woods around the time of Dare's departure, and after multiple eyewitness accounts of a horrifyingly ugly and frighteningly formidable beast living in a house made of human bones, many assumed Princess Dare was its first victim. "I've heard the creature is drawn to the aberrant," some say. "It has a penchant for the deviant," whisper others.

Then there are the Pursuers: a group that believes wholeheartedly in the monster, but also in the notion that Princess Dare is very much alive and in need of rescue. And not only from the foul beast; from her "abnormal proclivities" as well.

It should come as no surprise that the majority of Pursuers are thick-headed boys: hubris-driven imbeciles out to prove their manhood and worthiness of utmost respect and admiration by venturing into the woods, weapons in hand, and emerging with Dare cradled in a set of strong arms, her princess-y nature obscured by her frailty and filth.

(*Gross,* Dream thinks. And not at all because she just stepped into a puddle of muck.)

The hero of heroes would have a knapsack slung over one chiseled shoulder, and within that knapsack would be the severed head of the monster. Princess Dare would come to and fall madly in love with her rescuer, thereby transforming into the lady royal everyone would claim they knew she could be.

Only two would-be heroes—out of over one hundred—had ever returned from the forest. Both of them woefully empty-handed and driven too mad by what they'd seen to even speak of it. But the Pursuers were undeterred. In fact, Dream's current trek through the woods was spurred on by one of them: an admittedly *strapping* suitor—different from the one with the awful mother, delightfully tall and handsome, with skin the cool, dusky brown of a walnut shell—was so butt-hurt by Dream's rejection, he puffed his chest up and said, "Well, that's a relief. Now I can fulfill my *true* calling: taking down that wretched beast in the woods so I can return the Dare girl to her proper place."

Dream would've laughed in his face if not for the fissure of rage that opened up inside her chest.

Not only because these Pursuer boys see the "rescue" mission as their chance at glory. That they see the life of a young woman as little more than a proving ground for their bravado. And not only because they believe Dare—or *any* young woman—to be incapable of fending for herself. It's not only that, deep down, the intentions of these scoundrels are utterly dishonorable. That Dream *knows* what they really want is to be thought of as The Man Who Made Dare into a REAL Princess.

What makes Dream angriest is that she knows they're mistaken. It's why she's in these woods.

She's going to prove them wrong. About Dare, yes, but also about herself.

The townspeople, the suitors, they think of Dream as the dream girl. The dream wife. Pretty, sweet, compliant. Everything Dare was—is—not.

But they are incorrect. They don't know Dream, and they certainly didn't know Dare.

Dream, though, knew Dare.

Knows her.

Dream *knows* Dare doesn't need to be rescued. Not in the least. The monster does.

The sun is high in the sky by the time the monster—if you can even call it that—wakes in its treehouse made of fallen branches. (Not human bones like those nitwits in the villages claim; the monster always eats those.) Its belly burbles, and it releases a throaty groan. There's no doubt about it now: the monster's most recent meal had been absolutely rotten.

It groans again, this time in regret. It should've known: the moronic boy had smelled awful, and he tasted of sour milk and rancid meat. He was more pompous than the others, too. Hurling insults until the monster finally ate his face.

Now, staring up into the canopy of green and listening to the music of the forest, with a bellyache from the deepest circle of hell, the monster can feel the change in the air that marks the approach of an interloper—and potential meal. Perhaps this one will be better. A stomach-settler. It's happened before: the relatively nice boy who tried to use kind words to lure the monster into a rather obvious trap had been like a dose of milk of magnesia after the havoc wreaked on the monster's gut by the blustering, ruddy-faced chap the monster had previously eaten. *That* boy had attempted a curse-filled sword attack and tasted like dog dung.

A breeze rustles the leaves overhead, and the monster sits

up. Inhales. There's something . . . different. About this intruder. Different than the dumb-as-bricks boy-humans with their clubs and spears and bows and arrows—all objects now strung up around the monster's tree as an unheeded warning. The monster had devoured those boys in a blink and with abandon, though the monster is smaller than the boys had been. And they—the boys—were always so much less filling than they looked. Instead of heart and meat, full of hot air and utterly lacking in substance.

The scent in the air now is missing the mustiness of puffed-up ego and the pungency of presumed victory. There is . . . sweetness. With a smack of spice. Like a bouquet of flowers wrapped in a string of cinnamon sticks.

The monster hasn't smelled something so sweet in . . . well, it can't remember how long. It brings to mind someone the monster used to know but hasn't thought of in as long as it could think: a girl.

And she *was* a girl. Dare had been this girl's name, the monster recalls, and despite not fully comprehending the word *princess,* it arises beside the girl in the monster's mind. And she felt settled in her body and skin, though the monster knew, somehow, that there were many who assumed this girl not *fully* "girl" because of the way she refused to embrace frivolous things the silly townspeople decided were part and parcel to *girlhood.* Dresses and dolls and tea parties and stolen glances at their—presumed—boy counterparts.

What the monster *does* understand is that *princess,* whatever it means, didn't seem to *fit* this Dare girl. Her shoulders had stooped as though she carried the weight of a relentlessly cruel world on them. And her eyes rarely lifted from the ground around her feet. And beneath this Dare girl's sweet scent, there had been something incongruous. A tang. Something tinged with despair and broken dreams.

But what, the monster ponders, pushing up to its feet, had happened to Dare?

The monster is just about certain that it didn't eat her. It couldn't have.

The sweetness dancing up the tree trunks and spinning on the leaves intensifies, and the atmosphere crackles as warm, honeyed air rushes over the monster. It stumbles, shaken to its core—the monster has never experienced anything so *pleasant,* is the word that comes to mind. (It's a new one.) It lifts its rough hands and sucks in the monster equivalent of a gasp. The air burns going down the monster's throat, but that's nothing compared to the stinging fissures now snaking up, down, and all around the monster's body, leaving jagged gaps in its tree bark–like shell—skin?

Its gut rumbles, but there's something more.

An opening of the monster's mind.

Where had the Dare girl gone? And who is this delicious-smelling newcomer?

Without thinking too much about it, the monster leaps down from the treehouse.

Dream kicks a rock out of her path.

Most of the people back home—though she'd be lying if she said that word feels like it still fits when she thinks of the town she left behind—think Dream is no more than her name implies: cloudy-headed and moony-eyed. She has skin the color of coffee-splashed rooibos tea, and dark eyes typically turned skyward. A tendency that makes them sparkle like black sapphires in both sun and moonlight.

But those eyes are keener than anyone realized. They pick up on things overlooked by those too consumed with chasing the future to enjoy the present.

They are eyes that alight on the faint trail along the forest floor masked by an increase of broken twigs and divots in the earth that could only come from heavy boots.

It's true that even without these signs, Dream would've found her way through the woods just fine. Even now, with the sky beginning to darken as the sun makes its descent toward a horizon Dream can't see for the trees, Dream knows where she is going.

By Mother's orders, Dream stopped her daily jaunts into these woods when the town baker's right hand—as distinguished by a crescent moon–shaped burn scar along his palm—was found atop a pile of dead leaves three days after he took to the woods in search of his missing (Pursuer) son.

Prior to the monster's arrival, however, Dream had spent most of her time in these woods. As a young(er) girl, Dream loved nothing more than to spend her days slaying pine dragons with her stick sword while riding on the back of her stump steed. In a beautiful gown, no less.

Though the light is low now, Dream moves with certainty. A random gust of warm air caresses her face, and Dream knows she has almost reached the spot where she last saw Princess Dare with her own eyes.

On that afternoon, Dream remembers dreamily, Dare was wearing leather trousers tucked into boots that tied up to the knee. Her unruly black curls were pushed back from her face with a headband, and her skin, a deep bronze that glimmered in the sunlight, was exposed from neck to breastbone by her half-unbuttoned white shirt and glistened with sweat and confidence. Princess Dare's sleeves were shoved up above her elbows, and as she climbed a massive oak, her forearms flexed and pulsed.

It had warmed Dream in places that brought a flush to her cheeks.

Dream would never admit it to a soul, but she'd followed Princess Dare into the woods that day. In fact, Dream had been following Princess Dare for months, and though Dream was sure the princess would've welcomed the company—Princess Dare seemed so lonely back then—Dream could never work up the courage to step out from behind the bushes.

Dream had watched Princess Dare change as both girls got older. The same boys who tugged at Dream's skirts and whispered sugar-coated deceptions to her in passing would shout obscenities at Princess Dare and touch the princess without permission. Being a royal daughter meant nothing: Princess Dare's lack of interest in boys and refusal to wear the admittedly absurd fluffy froufrou dresses (the ones Dream couldn't get enough of) were treated as an abdication.

During their primary school days, Princess Dare appeared unfazed by the sidelong glances thrown in her direction as she blew by in her signature trousers, wild hair billowing like a lion's mane. But as they pushed into those years when a girl begins to blossom with the parts people claim make her a *woman,* the glances at Princess Dare turned to glares turned to whispers turned to outright disdain. By the time Dream and Dare hit thirteen, the princess walked with her head down and shoulders hunched.

Princess Dare was rarely seen in public at all.

But she would sneak off to these woods.

On the day Dream last saw Princess Dare, Dream herself had

been in these woods. Dream was up in her own favorite tree, daydreaming about what it would be like for the sky to be the ground. Dream's reverie was halted by the snap of twigs on the forest floor just beneath her perch.

Dream looked down just as Princess Dare stopped to spread her arms and inhale, and in that moment, with Dream's cheeks heating at the sight of Princess Dare's shiny curls, Dream knew she would follow the other girl wherever she went.

(At a safe distance, of course.)

Off Princess Dare went, deeper into the woods, and when Princess Dare had gotten far enough away, Dream shinnied down her tree, gathered the lace hem of her dress—which was already ripped in four places—and followed the trail Princess Dare had left in the underbrush with her heavy boots.

When Dream reached the edge of the small clearing where Princess Dare had stopped, Dream dropped down behind a thicket and just . . . watched.

She watched as Princess Dare scaled the gnarled shaft of a large oak tree and took a seat on a bough some thirty feet up. And there the princess stayed, gazing into the glowing canopy of leaves, her back against the heavy trunk, with one leg bent at the knee, and the other swinging free as the breeze.

Dream gawped, mouth open and everything. She felt like Princess Dare had shrugged off the cloak of contempt the townspeople daily draped over her shoulders, and left the wretched thing crumpled at the base of the tree. Seeing Princess Dare so open, so light, Dream had wanted to destroy that cloak somehow. To raze the kingdom, rid the whole world of anything that would return the stoop to the princess's beautiful, unbowed shoulders.

Dream wanted to step out of hiding in that moment. To climb that tree and perch beside the princess. Dream wanted to extend her own calloused hand in greeting—the rough palm Mother couldn't bear to look at because it reminded her of her daughter's "unpleasant" hobbies—as well as her heart.

But Dream hadn't had the courage.

Soon thereafter, a group of numbskull boys discovered Princess Dare's woodland sanctuary. Her tree. Dream hadn't been there, but she'd heard about the venom-slicked jeers and throwing of stones. The attempts to lure and then to knock Princess Dare down from her happy place.

That night, Dream dreamt that one of the boys had seized a filthy cloak from the muddy ground and climbed the tree to toss it over Dare's bent head and shuddering shoulders before shoving her down to where his cohorts waited with sticks, poised to strike the minute she hit the ground.

Two mornings later, Princess Dare hadn't been at breakfast. The servant sent to investigate found the princess's chambers empty.

When news of Princess Dare's disappearance reached Dream, Dream had run to the woods to check the tree.

Princess Dare hadn't been there.

And Princess Dare isn't there now as Dream steps into the small clearing and looks up at Princess Dare's favorite bough.

But there *is* a treehouse built from what look like fallen branches.

Dream takes a steadying breath and squares her shoulders.

Then she climbs.

∽

The monster hears and smells the person up in its treehouse before it sees them. But even without the sound or scent, the gathering of fireflies—a rare occurrence—makes it clear that there's an intruder. The last time the luminescent creatures appeared en masse, the monster discovered a small girl—she was no more than six—attempting to take a beautifully carved mahogany bow from the monster's collection of boneheaded-boy weapons.

The little girl had been lost. She smelled of honeysuckle and spun sugar. Of unbridled optimism and wanton naivete. So sweet, the monster lost its appetite. Instead of eating her, it led the girl back to the trail she'd wandered from so she could find her way home.

She'd even said *Thank you.*

This girl—for the monster is now sure there is a girl up in its treehouse, though an older girl than the one before—smells like fullness. Like dense, crusty bread and whipped, salted butter. Glazed, fatty meats. Like depth and breadth and wholeness.

It's been a long day. The monster failed to find Princess Dare herself, but it did find remnants of her in the bushes all around the tree. A bootlace here. A headband there. A strip of tattered fabric.

As the monster makes its way toward the tree, pulled as if by string to this new girl's delectable essence, a blast like the breath of a dragon (but less acrid) shoots down from the branches. The monster feels more of its armor-like skin crack and fall away.

But it doesn't care.

The monster is exceedingly hungry.

And *this* is a meal it will not miss.

Dream can hear *and* feel the monster approaching from behind.

It's starving. She can tell by the change in the air and the wet rattle of the monster's breath.

And Dream is afraid. Afraid she's wrong about the monster. Afraid the monster actually *doesn't* need her. Afraid Princess Dare truly *is* gone, and Dream herself is about to be devoured.

Dream wonders how much it will hurt.

She feels the monster stop. Feels that ravenous breath shudder through the air around her. Feels its hunger . . . for her.

Dream turns. Takes in the monster's face and looks into its fathomless eyes.

And Dream exhales.

Which appears to give the monster pause.

Dream wants to close her eyes but forces herself not to. This is the moment she's awaited for years.

"Princess?" Dream says.

Dare blinks. She's cold.

She's naked.

She's standing in what appears to be a treehouse built from fallen branches.

And there before her is a beautiful girl lifting the tattered hem of a dress—one that certainly has no place in these woods—to reveal a pair of leather trousers that the girl swiftly removes.

The girl kneels at Dare's feet and holds the pants out so that Dare can step into them. Then the girl stands and removes a rumpled tunic and a pair of thin, flat shoes from a satchel tucked and cloaked between the layers of her skirts.

"Sorry they're not your boots," the girl—a *beautiful* girl, indeed—is saying as she helps Dare slide the simple slippers onto her feet. "I had a hunch I'd find you here. One of the two boys who made it back has said literally nothing since his return but 'Those eyes . . . her eyes . . .' in a *deeply* disturbing voice, and it took me longer than it should've to figure it out, but once I realized—"

The girl stops talking. And swallows, it seems.

"At any rate," she continues (*so,* so beautiful), "I tried to pack as light as possible in case you *weren't* actually you, and I needed to make a run for it." The girl looks up at Dare and smiles. The warmth from those earlier breezes is nothing compared to the fire that has ignited within Dare's bones, marrow and all.

Which is . . . familiar.

"I brought you some food," the girl goes on, still down on one knee, removing more items from her hidden satchel. "Crusty bread and chèvre. They're your favorites, right? At least they used to be. I think. . . ."

At the girl's sudden shyness, Dare can't take any more. "You're the Dream girl," Dare says—well, croaks, really—finally finding her tongue and remembering how to use it. It occurs to Dare how disheveled she must appear. How . . . raggedy.

She hates it.

This is when Dare notices the chunks of bark-like armor littering the uneven treehouse floor at her feet.

The girl's—*Dream,* Dare believes her name is—eyes widen. Dare notices that they sparkle in the moonlight. Like black sapphires.

"What did you say?" Dream asked.

"That's your name, isn't it? Dream?"

The Dream girl rises to her feet but doesn't respond.

"I remember you," Dare continues. "You used to follow me into these woods when we were younger."

Now Dream's eyes *really* widen. "You knew?"

It's Dare's turn to smile. She wonders if her smile affects Dream like Dream's smile affects her—

Dare doesn't think she's ever hoped for anything the way she hopes for this.

"Yes, I knew," Dare says. "And I enjoyed every moment that I knew you were around somewhere. You followed me all the time."

Now Dream's chin drops. Is she . . . embarrassed?

"Yes, Your Majesty," Dream says.

"You saw me up there," Dare says, pointing to her favorite bough. It's still a good ten feet above the pair of girls, and Dare only does it because she wants Dream to look up. To lift her gaze from the ground. Set it skyward where Dare remembers it always being.

But Dream's eyes never make it beyond Dare's face. "I've always seen you, Princess." Dream takes a tenuous step closer to Dare.

It makes Dare's heart race, but she further closes the gap between them. Dare remembers the day she deliberately stopped beneath the tree Dream was perched in, hoping Dream would follow her deeper into the woods so Dream wouldn't feel so alone.

And Dream had. Dream did.

Though Dream had kept herself hidden (Dare could totally see her, but she'll keep that part to herself), Dream *saw* Dare.

Dream is seeing Dare now.

And Dare is seeing Dream.

They are (finally!) seeing each other.

Dream takes another step. The girls are about the same height, but Dream's figure, Dare notices, has dips and bumps where Dare is slim and straight lined.

Dare would like to run her newly barkless hands down into the valley of Dream's waist and over the hills of her hips. So she closes what space remains between them. "No one's ever called me that before," Dare breathes against Dream's lips.

Dream, who closes her eyes. Dreaming, it seems. "Called you what?" she says back.

"Princess," Dare says, barely above a whisper.

Then neither girl is speaking at all.

 WISH

JENNI BALCH

Words formed in the air this time, the edges of the letters iridescent. At first, Lane thought they were another weird symptom of his decades-long headache. They stayed where they were when he tilted his head, though, which was a clue.

"At last." Lane tossed the book he'd been rereading onto the other end of the sofa. "Took long enough." He pushed himself up and stepped to where the passage was slowly building itself in the wall of his den that wasn't occupied by his sofa, the tiny kitchenette, or the bookshelves full of used books. Lane bounced on the balls of his feet as he wondered where on Earth he would find himself this time. Maybe Istanbul again? Anywhere was good as long as they had good food. He would, metaphorically, kill for a fresh cup of coffee.

Telling how much time had passed out in the world was always chancy from inside the LAMP, but it felt like it had been much longer than usual this time. His supplies were running short, and he'd had to read everything in the place three times over. While Granters didn't need as much as people who lived outside a LAMP, it was still nice to have fresh supplies.

Each new word shimmered into being, solidifying in a way he felt more than saw, and as one after another slid into place, shaping a path between his rooms and the world beyond the LAMP, Lane could smell the edges of the place he was about to step into. A bit flat and metallic to his scent-starved senses.

Likely not Istanbul, then, but possibly still a place with some interesting foods to try once he got the Wish taken care of. If things went to trend, it would be something frivolous and easy that wouldn't really change anything. Three of the last four Wishes he'd granted had been for the latest sports car. The fourth had been some fancy exercise equipment.

After a minor eternity, with a stir of the air that felt like a Call, the connection between the LAMP and the world was complete. Lane was ready, hovering on the threshold.

He stepped through.

As the universe re-formed around him, he said, "Okay, what can I—"

No one was there. He saw consoles and computer equipment mixed with books and some mementos. A stuffed elephant sat on a shelf tucked under a corner of sloping ceiling at eye level, a creased postcard of the cliffs of Dover on its lap. The jumbled pile of odds and ends somehow seemed cozy. The wall was less than an arm's length away.

"Oh!"

The soft exclamation came from behind him and he spun around. A girl stared at him, wide-eyed. He glanced down and realized he'd forgotten to change. Not just his clothes, which were the jeans and faded *Star Wars* T-shirt he'd most liked growing up, but his body, too. People expected someone older, more mysterious when they Wished. But maybe it wasn't so bad. The girl seemed like she was about his age, not counting the centuries he'd been a Granter, which he never did. Seventeen at most. And already staring at him as if he had two heads, which he didn't. Just the one. He had unexceptional brown eyes and hair, and copper skin; he was as human as she was, mostly.

Though she was much paler, her skin somehow chalky, as if she didn't get enough sun. Even the brown of her cropped hair was washed out. Her eyes were sharp and quick, so maybe that was just the style now. Her clothes were a good hint that styles had changed since he'd last been Called. She was wearing the soft stretchy material he usually thought of as pajamas, but what she wore was much more like a uniform than he'd ever seen someone wear to bed. She had to be the new Wisher. The LAMP orb rested in her hand.

Lane smiled and bowed to her. "The contract is complete. What Wish would you have?"

The young woman cocked her head to one side. "The contract?"

That wasn't in the script.

"Yes, the contract." Lane frowned. How had she activated the LAMP if she didn't already know? "Hasn't someone explained what the LAMP does?"

She was still staring at him in a way that he wasn't sure how to interpret. It didn't really seem like a smile, for all that her lips turned up at the edges.

"Not in so many words. I've been trying to work it out myself for the last few years." She stood up. The battered old chair she'd been curled up on hit the far wall of the tiny room. "I didn't expect anything would happen."

A hint of wonder: he recognized that. He'd seen it so often by now that he could see it before they knew they were feeling it. Sometimes they liked to talk about themselves before they settled down to business. It used to be his favorite part, but right now, Lane just wanted to move on. She rolled the LAMP in her hand and studied him.

Then she smiled. She extended the hand that wasn't holding the LAMP. "I'm Ariadne. It's nice to meet you."

Lane froze. He really should have remembered to change. Wishers didn't interact with Granters as people, and he wasn't comfortable with this shift. As he glanced from her hand to her face, he could feel the energy sizzling through her, but she was outwardly still, ready to wait until he answered the unasked question.

He hesitated and then took her offered hand and shook it as briefly as he could. "If we could get to your Wish?"

She didn't let him escape that easily. She raised a brow at him and stared. Lane was sure Ariadne had never met his grandmother, but she captured her expression perfectly. Lane's cheeks heated.

"I'm Lane." He paused; then, hoping to get back to a professional tone, he added, "Ma'am."

At that, her smile grew into a grin. "'Ma'am' is my mother. I'm just Ariadne." She let go of his hand, and Lane stuffed it into his pocket. "Before we get to the Wish, you said something about a contract. I want to make sure I understand what I am agreeing to. Can you review it?"

It was unusual, but if she wanted to go over it line by line now, he could humor her. "Okay, point me to a coffeepot and we'll get to work!"

"We don't have any coffee on the station. Caffeine has so many side effects it was phased out a generation ago in anything more than ten milligrams."

Lane understood each word, but he still had no clue what Ariadne was saying.

"I don't understand," Lane said.

She said, "I'm not sure I do either, but regulations must be followed. We do have a tea shop. Maybe they'll have something that can help."

Ariadne grabbed a coat that was made out of the same jersey fabric as her pajama outfit, stuffed the LAMP into a pocket, and pushed open a door Lane hadn't noticed before.

"Come on," she said over her shoulder.

Lane stepped out of the room onto a metal stair and gaped. A vast lattice, like lace made from girders and glass, arced overhead. A vibrant neon-blue light radiated from every pane. Nestled in the hollow underneath, falling away from this tiny room tucked up near the sidewall, was a town. But it wasn't like any town Lane had ever seen.

"What is this place?"

"Welcome to Vale. The oldest research station in Venus's clouds."

"Venus?" Lane's voice cracked.

Ariadne leaned on the railing as she turned toward him. "Yep."

"But . . ." Lane inspected the dome again. "When did Venus turn blue?"

"It didn't. The glass is absorbing the energy, blue shifting the light as it processes it. That's used to feed the magnetic drive that keeps the station hovering."

"Oh, well, that's impressive."

She shrugged. "I suppose. I've probably just been here too long. None of it seems special anymore." She avoided looking at him as she spoke. "Come on. We should get to the shop before second bell."

Lane trailed behind her as they descended the stairs but couldn't help sneaking glances up at the wonders she so easily dismissed. What could she want to Wish for, if this was where she lived?

Ariadne passed the counter, answering the shopgirl's greeting and tossing out a quick order as she hustled Lane into a booth near the back, as far as possible from the big windows at the front. It could have felt like she was trying to hide him away. Instead it felt like she was hiding and had pulled him along with her.

The shopgirl had to be several years younger than Ariadne. Lane's best guess was she was around twelve, much younger than any he'd seen working in stores last time he'd been out of the LAMP. When the teapot arrived, the girl stared at him until Ariadne shooed her away. Once she left, Ariadne stopped peering around the corner toward the front of the store and started preparing their tea. Lane finally tried to find words to explain . . . everything.

"I've never had to do this before. The story is something you tell yourselves, as the LAMP is passed on. I'm Called and ask what the Wish is, grant it, and it's done. Then I can go back to my books."

"I don't need a novel," Ariadne said; "I need information. I have to know the consequences before I can make an informed decision." Lane fumbled his drink. She grabbed a cloth and wiped up the small spill. "I know. But my mother is the head of station. Unnecessary risks are not tolerated." Her voice twisted on the *unnecessary,* but she didn't give him a chance to ask about it.

She leaned back in her seat, her mug cupped in her hands, and said, "Tell me a story."

"There are stories about Wishes all across the world—I guess *worlds,* now that people have made it to Venus." A smile touched his lips, but just briefly, as Ariadne waited for him to continue. "Most stories get it more wrong than right. But we don't contradict the myth. We're not demons, or spirits of fire or air. We're people. Mostly."

"But you live in here?" Ariadne pulled the LAMP from her pocket and held it cupped in her palm. It glowed softly in the artificial light of the shop.

"The LAMP's more of a passageway or gate than a house. It's not like I shrink down and go live inside a glass sphere until the next Call. My place is pretty much the same as a regular apartment." Lane considered what he'd seen of where she lived and added, "Where I'm from, at least. It just connects to the rest of the world through that." Lane gestured toward the LAMP.

"Where are you from?" Ariadne asked. Lane hesitated. She hurried to continue. "It will help me understand this lamp."

"You don't really need to understand the LAMP." *Or me,*

he didn't add aloud. This was a transaction. Simple and easy, if she would let it be. "You just need to make a Wish."

She shook her head. "If there are rules, I don't know what they are. I won't know if you can help me or not until I understand how this works."

He needed to redirect the conversation. "The limits of my power to grant Wishes don't have anything to do with the LAMP or where I'm from. They come from the contract."

Confusion knit Ariadne's brow.

"I'm not explaining this well." Lane ran a hand through his hair and then tried again. "You know contracts, right?"

Ariadne nodded. "My mom runs this place. Sometimes she does more contracts than science."

"Then you know the basics. This whole thing"—he gestured to himself, the LAMP, and her—"is a contract. Everyone has their role and their obligations. You Called me. For that, you get a Wish."

"One? I thought there were three." Ariadne placed her elbows on the table as she leaned forward, interested.

Now that they were on safer ground, he picked up his mug again, letting the warmth seep into his hands. "That's just in stories. Wishes are a one-time thing. Because there's only sufficient energy if you Wish for something with all of your being. It has to be what you want more than anything else. Most people don't have three of those Wishes."

She drummed her fingers on the table. "Okay, I can live with that."

Lane nodded. "I'm basically a conduit. I am able to channel that Wish into something that can affect the world."

"And you can change anything?"

Something in the way she stilled after asking the question, leaning forward just a bit, fingers flexed on the LAMP, made him pause before he answered.

"I can do things; I can't change people." She moved, maybe to object, maybe to interrupt; Lane didn't wait to see. He continued, "Because Wishing another person different is never the right answer. Even if you figured out some way to make it happen, it doesn't end well."

"You think I want to change someone else? No, Lane, I wouldn't have spent this much time trying to change something I could fix on my own."

"Then what *do* you want? I can feel how much you want whatever it is."

Ariadne's mug clinked as she put it on the laminate and then pushed it away from her. "You already told me it wouldn't work."

"Tell me what you were thinking. There might still be something I can do. I've had a bit more time to know the ins and outs of this than you have."

"Maybe it was just company I wanted. Something new and different. Maybe I was bored, since all my friends are gone." The last words were bleak, cutting to the heart of whatever she wouldn't tell him. Her Wish mattered deeply to her.

"Where did they go?" The question escaped before he could stop it. And once it was out, he was surprised to find that he wanted to hear the answer.

Something twisted in Ariadne's face. "Oh, they went to Earth for school. Just like everyone when they turn fourteen." She held his eyes, challenging him to say something.

Lane was fairly sure whatever he said would be wrong, but he couldn't let the silence stretch. Not with the way she was staring at him. Still, he hesitated, nervous—for the first time in a very long time—about saying the wrong thing.

He took a moment to wish again that there were coffee instead of weak tea in his cup. He gulped down a swallow and almost choked in surprise as he tasted hot, strong coffee. "What?"

He'd been asking the cup, not Ariadne, but she answered anyway, her words chips of ice. "I know you haven't seen many people here yet, but you will when second bell rings in a few minutes, letting off the main shift. The station is home to service members, research personnel, maintenance people, and their minor children. Once you reach fourteen, there's no place for you here until you're ready to take on a job, which, due to labor laws about the dangers of work on stations, is twenty-one. No one stays."

"Except you?"

"Except me. Ask me why."

Anger simmered just under the surface of her words, but Lane could tell that talking about it was helping Ariadne. Somehow. He was already getting energy from helping with Ariadne's Wish. He wouldn't have been able to Wish himself coffee otherwise. "Why?"

"Just before I turned thirteen, I developed immune thrombocytopenic purpura, which means I have really low platelets. I bruise when I brush the corner of a table. Going through the acceleration of liftoff, I'd die. And if we got my platelets up enough to survive leaving Venus, it would wear off before landfall on Earth. It's been deemed an *unnecessary risk*."

Ariadne scanned the shop, but from her expression, Lane didn't think she really saw any of it. He recognized the restlessness, impatience, and frustration that he felt when he was stuck in the LAMP too long. Or, further back, before he was a Granter and was looking forward to being anywhere else. When that feeling hit, he was able to manage it, because he always knew that sooner or later he would be someplace new.

Ariadne met his eyes and said, "I can never leave here. I can't even try to get a job until I'm twenty-one, no matter how many certifications I collect in all this spare time. Just make work, like trying to figure out the LAMP. There is no place for me here. Everyone else is moving forward, and I'm stuck." Her voice broke as she continued, "If you can't change me, then you can't change that."

Lane finished his coffee. Ariadne had fallen silent, turning the LAMP over from one hand to the other.

The shop was filling up, and now that Ariadne had pointed it out, Lane saw she was right. No one else was anywhere near their age. Except a couple of people in coveralls with a delivery firm's logo on their backs.

Ariadne watched the waitress drop off another table's order. "Maybe all I needed was someone to talk to. Maybe that will be enough."

Lane was uncomfortable with the dull resignation in her voice. She couldn't be giving up, not when they were this close to a Wish that actually mattered. He was beginning to get a feel for how much she had done to get this far. Maybe her willpower and determination could get them close to her Wish. But, to be sure, he asked, "How could you open the LAMP if you weren't told how to by the previous Wisher?"

"I found a little information, as you said, in stories. Everyone was clear that there were limits. I got into the records from the black box of the ship the LAMP was recovered from too, which had some logs from the person who had the LAMP before." She grimaced. "It took a while to break the encryption and piece the information back together, but I had time on my hands. It took three years before I found a way."

Obviously, she had, but Lane was beginning to suspect that it wasn't the usual way.

"What did you do to open the LAMP?"

"I pictured a pair of giant doors, like in some old movie on Earth, as completely as I could—visualized it—and then pushed them open. Why?"

Lane laughed. "Most people just say it out loud."

"Oh. It didn't say in the instructions, and I'd said 'open' near it several times without anything happening."

"How badly do you want this?" Lane asked.

"With all I am," Ariadne said, then shook her head. "But it won't be enough."

"I can't break the rules of the universe. But I can probably bend them." Lane met her eyes. "I'm not sure that we can do it, but I'm willing to try if you are."

"Yes." There was no hesitation.

"It might be dangerous."

"Everything is dangerous. All the more so for me."

"Okay, let's go back to where we met." Lane stood up, but stopped when he realized Ariadne hadn't moved. "What?"

"Is there any danger to anyone else here?"

"No. It'll either work, which might be dangerous to you or me, but no one else. Or it won't, and then there's no danger to anyone."

Now she stood and joined him. "Let's go."

∞

Lane spread some foam padding under a thin blanket on the cleared floor, just in case. Ariadne did something on her wrist computer to set it to send a message if she didn't cancel it before their self-imposed time ran out, but Lane only caught the barest sliver of the technical details of what she was doing.

"Done," she said, pressing another couple of keys.

Lane heard the nerves in her voice, but she didn't hesitate to take his hand when he reached out to pull her to her feet.

"Okay," he said, "picture the place you've wanted to go the most. Hold that image as tightly and completely as you did to open the LAMP. And I'll try to make a portal like the LAMP's to send us there for a few seconds. Or however long the energy lasts. I just know that this'll burn through the power quicker than anything I've ever tried."

Ariadne nodded and closed her eyes. Lane stood behind her shoulder and rested his fingers against her temples. "Ready?"

"Yes." The word was barely a breath, but it was backed by her will and shimmered in the air. Lane pressed his will to hers, boosting it and channeling it. Then she raised her hands and pushed them out, as if she were pressing on giant double doors.

The world opened.

∞

206

"Ariadne? We're here."

Her eyes went wide as she saw grass rippling around their feet and then gazed out over white chalk cliffs to a choppy sea, and the blue sky beyond. Wind tugged her hair in front of her eyes, and she pushed it aside with a laugh. She tasted the sea salt on her lips and finally believed that maybe, one day, she would again be somewhere other than Vale. With that, the growing panic that had been building for years eased.

She turned to Lane, who stood beside her, a hand under her elbow.

She smiled. "See, you *can* change people. You just have to take the long way around. Like the rest of us." Her eyes fluttered closed, and Lane caught her before she fell, returning them in an instant to the little room in Vale.

He swore as he checked her pulse. But it was steady and strong under his fingertips, so he lowered her to the padded floor. As he sat, waiting for her to wake up, he studied her retreat, brimming with fresh Wish energy. For once, resupplying and moving on wasn't the first thing on his list.

He tweaked a few things in Ariadne's hideaway. The tiny room grew an annex, with a sofa and a pile of patchwork quilts, one of which he tugged over Ariadne. Next to it he Wished his bookshelf of favorite books. If he was staying a bit, he'd want those. He would have given her better computer equipment, but he knew when he was outclassed in a subject. Instead he Wished into existence a picture of the two of them at the top of the cliffs beside the old postcard. And, last but not least, he Wished a coffee maker, beans, and a battery-powered grinder onto a tray near the couch. Then he pulled out a book and waited.

Ariadne woke just in time to turn off the automated message to her mother.

"You could have deactivated it. I was fine."

"You passed out. Even if it was just to sleep, I'm not a doctor and I'm not a computer tech. So I wasn't going to mess with it."

Ariadne made a face at him but didn't continue to protest. Instead she asked, "What are you going to do now?"

"Stick around until I'm sure you're okay. That little stunt probably shouldn't have worked, and it took a lot of energy from both of us, whether you've noticed it or not."

She stretched and slid her hands behind her head, a grin lighting up her face. "It was worth it."

Lane nodded, only a little surprised to find that it had been, even if this new headache lasted a century.

THE
WEIGHT

DHONIELLE CLAYTON

Every heart tells a story.

That was what the Heart Scale Center advertisement whispered to Marcus and Grace as they stood outside the building. They clutched the newspaper between them, the paper flickering with promises pressed between black lines of vitalized ink. The scales in the picture moved up and down like the playground seesaw they used to jump on as children. Back when the city still made room for such things. Back when they were little and all that mattered was whether Marcus had remembered to bring the jump rope Grace liked when he knocked on her front door to play. Back before they'd been each other's first kisses, first touches, first loves.

The parking lot swelled with cars, an attendant stacking them like bento boxes in a vertical iron grid. This place had become the most popular spot in the entire city; lines of eager people hoping to get an appointment stretched around the block.

"You sure you want to do this?" Marcus asked, trying to control his face and keep his expression blank. His mama always said his eyes told the world too much about him.

"You said you were up for it." Grace removed their appointment card from her pocket.

He watched the calligraphy skate across the cardstock, forming and re-forming their names.

GRACE & MARCUS
MARCUS & GRACE

She cradled it like it was a golden ticket.

He studied her face; the honey glow from the center's lights reflected across the brown of Grace's cheekbones as she hid an excited smile. "We jumped the six-month wait list," she said.

"Coley got the appointments for us, didn't she?" he asked.

Marcus felt her bristle.

"Yeah. Why?"

"Nothing."

"Well, it's going to be great. Marisol and her girlfriend did it last weekend."

"Aren't they about to break up?"

"That's beside the point."

"And didn't Jacob and Keisha try this too? They've been fighting ever since."

They both paused to look up at the building. Marcus imagined the shadows from its towers growing larger, big enough to swallow him. Grace crinkled up her nose with curiosity, the pinch of it making her scattering of freckles hard to see. That look was usually his favorite, but maybe not today. He bit his bottom lip and fussed with his jacket.

"You scared?" she asked.

A shiver ran through both of their bodies, one colder than the few winter snowflakes starting to fall around them.

Marcus glanced away from her inquiring eyes. His heart did a somersault, and not because he was afraid of it being taken from his chest. Everyone said that part didn't hurt. He just wasn't sure he wanted to know exactly what his heart might reveal.

"No," he replied.

"Then let's go in." Grace barreled forward.

The lobby glowed red. Its walls enfolded them into a velveteen pocket. It felt like they'd walked inside a whimsical plush heart.

Grace figured this was how it should be. She blinked twice to be sure the walls weren't pulsing. She thought she could hear the thuds and thumps of a thousand heartbeats. Maybe it was the hearts sitting in golden sarcophaguses just beyond the door. Maybe it was just her own. Maybe it was all just part of the experience.

She'd heard so many great reviews about the Heart Scale Center.

Marcus's hand found the small of her back, one of her favorite ways that he touched her.

They walked farther inside.

Almost every couch was filled with a person. A motion picture flickered across a silk screen, showcasing scowling couples entering the Heart Scale Center and stepping into separate rooms, then emerging with smiles so big you could count all their teeth.

The montage ended with the words, **Welcome to a better way to love. Every heart tells a story. Find yours here.**

She wondered if she and Marcus would be like that. Though they hadn't been fighting lately, they hadn't really been doing much of anything else, either.

A woman in a tailored blue suit sat at a large desk. Grace smiled at Marcus, then stepped forward. "Hello."

"Welcome! We're so happy you've come to learn your hearts' story. Last names, appointment card, and registration paper, please," the woman said. A heart-shaped brooch began to vibrate on her lapel, drawing Grace's attention.

Is that a real miniature heart?

Marcus nudged her.

She flinched and pulled out the card, then the paper, tattered and worn from weeks of folding and unfolding, running nervous fingers over every line, and scanning all details of the procedure. She handed it to the woman. "Last names are Williamson and Tucker."

The woman gave her a clipboard with several forms and a writing stylus. "Fill these out together, and bring them back to me when you're done."

Marcus fumbled with the board. Grace caught it before it plummeted to the floor.

The entire room paused to look up at her. She flashed a sheepish smile. This wasn't the time to be clumsy. That's what her mama would say if she were still alive. She'd also probably tell Grace she had no business up in here. Some questions didn't need answers.

But for Grace, every question had one.

Grace and Marcus found a nearby couch to plop down on.

They scanned the forms together. The ink revealed questions, one set for her and one set for him.

IS YOUR HEART HEALTHY FOR REMOVAL?
LIST ANY HEART-RELATED SURGERIES OR
DISEASES YOU'VE HAD.
HAVE YOU BEEN IN LOVE BEFORE?
ARE YOU CURRENTLY IN LOVE?

Grace pointed the writing stylus at each one and searched Marcus's eyes, trying to guess his answer before he said it. She knew him very well and prided herself on being able to anticipate how he felt about most things.

Even though he hated when she answered for him, she liked knowing that she could—that she knew the shape of him.

HOW MANY PEOPLE HAVE YOU LOVED?

This question made her sit upright. It was the reason they were here. The tiniest tendril of apprehension curled in her stomach.

Her father had told her never to ask questions she didn't want answered, and maybe this was one of those times when she should've listened. She and Marcus were high school sweethearts destined to become lovebirds, together forever. That was what everyone always said. But this question bubbled up from time to time: *Has he ever loved another?*

They'd taken short breaks. It was possible. And what would that mean?

As soon as they'd gotten their college acceptance letters, more questions had crept to the surface. Did they love each other enough to make it through going to different schools, in different cities?

If the procedure showed that Marcus's love for her was heavy, then she'd know what they should do. She'd ignore her best friend Coley's warning that college changes you, silence her suggestions that she and Marcus break up and give each other clean slates. She'd have proof that they really belonged together. She'd have more faith and be able to stamp out those tiny doubts.

Grace nibbled her bottom lip.

"I don't know the answer to that question," Marcus said. "Do I include, like, my mom, dad, grandparents? How am I supposed to list everyone I've ever loved?"

"I guess we could skip it. The form says we don't have to answer them all."

"Okay."

Grace searched his eyes for how he *really* felt. He glanced around like they were being watched. She looked back down. The vitalized ink swirled, almost too eager to complete the form.

The last question revealed itself:

DO YOU UNDERSTAND THE OBJECTIVE OF THE PROCEDURE?

The goal was to have your heart weighed. To have the organ plucked from your chest like a swollen cherry and placed on a set of golden scales. To goad the blood-soaked flesh into exposing its imprints, the names of those you'd loved scrawled along striated muscle. To have a machine divulge whom you loved the most, whether you wanted to admit it or not.

Every heart tells a story.

"You ready?" Grace asked.

Marcus replied, "Yeah."

A line pulsed at the very bottom of the page.

PREPARE YOURSELF FOR YOUR HEART'S TRUE STORY.

Grace was certain she already knew her story. The largest name imprinted on her heart—aside from Mama's and Daddy's and her little sister Serenity's—was Marcus's. But her hands still shook, and she didn't know why.

"Finished, right?" he asked.

She nodded.

They walked together to return the clipboard to the woman.

A door swung open, and a man appeared. "Grace Williamson?"

Grace raised her hand like they were in school and the teacher had called her name from a roster. She turned to Marcus. "I guess I'm first. It'll be okay, right?"

"Yeah," he replied.

Grace kissed his cheek. It was warm with a deep flush she couldn't see beneath the rich brown of his skin. He always carried too much heat, like he'd swallowed the sun. It was one of the things she liked most about him. She'd never grow cold when she was with him.

He took her hand and squeezed it.

She thought maybe she should just turn around, pull him forward, and walk straight out the door. Maybe she didn't need to know. Maybe everything would be fine and her worries would drift away like rain clouds after a summer storm.

But maybe not.

Grace took a deep breath and released his hand.

Marcus scoured the waiting room for water. The answer he'd just given Grace about everything being okay lay thick and heavy on his tongue like cane syrup. He always told her those sorts of things, even if he didn't believe them. That was what you were supposed to do. His pops always made sure his mama was good, even if he had to wrap a little lie inside something sweet.

"You got dragged here too?" the man beside him asked.

Marcus flashed a false smile and mumbled something that wasn't *yes* and wasn't *no,* either.

When Grace had asked him to do this, he'd said what he always said to her: *Sure.* It was more reflex than real, mostly muscle memory. He didn't know how to say no to her. He didn't know if he had ever wanted to. When she cried, her hazel eyes appeared green, and her brown skin flushed pink, and he couldn't handle it. He'd seen the same thing happen with his mama. Those tears haunted him. He'd say just about anything to make Grace smile, to keep her smiling.

"My girlfriend thinks I'm cheating," the man said. "Yours too?"

"Nah," Marcus replied.

He'd never do that to Grace.

He'd never behave like his pops.

He'd leave her first.

Even if he had to see those tears.

Marcus's eyes darted around the room as more and more people disappeared behind the door Grace had gone through. He wondered what was happening to her.

"I didn't even love that chick," the man adds. "That shouldn't show up on my heart, right?"

"I don't know." Marcus knew what his heart would show: that he loved his mama and his sisters and his brother and his pops and Grace.

Always Grace.

But he didn't know if that would be the case forever, and he wasn't sure if the test would show that. If his curiosity about being with someone else might affect his love for Grace.

Marcus didn't consider himself a person with secrets. Grace probably knew all there was to know about him, and there wasn't much. His favorite things: the smell of a fresh pair of sneakers straight out of the box; the hum his grandfather's old albums made when he first put them on the record player; the way his dog waited for him every day like he was the best person in the whole world. She knew about the weird stuff going on between his parents 'cause his pop kept making mistakes, and she'd told him all his nightmares about drowning in the new pool on his block. She knew he sometimes worried that his little sister and brother might not return from school or that his parents' fights would get so big they'd turn into a hurricane and destroy everything. Or that maybe he couldn't be the perfect son, the one his mama counted on to put things back together.

He told Grace most things worth telling.

The man beside him loudly unleashed all the details of his affair while Marcus tried hard not to listen. The story of betrayal boomed like thunder, its rattle hitting him in the chest, excavating his greatest fears.

"Marcus Tucker?" an attendant called out.

Marcus leaped up, happy to be able to escape the man.

"Good luck," the man said.

"Yeah, okay. You too, I guess," Marcus replied. He didn't believe in luck and wasn't sure he needed it. He needed something else.

He ducked through the door and followed the attendant down a hall. Brass lanterns painted stripes across the floor. Marcus counted them as he walked. It was the only thing that kept him from panicking.

He felt like he was about to be outed in some way. That every half-truth he'd ever told was about to be laid bare and given air, a monster growing from it. He had always told himself he wouldn't be like his pop. He might not be perfect, but he wouldn't outright lie, the big kinds of untruths that were just too-small Band-Aids over hemorrhaging wounds.

No, he'd never do that.

But when did a lie become a lie? Was wanting to love someone else wrong? Was wondering about it the same as not telling Grace the truth?

What exactly would his heart show?

Would it betray him?

And her?

His stomach fluttered as they stopped in front of a door marked number three. That was a lucky number, or so he'd always thought. Gram said important things came in threes. Birds of good fortune. Auspicious news. Storms. Nightmares.

"You'll be in here."

The door slid open.

Was Grace nearby? Marcus gazed at the other rooms and sucked in a deep breath, searching for her scent, the pineapple of her lotion seeping from her skin as if she'd swallowed the fruit whole.

He stepped inside.

A female nurse entered through another door.

"Have a seat," she ordered.

He sat without thinking.

Always without thinking.

"Is there a fan in here?" he asked.

She didn't turn around.

"It's the perfect temperature for the procedure. The heart enjoys a specific climate. We like to honor that."

"Have you had this done?"

"Absolutely. All of us who work here undergo the procedure."

His hands quivered as she handed him a robe to change into.

"You afraid?" she asked.

Yes, he wanted to say.

"No," he replied.

She glanced down at his chart. "If you love your partner, there's nothing to worry about."

That had never been a problem for Marcus. The problem was what came after.

"I'm a heartician, and I'm here to complete your procedure," the man said to Grace. "Are you ready for answers?"

Grace turned her head in his direction. "I think so. But . . . like, how are the results presented?"

The corner of his mouth lifted. "First-timer?"

Grace smiled.

"A virgin," he added.

She crossed her arms over her chest, the cold of the room suddenly hitting her.

"You should wait and see. Plus, I don't want to ruin any part of the experience." He draped a blanket over her, tucking her in like the table was a bed.

"I want to know. I like to know things."

"Don't they say that good things come to those . . . oh, I've forgotten the saying. In any case, trust is what brought you here, so *trust* that you will enjoy the process. You're here to find answers, and the truth is always best."

The truth was always complicated. Grace didn't like the unknown. After her mom had died suddenly, she never wanted anything creeping up on her again. Her dad said she was scared of her own shadow now. But she chose to believe the world would be better if everything had its place and every question had its answer, like pairs of matching socks. So she could prepare.

She was about to get her wish.

The answers.

What if she didn't like what she found?

This is a bad idea. Her best friend Coley's warning grew louder and louder in her head, a wave about to crash into her.

As the heartician worked in a corner, Grace gazed around. She had expected a doctor's office—a sink, a chair, unmarked cabinets, the scent of alcohol, a few brochures. But the room's wonders unfurled: cabinets full of viscera, drawers spilling over with odd metal instruments, and a golden sarcophagus waiting to receive her heart.

"You'll love this process, and you'll come back," the heartician said.

"People do it more than once?"

"If you're lucky, you'll experience many loves in a lifetime."

Grace pursed her lips with doubt. She was supposed to be with Marcus.

MARCUS & GRACE
GRACE & MARCUS

She had never given herself room to think about having another love. Not really. He was the *one*.

The heartician's silver instruments hit the tray with a thud. "Some people don't like entering new relationships without a good sense of what they're getting into. To save themselves from heartbreak or have a starting place for couples therapy. I think it's smart always to be prepared."

Grace agreed about that.

"New relationship?"

"No."

His eyebrow lifted as he pressed a button on the wall. "Did he cheat, sweetie?"

The exam table rose beneath Grace. She flattened her hands against her sides. "No."

"Oh! Then why are you here?" The heartician gazed down at her.

"To see if we should stay together."

He paused. "We're not fortune-tellers."

"That's not what I mean." Her pulse raced. The man's

questioning eyes scattered her thoughts, disturbing them like a kicked beehive. "I want to know if we love each other enough. Is it heavy enough to, like . . ."

"I can't tell you what's on the road ahead. But I can tell you how much you love each other *right now.* Your heart will reveal its imprints. The deeper the imprint, the more love you have for a person. The fresher one is, the newer the love for a person. Scabbed imprints tell us about past loves that have gone away. And the weight of each will tell us the value of your love for one person in relation to your love for other people."

Grace filed that information away like a squirrel hoarding nuts for winter. She'd analyze it, study every word, to make sense of it later.

The heartician patted her arm. "Ready?" He retrieved a glass thermometer. "Need to make sure you don't have a temperature."

Grace opened her mouth like a baby bird to receive the cold instrument.

His eyes remained fixed on the thin rod as the red line of mercury rose. He plucked it from her mouth and said, "No fever. We're ready."

Grace gulped.

She wasn't so sure anymore.

The heartician placed a mask over her face.

It was too late.

A sweet-flavored steam entered her mouth.

In adjacent rooms, two hearticians removed knives from their trays. The lights dimmed, leaving only golden circles over the deep brown chests of Grace and Marcus.

Two perfect halos.

The edges of the knives were swift. Blood beaded along the lines they left behind, bracelets of crimson pearls.

The hearticians lifted the hearts of Marcus and Grace from their chests at the exact same moment.

"Healthy. Full of love," one remarked.

The organs sat upright, beating and thudding and racing and humming.

Two doors slid open to a viewing room.

Both hearticians clutched the beating hearts and entered the shared space between Grace's and Marcus's rooms. Twin scales sat on a table. Beside them, two golden sarcophaguses waited eagerly to be filled.

The hearticians nodded at one another. Their assistants removed the lids of the sarcophaguses. The hearts were placed inside. A latch unhooked to reveal a window into each vessel.

Gently, they poured a liquid thick as cream over the hearts. It crept down the organs' fibers, coating each muscle and chamber. "Prepare to note the imprints. Make sure to spell the names correctly. Aim for accuracy."

"Notation ready," an assistant replied.

The hearticians kneeled before the sarcophaguses, peering into the tiny glass windows.

Letters revealed themselves in the hearts' flesh like cursive burns. Names of beloveds.

FRESH.

SCABBED.

DEEP.

SHALLOW.

"The familial imprints are present on both hearts. I see the names from their paperwork," one heartician replied. "Make a note. Female heart has one large scabbed imprint and a small fresh imprint. Seems like a new love is budding."

"Make a note. Male heart has one major imprint. Three-quarters of it is scabbed. Seems like a fading love."

"Take a photograph," another ordered.

One assistant used a light box to capture the hearts' likenesses. He pressed it to the transparent side of one sarcophagus, then the other. The flashes made the thudding hearts illuminate like bloody stars.

"Time to weigh." The hearticians removed the hearts from their coffers and placed each on the left side of a scale.

"Now to measure each imprint's weight to determine its importance and hierarchy."

The assistants set velvet boxes beside the scales and flipped open the lids. A medley of small weights, tiny golden eggs, sat tucked into pockets.

"Read each name. The liquid will react. I will watch the heart and add to the scale until it levels," one heartician said to the assistants. "You write down the official weights."

The thudding hearts were gilded cherries, their secrets ready for plucking.

Grace and Marcus woke with a start. They gasped for breath. They touched their chests. They clamped their eyes closed and listened for the beating of their own hearts. Grace turned her head to the right to find Marcus staring back at her from an adjacent bed.

"You okay?" he asked.

"Yeah. You?"

"Of course."

She reached out her hand. Marcus let his fingers graze hers. They twirled them. Twists of brown sugar and chocolate ganache.

"How was it?" she asked.

"Okay, I guess. I don't remember anything."

"How long have you been awake?" she asked with a yawn. "Are the results in?"

Marcus knew what she really wanted to ask: *What do you think the results will say?*

"Only a few minutes. I don't know," he replied. "Do you think we need to know?" His question sizzled, almost like a lightning strike in the quiet room. "I love you."

"I love you too," she replied.

"Are you worried?" He squeezed her hand tighter.

"Are you?" Her eyes stretched wide, so wide they could've taken him in completely.

Neither of them answered.

"Do you think love lasts forever?" he asked.

Grace's eyes watered, the hazel of them starting to lighten. "When my mama died, she told me that it did. She said, 'Nothing real can be threatened. Not even by death. That is love's greatest secret.' Feels kind of silly. Ridiculous."

"It's not. Even when I want to hate my pops, I can't stop

225

loving him. Even though I try." Marcus watched as fat tears left her eyes, a tiny rainstorm spreading across her cheeks.

One of his greatest fears.

A silence stretched between them.

"Do you think *this* will change anything?" he asked.

The door swung open.

"Yes and no," she replied.

The hearticians walked in holding sheets of paper. The vitalized ink skittered across the pages. "Results are in."

Marcus and Grace didn't turn their heads.

Instead they faced each other.

UNMOOR

MARK OSHIRO

F elix waits.

He paces the room, his parents' eyes searching his nervous frame, his hunched shoulders, his drooping face. He knows what they want: assurance. Papá clears his throat, and it is thundering in the silent living room.

"Are you sure esto es lo que quieres, mijo?"

Felix freezes. He knows that if he looks at his parents, he might lose his grip.

"You've been saving for months," his mamá adds. "I know you were saving it for . . ."

She doesn't finish. He squeezes his eyes shut, forces the lump deeper into his throat. He knows what she was going to say: that he was saving the money so he and Arturo could travel abroad

227

together. Two weeks in Amsterdam, Paris, and London. Two weeks discovering new cities and each other. Together.

Not anymore.

He looks at them. Sees his mamá's lip tremble, catches his papá averting his gaze, and he knows he has to do this. "It'll help," Felix says. "I know it."

There's a chime behind him. He spins, draws a circle in the air with a finger, then uses both hands to widen it. His magic shows him the other side of the door. She's tall. Lanky. Skin the same brown as his own, down to the red undertones. There's a blond streak bleached into her hair, and her jewelry sparkles from the porch light. Otherwise, she wears dark colors. Her cloak is a deep red, perhaps purple. He isn't sure and wishes he had cast a stronger sight spell, but he is lethargic lately. Unmotivated. Tired.

She's definitely Unmoor.

He rushes to the door, then stops before it. Collects himself. Takes a deep breath. He runs his fingers down the lock and whispers the spell to open it. There is a buzz, the magic whirring like an electrical current, and then it clicks.

The door opens, and he is face to face with the Unmoor rep. She smacks a piece of gum, and she's staring at her phone, swiping through something by waving her hand upward.

She looks up.

Squints.

"Felix Serna?"

She flicks her wrist.

Right next to him, there's a projection of the photo he used in the app. He's not wearing the thick black-framed glasses now, but all the rest is the same. Tight fade, a dust of facial hair above his lip and on his chin, the scar from falling off his bike cutting through his left eyebrow.

He nods.

"I'm Mirella," she says. "Where do you want to get started?"

He watches her wiggle two fingers on her right hand, then gesture downward, and the phone in her left hand gently floats to a pocket on the inside of her cloak. She doesn't verbalize her spells, he realizes. Just moves her fingers. She isn't even concentrating on what she's doing.

"I charge by the hour, you know," she says, and her voice is husky, her tone clipped. She's staring beyond him, and he clumsily moves out of the way, gesturing to invite her in. Her cloak—which he now sees is actually a midnight blue—flows behind her. She's got matte black nails, too, and there are graceful tattoos creeping up the back of her neck. They must have sensed him staring, as the green tendrils and colorful petals scatter and hide under the collar of her shirt, away from his gaze.

His parents are still there, still huddled together on the couch. She looks from them to him, then back again. She waves her hand, this time to the side, and Felix keeps his eyes on her lips, painted delicately in black, but they don't part, don't move. Yes, her spells *are* silent.

She's the coolest person Felix has ever seen.

An image materializes in the air, crackling as it does so. It's the contract Felix and his parents signed. She narrows her eyes as she reads over it. "Huh," she says, more to herself than the others in the room. "They didn't tell me I was doing a minor case tonight."

She turns to his parents. "You signed this, right?" Two of her fingers pinch together, then widen, and the contract focuses on their signatures. "He didn't forge this?"

Papá shakes his head. "No, that's definitely us."

"We all signed it together," Mamá adds. "Como una familia."

There's a spark in the air, just beyond Mirella's fingertips. *Runes*. She draws one in front of his parents, and he doesn't recognize it. A curtain of light drops down, then sparkles. It's a sheet of magic, one that helps determine if someone is telling the truth. Everyone learns basic runework in school, but this shit she's doing . . . it's way more complicated than anything he's ever seen.

Even his parents are impressed as the magic shimmers for a moment, then fades away. "That's incredible, magiquita," Papá says, using the respectful term for a younger mage. "Where did you go to college?"

She barely looks at him. "Didn't."

They all still, and Felix is thankful his parents do not lecture her about their belief in school-sanctioned magework.

Mirella looks to him. "You ready, Felix?"

Panic slips over his skin, like she has cast one of her rune curtains over his body.

"Yes," he says.

This *is* what he wants.

No.

This is what he *needs*.

"Just take me to the first place," she says. "Wherever you want."

Felix leads her out of the living room and toward his bedroom. "Take your time."

Mirella's voice is calmer. She does not seem as detached as she was just seconds ago. When he arrives at his room, he lets her enter first, then regrets it. Books are piled on his desk in a haphazard stack; his dirty laundry hangs out of the basket. He curses under his breath. "Sorry," he says, then whispers one of the organizational spells his mamá drilled into his mind when he was younger.

The books straighten. The clothes fly into the hamper, and the lid closes it off. The duvet on his bed stretches to cover the unmade sheets underneath it.

"I've seen worse," Mirella says, and she sits in the chair at his desk. "And it's fine to leave it like it was; it might work better."

He slinks over to his bed and falls onto it. "I've seen the ads. And I had a friend use Unmoor last year. But . . . I don't really know what I'm supposed to do."

She smiles, and it warms up the whole room in an instant. Felix relaxes as she takes off her cloak and hangs it over the back of the chair. Rubbing her hands together, she focuses briefly on Felix's face, then blows on her cupped hands.

The image before him is of Mirella and another stranger, someone who is sitting at a wooden table in . . . a kitchen. It's definitely a kitchen. Mirella reaches out to hold the person's hand, and she speaks. "Just think of the memory," she says, and her voice is soft, just like it was once they were out of earshot of Felix's parents. "Bring it to the front of your mind. My job is to 'unmoor' it from this location, from this physical space."

The person brushes hair out of their face; their image is just blurred enough that Felix cannot make out any real details. Their identity is protected. "Okay, I'm doing it," they say, and then the image fades away, and Mirella is still there, looking at Felix with anticipation.

"It's that easy," she explains. "You just sit there and recall the memory you want unmoored. The more detail you can remember, the easier it is for me to grasp it with my magic. Then one quick tug, and that's it."

"That's it?" Felix says, raising an eyebrow.

She nods. "It really is exactly as we promise."

This is what he wants.

This is what he *needs*.

"Let's try one," Mirella says, and she tucks her blond streak behind an ear. "Take a deep breath."

He does.

"Another."

He does.

"Bring it forth, Felix."

Arturo stood on his tiptoes. He strained to reach, and Felix could smell . . . something. A fragrance, floral and earthy, and he knew then that Arturo had found one of those dudes on the corner who could enchant the collar of your shirt with a scent. They yelled at you when you got off the train, told you that "she won't be able to keep her hands off you, pa," and it delighted Felix that Arturo had done this, had probably not told them he was doing it for another guy.

It worked. The smell was heady, intoxicating, and Felix leaned down, rubbed his mouth over Arturo's neck, took in another whiff. His lips traveled upward, and the fear was gone. Maybe his parents would catch him, but he had wanted this for a long time. It had been five weeks, and he'd only been guilty of wandering hands. But this . . . this was right.

He leaned down into Arturo's lips. They were soft. Tasted sweet, like . . . peach. Maybe honey. It was his lip balm, and then Felix didn't know what to do with his tongue. No one taught him that. But he kept his eyes closed, and he pushed closer, and he felt alive. . . .

Felix opens his eyes, and there's a shadow before him, but it fades away gently. He sees Mirella, still sitting there, her breaths heaving her chest and shoulders up and down. Rune magic. Again. He thanks her for it.

"No problem," she says. "Just part of what I do."

He tries to stand, but a wave of dizziness pushes down on his skull. Mirella rises quickly, keeps her hands out. "No, no, take a second," she says. "This is how it usually feels on your end. Just breathe for a bit."

He rubs at his temples. "What's it like for *you*?"

She sits back down. "Depends on the memory. It can be more intense if I'm dealing with deeper trauma. But mostly . . . I just get vague images, these hazy feelings from the other person."

His heart beats furiously in his chest. "What kind of images?" *Had she seen everything?*

"Don't worry," she says. "We're bound by confidentiality laws, just like anyone else working in the mental health field." She smiles again. "Trust me, I've seen so much worse. So much *weirder.*"

He laughs. "Yeah? Like what?"

She crinkles up her nose. "Confidentiality, remember?"

"Ah, right. So . . . what happens now?"

"Well, we can move on to a few new locations if you want, but basically? The memory isn't permanently gone. It's just no longer triggered by this location. I've 'unmoored' it from this place. You can still think about it if you want, but this helps make the world a little more livable."

"Wow," he says. "Just like that?"

She nods at him. "It's a stopgap, of course, not a full solution. Living day to day is a little easier for those who've gone through the treatment. There are high-demand spells that I've done for those dealing with more intense trauma, and they can be far more permanent, too."

"So . . ." He pauses, lets another wave pass. "You could do that for me?"

"For a standard Heartbreak Package?" Mirella shakes her head hard enough that her blond streak comes loose from behind her ear. "No. Too much. And too *expensive.* I doubt you could afford it."

Well, maybe this will be enough, Felix thinks. *Maybe I can finally move past this.*

He guides her to the next room, only stumbling once. His energy is slowly returning, and he otherwise feels exactly as he did when he started. It's hard to tell if this is working when all he can think about is *him.*

But he wants to do this.

He *has* to do this.

They stand in the silent kitchen, next to the corny thermometer that Mamá found at a yard sale long ago. There are no numbers on it. It just says TOO HOT or TOO COLD on opposite ends, and Felix hates it because it's never wrong.

The memory is already coming to the surface, so he tells Mirella to begin.

Arturo stuck his hand out. He was a full head shorter than Felix's papá, but he carried himself as if he towered over everyone in the room. He puffed his chest. His grip must have been firm; Papá's eyes bulged a little when Arturo squeezed.

"Nice to meet you," Papá said. "We've been looking forward to meeting the one who's got Felix all distracted."

*While Arturo went red in the face—and he looked so cute when he did it, god*damn!*—he changed the subject. "What's that thing on the wall?"*

Mamá swooped in on them, swallowed Arturo in a hug. "I'm so glad you asked," she said, and Felix groaned. "I found this up by the Ashby BART station. You know all the people selling stuff there on the weekends?"

"Of course," Arturo said. "That's where I got my kicks." He lifted a foot to show off the Jordans he'd copped from some dude there.

His mamá beamed. "Sometimes, we do brunch there on Saturday mornings," she said. "Just hopping from stall to stall."

"Yes!" Arturo exclaimed. "My mom used to bring her ube cupcakes to sell there after we moved here from Manila."

Ah, *thought Felix.* He's going for the immigrant angle. *And sure enough, Felix's parents opened up immediately, and it was over.*

Arturo had said the right thing, and a calmness radiated out of Felix, starting at his chest and spreading through his veins. They liked him. He needed them to like Arturo, and he'd already passed their tests.

Felix floated.

He gasps.

Mirella steadies him, her hand on his back. "Deep breaths again," she says, her voice low. "Tell me if you'd like a booster at any time."

He shakes his head, though he is impressed she knows how to do runework that can change chemical relays to the brain. *Where did she learn all this?* Felix wonders.

He breathes out. "There's one more here," he says. "That okay?"

"Sure. If you think you can take it."

"I have to," he says.

She frowns at him, but they begin.

It was dark. Middle of the night. Felix could not sleep. He crept into the kitchen, edged open the pantry door, and grabbed a package of Oreos. He floated them the rest of the way to the counter once his two working brain cells were ready for thought, then dug into the packaging. Golden Double Stuf, his favorite.

He popped one in his mouth. Sugar wouldn't help him go to sleep, but it gave him comfort, and hopefully it would stop his mind from buzzing. He found himself staring at that damn thermometer. Had he imagined it all? Was he just too sensitive? But Raquel wouldn't tell him something like that unless it was true. . . .

He swiped in the air in front of him, and his phone lifted out of the rear pocket of his pajama pants, then dropped down in front of him. He pulled up Arturo's Twitter page, then went to the Likes tab, just as Raquel had instructed.

"It's just weird, that's all," she had said before leaving his house that night. "I mean . . . you guys are together, right? Like, together together?"

"Two months now," he had said.

"So why is he still doing that?"

His best friend had never lied to him. Why would she start now?

Every photo that Arturo had liked was of another boy. Most were of one guy, a quarterback from a high school up in Piedmont. He had liked all his selfies, one just a few hours ago. There were a bunch of selfies from other guys, too, most of them shirtless.

There were only two likes of anything Felix had posted.

He closed his phone. He shoved another Oreo in his mouth.

When he opens his eyes, Mirella is shaking her head back and forth. "Sorry," she says. "Sometimes, the client comes through more clearly. That was . . . wow. You're really angry, aren't you?"

He does not respond. It's too raw.

He looks back at the thermometer.

He tries to remember . . . something.

What was he angry about again?

He turns back to Mirella. "There are two more places," he says. "Can we go to those, too?"

She scowls for a moment. "I don't know, Felix." There is a reluctance around the edges of her words. "Most people do this in multiple sessions. It can be disorienting to keep going, to test your mind and your body this much."

"I'll give you a fat-ass tip," he says, and he knows he shouldn't have—he doesn't have *that* much money saved up—but he says it anyway.

She blinks. Then shrugs. "Well, I need the money," she says. "Let's go. Off-site?"

Felix confirms, and Mirella retrieves her cloak from his bedroom. He dons a hoodie in the living room; Mamá and Papá are pretending to read. He bids goodbye to his parents before he and Mirella leave the house, and when they look at him, the pity is still there. *Is it working?* their gazes appear to ask. *Will you be okay?*

He just inclines his head, purses his lips, then leaves.

They walk to Felix's school, passing the garbagemen at the end of the sidewalk, who are on the block later than usual. One of them draws a rune in the air as the other uses his powers to lift the garbage bags above the truck. Suddenly, the bag is torn open and the garbage is separated from the recycling, raining down into its respective receptacle. Felix jams his hands into his hoodie, shrinks down, makes himself smaller.

He knows the worst is coming.

They dodge the mail delivery as packages and envelopes zip to mail slots and porches, and Mirella clears her throat.

"You'll be fine," she says. "With some time, it'll be okay."

"I guess," he says. "Everyone tells me that."

"Maybe everyone has a point."

He fidgets.

"But they're all on the other side of it," he says.

She grunts. "True."

"What makes the pain go away *now*?"

She doesn't say anything for a few minutes, and the silence spreads between them until it feels unbearable. But then she speaks.

"Nothing does." She twirls her fingers in front of her, and then there's an image of a man smiling, his hair dark with curls. "He cheated on me. For months." She whisks it away with a flick of her wrist. "And now I can look at that photo and laugh about it all with my girlfriend. But for a long time, just the *thought* of him made me want to never wake up again."

She nudges Felix with her shoulder. "Feel the pain. And the sadness. And the loss. That's the only advice I can give."

"Thanks," he mutters, and he means it, even if his tone doesn't sound like it.

The school grounds are dark, shadowy, and it looks like another world, not the one Felix is familiar with. Mirella heads toward the front steps, but Felix stops her. "No," he says. "Out here first."

She glances around. "Here? On the . . . grass?"

He nods. "It has to be." Pauses. "For . . . reasons."

They stand across from one another, and they begin.

Felix rolled his eyes at Raquel. "Te lo dije," he said, "don't trust him."

She slapped his arm playfully. "Well, look who's walking by again today," she said. She gestured behind Felix with her head.

He tried not to be too conspicuous as he looked, but he made eye contact with Arturo instantly. Shit, *he thought, then cast his eyes downward to the grass.*

"Nice Jordans," someone said.

He looked up.

Right into Arturo's eyes again.

They were brown, nearly black. Soft. Sparkling.

He wanted to get lost in them.

He had.

"Uh, thanks," said Felix. "Got 'em from a place in Alameda."

"Dope," said Arturo.

He walked away.

Raquel giggled, and she was saying something, but Felix heard none of it. He stared after Arturo and admired the wideness of his shoulders, the way his ass looked in those tight jeans he wore.

It's impossible, *he told himself.* He's probably straight.

Felix takes only a few moments to recover, though Mirella gives him another look of concern. He is thankful she says nothing as he leads her around the front of the school to the west side of the main building. They're outside Mrs. Cho's science class, and he points in through the window.

"Is this close enough?"

She peers in through the filthy glass. "As long as you can see the root of the memory . . . sure."

He can. He knows that he has to cleanse this place or he'll never be able to concentrate here again.

They begin.

Felix tried to ignore it as best as he could. Mrs. Cho hated interruptions, and she hated when people didn't pay attention. But he felt Raquel tap him on the back again. And again. And again.

He turned around and gave her a glare he hoped would send the message.

She held out a folded square of paper.

Is she serious? *Felix thought.* Is this elementary school?

He took it.

He spun back around.

He didn't read it . . . at first.

As Mrs. Cho continued to talk about singularities, he ran his fingers over the edges of the paper. He wondered what was inside. Why would Raquel pass him a note when she could just text him?

He did it as quickly as he could. He drew the shape on his desk with his index finger and then whispered the spell. He flung his hands out, and the silent bubble was there; it would last thirty seconds before anyone was aware that he was using it.

Tearing at the corners, Felix pulled the paper open.

He read it.

Then read it again.

What the hell?

The bubble snapped back without a sound. Should he turn around? Should he even look at Arturo? Was this just a joke that one of his homies set him up for?

Felix tried to pay attention to what the teacher was saying, but the words he'd just read repeated in his head:

Think you're cute. Hopefully you think notes passed in class are too.—Arturo. <3

He couldn't resist. He turned around.

Arturo winked.

Felix was in another world for the rest of class.

A wave of sadness floods Felix, though he keeps himself upright this time. In his mind, he sees the image of Arturo winking, and then it begins to fade away, and he stares into the classroom. Looks to where Arturo sat that day. Tries to remember.

It is hollow. Something should be there, but it is not.

He puts a hand to his chest. Is he leaving a piece of himself behind with each memory?

"We can stop, Felix," Mirella says, her voice piercing his thoughts. "This is far more than enough for one session."

"No." He breathes out. "I want to keep going."

"I can do another session next week," she says. "On the house."

"No," he repeats. "You need the money."

"Not at your expense," she shoots back.

He shakes his head. "We keep going."

She stops trying to convince him otherwise.

They wait at the corner across from the school, and Felix floats up a lighted signal with a spell, notifying the bus driver that they need to be picked up. They board and pay, then sit in the middle of the bus without a word exchanged between them. Felix has a lot he wants to say, but he says nothing at all. This next location . . . it's going to be the hardest.

The Night Market is up near Berkeley, nestled in a

neighborhood that is just on the edge of Oakland, before the street signs change color from green to brown. It's tucked in between rows of colorful houses, and the bus lets off right at the entrance. There is already a large crowd milling about, and the sounds of a drum circle clash with the din of voices negotiating. Mirella pulls her cloak tighter against her body as they squeeze through pockets of people.

"It's this way," Felix says.

He points.

He leads her to a jeweler, one who enchants her pieces with a magic that pulls light in, that gives her gems a sparkle, no matter how little light there is.

"Here," he says.

Felix can see Mirella trying to hide it, but the pity slips over her face long enough that he catches it. "Oh, Felix," she says. "You didn't actually—"

"Can we just get started?"

She sighs.

They begin once more.

He handed the charm back, though he knew it would look good on the chain that Arturo wore. The jeweler smiled. "Is this for someone special?"

"Yes," he said. It was the truth.

"What makes you hesitate?"

He wasn't sure he should answer that truthfully. Could he tell a stranger that he was trying for a gesture of peace, of promise, of reconciliation? He just wanted to believe in the potential of him and Arturo again.

Instead, he gave her a smile. "Just the cost, that's all."

He did not buy anything.

When he opens his eyes, he realizes that Mirella has damped the sound around him. The Night Market comes back to life, and she breathes out. "Okay," she says, "I thought you had bought him a *ring* or something."

"No," he says. "I wasn't *that* in love."

"So that was the last one?"

He bites on his bottom lip. He'd saved the worst for last, and so he shakes his head at Mirella. An exhaustion has settled into his bones, and he wants nothing more than to go home and bury himself under his cobija.

But he has to do this.

"One more," he says.

"No."

It's a complete sentence. She glares at him, her hands crossed in front of her.

"Just one more, I promise," he begs, and he knows his voice sounds pitiful.

"This is way past the—" she begins, but then he is crying, and he knows it's manipulative, but it's also real.

"I need this one gone," he explains, wiping at his eyes. "More than the others."

She raises an eyebrow.

"Fat. Ass. Tip." He says each word with force. He means them.

She closes her eyes. Opens them again, nods her consent, and they glide through the crowd, Felix's heart flopping and dancing in his chest, a scowl permanently etched on Mirella's face. He knows she wants to stop. But then he can see the stringed lights, the sparkling orbs, the enchanted birds flying about, and he brings Mirella to La Estrella Mágica and stands off to the side of the outdoor patio.

"Here?" she says. "La Estrella Mágica?"

"Yes." He stills. "I want to be able to come back here someday, and right now . . . I can't."

The memory is pulsing in his mind, the images flashing over and over.

"This has to be the last one," Mirella warns. "Even *I* am starting to get tired."

He agrees.

They begin, for the final time.

Felix sucked air through his teeth. It had taken him two weeks to get this reservation, and Arturo didn't seem to care. His phone was floating just in front of his face, and he swiped down in the air. Scroll. Scroll. Scroll.

"Arturo," Felix said.

Arturo looked up over his phone. "Damn, sorry," he said, and with another swipe, the phone was turned off and floating down to the center of the table. "I'll leave it there for the rest of dinner."

He smiled then. It sent a pang of desire through Felix. He wanted to leap up and over the table, to take Arturo in his arms, to feel his tongue in his mouth.

But then the waiter arrived. Arturo ordered first, and the waiter scribbled runes in the air as Arturo spoke. Then he waved the order toward the kitchen and turned to Felix. He studied the menu, unsure of what he wanted, and when he looked up, he caught it. A short glance at the waiter's ass and then Arturo licking his lips. He probably thought he got away with it.

Felix stuttered through his order, then off to the kitchen it flew, and he watched it. Focused on it. Tried to keep his thoughts off all the doubts that now swirled in his mind. Why couldn't Arturo just appreciate him and him alone?

Dinner arrived, carried by los pájaros mágicos, and by the time it settled on the table, Arturo had made eyes at two other guys, one of them a forward on their school's soccer team. Felix told himself to ignore it, told himself he was being too sensitive, told himself that this was just how guys acted.

Felix picked up his fork.

Looked up.

Arturo was still staring at the boy on the soccer team.

He winked.

Raquel's voice rang through his head. "Felix, he should at least make you feel special. Like he actually wants *to be with you."*

They ate mostly in silence. Arturo made a comment on how bougie the meal was. Felix tried to laugh. It came off more like he was choking.

"Come on, boo," Arturo said. "Liven up. Can't you relax just this once?"

Rage pulsed through him, out from his chest, up into his throat. The words spilled from his lips before he had a chance to stop them. "It's hard to relax when you keep checking out other guys."

Arturo dropped his fork, and it clanged loudly against the plate. "You just can't let that go, can you?"

Felix scowled. "So you don't deny that you keep doing it?"

"It doesn't mean anything. I'm here with you, aren't I?"

"But are *you?" Felix shot back. "You might be sitting there, but your attention is elsewhere. I organized this whole thing for*

us. Why can't you just be here in this moment?"

Arturo's napkin plopped on the table. He stood, letting his chair scrape against the cement. "I don't need this tonight," he said. "You always stress me out."

Felix stood up, too, but a force shoved him back down into his chair and kept him there. His words stuck in his throat when he saw Arturo, his hands raised, the spell leaving his lips. "No," he said. "You stay. Don't come after me."

Arturo stormed off.

Felix sat in silence for half an hour.

He paid the entire bill by himself.

Tears pour down Felix's face. Again. He opens his eyes. Mirella is crying, too, and her chest heaves.

"Wow." That's all she says as she wipes at her cheeks.

"I know," he says, and he sucks air into his lungs, but the memory is fading, disappearing, unmooring from this place. He sees more pájaros, their shiny wings flapping as they deliver food, and he knows there is a reason this should hurt, but it's . . . it's . . .

Gone.

He turns to Mirella.

Her eyes go wide.

She grabs his arm. "Come this way," she says, and she's pulling him back toward the bus stop, toward the way they came, and he asks her what's wrong, but she won't talk, won't answer, and he looks the other way, looks at La Estrella Mágica and its lights and sparkles, and there's a man on the other side of the restaurant, standing next to—

No.

He looks down, and it's those Jordans.

It *can't* be.

Three weeks. In three weeks, Arturo has found another guy.

The thought pulls Felix to a stop. "How can he?" he says, and he doesn't even know who the words are for. "How can he just *move on* so quickly?"

She tugs on his arm again. "No, Felix," she says. "It's not what you think."

He whips around to her. "Why? What else could that possibly be?"

"My coworker."

The other man. Felix squints. He's doing some sort of magic, waving his hands, and Felix almost falls over from the shock. *How can Arturo do this? How can he want to purge his thoughts of me? Wasn't I the good one? Didn't I try my hardest to make this work?*

The last thought devastates him the most:

What does Arturo want to erase of me?

"Do it."

Mirella doesn't know what Felix means at first.

Arturo turns.

Sees Felix.

Confusion passes over his face.

And he starts walking toward them.

"Do it!" Felix yells, and he is grabbing at Mirella. "Whatever it is, whatever you said earlier!"

"What are you *talking* about?"

"The spell you mentioned! The one that's stronger, that you use on bigger cases."

She is shaking her head, her hands up, her palms out. "Absolutely not! You don't *need* that!"

"I'll pay you twice what I owe."

Her mouth drops open.

Arturo is closer.

"No, it's not right—"

"Please," Felix begs. "I can't face him. I can't have him hurt me all over again."

He watches her struggle. She glances at Arturo, who is now calling Felix's name, and then her fingers are tracing a rune in front of her body, and her mouth isn't moving, and Felix is trying to ignore Arturo, but his voice is so loud, so high-pitched, and he can hear the worry in it, and he's yelling now—

"Felix! Felix! What are you *doing*—"

Pop.

Felix sways.

He looks to the man who had been with Arturo.

Sees the horror on his face.

Mirella gasps for air.

"I had to," she blurts. "He wasn't ready."

The man reaches out, puts his hand on *something.*

"Arturo, I need you to calm down," he says.

To *nothing.*

"Come this way," the man says, and he turns away, and it looks like he is guiding . . . nothing.

Felix sees nothing.

Hears nothing.

Tears brim his eyelids as he faces Mirella. Her face is contorted; she is out of breath.

There's an image in his head: brown, soft eyes, so dark you could—

No. The shadows swirl. Dissipate.

It's gone.

Whatever the memory . . . it's gone.

Felix tries on a smile.

He's not sure it fits.

THE COLDEST SPOT IN THE UNIVERSE

SAMIRA AHMED

June 21, 2031, First Day of Summer

The bodies are all broken.

Stuck in the ice, all the color drained from their skin. Once they saw the water coming, they tried to make it back to shore, but the waves were too fast. Too frigid, crests crystallizing as they arced through the air, trapping people in the glacial swell.

Ummi said they took a foolish risk, rushing toward the last supply boat, trying to get to it before it capsized and the grain was ruined anyway. "That kind of courage gets you killed," she warned me. She didn't add "sooner." *Gets you killed sooner.*

But they took the risk for us. And now they're like dead trees, limbs bent at nightmarish angles, breaking against the waves. And we are slowly starving. They lost their lives for nothing. Like so many others. Like all of us will.

The few who were still in the shallows made it back, toes and fingers blackened by frostbite, but alive. Or at least not yet dead.

But the others—the dumb, brave ones, the ones who were more athletic and rushed the ships—first the slushy depths grabbed them, slowed their movements through the viscous waters. Then came the waves. Relentless. One after the other, crashing over the ship and onto their stuck bodies. Not the normal waves we used to see in the dazzling, ferocious thunderstorms, which crashed against the rocks at three or four meters. No. These were monstrous. Tidal waves. In a lake too wide to see across. Perhaps this great landlocked sea is landlocked no more. Maybe those last lingering appendages of land that connected us to other states, other countries, are ash now; maybe that's why the ocean rushed in. But there is no way for us to know. All we know now is what we can see, and our vision ends at the horizon. I'm too terrified to look any farther.

I pray that their eyes froze shut before they saw the wave that would kill them. But I'm too old now for fairy tales. Nearly an adult in this age that ended childhood.

I know they faced the horror of their death, eyes wide open.

I saw it all from our fortified tower.

I wonder if it will be the same for me and Ummi and sweet little Zayna. I can't bear to think about Zayna, whose only real memories will be this, the *after,* and not the *before,* messed-up as it was.

Inshallah, may our end be fast and gentle, like falling into a dream. Because *this* world we're living in is the nightmare.

Voice Log: Planet Mirzakhani, Diin I Saal 3027

The bodies are all broken.

And they are everywhere. Frozen in ice, half-buried, stop-motion hands in the air, lips blue, eyes open. They must have faced the end totally aware. Frost creeping up their immovable bodies but the synapses of their brains still firing. Still screaming.

Abba—whom I only call Salar while on mission (yes, it is strange to call my father "Commander")—says the bombs fell and the clouds rose high into the atmosphere, hundreds of saal ago. Or longer. And here they all still are. Planted like the carcasses, like trees in a lake, limbs shattered by a storm, on this frozen dead planet. Preserved like fossils for us to find. Like a warning to show us how easy it is for a planet to fall.

On approach, the planet was beautiful, quiet, the blanket of snow and ice beginning to recede back to its poles, quietly revealing brown dirt, even tender buds of green dotting the landscape, waiting like a breath held in secret ready to exhale.

July 4, 2031

There are no fireworks today. No celebrations of our independence. People gathered briefly on the first terrace, where the swimming pool reeks of composting food and human waste. We pretend not to notice. Pretending helps. Long ago we salvaged and filtered what water we could. Not to drink—too much of a risk, since we couldn't be sure what direction the wind had shifted the fallout—but for cleaning and washing and failed attempts at indoor gardening. That was a few months ago, when people still had hope in their eyes. And yet there must be echoes of faith and optimism, because the families left in the tower all came down to sit in a corner, consoled by the cold rays of the sun—at least the sun shone today—to trade stories. To reminisce. All of us, save the very youngest, like Zayna, know that nostalgia is dangerous.

It keeps you looking backward at what you've lost and how things used to be, when we have to keep our eyes forward to try to make it another day.

Supplies are getting scarce. Ummi won't tell me exactly how little is left; I know she is still trying to shield me from horrors. So she can feel like she's doing her job as a mother. Her face betrays her, but I pretend not to notice. It's a small gift I can give her.

Later I will climb the stairs of the tower again, as high as I can go without worry, twenty floors, to the apartment I have claimed as my own hideaway. All the families—the ones who stayed, the ones who were either too scared or too realistic to hope that traveling south would be a salvation, everyone who remained—live below the fifth floor. It's safer and, honestly, it doesn't make sense to try to make a home any higher. The higher you go, the more dead bodies you have to see on the lake. No one ventures to the shore anymore; we're too scared of ghosts.

Is it strange that even with so few of us left in this once-teeming city, I need to be alone sometimes? I mean, we are *so* alone. No phones. No TV. Soon after the bombs, someone was clever enough to break into the Museum of Broadcast Communications to steal an old-fashioned radio, the kind that has a crank. The kind that doesn't need batteries or electricity. That's how we knew there were others who survived—that's why some people tried their luck on the open road, heading south. There was a voice on the radio, and some people decided to trust it.

I'm glad we didn't go. At least here, we salvaged part of our lives. There are people. This is home. And if Papa-ji is out there somewhere, this is where he would come to find us. But it's been six months, and if he could've found food and weapons and if he could have survived the unbearably cold nights in the open air, he would have been here by now, even walking all the way from the East Coast.

Maybe that's why I need to be alone. So I can believe. I have to believe. Magical thinking is the only thing that gets me out of bed.

Tonight I will walk back into this apartment that I've taken for myself—one that faces the lake and the pier—and close my eyes and pretend that there are bombs bursting in air in glittery pinks and blues, reds and greens, lighting up the night sky, to fill our eyes with wonder. Sentimentality can kill you. But we are all dying anyway. I still have my imagination. I still have a bare flicker of hope. And this is a small gift I can give to myself.

Voice Log: Planet Mirzakhani, Diin 2 Saal 3027

We have set up camp in the fields near the immense metallic bean that reflects our faces and the jagged broken towers they built into the sky. Abba said this was a place of gathering, perhaps worship—that its higher elevation and the wide stone platform on which it was mounted indicated reverence. That the sinuous low bridge that leads from these fields, snaking its way toward the shore, was meant for the masses and that the curlicued and bent-metal exoskeleton structure, which spans a distance nearly as large as our ship, would have been a place where music was heard, a place for the smiles and laughter of a people who did not realize how near their end was.

This is where we landed the *Khawla*—in this dead place once so full of life. Both my fathers had concerns that I would be overwhelmed with the weight of what had happened here. That my heart would be too soft, that I was too young. I promised them I was ready. I had studied. I had learned their language, their consonants so similar to our own but the irregularities still twisting my tongue. I did not expect Salar to treat me any differently than he would the rest of the crew—to baby me. Not after he'd assured Papa that he was allowing me on this journey only because he had already been to this planet on five previous missions and because the atmosphere was no longer toxic to our people. The Great Melting was under way, and our Terrapathos work would resuscitate this planet. It is a profound thing to bring life from death, Salar had said. I could bear witness.

Looking around, maybe Papa was right—he is a poet and softer than Salar, after all. Perhaps sentiment does get the better of me sometimes; perhaps our people view that emotion as dangerous. But I see it as an asset in the future I want for myself, studying the archaeology of ancient civilizations.

Still, I am only seventeen suraj, the youngest by three saal on this voyage, and I intend to show my value. While Salar sees to the botanists and terraformers and hydrologists, I take my pack and set off toward a tall tower in the distance, still standing relatively intact.

There is no hope for survivors on Mirzakhani, but if any lived through the first melting *and* the bombs whose mushroom clouds blocked their sole life-giving star, then surely they would have sought shelter in structures built to survive the great storms that inevitably came.

The *Khawla* historian says the people of this planet were like a virus—multiplying endlessly, consuming every resource they could wrench from land and sky, acting as if all they could survey was theirs for the taking and the ruining. Every time their planet cried out, they ignored its pleas. Instead of curbing their wasteful desires—their fossil fuels and their petroleum-fueled lives—they simply expanded their settlements, moved to new places, plundered more ground, until their land could bear it no longer and erupted in fire. There were many among the young who had spoken the truth, who gave warning of what their future could hold, but on this planet, old men didn't plan for futures they knew they wouldn't be there to enjoy. They couldn't see past themselves.

July 20, 2031

We thought it would all end in fire. In the ice caps melting and the oceans rising, seizing back the land we stole, abused, treated as an endless resource, when all along it was finite. I wonder if one day we will be the example they use on some distant planet to teach their children about hubris, when they read the morality plays and mythologies, just like we did about the mortals who angered the Greek gods. It was all fiction, of course, the legends we learned, but it was what we should have known. What we knew, maybe, but denied was that for as long as humans have lived, we wrote fiction to tell the truth. Somewhere along the way, we decided telling lies to ourselves was the easiest way to live.

The Earth disagreed.

Voice Log: Planet Mirzakhani, Diin 3 Saal 3027

The tower was an incredible trove. It feels wrong to be excited about bones of an extinct species, but bones give us information. Our biochemists will be able to test the level of toxins that seeped through the skin and blood of these people. Unlike people, bones don't lie. They don't try to make themselves look good by covering the wrongs they've done or by twisting them to hide the real truth.

It's not just bones I found, though. Bones give us facts, but the other vestiges of people's lives tell us who they really were. What they valued. What they loved and hated. Who they wanted to be. These people *tried* to save themselves, but they started too late.

As soon as I realized what I'd discovered, I hurried back to camp, and Salar returned with me and a small team of archaeologists and biologists and structural engineers, who tested the building to make sure it was sound for us to enter. Of course, I had already barged in without regard to safety, and, wow, did I get a tongue-lashing when I revealed that I'd breached protocol.

I wanted to rush in, sweep through every chamber and floor, but that is not how scientists work, even if that is what every fiber of our being screams to do. Curiosity may be my calling, but logic must be my guide. Waiting for the engineers to clear each area was tedious, but as I stood in the entry, with the debris and dirt and tiny green shoots that lay ready to reclaim this space, I found a wood-and-metal rectangle—a *plaque,* the historian called it—engraved with words in their language:

DON'T BE SATISFIED WITH STORIES,
HOW THINGS HAVE GONE WITH OTHERS.
UNFOLD YOUR OWN MYTH.
—RUMI

The historian bagged and catalogued this plaque right away. These people did terrible things to each other and their planet, but they were beautiful, too, they said. What the historian doesn't say is that they have a fondness for this people, more than a historian should. They have been with Salar on all five previous missions to Mirzakhani, and to be unmoved in the face of this tragedy that wrecked the world of this precious, broken species surely would be impossible.

August 1, 2031

We burned through the last paper today. Everything we could find. Everything that hadn't been scavenged. All the old books in the library. The ones that no one had cracked open in a million years, because physical books were relics. A quaint throwback. They say a story can change your life—those books were what got us through this endless winter. It felt wrong to burn them, so I said a prayer as the ashes of words rose to Jannah. In gratitude, for all the stories that saved us, that helped us live a little longer.

God, I wish I had paper.

It's a little ridiculous, because we'd all but eliminated paper from the world a few years ago. Planted more trees. A last-ditch effort, hoping they would help suck in the toxins from the mess we'd made, since we'd already poisoned the oceans.

No one missed paper. Except for a few curmudgeons who you could hear mumbling about wanting to hold the *Tribune* in their hands. As if that were even a choice. Journalism was already a relic long before we banned new paper.

I can't explain it: longing for something I never particularly thought much about. Maybe the idea of tangible things—of holding someone else's story in my hands—reminds me that I was once part of something bigger than what we've become. Yes, we could be monsters to each other—our crass, controlling politicians telling us who we could love and how we should worship and which of us were more deserving because of the tyranny of demography, while too many silently stood by. But we were also once a people who dreamed. We had moments of greatness, of tenderness toward each other. There were times we were beautiful. Alive in our songs and dances, in our words and our art. We didn't always exist in this numbing state of deathlessness.

I don't share this with Ummi or any of the others. It feels too selfish. Too small. But I don't just want paper. I want my old life. I want homework. I want chocolate cake with too much buttercream frosting. I want my friends. I want Adnan's smile greeting me in Calculus first thing in the morning. I want his holo-message waiting for me by the time I get home from school. I want to hear his voice.

Sentimentality for dead things can kill you.

And today, as I sit down to watch the haze of sunset on this terrible, beautiful dying world, I am hungry.

Voice Log: Planet Mirzakhani, Diin 4 Saal 3027

The engineers have cleared the building, for inspection and cataloguing. They were impressed with how this tower was fortified to withstand blasts and cold and swirling storms. Working with our physicists, they have planted buttresses of light beams around the perimeter to hold the building up and stabilize it if the foundational integrity has been compromised or should we experience any seismic shifts. It is unlikely, our geologist assures us, but this planet is waking from a deep sleep and we don't know how much anger it still holds deep in its core.

I have only a few diin left. I will be returning to *al-Fihri*, our orbit ship, because Salar is afraid that an extended on-planet mission will be too much for me. Though the air is no longer toxic to life and even though I spend my allotted time on the decontaminant filter each night before I sleep, my return to our orbit ship was always part of the deal. The doctors aboard will want to run me through a battery of tests since I am the youngest to touch this planet's surface. And it is only dawning on me right now how profound that is. Maybe that's why the historian had tears in their eyes when I asked them what the young people of this planet did when they weren't in school or training. Swim, they said, pointing out to the frozen water. Once those depths teemed with life. Long ago, their old and young would walk to the water's edge, enter, and let their bodies lie still, buoyant on the freshwater surface, eyes transfixed on blue skies.

I couldn't imagine it until they pulled up an old image archive that had survived, uncorrupted. And there they were. Frozen in time. Hundreds of people on the sand, some shielding their eyes from the brightness of their star. Some floating in the water. Some riding on boards through the waves. Some sailing. I wonder what it must have been like to have all that potable water and then to poison it.

I zoomed in to see a little girl—maybe two or three saal, with saucer-like eyes, and another girl, an older one, perhaps a sibling, who looked to be my age. Brown skin and long black hair running down her back. She has her arm around the little girl, who is focused intently on a collapsing pile of sand before her. The older girl looks protective and proud of the little one. She wears a wide smile and is looking straight through the image, at me, another girl many saddi into the future. She looks unbothered. Happy. Blissfully unaware of the fate of her planet and her people. Seeing her, staring at her, I sucked in my breath, because she looks like me. Now her oval face, the tilt of her chin, the evenness of her teeth is etched in my brain. She looks like she could be my sister, too; she could be a twin.

The historian said this was only two saal before the end came. But what we both know is that when this moment was captured, the end was already upon them.

When I zoomed in again, I saw a trinket, a jewel around the older girl's neck. It is their letter *R*. And in their language, that letter would also be mine.

It is not logical to be emotional for a stranger's life. Sentimentality has no place on a mission. But I want to find R— this proud, smiling girl who looked full of life. Who was once alive. This girl like me, who must have had her own story to tell.

August 7, 2031

I play with my necklace. It is all I have left of Adnan. This stupid fake-gold initial necklace is somehow supposed to represent what we were to each other. The time we didn't get. The things we never said. Like goodbye. I didn't get to say goodbye to anyone. Not to Adnan. Not to Papa-ji. Not to my other friends.

We were all told to shelter in place, because the bombs they were releasing were the last countermeasure. The last hope to cool the planet. Can you imagine? Putting our hope in bombs? Having faith in the same politicians who had gotten us here because of their willful denial of how we were choking our planet. They chose the nuclear option. Literally. There would be three, maybe four, degrees of planetary cooldown, some of the scientists had said—the ones cherry-picked to agree. Almost instantly. It could be a miracle. Like a shot of high-dosage antibiotic for the planet. What they never said, what no one would ever admit, was that we were the infection that needed to get wiped out for the Earth to heal itself.

This is the way the world ends: with guns and plastic and denial about bombs bursting in air.

I have been spending more and more time here, in my perch, away from the others. Hiding. Our rations are thinning, and Ummi looks like she hasn't slept in a hundred years. And Zayna, she was always small, but now she is the tiniest thing, a small spark, when before she was a laughing, twirling fiery ball of joy and chaos. I gave her my dinner last night and the night before. Ummi tried to force me to eat it, but I lied and said I wasn't hungry. I'm not anymore. Not really. Not for another protein bar. Not for sawdust. I long for fresh food. But even if it still existed somewhere, even if by some miracle there was a patch of green earth, it would still be poisoned. For a moment, though, it would be ripe and delicious.

In the early days, Ummi would play a game with Zayna, pretending they were actually cooking a meal in the defunct kitchen of our apartment. Together they would get the imaginary ingredients from the cupboard that is mostly bare and from the fridge that has no light, to prepare dinner on the stove that gets no heat. Ummi would sing as Zayna banged around the pots. Ummi has the most beautiful voice—when I was little, her voice sparkled; it once filled me with hope.

I had a theory, once. But I stopped working on it, stopped believing. Early on, I spent time carefully hand-drawing the space vectors of the Cold Spot—charting the great void I thought was a door we could open. I have no way to access my work from my data chips anymore, but I save them anyway. And I have my memory. I have my ideas. For a while, it was a way to pass the time and hold on to the possibility of tomorrow. It feels hollow now, like Ummi's voice when she tries to sing.

Now I hide from Ummi and Zayna and the reality of what we've become. I'm a coward for hiding. Truth is, I've been lost for a while now. And no one is going to find me. No one will ever know I was here. We will all be forgotten, and that is the saddest thing of all.

Voice Log: Planet Mirzakhani, Diin 5 Saal 3027

I found her.

The archives the historian showed me were full of her. She was a champion. An athlete. A scientist. A girl who followed her curiosity. A girl who could be me.

Before the adults of her world set her planet on fire, she studied the Cold Spot in her universe. The bubble where her universe collided with its mirror. She was so close to proving the multiverse exists. Though we have mastered travel at the speed of a star's light, we have not yet broken the boundaries of the multiverse. We know they are out there. We have seen the trace particles, the barest evidence of quantum entanglement. And here was this girl, R, hundreds of saddi ago in this brutal world with primitive technology, on the cusp.

To be so close but to not have enough time. My chest contracts, thinking of her. She deserved more time. Salar says these people were undone by their own deeds—that this was their qismat, the fate they merited. Perhaps I am spending too much time with the historian, but I'm starting to believe that they were more than the sum of their parts. R certainly was, and records show there were others who fought and worked to save this planet—who spoke out against its cruel inequities. They needed more time, too. As a student archaeologist, it is my job to study the material culture of this people, to unearth and study their artifacts, to catalogue, date, examine. I am trained to tell a story through facts. But what I'm learning is that facts don't tell the whole story.

The story of R is the story of her people, of this planet. That is the testament I will give. I am not the ancient peoples I study. I can never fully understand them. I lay no claim to a so-called expertise that some anthropologists and archaeologists believe they have. That, to me, is hubris. But I hope I can lift up vanished stories. I hope I can be a steward, so that R and her people are not forgotten.

One day I will be chief archaeologist on a future mission like this one. On Mirzakhani I face a test, too. I want to be worthy of sharing the stories of these lost people—the sacred lives of strangers. But I have to understand my limits because I want to honor them without intruding on what they were.

August 15, 2031

The walls are filled with my drawings and my theories. I no longer have the luxury of computer simulations or the internet or even a calculator to help me. And what am I doing anyway when there is no one to read this? When no one left on this Earth cares about the Cold Spot in space, because this entire planet is frozen. Maybe if I'd been faster, smarter, I could have found it, our mirror. Pushed light particles through from our side to theirs, sent them an image, a pulse, a cry for help. Maybe they could have pulled us out through a wormhole, an Einstein-Rosen bridge. But then what? We probably would've wrecked their planet, too.

If only we had more time. If only I had more time. Time and a cold atom lab so I could test my multiverse theorems and run my models. But time is indifferent to our needs and our lives. Once I would've said nature was indifferent, too. After all, no one killed by a hurricane or tornado deserved to die that way. What I think now is so different. We had a job to keep this planet alive. We failed. So the Earth rose up and defended itself—from us.

I wish I could've seen the planet and its abundance at its best—at its most lush and vibrant. I wish I could have breathed fresh clean air. How good that must have felt. How pure.

I wish I could've seen us at our best, too, tapping into the greatest resource we had: us and how we could make dreams real like they used to talk about in the old documentaries we saw in school of leaders who once inspired people to change the world, to overcome the odds through the power of hope; and kids my age who marched and fought for equality and who lifted each other up.

How ironic that one dream would take me to the past that is long dead and one to the future that we'll never have.

Humans destroyed things, but we were also curious and brave. I think of the first humans we sent to space. That must have been terrifying—the unknown darkness so far from home. I've seen those old spacecraft—tin cans with the technology not even equal to our old microwaves. I watched in awe as Amina Zazzua stepped foot on Mars. I joined every other human being in prayers as the *al-Nisa* team sped off into the stars from the Chawla Deep Space Gateway in hopes of finding us a new home. They flew with the fastest engines we'd ever created, but they still weren't fast enough. I hope they survived. I hope they found a new place to call home. They carried our dreams with them. They carried the seeds of our earth.

Voice Log: Planet Mirzakhani, Morning, Diin 6 Saal 3027

She lived in the tower. I want to discover more than her photo, than her archive. I want to unearth everything she was. I want to find *her*.

August 25, 2031

Last night Ummi held Zayna in her arms and sang to her in a soft melodic voice, like she used to. It's been so long since she sang our favorite Urdu lullaby:

> *You are my moon.*
> *You are my sun.*
> *Oh, you are the stars in my eyes.*
> *I live just looking upon you.*
> *You are the solace for a broken heart.*

I listened through the door. I listened with dry eyes and a heart that has already been broken into so many pieces that all that is left is dust.

I mouthed the words as she sang them, over and over. I never imagined a lullaby would be the sound of the end of the world.

Zayna never woke up.

Voice Log: Planet Mirzakhani, Afternoon, Diin 6 Saal 3027

Razia Sultana.

She had a life. She had a name. And it is mine.

My fathers told me I was named after a woman warrior of ancient myths. A queen. I do not understand how this is possible. The historian explained that these people held strong beliefs about fate and the correlation of seemingly random events.

Coincidence, they called it. *Synchronicity.* No such idea exists in our language.

There are scant traces of Razia in the dwelling she seems to have shared with her mother and younger sister—I recognize the little girl from the archival image at the shore.

We found only two skeletons—an adult and a small child, their arms intertwined, and a small metallic canister, a rubber seal around its lid, on the floor next to them. In it a faded photograph encased in a kind of resin with their names scratched on the back and two computing devices the size of my thumb that our data forensics team is attempting to decrypt and read.

There was also a key.

August 27, 2031
Ummi's spirit died the same day as Zayna. It took two more days for her body to catch up. When she was finally gone, I laid her body down, wrapping her arms around Zayna as well as I could. There is no ground to cover them. No caskets to bury them in. No one left to mourn them but me. We bury our dead in unmarked graves, wrapped in simple shrouds. We came into this world with no earthly possessions, and we leave the same way, humbly, carried off in prayer.

I don't see the others anymore. Some headed south. Trying to find the warmth of the old sun. Last night I watched from my twentieth-floor perch as a lone figure walked onto the ice, toward the horizon. I followed them a long time until they were a dot. Until my eyes blurred and I blinked and they were gone. Maybe they wanted to be alone when their time had come. Maybe they just wanted to be away from this place. Maybe they wanted to remember what it was like to stretch and use their muscles and breathe the frosty air, because that was the last way to know they were alive.

I found a book in Ummi's belongings. One she'd safeguarded. One she didn't burn for heat: *Forty Rules of Love*. There is no one left to read it. I ripped out page after page, twisting the centers into stems until they transformed into a shape that looked like a flower. I scattered the paper flowers over Ummi's and Zayna's bodies while whispering a prayer. It is not much. But they look peaceful together. Like an infinity poem that repeats itself forever. That is how I will remember them for whatever hours I have left.

I left a small vacuum-sealed capsule next to Ummi. I had almost nothing of ours to leave behind. A small photo that Papa-ji took of his three girls and encased in flexible acrylic, our names and the latitudes and longitudes of our birthplaces etched on the back. I left my Cold Spot data, my notes and models. I left my key. There is no reason to lock anything anymore.

I whispered goodbye when I left the old apartment. It is the last place for Ummi and Zayna to rest. Peace be with them.

Voice Log: Planet Mirzakhani, Diin 7 Saal 3027, Last Day
The key was to a dwelling on the twentieth floor. Her place. Perhaps a quiet room she could go to when the terrible silence and fear grew too loud.

There she was, body curled up in a corner, the golden *R* pendant dangling from her neck.

Words cover the walls. Her words. Every inch of free space. Math problems and diagrams. Two-dimensional maps of the Cold Spot. And a log. A diary of days. Of the horrors she faced. Of the wonders she saw. Of the curiosity she tried to follow.

I sat next to Razia Sultana, my namesake, for hours, through the entire night. Letting her know she was found and will not be lost. Thanking her for her courage, for her story. For this unexplainable moment that drew us together.

We study the ancient ones to learn about ourselves. They are not a monoculture, not a song with a single note. They are a collection of stories, an endless symphony, a galaxy of stars. Perhaps my people are too logical to believe in synchronicity; perhaps the notion is absent in our language. But on this planet it meant something. Improbably, Razia called to me, through the vast emptiness of space-time, and asked me to find her, to tell her story.

I honor that request.

September 1, 2031

I don't think I'll be able to write anymore. I think this is the end. The sun is rising over the lake, and I am thankful that for a moment it covers me in its golden light. So that I will be able to close my eyes and remember what it was like to be warm. To remember what it was like before we lost everything.

If you have found this, if you are reading this, tell *our* story. The terrible and the beautiful. The horror and the wonder.

Tell *my* story.

Say I lived.

I wondered.

I dreamed.

I loved.

I gazed into the stars, hoping to seek you out. And here you are. I looked to find answers because I refused to believe we were alone.

Strange, now as my light dims, I've found a flicker of hope again that you might find me. That you have heard my call and will answer.

I was here.

We were all here.

Remember us well.

THE BEGINNING OF MONSTERS

TESSA GRATTON

The College of Dedicated Renovation had agreed to make Lady Insarra a new body because she was tired of being a woman.

Insarra was one of eleven small kings of the nameless crater city: rich, powerful, and spoiled enough that boredom was all it had taken for her to commission this expensive redesign. Most people who wanted a new body but not chimerical accentuations or augmentations did so because of their gender identities, and of those, most couldn't afford this level of work. But Insarra could've afforded wings if she'd had a sudden hankering to fly.

Elir was the designer assigned by the college. She was a sixteen-year-old prodigy born with crystal bones and retractable crystal claws that allowed her to lift and knot pure threads of power with her bare hands. A stylus was often necessary for heavier work, but not that day.

In the initial design phase, Elir spent hours alone with Insarra, a magnifying circle, pencil, and paper, drawing every tiny detail of the small king's current body.

Insarra reclined, naked, on a low sofa, presently on her side and smoking a long red cigarette. She was careful not to blow the smoke toward Elir, as she must have known its effects would limit the girl's capacity for detailed drawing, but otherwise Insarra ignored her. Elir knelt on a thin pillow, a sketching frame set over her knees to support the sheaf of papers upon which she drew the dips, shadows, jutting lines, and folds of the small king's right hip. This phase was for overall design: color, freckles, blemishes, and hair texture would come later, once Elir'd finished the structural design mesh. Though it was possible Insarra would request a new skin color or hair texture, Insarra was Osahan dynasty, with the rosy-tan skin and wavy thick hair of her people, and for pride would very likely keep it.

Such concerns were for another day. Elir licked her bottom lip to make it more sensitive to the eddies of force-threads as they curled against Insarra's hip and belly. She made a note in the corner of her paper: Insarra was heavy with flow force, which affected the other three forces—falling, rising, and ecstatic—in difficult-to-predict ways. Some said impossible-to-predict, but those people didn't understand the math as well as Elir.

The chamber in which Insarra posed for Elir was octagonal, with eight pillars holding up a mosaicked ceiling, and the walls were latticework quartz, thin enough that sunlight penetrated not only the cutouts, but the pale-pink stone itself. It made this room ideal for sketching at all hours of the day: the pinkish glow softened the harsh desert sunlight.

"Irsu," Lady Insarra drawled, arching her neck to glance toward the eastern archway.

Elir paused, not because Insarra moved, but because the small king's only child had entered. Irsu walked on bare feet, which slapped gently against the marble floor, ans chin lifted arrogantly. An wore a loose white robe and pantaloons tied at the knee, and ans hair fell in sleek black lines around ans face and neck. An was so much more beautiful than ans mother.

"I came to tell you, Mother, I am not attending dinner tonight. I'm tired of the games you play with Far Dalir." Irsu drooped one shoulder in a lazy, disinterested affectation that Elir wanted badly to draw. An was the sort of person inherently talented at using ans body to the fullest. Inhabiting it completely in a way even Elir, who understood the very design of her own, could not quite manage. And an was only eighteen, barely older than she was. By the time Irsu was thirty, imagine the devastation an might cause, or the emotion an might encapsulate with the slightest gesture. Elir wanted to imagine it. She wanted to imagine Irsu doing a great many things.

Lady Insarra groaned and flicked cigarette ash toward her heir. "You would be dour company. I give you permission."

Irsu stiffened so slightly Elir might not have noticed if she hadn't been staring at the play of musculature on ans face. But an loosened the tension instantly. "My thanks, Mother." An turned to go, glancing at Elir.

The designer lowered her gaze to her work. Irsu paused, studying her, Elir was sure. Then an strode out.

"I am exhausted, Eliri," Insarra said. She stretched her back with a pretty sigh, then reached for her long silk robe.

"I have enough for today," Elir said, remaining on her knees.

"Good." Insarra stood and snapped the corner of her robe as she wrapped herself, in a slight display of irritation. Unlike Irsu, she swept out of the chamber loudly.

Elir gathered her things and retreated to the workshop.

The workshop was deep in the heart of Insarra's fortress, where no light penetrated that Elir did not invite, and no breeze or errant force-thread was allowed. Cubbies were built into the floor for storage, and sections of it lifted to become worktables of various heights. Everything an architect might need, Elir could find right here.

She pinned her day's drawings to the south wall, made of smooth stucco to discourage sticking forces. It had been built to her specifications when Elir's college accepted the commission to redesign Insarra's body for her, and Elir was satisfied with it. She sealed the door behind her and opened the long box containing the delicate wire mesh into which she was building the structural design. She rotated it so that the right hip was level with her chest and flexed the forefinger and middle finger of both hands so that her crystal claws slid out.

Slightly curved, the claws acted as precise styli, and Elir plucked a humming thread of flow force that had entwined itself around one of the wires of the design mesh. She pulled it in two places to readjust, and with it the thread drew the mesh into a more accurate peak of hip bone. For several minutes Elir worked by memory and instinct, before turning to the sketches to refresh her familiarity with Insarra's physical design. Elir needed to understand the design intimately; not only to successfully convince everyone the redesign would work, but so that she could sabotage it when the time came.

A chime shivered around the seam of the workshop door: Elir had a visitor.

She took a moment to fix the mesh in place before answering. She tapped her key into the small panel with her claws before retracting them. The door unmade itself, flowing smoothly into the design of the walls, as if it had never been.

Irsu stood there. An leaned ans bare shoulder against the entrance frame and said, "I'd like to see it."

Silently, Elir backed away, allowing Irsu entrance. An walked to the mesh, where it hovered over its box on a cushion of rising and flow forces. In ans wake, eddies of rising force lifted, tingling the hairs along the back of Elir's neck.

"You never speak to me," Irsu said, examining the wire mesh vaguely shaped like ans mother.

"I was not hired for conversations."

Irsu glanced over ans shoulder at Elir. Wryly, an said, "Do I need to compensate you for this then?"

Though she might've earned a tip for herself that she wouldn't need to report to the college, Elir tilted her head no. The excuse to study Irsu's face and the lilt of ans voice would be compensation enough. An stood still, staring at what would eventually be fit over ans mother and irrevocably alter her design. An said, "How are you so good at this, and so young?"

"I have trained for it my entire life. How many languages do you speak?"

"Six."

"I only speak this."

Irsu fell silent, staring at the complex wires of the mesh. Maybe an could see or sense the force-threads, too.

"Why are you here?" Elir asked carefully.

"I'd like to ruin it."

Elir's eyes widened. An could so easily touch the wrong thing and undo days of work.

Irsu turned to her, smiling. "But I won't," an assured her.

"That was unkind," she said, unable to stop her gaze from darting along every line of ans face. Irsu was slightly taller than she was, more slender, and graceful. Ans mouth looked too thin to be soft, and a slight rose-gold darkness bruised the skin under ans honey-colored eyes. Copper studs pierced both ans ears, curling up around the cartilage. As Elir stared, she realized that hidden among the sleek black hairs on ans head were long, narrow feathers. Her lips parted.

Irsu sucked in a quick breath, surprising Elir out of her trance. She raised her hands to touch her eyelids in brief apology and murmured, "I look with a designer's gaze."

"And?" Irsu asked just as quietly.

"I wouldn't change a thing," Elir answered immediately. She felt rising force climb her neck to flush her face with heat and wondered if Irsu was studying her intently enough to notice the dusky tinge it would give her light-bronze cheeks.

"Neither would I," Irsu said, glancing back at the design mesh that would change everything about ans mother's physical body. "My grandfather had the eyesight of an eagle, and a related chimerical redesign aesthetic."

The sudden change of subject startled Elir until she realized it was no change at all. If Irsu had been born with feathers two generations after ans grandfather's redesign, that was amazing! "That is indicative of a stunning level of design," she said breathlessly.

Irsu shot her a look just as wry as ans earlier comment.

Elir raised her right hand and flexed the appropriate muscles to slowly display her crystalline claws. "My mother used a fetal mesh to redesign the development of my bones. My body is a perfect machine for architecture."

Irsu's gaze swept down her body, and when an lifted ans eyes, they held on hers. An touched the pad of a forefinger to the tip of her claw.

"Be careful," she whispered.

"I think everyone should be careful around you."

Elir stopped herself from asking what Irsu saw when an studied her. How did an suspect her when nobody else did? Or was it something else an meant with those words?

She wanted to find out.

The crater city did not have a name because for over a hundred years everyone had been arguing about what it should be. Small kings, cult leaders, the commander-philosophers of every design college, boss artists, and crime lords, all had their own names for the city, and nobody could earn a majority preference or the favor of the god whose fall had caused the crater itself. He lived in the center of his city, sometimes benevolent, sometimes razing an entire precinct with his temper.

Every neighborhood had a name to make up for it, and Lady

Insarra's fortress rose in a spiral of elegant towers at the center of the Rivermouth precinct. Stone designers had carved tunnels through the side of the crater to draw the clean water of the Lapis River into the city, where it bubbled up in private springs and carefully monetized pools. It was this water that made Insarra rich.

Elir lived a twenty-minute walk away, in the Chimera precinct, where several design colleges made their homes. There the buildings burst with strange angles and open rooftops lined with toothy force-hooks, swaying towers, and cloud bridges connecting floating apartments, each style a secret of its birth college.

Some days Elir was allowed to walk through the twisting, layered streets of the crater city on her own, with nothing but a linen cloak designed to bend threads of ecstatic force to make her slightly hard to spot. She didn't like wearing the hood, as it muffled the singing of skull sirens and the hum of graffiti and street advertisements. Elir was not worried about thieves or assaults, for her crystal bones were strong, and her claws viciously sharp.

It was on the days when her neighborhood and the Rivermouth were under small-king alerts or the god's interdiction warning of sky-whales roosting nearby or diamond rain—both remnants of recent wars between city factions—that Elir took extra protection with her: a contingent of mercenary combat-designers trained to turn air into ice or pull blood out through an enemy's pores. Paid for by Lady Insarra, of course. Those days, Elir was bundled into a force-suit woven with ecstatic wires, which she could activate with a sharp cry. Even a sky-whale would hesitate to chomp on such a spiky treat.

Elir arrived at Insarra's fortress exhausted those mornings, needing to rehydrate herself from the effort it took to move under the weight of the suit. She stripped it off piece by piece in the sunny courtyard just beyond the fortress's third-tier gates. The mercenaries teased her, easily moving in their own armor as they left for Insarra's private barracks. Usually a kitchen servant awaited Elir with a flask of water and cup of mint tea, as well as a small basket of sweet cheese and olives to take with her to the workshop.

Today it was Irsu holding a juniper-wood tray inlaid with gold sigils spelling out a poem Elir could not read. She took the water flask and sipped from it, then dribbled some into her palm to splash her hot forehead. All the while, she kept her eyes on Irsu's, trying to exude confidence.

But ans nearness shook her. Especially when one half of ans mouth lifted in that wry smile as she pressed some water up into her scalp, hoping to stick her baby hairs where they belonged.

"Don't you have a design comb for that?" Irsu asked.

"Not with me. Can I borrow yours?"

An shook ans head, and that sleek, straight hair brushed along the embroidered silk of ans sleeveless robe. "I don't need one."

Elir licked her bottom lip to feel the threads of force dancing around Irsu, and when ans gaze flicked down to watch, she realized a non-designer might think it was a different sort of habit. But when Irsu kept ans gaze on her mouth, she also realized she didn't care why an thought she'd done it, because it was clear an liked it.

She took a deep breath. "I need that tea, please." She plucked a small square of cheese off the tray. The sweetness was complicated by essence of roses. A good restorative.

"What is the alert for?" Irsu asked.

"An old spider mine was tripped last night, arming a whole web of them between Chimera and Ribbonwork. Everything around is on the god's interdiction."

Disgust crawled over Irsu's beautiful features. "It is these wars that make the small kings small."

"When you are the small king of Rivermouth, will you stop them?"

"If I survive to ascend."

An would, Elir thought, because ans mother was not long for life.

They walked in the labyrinthine pearl garden in the residential section of the fortress. Near the center, four towers were connected with flaring balconies like petals spiraling up the stem of a vibrant suncup. The pearl garden wove around the bottom levels, looping over itself in puzzled layers, tucking under to make surprise rooms or corners that flared with shade bushes. The paths were laid with crushed marble, gleaming white and iridescent blue-purple, which is what gave the garden its name. Irsu led Elir to a tear-shaped grotto with a thin lattice roof laced with blossoming drop vines— the flowers hung in near-perfect spheres of white and deep pink. They bobbed happily in the artificial breeze of force-fans.

"I can relax here," Irsu said, sinking onto the gleaming granite edge of a crescent-shaped pool. Fish with fins like a peacock's tail swam lazily in the clear water, blowing bubbles that lifted above the surface before popping to release a sweet smell. Decorative chimerical design could be the most fun, but it wasn't intense enough to hold Elir's interests.

She perched beside Irsu, watching the way sunlight filtered through the vines to mottle ans black hair. She could see the slight waver in the light-prints indicating that a force-roof covered this entire garden.

"Do you think you're making my mother better?" Irsu asked, tilting ans head back to look at the nearest bobbing drop flower.

"Is something wrong with her?" Elir asked, sliding her gaze along the lines of Irsu's throat. Her pulse popped with little bursts of ecstatic force.

Irsu laughed and jerked ans chin down to grin at her. "So many things. But nothing a redesign of her body will improve."

"Oh." Elir missed the visual access to ans neck, and traced the lines of ans bare shoulder with her gaze instead. "But what will a redesign hurt? And if it improves her state of mind, surely it helps."

"Her state of mind is boredom, so I suppose. . . . But your skills are wasted giving her a new aesthetic she doesn't need."

"It's never a waste!" Elir was startled out of her obsession with Irsu's features. "At the very least I am practicing, and together, your mother and I create art."

"But you could be practicing your art by making the world better."

Elir narrowed her eyes. She knew this philosophy. "You're a cultist."

Irsu glanced away and rubbed ans thigh nervously. Then an curled ans hand into a fist and looked back at her, hard. "So? Cultists have good ideas. There is even a cult approved by the fallen god."

"My parents were both architects in my college," Elir said.

"The College of Dedicated Renovation."

"It sounds cold, and we have many necessary regulations that help us direct our designs so we don't end up hurting anyone. My ama taught me to work architecture without doing harm."

She put her hand over Irsu's and wondered if her ama would approve of this sabotage assignment. It was a small harm to prevent a greater one. Like cutting into a body to revive the heart, the commander-philosopher of her college had said.

An loosened ans fist and nodded. "Good."

"Good?"

Turning ans hand beneath hers, Irsu laced their fingers together. "I wouldn't like to want to kiss someone who believed in weaponizing architecture or death-design."

Elir's breath caught in her throat, and instead of replying, she leaned up and put her mouth against Irsu's. Ans lips were dry, and softer than she'd expected, and an pressed gently. Her eyelids fluttered, and she thought of the contours of ans thin lips even as she touched them with her own, even as rising force teased up her spine, tingling with ecstatic, and flow pounded through her veins with every beat of her heart. Falling force dripped through her stomach like the hundred tiny feet of a tunnel snake.

Irsu tasted her, and Elir gasped into ans mouth at the touch of ans tongue, leaning away.

It was lovely and strange to feel the eddies of design dancing in the air because someone else had licked her bottom lip.

Irsu kissed her almost every day.

In one of the pockets of the pearl garden, or in her workshop, or quickly in a turn of the corridor, just a breath or lick of her lips. It added such a tension to her days that Elir relished nearly as well as the kisses themselves. Frequently, Irsu came to observe during Lady Insarra's posing sessions, leaning over Elir's shoulder to watch the sweep of her pencil. She'd moved on from the contours to the details, and marked extremely precise maps of Insarra's body. The lady wanted as little change as possible, except what was required to forward a male aesthetic. Irsu rarely spoke to Elir during the sessions; an wasn't cold exactly, but seemed indifferent. When Elir asked why, Irsu said ans mother would lose respect for her if Insarra realized she was carrying on with an. "I'm lazy and unambitious," an said, drawing the words out like ans mother.

Insarra did wish to retain her perfectly shaded Osahan skin, but said she'd take a darkening of her hair with undertones of auburn, as such was the perfectly realized beauty of her ancestors. Elir nodded her agreement, but she was disappointed.

Irsu noticed, and inquired why when they were alone.

"Beauty should be surprising," Elir said. "She could have blood-red hair, or iridescent scales spilling down her scalp, for the price she's paying. I could fit her irises with ecstatic shifting flecks! And she merely wants the physical appearance of a man's aesthetic. How is that better? For her or anyone? It is merely different."

The heir to Rivermouth smiled in such a haughty manner Elir snapped her mouth shut. But an said, "You're frustrated with the art."

Elir reminded herself that the ultimate point of this redesign was assassination. She could not meet Irsu's gaze that afternoon, and put off ans kisses. An teased her for being a grumpy artist.

Elir carefully controlled the release of her breath to keep her claws from trembling as she linked six separate threads of force over the mouthpiece of her design mesh. They latched as they should, shaping a perfectly specific lip-corner. Insarra had approved the final design two days prior and so Elir had begun the real construction. This part was even more delicate than the initial phases, especially because it would be examined closely by security designers and the small king's mercenaries, for weaponry or false-design. Elir had to get it right, and still leave a ripple in which to pinch the sabotage at the very last moment.

Every stroke and pull of her claws could unravel it.

When the alarm ripped through the walls of the workshop, Elir gasped and instantly splayed her hands away from the mesh. Then her mind caught up, and she realized what the alarm meant: the fortress was under attack.

She carefully opened the long box and settled the mesh inside it, sealing the box with null spikes to keep every possible combination of forces out. The workshop was a good place to hole up, as it was suited to defense here in the depths of the fortress.

But Elir didn't stay there: she clawed the door open and dashed out, heading up the spiral stairs. Irsu spent ans afternoons in the tiny fortress library, practicing rhetoric with a tutor or listing Sarenpet declensions, and occasionally writing poetry an refused to share.

It was stupid to leave the workshop sanctuary, but Elir wasn't thinking. She pushed past a quad of Insarra's personal soldiers and avoided people rushing to one of the underground shelters by darting through the gardens. The air was tinged dark, despite the daytime hour, and rang with the alarm. Just as Elir reached the side arch leading into the minaret with the library and a honeycomb of guest rooms, she slammed into Irsu.

An caught her shoulders, but was given no moment to speak, for the soldiers swept them both along to the private shelter, disregarding that Elir was not allowed, because Irsu refused to release her.

Once they were buried under not only the red rock of the crater floor but layers of defense-design, a combat-designer in Insarra's employ lit force-lights in a web against the cave ceiling. The shelter was small but luxurious, and Insarra herself was standing with a flask of some fuming liquor in hand.

When she saw Elir, the small king tapped her foot angrily. "What is she doing here?" she asked, not exactly hostile, but annoyed.

"She was with me," Irsu said. "And so I brought her. She's too expensive to risk losing to your enemies."

"*Our* enemies," Insarra said sourly. She drank from her flask and stalked to her combat-designer, dismissing Elir.

Elir hugged herself. Irsu touched her shoulder. Ans hand was a weight grounding her, and she wanted to lean into an, but she settled for closing her eyes and licking her bottom lip. The forces in this shelter were perfectly aligned and in order.

She felt a hum in the soles of her feet. Then the vibration traveled up her crystal bones in uncomfortable dissonance to her ears, becoming a sound she doubted anybody else could hear. "Null the gates," she said. Then louder, glaring at the combat-designer. "Null the gates! Can you do it from here?"

"Kid, I don't know what you—"

Elir unsheathed her claws, gripped the lines of force tightly woven across the arch, and bent them, slipping out enough to see the air of the tunnel turning hard yellow in billowing clouds. A gaseous design, and it was strong enough to turn on elements too tiny for her to see—that was the only way through the defenses they'd passed. The elements of the air screamed as they were violently redesigned, and she could feel it in her bones.

She reached out and dug her crystal claws into the stone wall, hunting for the right threads: they were so thickly woven here she had to strip some apart to find what she wanted. Knots that could be undone and redone into null knots. She gripped a thread of rising in her teeth—bless the crystal in her bones—and worked fast. Behind her the combat-designer grunted and grabbed another thread with the tip of his stylus. He twisted it and held it at the angle she needed, then Elir flipped the final thread and hissed to speed the ecstatic force, and the null knots imploded.

As Elir fell back, Irsu caught her, dragging her inside while the combat-designer sealed the arch again.

Irsu lowered Elir to the cold floor of the shelter and stroked her braids.

"What was she doing with you?" she heard Irsu's mother demand, though Elir was slowly drifting into force-loss sleep.

"Drawing my picture," Irsu said tenderly.

Elir's last thought was that her quick actions had saved Lady Insarra's life.

Four silver-moon months ago her teacher Sahdia had interrupted Elir's practicum for her final project and dragged her into the commander-philosopher's office. The view from the spire opened in three directions: east, south, and west, leaving the ecstatic north closed off with black-fired tiles. The commander's crescent desk curved against the wall, and she stood behind it, flanked by trees of pale-yellow force-fire.

The commander beckoned Elir close with her milk-pale hands. Her vertical inner eyelids blinked one at a time so she never took her gaze away. Though not truly a parent to Elir, hers had been the father-seed Elir's ama used to grow her in az womb. When az died of a miscalculated force-feedback, Elir had been thirteen, and the commander had told her they both had been proud of her and that she could serve that familial pride by climbing the ranks at the college fast and well.

Elir had: she was only sixteen and already prepping her final project.

"I have a new final for you," the commander said, Sahdia thrumming with restrained ecstatic charges at Elir's side. "I've received a commission for a redesign of the small king of Rivermouth. She requests a body with a male forward aesthetic."

"That's all?" Elir wrinkled her nose.

The commander grinned to show her crocodile teeth. "That's not all, girl. The small king of Rivermouth, we've learned, supports the heresies of the hope cult with quite a bit of money, and you will use your access to design a poison to kill her when she undergoes the aesthetic surgery."

Murder! Elir could not hold back a gasp of ecstatic surprise.

Sahdia touched the nape of Elir's neck. "Use your imagination, sky-heart. Impress us."

Elir thought of her ama excoriating the Cult of Hopeful Design for its philosophies, for the scandal five years before that revealed how many children were buried in their catacombs with ruined bones and crushed skulls.

Lazy architecture, her ama had exclaimed. *The worst crime. A careful moderation is necessary for the long-term benefit of humanity's design! Fetal mesh is not meant to change human children into chimeras—merely for slight changes like your perfect bones. I drew out the crystal already written into your design, nudged you better. Aren't you better, baby?*

Yes, ama.

That's right. No lazy designs to glorify the possibilities of human design!

Then most colleges had banded together for once to demand that the hope cult be stopped—the cultists were too wild, too bizarre! Of course, the fallen god of the red moon had dismissed the complaints of the city colleges, saying there should be no limit to the possible achievements of human architecture. The fallen god rarely took sides, preferring, some said, chaos.

Elir understood, though, that her family and college believed the design of the world would be better if the hope cult fell. It made sense. The cult took too many wild risks. They were not regulated.

And so she had walked to the inner curve of the commander's crescent desk and, with her crystal claws, touched the skin over her heart. "I accept," she'd said, meeting the dangerous gaze of the commander-philosopher.

Elir woke to the touch of light silk sheets and a warm breeze fluttering her lashes.

She opened her eyes and saw first a vaulted ceiling set with tiny shards of blue and green chipped tiles, in a mosaic like the waves of the sea.

"Elir," said Irsu, coming to kneel at her bedside. "You've slept more than a day, and I brought you to this room, a guest room. It's yours until you've recovered, but I'm afraid you'll have to remain while the fortress is interdicted." An spoke more quickly than usual.

Elir blinked slowly, thinking of the commander's vertical inner lids. A shiver dragged down through her bones, and Irsu kissed her forehead.

"Are you ill?" an said. "Curro thought it was force-loss faint, and that you'd recover quickly."

"Yes," she whispered. "Water?"

Irsu left, but Elir heard an moving and the trickling sound of water being poured. An set a shallow cup down on the rug and scooped an arm around her to help her sit up. Then an brought the cup to her lips, and she drank.

"You'll have to draw me now," an said. "I told my mother that you'd offered a portrait."

"No extra charge?" Elir whispered, managing a little smile.

Irsu laughed and kissed her cheek, then pressed ans forehead to hers.

Elir remained at the fortress for six days while the small king's combat-designers cleansed the air. They were wonderful days, because Irsu spent them with her and allowed her to draw an.

Elir went carefully, first focused on ans eyes, then jaw, then mouth, before letting her gaze travel down ans throat to the bend of ans collarbone.

"Shall I remove my robe?" an offered quietly.

Elir's heart popped with ecstatic hope, and falling knots twisted in her belly. She parted her lips to answer but could not.

Irsu took the paper and the pencil from her numb fingers, set them aside, and tugged at the small hooks holding her robe closed below her breasts. She allowed it, barely breathing, and took ans face in her hands, fingers flicking over the copper studs in ans ears, and kissed an without a thought to eddies of force. She wore a sleeveless linen shift under her robe, and Irsu kissed down her sternum, teasing her with warm breath that easily drifted through the linen. When an kissed one of her breasts, Elir flexed her claws. They sliced through the silk of ans robe, snagging a line of embroidered succulents. Elir gasped, and Irsu laughed. "See," an said, "I should just take it off."

Nudging Elir away, Irsu stood and easily untied ans robe, letting it slip off one shoulder. An lifted the shoulder and turned to gaze flirtatiously over it at her. Where the robe slunk low on ans chest, the hem of pretty purple binder showed.

"What do you want me to draw?" Elir asked, staring at Irsu's languid beauty.

"You're thinking about *drawing* right now?" an murmured.

"I can't stop thinking about the lines of your body, the tucks and shadows, the curves and planes," Elir whispered, slowly standing. "I'll draw it however you like, you know, however you want it."

Irsu put a hand out to stop her approach. "I like it as it is, Eliri. I told you that."

"Then that's how I'll draw it. Though I think you'd look magnificent with wide drooping wings to match. . . ." She caressed one of Irsu's head feathers.

An kissed her again, hands on her hips, and she tasted the threads of ans design on her tongue!

"Why are you a cultist? What is your cult?" she asked Irsu, draped against an later, half-dressed but lazy with kissing and touching and sharing knots of force between them. She knew an would say the hope cult that Insarra supported, but she longed for an to say something else. Give her a reason to argue.

"Roc Aliel is the leader. Have you read any of his philosophy?"

"No," she said, though she knew the name: he was the founder of the hope cult.

"He writes about possibilities. About being better than our design, pushing past what we know and believe, into a realm of infinity."

"What does that mean?" Elir asked, trying not to sound intrigued.

"Well." Irsu kissed her shoulder. "For example, he thinks we should have names for more than four genders."

Elir snorted softly. "More between? Or beyond?"

"Either. Both. I know you are stuck at four in the same way most are, especially because you are an architect. Four-way thinking is the foundation of our entire society. Four genders, four directions, four forces! But there are more ways to walk to the horizon than east or west or north or south, and there are more possibilities between bodies and what different designs— physical and inner—signify."

Elir hummed, staring at the tiny whorls of hair on Irsu's forearms.

"Isn't it more wonderful to imagine *more* than to limit your thinking?" an said.

That made her sit up. She stared down at an, stunned.

She'd had the same thought about architecture. About life itself.

"See?" Irsu grinned. "You're imagining possibilities."

But this was the thinking that had led to catacombs of dead babies and rampant sky-whales. Imagination and power running wild together. It sounded exhilarating—and dangerous.

Irsu said, "Soon, Roc and I will crash over the city, and everyone will change in our wake."

"You and Roc? The leader of the hope cult."

"I'll take you to meet him." An lifted her hand to kiss the pads of her fingers, trailing them against ans lips. "I've been going to meetings and funneling cash. Mother has no idea. Rivermouth will be the stronghold of hope."

Elir's pulse pounded in her fingers. Irsu was the one supporting the cult, not ans mother. An was the one her college should have her kill.

She could never do that. She loved an. She agreed with an. Elir wanted to imagine more.

Irsu sat up, holding her close. "Eliri, stay with me. You were made for infinite design! Born for this—for me. It is a fight worth fighting. Limitless potential! Hope!"

She pushed away, climbed to her feet. She had to think. "The fallen god will not let you amass against him."

"He likes ambition!"

"I should design you those wings," Elir said, picking her robe up off the floor. "You would fly all the way to the stars."

Irsu laughed, and an was so beautiful it took her breath away. "I'll let you, if you design a matching pair for yourself. I'm a little in love with you."

"A little?" she laughed, giddy and horrified—she'd not realized before they were so much the same feeling.

"With all the possibilities ahead of us for more!" Irsu said, finally rising to ans feet, too. "A little love is only the beginning. This is the beginning."

Elir stared at an a long moment, at the curve of ans thin

lips, the brightness of ans eyes, and the perfect haughty lines of ans bearing.

She fled.

Her personal room in the college complex was tucked among those of other final-year students, in a honeycomb tower grown from the red rock of the crater. Elir hid herself within, curled on her pallet with her knees drawn up. She stared at the wall, papered with chimerical diagrams she'd drawn as a child: a griffon, its bones, muscles, connective tissues, feathers, and wings all on separate tracing papers; a thorn tree with bisected branches to show rings and veins; a rainbow bee, stingers drawn in large scale to show their mechanism; pear blossoms randomly sketched in corners; lips; her own name repeated over itself, again and again, to form a complex heart-design that might suit a massive monster like a sky-whale. From the ceiling hung the real wing of a tree dragon, furry chimeras made of lizards and rain-forest megabats. The wing's long bones splayed like an open hand, with white-gold membrane stretched between, and the longest bone arced down, glinting pearlescent in the small bobbing force-lights.

She thought of Irsu with such wings, though an probably would prefer graceful feathers, the black-and-white patterns of an oasis vulture.

Elir thought of many things that long week she confined herself, sketching wings for both of them, various models and skins. Avian, draconic, mammalian, insectile. She thought of the first lessons of architecture, that there were only four forces; of the special blaze she felt when ecstatic pops fizzled into something more like flow; of what made the fallen god a god—his ability to change his design at will, without architecture, without external design; of her parents, especially her ama, who had so strongly proselytized moderation yet had worked design on az own womb to give Elir this crystal gift. Az had certainly imagined possibilities. Maybe the difference between college and cult was merely education and skill. Or only regulation. Maybe the cult needed someone to describe the distinction between true possibility and doom.

Maybe Elir was arrogant to think she could make any kind of choice like that.

She was only sixteen.

But maybe only somebody at the beginning of their life could change the course of the future.

A little love is only the beginning, Irsu had said. Maybe a little arrogance was only the beginning, too.

The song of the riot did not vibrate through the intricate security of the college, but Elir heard the noise. She was already on her feet when Sahdia came to drag Elir out of her reclusion, rolling her sharp eyes. "While you pouted, never finished your work, the hope cult has risen, Eliri! The commander will see you now, and you need a good explanation for your failure." She pulled Elir into the corridor.

Elir grabbed Sahdia's wrist, jerking free. "What do you mean it has risen?"

"That leader, Roc, has taken over Rivermouth, and you are the only one who can stop him."

"Why?"

"Because Insarra wants her new body, and she trusts you. Her household knows you."

"No, Sahdia, why must the cult be stopped?"

"Ah! Eliri! If they have their way, someday there will be no humans left."

Elir flexed her hands, unsheathing all ten of her claws. "What is human?"

"Has Insarra been preaching? She is corrupt. Remember your ama, and listen now to your commander."

"I never spoke to Insarra about hope." Elir smiled before she could stop herself, recalling the passion in Irsu's voice. She'd made her choice days ago. "Sahdia, I forgot something in my room. Go, and I will come after to the commander-philosopher's office."

Sahdia frowned. She'd assisted the commander for years and knew well how to look for subterfuge in students. "You promise?"

"I promise," Elir lied.

But the woman left her, and Elir hurriedly packed a small bag with only her favorite slippers, a set of styli, and the tracing-paper griffon diagram. She did not need any of the winged designs. After putting on her best robe she went out of the honeycomb student rooms and across the eight-star courtyard. The sky blazed red with bright lily-bombs, and intricate spirals of purple smoke rose. There came a roar in the seven-note chord of a raging sky-whale.

Instead of turning into the command tower, Elir walked for the massive gates of the college.

They spread like wings, cut of mountain crystals, with veins of red crater rock. Fuchsia blossoms trailed over them, from vines rooted in place, for the gates of the college rarely opened. Instead, a tiny arch cut into the granite wall beside them served as an entrance—and an exit.

Elir drew a deep breath and unsheathed her crystal claws. She dug them into the gate, and baring her glittering crystal teeth, she tore through a knot of falling force. It snapped free, and she hooked a pop of ecstatic force, redirected it with two claws to disrupt the flow force binding the gates together.

They groaned; the fuchsia blossoms shivered and began to fall around her like vivid rain.

Then the gates of the college opened, scraping the street in a raw cry that would call the sky-whale here to distract the commander-philosopher.

Elir walked through it, and there was Irsu with a streak of dark blood on ans cheek.

Her lips parted in surprise and eddies of chaotic forces tickled her tongue as she stared. The crater city lifted around them in gleaming towers and arched bridges, floating apartments and rising ribbons of force, all a-shudder with the peal of alarm bells and the chanting cultists, with booming explosions and something like distant laughter.

"I came to see you," Irsu said. An wore a dark-blue robe, sleeveless and tight to ans chest and waist. It flared around ans hips like a skirt, and for the first time Elir had seen, an wore shoes, to protect ans feet against the dusty flagstones. She lifted her eyes from the soft brown boots, dragging her gaze up and up to ans face again, and the straight lines of ans hair as it gleamed in the hot morning violence. An added, "I came to implore you."

"I hoped you would," she announced, letting her bag slide off her shoulder.

Irsu stepped closer and took it, smiling ans wry smile. An offered ans free hand.

Elir scraped her claws gently against Irsu's sensitive palm. She said, "This is only the beginning."

LONGER THAN THE THREADS OF TIME

ZORAIDA CÓRDOVA

Belvedere Castle in Central Park was an extraordinary building, but not everyone knew that. When construction began in 1867, the building was designed to be a folly. Danaë always thought that a folly was a mistake. Something people did by accident or an eternal flaw, like heroes in fantastical stories who tried so hard to beat a cruel destiny that would always be against them because of their foolish actions. But for architects, it meant a replica.

The thing that made Belvedere Castle magnificent, to those who could see it, was the additional tower, a thousand and one feet tall, shrouded in a magical barrier. For everyone else, the folly was magnificent in a mundane way, meant to be whimsical but nothing else.

Danaë felt that way sometimes, but then she remembered

that, imprisoned in the top of her tower, she was not a folly. She was just forgotten.

Fabían Macías had the Sight, and it sucked. Coming from a family of brujas meant that he always smelled like incense and buried his moms' good-luck trinkets at the bottom of his book bag, where they lived next to a city of pencil shavings, broken erasers, the MetroCards he kept forgetting about so they each only had seventy-five cents, and sticks of gum so old they were smooshed into the cheap polyester fabric.

Fabían wished he could shove his family's magic down in the bag with the rest of the forgettables, but he wasn't about to piss off his gran. Besides, there was this girl down in Brooklyn everyone whispered about, Alex Morticia or whatever, who had some big type of magic that she tried to curse away, and it had backfired, turning all her family members into frogs. At least that's what people said. What. A. Dum. Dum.

See, Fabían's beef with magic wasn't that he didn't like it. It was that he liked it so much. But he wasn't chosen. Why couldn't he have been an Encantrix or a weather brujo or even have the ability to guess Lotto numbers so he could buy his moms something nice. His cantos were weaksauce. One time, he tried to cast a canto to make his beard grow out so he wouldn't look like an alley cat with patchy hair. Instead, he ended up with tiny green shoots, like he'd sprouted grass.

Meanwhile, his brother, Gabriel, had that nice beard all slick and curly. They were otherwise the same, he and Gabriel. Both had their parents' brown skin, thick eyebrows, and round eyes framed by lashes so long it made girls angry because the Macías brothers didn't have to try. He wished that his family had been blessed by the gods of old, the Deos, the ones that their ancestors had brought with them as they migrated from Ecuador to Colombia, picking up magic tricks until they settled in a dank little building in El Barrio.

Most days Fabián wished he'd been born ordinary. Knowing about the magical underbelly of a city like New York just made him want more of it. Other days, he felt lucky to just be part of the most exclusive club in the world. A brujo. Even a not-so-powerful one like him. He might not be raising the dead any time soon, but he could do what regular humans—magical ones, even—could not.

He could See. That's *See* with a capital *S*.

The Sight was said to have been passed down in his family ever since his ancestor Túpac Pachaquil made a bargain with a goddess. He'd sacrificed something or other—Fabián couldn't always remember if it was fifty guinea pigs or fifty rabbits, but that was the gist. The goddess blew in Túpac Pachaquil's face the way Fabián had seen curandera witches blow holy water on the body of a possessed person to banish an evil spirit. The goddess banished Túpac's human ignorance to the supernatural. Dispelled the layer that exists between the mundane and that which is magic.

Of course, not everyone in his family had the Sight, which was sometimes a good thing. It was like how his uncle Marcelo had a crooked finger bone just like his great-granddad, and how his moms had the same beauty marks on her shoulder in the exact same spot as her father, and how his cousin Willie had the Macías ears but not the Macías nose. It was just another thing he'd been lucky enough to inherit.

Fabían was unique in his own way. Even though he'd never been to Ecuador, he had something from the Earth's belt. Something no one could take away from him.

And he could see when he was getting a rat deal from the fairies in Central Park, when the mermaids were wearing their legs but didn't hide their scales or strange ears and stranger eyes.

He could see when vampires tried to glamour themselves a tan. Creepy AF.

His Sight helped him survive the streets of New York City in a different way.

That's why it was so tragic that the Sight, the very thing that should have helped him See, was the very thing that would lead to Fabían's undoing. There is only one thing that can trick a gods-given gift like his.

Love.

Up in her tower Danaë could see the entire city and beyond. When she first came to be trapped inside its stone walls, she thought that someone might eventually come for her. But the only person who might have once remembered Danaë was her mother.

Decades ago, they'd gotten off a ship to Miami, taken a train to New York City, and finally hopped on the subway as far as 116th and Lexington and walked down to their apartment on 114th. They had one suitcase between the two of them, plus a handful of seeds her mother had smuggled in the hidden pockets of her skirts. They'd been wearing the same dresses for days. It was lucky that her mother was a seamstress, able to repair their rips and seams, their buttons that kept falling off as if even they didn't want to be attached to the Santiago Aguilar girls.

Danaë could still picture her mother back then, with her thick curls carefully waved beneath a smart wool hat. Her dress perfectly fitted to curves that Danaë always believed she'd grow into herself. But over half a century later and Danaë was still stuck in the body of a sixteen-year-old.

She pushed aside the curtain, like that might erase the memories of her life as it had been. She could divide her life in two segments: before and after the tower.

Before the tower went as so: they rented a studio apartment in Spanish Harlem that had once smelled of urine and the carcass of an abandoned dog. Her mother always reminded her, "We might be poor, but at least we're clean," and soon enough they transformed their living space, polishing the wooden floors and adding a fresh coat of paint in a color that reminded them of the blush of spring. No rats or cockroaches dared sneak under their clean sheets. Even the ants that crept up the rusted fire escape avoided their space. Their little home smelled of bread after her mother learned to bake from a Polish woman on the second floor, who didn't speak English either and didn't seem to mind the mother and daughter who kept to themselves. For a time.

There was a moment in between the apartment and the tower: a bad bargain, a betrayal, a terrifying limbo where Danaë slept until she woke in a stone room so high above the city, she could eat the clouds for breakfast.

After the tower was an adjustment: there were months of screaming and tears. At least she had a soft mattress with silk sheets. At least the stones warmed in the winter and cooled in the summer.

Danaë longed for a stove to bake bread. She longed for sugar to dissolve in fresh coffee. She longed for mangoes to bite into like a ripe, juicy heart. She longed for more than the three books the sorcerer had left on a single shelf, and the copper spyglass to let her peer at a world that was passing her by. Danaë was filled with so much longing, but none of the promise of possibility.

There was no possibility for her. She was like an insect frozen in amber, a fossil waiting to be unearthed.

All because her mother had made a bad deal, and Danaë had paid the price.

In the beginning, she used to cry. She cried so much that she thought she'd fill the entire room with her tears. But the space was too large. It turns out that tears only feel like a lot to the person crying them.

When she'd tire herself out, she'd stare out the window and feel terribly, hopelessly small.

After that, she would scream.

"Help me!" she shouted, in a city where everyone needed help. In a city where people got lost and killed and crushed and swept away in different ways. Who could help her when that city could not even help itself?

Still, it was a particular type of punishment that they couldn't hear her supplication, but she could hear them. Their voices carried up to Danaë's window. Lovers sneaking in the dark shadows of Central Park. People screaming. Police barking. Sirens wailing. Bands playing. It was all the same cycle of sounds. New York only changes on the surface, after all.

There were the occasional taunts from the solitary fairies and werewolves that lurked in the trimmed wilderness below.

Her entrapment was a discovery of the magical world that existed in the betwixt spaces, the twilight, the midnight, the halves of the world. Unfortunately, her own magic was bottled up.

"Rapunzel, Rapunzel! Let down your hair!" a gnarly troll shouted once. She couldn't see his face through the foggy view of her spyglass, but he *looked* like he could be a troll. She wished she had something to throw at him, but mostly, she wished that someone would try to free her instead of chiding her.

While she possessed very little, the tower apartment did come equipped with some necessities: a bathtub, soaps and sponges, a gilded mirror, and a few dresses her mother had left behind.

Danaë had a very meticulous hair routine. When she'd first been locked in the tower, her hair was the fashionable bob of working girls. The year she'd immigrated to New York City had been 1946 and it felt like a new era. With hot curlers at the salon run by a fellow Dominican woman named Yennifer, she'd turn her ribbon curls into the sculpted waves.

The first week without her products had been torture. Being among the clouds meant there was nothing but moisture. The sorcerer, whom she'd met thrice (once when her mother made the deal, once when he'd collected his payment, and once more) had granted her a never-ending coconut oil vase and an ivory comb. Perhaps it was the magic he'd used, but she could never quite remember his face, only the strange weariness that overtook her when he was around. It was as if his power came from some long-gone god of slumber. Either way, for a time she was content with keeping her hygiene. She bathed every day and spent hours brushing tangles out of her hair, until, before she knew it, her hair was down to her ankles. She braided it, and as new buildings were erected and the city changed, her curls spilled in ropes longer than the threads of time.

She slept in a nest of her own hair. Her tower, being enchanted and all, provided magical remedies. She couldn't age. She couldn't get sick. She was never hungry. She was perfectly preserved in most ways. Even her menstruation stalled. The things that magic couldn't take away were the hairs on her head and the strain on her heart.

Why would someone want the heart of an ordinary girl who sometimes worked at a pastry shop with her mother?

At least her heart couldn't get tangled and snagged on furniture. She once broke the mirror and used a long shard to try to cut her hair. But the strands were like metal cords. The mirror re-formed. The gash on her palm healed. Then she'd tried to bite her hair off, rip it with all the strength she could muster, but only managed to crack her front tooth. It healed that very night.

So her hair grew, year after year, like the berries on her window that gave her the only sustenance she required.

Eventually Danaë had stopped counting how long she'd been in the tower. Sometimes it felt like a century. Sometimes it felt like she was already dead, and this was her punishment from a cruel god for reasons she couldn't understand.

But then one day, while she sat on her windowsill picking at her split ends and singing a song she'd heard on a jukebox nearly seventy years before, she heard a voice call back.

Not taunting.

Not far, either.

She couldn't see him well at first, as it was a particularly rainy day and her spyglass was warped. But she knew she wasn't imagining him.

A strong breeze shoved the clouds away and there he was. He was standing on the edge of the pond behind Belvedere Castle and looking straight up at her. A boy with a flop of black waves, dressed in a brown leather jacket, twisting something in his hands. Everything inside her was torn. Was he real? Did he really, truly see her? Her heart gave a painful pump, like after so many years she'd forgotten that it was actually still beating.

"Hello," he said. "Can you hear me?"

Fabían Macías knew about the tower. Every magical person in New York did. They knew it had been built as a prison by those who hunted people like him. It trapped strong magic inside and out of the way. He knew that everyone pretended it didn't exist because there was already someone in there, and if it ever became empty, then the hunters would want to fill it back up.

But how was he supposed to ignore the structure that split Central Park in half? How could he ignore the girl who sang every night, sometimes off-key? He could hear how lonely she was because he felt that way sometimes too.

That night, he was crossing the park to get to the movie theater and meet his friends, when a strange feeling gripped him. It said, *Wait. Listen. Speak.*

So he spoke.

He yanked the beanie from his head and wrung it out like fresh laundry as he waited for her to answer. He heard her before he saw her. She was sitting in the south-facing window of the tower, touching the curling end of her hair. He didn't recognize the song right away. It was one that his grandma used to like to play, but his Spanish wasn't all that good.

He saw her get scared. He'd seen boys around the block talk at girls from the street. Call them out from their windows. The girls would stand at the fire escape until their mom or dad or big sibling came out and got tight. Then the guys would run off.

But here, on an evening where the staff had left for the day and there was no one in the park except humans looking for trouble and magical beings coming to life under the moon, he finally worked up the nerve to talk to her.

"Who are you?" she asked. There was something defensive about her voice.

"Um—I'm just Fabían. My friends call me Fabe. Like Gabe." He wished he could smash his own face against the side of the brick building. *Fabe like Gabe?* Who said that? He'd never said that in his life.

But then it was worth it from the sound of her laugh.

"What are you doing up there?" he asked.

"Taking in the view, naturally."

"Yeah, but why are you up there?"

"Someone I loved very much left me behind."

"You loved a hunter?" Fabían grimaced.

"What? No! What do you want, Fabe like Gabe?" she asked, leaning just slightly out the window.

"The song you were singing reminded me of someone. Usually I just keep walking, but today is different. I felt like I should say something. I don't know . . ."

"So you've heard me before?"

307

"Well, yes."

She set her chin on her wrist. "Then why talk to me now?"

"Because everyone tells me not to."

"Do they?" She sounded so sad, and he wanted nothing more than to make her not sad.

"Everyone knows that this is a prison and that you never talk to anyone."

"Who am I supposed to talk to?"

"Me. If you want."

"It's kind of hard to have a conversation while we're shouting."

He knew he should go home. If he didn't leave that minute, he'd miss the movie and his moms would be pissed if he bailed on dinner, but it was ceviche night. He hated ceviche. Fish cooked in lemon juice? No, thank you.

But it had taken him too long to work up the nerve to talk to the girl in the prison tower. He couldn't turn back now.

"Is there a ladder or an elevator?" he asked. The structure couldn't just be a cylinder of stacked stones, right? Of course, he knew that though magic had rules, they didn't apply to everyone in the same way.

"No . . . but there's another option. Would you do it?"

His heart felt like the time he took a beating at the boxing ring. Gloved fists popping against his chest. Only now that sensation was coming from within.

"Yes! What is it?"

There was a long pause and she vanished. He could see a silver ripple in Turtle Pond beside him. A slender green creature with a bald head, wearing a lily pad as a skirt, giggled. "But how will you get down, little one?"

"The same way I come up," he snapped.

She raked her sharp, webbed fingers across the surface. Smiling with pointed teeth, she said, "I'll be here to break your fall."

Horns blared in the distance, and a whiff of pretzels and hot dogs somehow made its way here, too. With his true Sight he could see the world come alive. New York City was magic in a way that no one ordinary would ever know. Fey creatures wearing human clothes slunk around smoking cigarettes, and down below across the sprawling green mounds, there were young vampire girls moon-bathing in string bikinis. They drank something dark and syrupy from 7-Eleven Slurpee cups.

He suddenly felt his fragile mortality so much more. There was a reason his mother didn't want him running around at night, and it was more than the usual human worries. It was more than getting mugged on the 6-train platform. It was getting mugged by a werewolf breaking the peace treaty because he hadn't eaten in days. Or a renegade cult using his bones to summon an interdimensional demon. It was an old worry, in their time of supposed peace, but it was New York City. Anything could happen. Why was he expected to live afraid all the time? Why was he expected to be the scared one, unlike the great, terrifying, fearless brujos he'd heard of in the past?

Then he saw the rope. It cascaded down in front of him. His heart stuttered, thinking it was a snake or some sort of octopus thing. He needed to stop watching scary movies was the real truth of it.

It was just hair.

He smiled at himself. He grabbed the rope braid and wound it around his hand.

Then he climbed.

∞

Danaë gasped softly. "He's really coming up."

She felt the tug at the roots of her hair, and she yelped like a cat that had been stepped on. She held on to an arm-length chunk of braid and propped a foot against the windowsill. She pulled to help him up, her heart like the tap of tambores in her eardrums. A strangling sensation wrapped around her throat, like the times she'd fallen asleep tangled in her own braid. She'd imagined this moment for years, decades. For so long that it was only ever a fantasy. She had only ever hoped to be like the girl in the stories, but stories never ended happily for girls like her.

Then she could hear him. Did all boys grunt so loudly?

She saw the moment when he looked down and the fear of falling overtook him. His eyes went wide, and then she was reaching for him. He grabbed her hand and tumbled inside. She staggered back, pressing her palms on her thighs, watching him.

He stood to full height. He looked about the age she'd been when she'd been frozen forever—sixteen or seventeen. His dark curls were smooshed at the top, probably from the hat shoved in his back pocket. His nose reminded her of a bird's beak, but it was lovely on him. High cheekbones and lashes so black she took a step closer to see if he was wearing makeup. It wasn't something men did in her time, but times changed always. When he smiled, the flutter of wings took off in her belly. Her mother had once said something about beautiful boys with crooked smiles. But her mother wasn't here. Her mother had left her behind.

This boy was here now.

"Hey," he said, brushing the front of his leather jacket. It looked soft to the touch, but she kept her hands around her torso.

"Hello," she said.

He looked out the window and grinned. "You know, I'm glad my friends dragged me to that rock-climbing wall in Brooklyn. It came in handy for this."

"Rock-climbing?" She searched her memory for something like that from her time before the tower. But the closest she came was from her time in the Dominican Republic. There had been this sea-facing cliff the local kids would leap off on sweltering days. "Is it dangerous?"

He laughed, and his laugh was so sweet and musical. "No. Well, sometimes. My cousins have been trying to get me to conquer my fear of heights."

The tension of strangers dissipated with every direct eye contact, every moment he fidgeted and his full mouth tugged in a playful way. She found that her whole face ached. Muscles that hadn't moved were stretching, and it was painful.

"Yet here you are scaling the side of a building a thousand feet in the air," she said.

"I'm going to be real with you right now," he told her. "This is scarier. I've thought about you for so long and now here you are."

She walked to the window, around him, and stared at the city night, lit up with a million lights. She reeled her braid back. "Are you disappointed?"

"No!" he said, reaching for her quickly. His fist closed around air, like he was afraid to touch her. "I guess I never got to the part where I actually met you. How long have you been here?"

When she got the last of her hair up into the tower, she sat on the neat pile of it, a throne made of her own locks. She gestured to the pillows on the floor. He kicked off his sneakers, and though there was no door anywhere, he left them neatly pressed against the wall under the north-facing window.

He sat cross-legged across from her and waited.

"I used to count." She twisted the end of her braid around her finger like a garden snake. Her brown eyes darted to the wall beside him.

He pushed the curtain aside and noticed long scratches in the smooth gray stone. There were dark spots, and it took him a moment to realize they were blood. She'd clawed those tallies, or used something so sharp she drew blood.

"And then I stopped counting," she said. "I tried to train pigeons to fetch me things, but they're incredibly flaky. I was brought here in 1947, a year after my—my mother and I moved to Spanish Harlem from a little town outside La Romana."

"Is that in the DR?"

"Where?"

"The Dominican Republic," he clarified. "The kids from the floor downstairs call it that."

"It's strange having once been from a place and not knowing what to call it anymore. It hasn't been home for a long time. But then, this tower is not my home either."

"What did you do?" he asked.

At that she felt her blood run cold, and her words sharpen. "What makes you think I did anything?"

"I—I'm sorry. It's just. Well. Everyone knows the hunters built this tower as a prison. Don't get me wrong. Everyone hates them and they hate us."

"I was put here by a sorcerer."

"Well, they do employ magical beings when it's convenient for them. No one is supposed to come near here. That's what my moms says, though. I don't think anyone knows the real truth."

Danaë breathed fast and short. Was that why no one had bothered with her? What did she know about the man who brought her here? "I can't always remember the day it happened. I just know I saw him twice more. He'd checked up on me once after locking me up . . . and then he never came back."

"And you've been here all this time." He shook his head. It was like his world was inverting.

"What did you expect? A dragon? A witch?"

"I'm a brujo," he told her. "So that wouldn't be very shocking."

She perked up. "You are? That's why you can see the tower."

He waved a hand, like he was trying not to brag. "I have the Sight, too. I can See through magical shields and glamours. I can cast some cantos, but my brothers are better than me."

Tears pricked at her eyes. Her very distant memory remembered magic. It remembered a bright golden light that burned her retinas. Then darkness. Then the tower.

"Fabían, tell me everything."

Danaë said his name in a way that didn't make his shoulders bunch up and his insides cringe. *Faaahb-eee-aaahhhhn.* She dragged the syllables like she was singing just for him. It made him feel light-headed. He'd had as many crushes as he had digits, but this strange girl made him feel something no one else had. She had a heart-shaped face and a small round nose. With eyes like that and lips that always looked pink, she was the closest thing to a Disney princess he was ever going to see up close. She had the weirdest freckle on the mound of her cheek, misshapen like it didn't know if it wanted to be a circle or a star. It was pretty, no matter what, and the longer he stared at it, the more he decided it was a star. Definitely. One to guide him back.

He thought of that as he inched back down the tower with her rope of hair wrapped around his ankle and his heart lodged in his throat. The sun was breaking, and when he glanced up at her, she was there in the shadow of the window. How wack was it that she could send down her hair, but never leave herself?

These damn hunters.

As he ran all the way home, trying to beat the rising sun, he thought about his tasks for the day. Gather as much junk food as possible. She could only eat these tiny purple berries growing from the vines at her window. They kept her alive and healed her. He wasn't sure what kind of injuries she could sustain in a circular room, but he'd heard stories of people who got locked up. People who couldn't leave their homes because their fears took over. People who had no choice. He shook his head. If she was going to be stuck up there, then he could at least give her a crash course on the last sixty years.

When he walked into his house, he stopped to think. He had a crush on an older woman. Technically, *technically,* she was, like, eighty-two. But she still looked sixteen. One year younger than he was. She'd been frozen in time for so long. What must it be like for her to age mentally but not physically? Weird.

Then he stopped for an entirely different reason.

His mom was standing in the hallway. The dark skin under

her eyes was pinched. Her rollers were tied in that silk net she always put on before bed. The long bata she wore to sleep wasn't even wrinkled, like she'd been awake sitting up. And then there was the rolled-up newspaper in her hand.

When she was angry, she only spoke in Spanish. But this was next level. It was on some Satanic ish level, like when the Irish kids in the apartment down the hall tried to play their granddad's records backward. He thought it sounded like "Where have you been?" Or maybe "I'm going to kill you."

"I'm sorry," he said quickly. "I went to Central Park and there were these fairies. You know how time stalls when they're around. I'm sorry!"

One thing he'd learned from fairies was how to lie without lying. He *had* been in Central Park. There *were* fairies in Central Park. Time *did* act weird at their magical raves and gambling dens. His mom did know all that.

She touched her forehead. Her heart. Her throat. It was like a prayer, but for brujas asking or thanking the Deos for a miracle. Why did she always worry? He was fine.

"If you're not home tonight by dinner, I'm going to invent a canto that will ground you for the rest of my life. Go put on the coffee."

He did as he was told, scooping the grounds of Bustelo into the coffee filter and hitting the on button. The whole time he thought about Danaë. Her face. Her hair. He'd never seen so much hair in his life. The way she sat there in the pale blue dress that brought out the freckles on her arms. The way she spoke about her old life. The things she remembered, at least. The songs she liked. He was already making a playlist on his phone for her. He didn't understand why she'd been put in that tower, but he was going to find a way to break her out.

It took him three days to come back. In that time, Danaë tidied up her belongings. She scrubbed her skin. She changed her dress. She gathered the tiny, fragrant flowers growing in from her window vine and rubbed the sticky floral scent on her wrists and throat.

Her mother had once told her about boys. They'd been on the ship, and several young men had called her attention with sharp whistles and sultry glares. Her virtue had been the most important thing about her, it seemed, until the day her magic surfaced.

"Danaë!" he shouted. "It's me."

When he made it back up, she dug her fingers through her hair and massaged her scalp. "Did you double in weight while you were gone?"

"I came prepared." He only laughed. He shook off a backpack from his shoulders and a satchel from across his chest and got to work. A black cylinder. Bags of what looked like food. Candles. Jars of powders and sticks of palo santo. Clear boxes filled with more food. Coca-Cola in tin cans instead of glass bottles. Her longing for the world outside grew.

She picked one up and held it in her fingers. "Can I?"

"It's for you," he said. Then, as she popped the top, he added, "It's all for you."

For a long time they feasted. She cried when she crunched on the salty platano chips. She wept harder when the black cylinder, which he called a portable speaker, plugged into the smallest telephone she'd ever seen and played the songs of her childhood.

They spent the day following the sun as it filtered into her small room. They reclined on cushions, and then as the sun began to sink and they'd nearly finished eating everything, they lay side by side with their shoulders touching.

Touch was something so strange to her, after decades of being alone. She reached out for his hand and he didn't move. His skin was warm in hers. It sent a spark across her chest, filled her with a heat that felt like it could burn her up if she let it. A simple touch could do that?

"How does it work?" he asked, tracing his thumb across her knuckles. "The magic of the tower? Every spell can be broken."

"If I knew, I wouldn't be here."

"The hunter—the sorcerer—he didn't give you any hints? Usually bad guys like to give out their plans in long monologues at the end of the movie. Gods, I want to take you to a movie. Special effects have come a long way since, well, your time."

She wanted to tell him not to give her hope. "No charms or incantations. No blood sacrifice. No true love's kiss." Then she pictured the sorcerer standing in the hall of her studio apartment. Her mother's flowers were taking over the windowsills, growing wild out of their ceramic pots. He wore all black and a long coat with a metal pin over the breast. A knight riding a horse with an eight-pointed star over his head. He'd said he was from the Order of the Knights of Lavant. He said he would help them. That there was a place Danaë would be safe. No charms or incantations. No blood sacrifice. No true love's kiss. Nothing could set her free except a willing exchange.

"No true love's kiss?" Fabían said. His fingers were completely entwined in hers now. "Damn. There goes my shot."

"We can try," she said. Good girls weren't this eager to kiss a boy. But she had stopped being a good girl long ago. What did that even mean, anyway? She'd been alone for so many years, she'd forgotten what shame felt like. After all this time, Danaë did not want to be good or bad. She wanted to simply *be*.

"Really?"

"Kiss me." Then she added softly, "Please."

They leaned in, and when his lips brushed hers, Danaë felt time itself slow down. She stopped breathing, and her heart felt like it was growing. She thought of berries ripening on the vine. The sun coming out from behind clouds after a long, terrible winter. His lashes fluttered against her skin. His hand wrapped around her hip and pulled her closer. She'd never kissed anyone. Not in her sixteen human years and not in the petrified decades that followed. She felt the tip of his tongue and she gasped.

"Was that okay?" he asked quickly.

She answered by scooting on top of him so her torso was at an angle across his chest. She kissed him, and this time she was in control of it. When their lips touched again, she could taste the sugar of the dozen lollipops they'd consumed. She tasted her own tears because she was overjoyed. There was the rush of the oceans in her ears, and she remembered standing at the edge of the shores back home watching the crystal waters of the Caribbean.

"You're crying," he said. "I'm sorry. It didn't work."

She sat up and wiped her cheeks. Here he was trying to fit an entire lifetime into a few days. It was so much. So much.

"I told you not even true love's kiss could free me," she said, and held him closer. "I wouldn't even know what true love felt like, but we might be on the right track."

He grinned that soft, adorable grin of his, and her insides felt like they were being hollowed out to make room for more butterflies.

"Cool, cool, cool."

"What else did you bring?" She picked up a bottle of shimmering red dust.

"This? Well, you said you missed magic."

Magic was the reason they had left the Dominican Republic. Chased out of their little town outside La Romana. Her family had moved there to work in the sugar factories. Even now, sugar was the closest thing she'd get to home.

"Show me," she said, eager to hear more about Fabían's magic.

He unstoppered the bottle and bright sparks flew.

It was a cheap trick. There were some herbs. Ground jasper. The crushed bones of fire salamanders native to regions in Mexico. The botanica shop had everything he could ever want. Lady Lunes, the owner, had given him *the eye* when he'd purchased it all, but he'd said he was having a little birthday party. Brujas were gossips. There was no question about it. Besides, these items were trinkets. It's not like he'd bought anything dangerous.

"I might not be able to summon the dead like some brujas, but my uncle taught me how to make fireworks of the magic variety."

He tested it by making the shape of a bat. He held the powder in his hand and envisioned the winged creature, felt this cord in his gut that pulled real tight. It was the same feeling as when he and Danaë had kissed. He wanted nothing more than to do it again, but he didn't want to push her. He could stay with her all night.

He should be getting home, but he kept lighting up the room

with animals made of sparks and smoke. Each time, she clapped and squealed like he was the world's most brilliant brujo.

"What about you?" he asked when the bottle was empty and the moon was out. He brushed a stray curl from her face and leaned back on his hands. "What kind of magic do you miss?"

"I used to be able to conjure light," she said.

"Cool," he breathed out.

"This place won't let me."

He took her hand in his. "I'll find a way to get you out of here. There are brujas who know things. My moms is afraid. But she's afraid of everything. There's this family in Sunset Park—three sisters—they're always getting into some sort of mess. I could ask them. Or, if they can't help, there's the Alta Bruja, Lady Lunes. And if it's bad, real bad, we can go to Angela Santiago."

He watched her face go still. He'd seen that happen to his mother when his uncle had been attacked by a stray vampire and left for dead. He'd seen fear in people's faces his whole life, not just magical people, but the creatures trying to survive.

"What is it?" he asked. "What did I say?"

"It's nothing," she assured him. A deep frown darkened her features. "I just haven't heard my last name in a long time."

"Danaë Santiago."

She blinked quickly, like there was something in her eye. Her gaze fell to his, and she smiled. "There are many Santiagos in this city, I'm sure. Do you know this woman?"

Fabián scratched the side of his head and went through the bags of empty chips until he found a single bag of Takis with a few bites left. He sucked the powder off his thumb and fingers. "I'm not allowed to go there, but you hear stories. She has this greenhouse full of poisons, and the funny thing is, she grows everything inside her bakery. Has a special room. My cousin's friend's girlfriend goes to her when she wants a curse. The kind that takes generations to cure. I told JP he needs to stop hanging out with those girls, but no one listens to me."

She stood up and walked to the south-facing window. She touched the empty space there, sticking her hand out as far as it would go before a rippling force pushed her back. Reminded her that she was trapped inside.

"I promise, Dani. I will find a way to get you out of here."

"Don't say things you don't mean."

He stood up and went to her. He was a head taller, and one day he'd fill out his taut muscles. He'd be strong and powerful. "I would learn how to wield the power of the moon for you. I would do anything, Dani. I would trade places if I could. I—"

She sucked in a sharp breath. Held his hands tight in hers. She tipped her head back, and when she blinked this time, tears ran down her cheeks. "Don't say that."

"Too late. I already did." He brushed her wet cheek with his thumb.

Danaë leaned in, meeting him halfway for another kiss. This time, the fire built up inside his chest and spread through his lungs. She ran her fingers through his hair and down his back. They kissed each other until their mouths were swollen and the orange haze of sunrise began to break. He didn't remember falling asleep. But he remembered waking up alone.

He sat up in her bed. His shirt was on the floor and a cluster of vine flowers were on her pillow.

"Danaë?" he called out to someone who was not there.

∽

The Knight of Lavant stood over Danaë's figure curled up in the bed. Her hands were clutched against her chest. Even after the accident, after she set the other apartments on fire, her light was still glowing.

"Don't worry, Mrs. Santiago," he said. "We have a way to fix these kinds of things."

"How long will she be in there?" Angela Santiago asked.

"A few years. Our organization is here for the sole purpose of protecting the human population."

"And you're sure she can't get out?"

"No charms or incantations. No blood sacrifice. No true love's kiss. Nothing could set her free except a willing exchange, and I doubt anyone would ever risk such a thing. Moving on, we've taken care of the survivors and we'll find a place for you."

"Where?" she asked sharply.

"Bay Ridge."

When she peered up, her mother held a bit of foxglove in her fingertips. Danaë felt the effects of her mother's medicines, the ones that kept Danaë's powers at bay. The last time she had stopped taking them, she'd burned their neighbor's house down and they'd had to flee.

"Please don't," Danaë cried. "Mamá!"

"You're doing the right thing," the Knight said. "We'll come get you when we find a cure."

"There is no cure," she heard her mother say. But the next thing she knew, she was awake in a gray stone room, petrified in time.

∽

Danaë climbed down the tower using her own rope of hair. She trembled the whole way down, shrouded in Fabían's jacket. The strain on her temples was enough that she wanted to pass out, but she focused on the climb down, moving one hand and then the other. When her feet touched the ground, she was amazed at the feel of the grass tickling her ankles. The cold air against her legs and face. A creature hissed at her from the pond, but then sank beneath its murky surface.

She searched his pockets and found a knife. With shaky fingers she cut and cut and kept on cutting until her hair was free and around her shoulders. She yanked on the other end and the rope pooled at her feet. She wrapped it around her torso. She'd have to hide it . . . or burn it. But she couldn't leave it behind. A bruja never gave away parts of herself, lest they be used to bewitch her. Her mother had taught her that once.

Danaë thought of Fabían.

He'd be waking soon, and she didn't want—couldn't hear him cry for her. She knew the ache of that first loneliness. The jolt of realization that there was no way out.

She tried to run, but her muscles were out of practice, and before she could get far enough, she heard his voice.

"Dani! Danaë!"

Nothing could set her free except a willing exchange.

"I'll come back for you." She spoke the promise into the air.

If the noise had been terrible up above, it was worse as she took the labyrinthine roads out of Central Park and found a subway. Everything was different. She was different. Changed from the inside. Would her mother recognize her?

She boarded the train to Bay Ridge, muttering her own charm. The tips of her fingers lit up as she said, "I'll come back for you." But first, she was overdue for a family reunion.

HABIBI

TOCHI ONYEBUCHI

DEAR OMAR—

Solitary kills niggas, but it ain't gon kill me. That's facts.

After everything I been through so far, I know it ain't for me. They got me in here, but can't no kinda block hold me. I'm too big for that shit. Like, you know how shit just sometimes leaves you alone? Or, like, passes you by? I don't know how to explain it, but it's like bad shit just be missing me, bro. I'm not about to snitch or nothin, but one time the homie Victor and I—Victor's half-and-half, like half-black, half-Mexican but he ain't been jumped into no cholo gangs—we was headin back from school early on some bullshit. And I remember what day it was too, because Miss Frazey, who was always on our ass about something or something else, she took me to the side and she was like "you're

325

gonna have to make a choice between your future and your friends" and you know how much it can mess you up to hear that when you're twelve? On the set. All I know is this gang-banging, you feel me? But Victor and I are leaving school and we on our way to the Lakewood Mall when I see some Pirus literally headin right toward us. Now, they used to go to the other school around the way, and we used to play football against them until their set started showing up to the games carrying hammers and the schools were like "we ain't tryna see no dead kids on this football field," but these Pirus are headin straight for us. Like, we're about to get caught slippin, and it's just me and Victor and these four brolic-ass Bloods headin our way. So I figure, they bout to get the drop on us. And, like, if you're gonna get stomped out, you can't just go down like no bitch becuz people talk and it's gonna get around and maybe it's gonna turn into a thing where they give you the whoop-dee-whoop and now you gotta kill one of them and then they gotta kill one of you and it's just a lotta cryin mamas and a lotta wakes and, on the dead homie, I'm tired of that shit, you feel me? Like, this gang-banging shit ages you, bro. Anyway, they're bout to get the drop on us, and, you gotta understand, I got the rag out, yo. I'm Cripped up, all Crenshaw everything. I can't tuck nothin. And I left my hammer at Mac's place becuz we sometimes hang there after school and chill in his studio while a bunch of them make music and all that. But, get this, just when I think I'm bout to get the whoop-dee-whoop, they walk right past us. I'm talkin, right past us, bro. They don't even see us. Like we ain't even there. Victor notices it too, and at first we were like okay what if they're just waitin till we alone, you know? But, nah, we catch up to the homies at the Mall and it's on and crackin again. And at first, I ain't know what happen and I ain't even tell the other homies, but now I know what that was. I'm special. I'm Protected, yo. Like, I been shot at but never shot, you feel me? 16 years here and damn near everything's tried to kill me. but I ain't die yet. It's weird to say at 16, but sometimes it feel like forever yo.

But that's how I know, fam. I'm special. Like, that happen and so many other things. Like this.

I still don't know how this started or how exactly your letter got to me here. I swear, one second I'm takin my shit, then there's this piece of paper lyin in the dookie water and I'm so sick from bein in solitary without hearin or seein or talkin to nobody that I'm like "is this for real?" and I get the letter out right before I flush, and I look at it and it's all in these letters I ain't never seen before, like backwards cursive. And I don't know how you write like that, all the letters connected. Least, I think they're letters.

If this were happening to anybody else, they'd have all these questions. But not me. I know exactly why this is happening to me. Same reason we ain't get the whoop-dee-whoop from those Bloods. Same reason I ain't never been shot. And you gotta know this before I eat this letter and send it to you.

I'm special. They ain't gon kill me here. They can't.

QUINCY—

I think I know what you speak of. That feeling that you are special. That Allah has wrapped His blanket over your shoulders. I saw it once. Outside. In Gaza. It is hard to imagine Gaza City if you have not already been there. Everything is close. We live on top of each other. There is garbage in the streets and it is tough to escape the smell even if you go all the way to the sea. And when you're young and you get to the sea, you might think you've found a moment of freedom, of peace. But there are Israeli ships in the distance—you learn to notice them from an early age—and there are people arrayed on the water to shoot you if you go too far out.

That happened to some fishermen I knew. The tide was receding and it had been a bad day for them. Everywhere they went, the fish fled. As quiet as they tried to be, as much as they'd tried to still themselves, to vanish and be like the air around them and the sea beneath them, they were always too clumsy. Their bodies would get in the way of their mission. So, frustrated, their boat kept moving further and further away from shore. Normally, it is an easy thing to keep track of. You don't need the buoys, you just learn early on, first from your parents, then from your friends who disobey and are punished, until the lesson lives in your bones. But some days, if you haven't caught the fish you need to cook to feed your family for that night and if you've had several days like this now that build up and cloud your mind and bring fog between your ears and behind your eyes, sometimes you forget the lessons in your bones and

328

you drift far out and you don't even hear the gunshot.

Your friend collapses. Their legs just fold beneath them. And a part of you is angry that they've fallen so gracelessly, because maybe some of your supplies have now slipped into the water and these are things that you paid very hard and dear money for that you will now never have back. And maybe you're angry because your friend falling the way they did threatens to capsize your boat, tossing you all overboard. And the water is clean enough to swim in if you needed to, but then it would be easy for the snipers to say you and the others abandoned your boat simply to swim further out, as though that were a thing we would ever want to do.

Your friend doesn't capsize the boat. You don't tilt over. But you know from the way that red blossoms on their chest that they're dead. A sniper has shot them.

But that's not what I was talking about when I said I knew what you meant. There was one time, by a border crossing with Israel, several of us were protesting. It is often a family affair. People bring their instruments and we have signs and, because so many of us live together, we make the trip together.

We get to the beaches and there they are waiting for us. Soldiers. Some of them sit in armored personnel carriers and other huge vehicles. They have put up towers from whence they can snipe us. And soon, after a few warnings in Hebrew, they fire the first tear gas canisters at us. And the smoke, thick and white, swells towards us. The wind did not like us that morning and swept the tear gas right in our direction and soon we were all choking and crying out for milk.

It looked as though we would end our march as soon as we began. But then wind came and whisked the tear gas away. Someone had set fires nearby, or maybe the soldiers had shot at our electricity generators, setting them on fire, but large columns of black smoke seemed to rumble along the horizon on the beach. They made a sort of fence, as though this portion of beach were all that was left of Gaza.

And I look, as the tear gas clears away and a friend is pouring milk on my face and my eyes to stop the burning, and there, in the center of the fence, with smoke billowing around her, is my sister in her denim overalls. She's with several of her friends. All of them wear keffiyeh around their necks. And in their hands are strings of beads, and they swing them as they dance the dabke.

It is a joyful thing to watch the dabke. It is danced at weddings and other joyous occasions. It is a sort of line dance, led by one person in particular who is supposed to be like a tree but with legs that stomp into the ground like roots, and arms that wave like tree branches caught in autumn wind. There's chanting and the leader drives all of it, kicking and hopping and flaring their legs and skipping and spinning. And there is my sister, kicking and hopping and skipping and spinning, and she twirls her string of beads and leads the chanting. She is a warrior, the bravest thing I have ever seen.

Then I hear the thwip sound that rubber bullets make when they buzz by you. Sometimes they make a crackling sound when they hit rock or a thudding sound when they hit your chest or your stomach or your shoulder. But around her, all there is is thwip thwip thwip. As though she is dancing around them. As though she is dancing through them.

Do you think it ever stops? The protection? The thing that kept bullets from hitting you and that shielded her that day? Do you think a day comes when you wake up and suddenly you're no longer protected? Do you even know it? What would it feel like?

Would it feel like going to sleep, thinking that you can control what you see and hear and think in this nightmare, and hoping that you might finally wake up somewhere familiar where you are loved, somewhere filled with the sweet smell of kanafeh, somewhere busy with the voices of your siblings and your cousins, where everyone is alive and loud and happy to see you . . . then waking up to see that nothing has changed?

You are still here. In this cell. Alone. So alone that the magic of this letter, which I will eat and chew up and swallow and which I will somehow pass to you, feels hollow. Morning comes when I wake up and chastise myself for having spent so much time talking to a ghost.

Please write me back.

Even if you aren't real.

OMAR—

I'm real, bro. I'm here. And whatever it is that's going on, it's real too. And if it ain't, then that means we got the same dream going on at the same time, and that's gotta be its own type of magic.

But, bro, so much of this is mental, you feel me? It's like say I'm a ballplayer in the NBA and my pops manages me and he says I'm better than everybody. You ask him, "is your son better than Steph Curry?" and Dad's like "he could be." "Is your son better than LeBron?" "Well, he could be." And you know for a fact that all those kids that play ball in college maybe 50 percent of them make it to the League, so it's all mental. Mad people got talent and can learn skills and all that, but to get to the next level, yo? You need to be gassed up. Let me find out my dad's gettin asked if I'm better than people and he's like "oh man I don't know." Get outta here, for real? You my dad and you not gonna call me the best ballplayer that ever lived? But I hope you get what I'm tryna say.

I guess what I'm tryna say is that you gotta keep your mental straight, you feel me? Becuz sometimes when that shit gets broke you can't put it back together.

I seen some shit the other day, they was walkin me out of my cell for my hour of rec time in the yard, and on the way out, we passed by this other cell in solitary and there was a bunch of guards outside this one door and they had the door open and they were talkin all quiet and whispering and you could tell they was tryna frame someone or build a lie around whatever it was that had happened. And that's when I seen the nigga foot like stickin out past the door. You can't see all his body because of the way the guards are standing, but you can see some of it, and he's lyin face-up on the floor, with his head and upper back propped up aginst something and there's just that shiny stickiness ALL over the floor. It come back that he slit his wrists while he was in there, and you're not supposed to be able to do that. They give you the suicide blanket for that reason, and it's not even a blanket thing, it's like this thing they just basically wrap you in and zip up to your neck. It's like nylon or something and they basically trap you in it. You can't mov for shit. And they call it a suicide blanket becuz you're not supposed to be able to tear it open and make a noose like how you would normally do if you were gonna do yourself like that.

But I guess the guards thought that he was better. He looked like he could be about my age. I don't know if I ever seen him around on the outside. He coulda been from any block really. But I'm glad it wasn't me. Coulda been. He and I got the same setup. A bunk. A toilet. And a mesh window. There's a slot they slide your food in and that's how the roaches and all that get in to your cell and sometimes they make so much noise it gets hard to sleep. It don't feel like you have company, tho. The Box could be fulla bugs, but you still feel alone.

Sometimes I cry and that helps. Not loud or nothin, but real quiet. You know the type where your shoulders heave and it feels like the sadness is tryna bust right outta your body. Just like that.

DEAR QUINCY—

I am sorry to hear about your fellow prisoner. May his soul be blessed. May Allah guide him. Suicide is sin here. But I know many who have taken their own lives, and I do not blame them.

There was a boy in our neighborhood, Mohanned. He was a writer. He was older than me; thus, we all looked up to him as an older brother. When he wrote, you could feel the despair that moved through him and see that it was the same despair that moved through the rest of us. By the time I was 7 years old, my home had been bombed by the Israelis three times. Three times our memories had been reduced to rubble. And three times we had to rebuild. For some, it was like starting from scratch. Like the whole of your life until that moment had been wiped away and was nothing more than broken stones and metal and dust. But some of us could still recover the toys we had played with or the shoes our parents had purchased for us when we were children.

Mohanned used to write and write and write. He would shut himself up in his room for entire days, just reading and writing. We all thought he was a sort of prophet and that he simply lived differently than the rest of us. He had a direct line to Allah that the rest of us could only hope one day to have. He would post his stories on Facebook, and as soon as they went online they would get hundreds of likes that would then turn to thousands of likes. We loved him. So when his mother found him in his room, no longer breathing, it was not just she who grieved. It was all of us. Then, on the heels of that grief was fear. Because he was suffering just like the rest of us. And now we knew that what took him could take us as well.

You see it sometimes in the way that we practically throw ourselves in front of their bullets. Everybody protests, no matter your age or whether you are a man or a woman. But often you will see the young boys in the buffer zone, and if you ask them, they would say that they didn't care if they died. During the siege, we live without electricity, without running water, and without any sign that things will change. So hopelessness is logical. But we are taught to be stronger. There is always a family member or a member of someone else's family who would feel a loss too great for you to ever want to inflict on them. And we have been suffering for over 70 years, so what is another month of this sort of life?

Even if I wanted to, there is nothing for me to do it with here. We had our blankets taken away when it was announced that several of the prisoners had begun a hunger strike. They are protesting their conditions. There is nothing in our cells to regulate the temperature. The food is crawling with insects. Occasionally, we are taken out and beaten for no reason. There is no interrogation, only the beating. And we are not given prayer mats for salat. All of this because I once threw a stone at a settler's car.

But maybe I am safer in here than I am out there.

Still, I dream of the Rimal district and all of its leaves. It is like an oasis in this desert of misery. It is where the wealthy in Gaza congregate. It contains the Governor's Palace and the Presidential Palace, but it also has the school for refugees, maintained by the UN. The Gaza Mall is there. But also there is coastline. Mohanned went there often to write. Also, foreigners who came to Gaza would bring books. And we would sometimes fight over them. They were portals to different worlds. And in them you could sometimes see yourself. Even though they were rarely about Arabs, and rarely about young Arab boys like me, if I squinted, I could see in the contours of their heroes something of my shoulders and my hair and my hands and feet. If I closed my eyes, I could imagine myself as the main character. And I was a hero who did not destroy things but saved them.

You are right. We are special. Because when I hear of other prisoners, I always feel as if their loneliness is bottomless. But, because I have you, that is not the case for me. We have this gift. And you give me courage.

I think I will join the hunger strike. It is an opportunity to build something. I do not see it as destroying my body. I see it as transcending it. I am preparing myself to live on a higher level of existence. I am flower petals being whisked on a breeze ever upward. Heroes take control of their destinies.

I will be a hero.

DEAR OMAR—
We heroes?

I like thinkin I'm a hero, but do kids like us get to
be heroes? My homie got shot like 8 times over some
bullshit and he ain't stop no bullets. He still alive tho, so
maybe he is. But like we just kids. We beef with other
sets and stomp kids out and get stomped out and laugh and
sometimes I go to Cee's house to listen to the music he
makin with Mac and them but I gotta leave the hammer in
a locker cuz he don't like guns in the studio and I can't
forget it on the way out cuz I have to cross the way to
get back to Artesia and that's Bloods over there.

There's lots of empty houses in the hood, and when
I was little, we didn't think nothin of it. Maybe ghosts
was in them, but couldn't be nothin scarier than what was
out on the streets. Still it was fun. We was havin fun.
I mean, that's Long Beach. Everybody from everywhere so
really we don't do that whole "where you from, cuh?" and
all that stuff. But that's the thing is like heroes gotta
have origin stories, right? Like Superman is from Krypton,
he some undocumented immigrant or whatever. And Batman's
from Gotham. Spider-Man's from somewhere in New York or
whatever. But Long Beach, do you even have history before
you get to Long Beach? Our parents and grandparents, they
came back from the wars way back when and it was like ownin
a home was the most important thing in the world so they
bought up all these houses and you get these families movin
in but then the houses get foreclosed on and the government
snatch them right back up and ain't nobody livin in em no more

so all you got is ghosts maybe. I don't know why I'm so hung up on needin to know where heroes is from.

Maybe it has somethin to do with order, you know? Heroes are all about restorin order or bringing balance back to things. There's a bad guy who's messin everything up and the hero's gotta get rid of the bad guy, but it's like, what does a bad guy look like here?

Before I got put in solitary, there was a couple East Coast cats who wound up here (everybody's from everywhere) and they was talkin about street justice. And I ain't really know what that meant and they was talkin bout how if somebody did something wrong they'd have somethin happen to them. Everybody was talkin about some kid or another who got boo-bopped by the cops and street justice meant that "aight, you goin after the kids, you gon get got" and one of them was in here and is actually servin life becuz he capped a cop who he said had killed a little black kid and gotten away with it. And it's like, over here anybody could get it. It just happen here. Like "Oh that cop boo-bopped cuz? That's craaaazy. Oh they robbed the bank and the little girl AND her mama got boo-bopped? That's craaaazy." And you just go about your day. Street justice? They talkin bout some dude from the streets puttin all they beef to the side to go down to Florida to pop George Zimmerman. Niggas in the streets got bigger things to worry about, feel me?

But I been thinkin that when I get out, I might try to learn, you know? Cuz kids out here is smart! My ex-girlfriend's son autistic, but you give that kid a math problem? He a genius. Long division. Algebra. Three seconds, he got the whole thing figured out. And they got a Youth Program at the YMCA in Long Beach. You can learn the piano, play pool, do gymnastics stuff. Get strong and smart.

It's tough, tho, cuz you gotta ride the Blue Line to get there and niggas be gettin in trouble for not havin a ticket. That's one of the first cases I caught. Ridin the train without a ticket. Then they give you a ticket that's like $500 and I can't pay that cuz I'm 12 years old. Where I'ma get the money to pay that off? So, boom, I got a warrant. And if you already on probation on some other shit, boom, straight to jail.

How I'ma be a hero if that's part of my origin story?

But I like what you said about not bein a hero that destroyed things but a hero that saved things. That's how I be feelin these days. It's weird. I thought bein in the Box would make me more selfish, you know? Make me think more about myself and about survivin. But I seen what happened to dude across the hall and one of my first thoughts was "what could I have done to keep him from doin that," you know?

Sometimes I be hearing things and seein things that ain't there. Feelin them too. On the dead homie, I swear the other day I swear I musta transported myself to some other nigga hood I ain't never been to before. I know it wasn't no kinda memory or nothin because it was all strange and new and different.

Shoes dangling from power lines like some kinda ballet over this potholed street with cracks makin a spiderweb from one small crater to another, and they was gettin made bigger from the wheels of Camaros and Hondas and beat-to-shit Subarus, all these worndown four-doors takin kids to and from school or this local park with a green-and-orange jungle gym for a afternoon where they'll learn how to ride bicycles and where they'll fall while speeding down that hill by the parking lot and realize that the natural way to deal with pain is to cry. There was weeds poking out above freshly mowed grass where the men in tanktops was maintainin their yards, and there was these gates of green and white and yellow, with grasshoppers playing tag, in front of two-story brown and black brick project towers where extension cords tangle and hang, pulled by gravity into a slump around their middles, between windows, and people siphoning power, sharing it, experiencing the same electricity that sparks the small satellite dishes on top of certain roofs and the bootleg cable boxes in other windows, and some other ledge was taken by an air conditioner, and it was groanin beneath the weight of this oppressive heat that just sits on your shoulders and bends your knees and soaks your shirt and makes everything too heavy. And the kids was comin out with their magnifying glasses to aim the sun on the ants scurrying out from under their badass attentions, intentions, and a crow's head is gettin all moldy in the middle of the yellow-striped street, its body lost somewhere in the weeds of a nearby hill where other kids had tossed it. Beer cans lost in the tall grass, half-eaten chicken with the meat smoldering at each end of the wing's bones.

And I swear on the dead homie that I was there. It was just for a second, but I was out. I was out of my cell.

Maybe, next time, I could take someone else with me. If I can figure out how to do it again, maybe I can take you with me.

DEAR QUINCY—

I am sorry it has taken me so long to respond to your latest letter. What you described sounds magical. Through your words, I could feel the heat on my chest. And I could feel the beginnings of a breeze on my face. I could smell the grass. I could hear the sizzle of electricity and the hum of the air conditioners. You say that it is difficult to imagine yourself a hero, but perhaps Allah has gifted you with abilities beyond our comprehension.

I have been seeing things too, but I don't know that it is because of any gifts.

The hunger strike has entered its second week, and everything hurts. My entire body sometimes feels as though it has been swallowed by fire. My throat is a desert as I have also refused water. There is talk of forced feeding. It is when jailers bind you to a chair and insert a tube through your nose into your throat and inject liquid nutrients so that you do not die. They say it is to protect us from ourselves, but I have heard from some of the older prisoners that it is the most painful thing a man can endure. Many have been left weeping and broken by the end of it. They say it lights your brain on fire, and the whole world explodes into whiteness. It is like dying, but there is no release.

I'm scared.

I don't know what I'll do if they come for me. I will try to pray if they ever put me in that chair, but I fear my thoughts will become too scattered for me to form the words. I fear I will already start crying before they begin.

I am sorry for how messy my writing has become. My

hands have begun shaking. I don't know if it is because I am afraid or because my body is breaking down.

There is no real way for me to communicate with the others. We have our secrets, but they are all coded messages with instructions. I have not seen my family in over six months. I don't know who is alive and who is dead. I don't know who has celebrated a birthday. I don't know who has married. The world moves on outside this cell, and I feel like the only way for me to rejoin it is to die. And I'm scared. I wish that just once I could receive a message from another one of the hunger strikers that was not a set of instructions or a number for how many days we have been doing this for already. I wish I could receive from them a poem. Or a photograph.

All I have is you.

OMAR—
Whatchu look like?

I'm asking because when I take you to where we're going, I want to recognize you. I don't know if I'll meet you alone or if you'll be in a crowd, and this might sound mean but I don't know if I'd really KNOW it was you. Even with all of what's been happening to us. Like, you think that with this thing we got, we'd know each other instantly, but, like, I have no picture of you. I ain't never seen you before. And before that first letter, I had no idea you even existed.

But now sometimes when I close my eyes, I try to picture you. I try to put your face together. At first, it's kinda like a Mr. Potato Head thing where the lips are too big and the nose is way too big and the eyes are kinda googly, but then it starts to come together, you know?

Here's what I picture, and you can tell me if I'm wrong.

I never met a Middle Eastern person before and I don't think I know any Palestinians, except DJ Khaled. He's a Palestinian, right?

But I picture you having this straight nose that juts forward a little bit with tiny down-facing nostrils. And your bottom lip is a little plump, but you got your lips pursed together in this straight line. And your eyebrows are bushy and curve sharp-like towards the ends. And your eyes are shaped like almonds. Like the kind Mama was always eating. And your skin is dark but not dark-dark like mine. More like when water wash up on the shore but the sand ain't dry yet. Like, dark but not dark-dark. It's the type of brown that's nice to look at. And you got this sloping jawline. It's smooth and curved. I think you're my age so you don't got no baby fat left. Maybe you hit your growth spurt. Some of the cats who play basketball around the way call it your Mango Season. Maybe that has somethin to do with the South, I don't know. But maybe you're tall. And maybe you could hoop too. When you get out, you should think about playing ball.

You ain't gotta say what you think I look like or nothin. Ur a good writer but my face too pretty for words. Haha, I'm just kiddin. I'm just a regular nigga. Regular-degular. Nothin special.

But I think that's what you might look like. It's what I think a hero might look like.

QUINCY—

Do your hands have long fingers? Like those of a piano player?

I imagine you with strong hands. Your grip isn't bony, it's iron. You hold tightly to what is dear. I imagine your skin dark as seabed on the backs of your hands and your palms are the color of milky coffee, and I can now imagine every line, every crease, every crevice. Once upon a time, your knuckles were cracked, and I think they have bled often. You have broken the skin of them on many things, trying to survive. But what has grown over that broken skin is rough and safe and secure. That's what I imagine when I imagine your knuckles on my cheek. Security.

It is more difficult to see your face. I think that my sight is failing me. It took me a long time to read your last letter. The words themselves were slipping away right before my eyes. I cough now and when I cough, I can feel the blood moving in my chest. If I cough into my hands, they come back red. They have started trying to force feed us, but I have remained resilient, and I find the occasional message of support and congratulations waiting for me in my cell. I can barely lift my arms, and I have stopped trying to walk the length of my cell for exercise. My legs no longer support me. Sometimes, I feel nothing at all. I don't feel my bed beneath me, nor do I feel the heat of this cage on my forehead. Sounds come as though from far away. I sometimes hear screams, but I tell myself I am only dreaming them. If it is a lie, then let it be mine.

When I try to imagine you, I imagine your hands, but I also imagine your arms. They are thin and sinewy. Strong but light. Running is easy for you. And your legs are the same, and I can see them kicking behind you as you dive into the water. You are an arrow fired into it.

We are just off the shore, swimming into the Mediterranean. The sun is shining so bright it turns the rippling waves into a bed of diamonds. And I see you swimming and swimming.

I hope you get this letter. My stomach has stopped working. I don't know if I can pass anything through it anymore. I think I'm dying.

I am sorry if my writing is messy. My tears are falling on the page, and I can't stop them. You told me that crying helps, so I am trying it now.

Habibi, come to Gaza some time when you are able. You will find me.

Now that you know what I look like.

OMAR—

Bro, I'm not gonna lie. Your last letter had me shook. Your eyes aren't getting bad. It's just these new pencils they're making us use. They're all made out of rubber and they don't have any led in them so that we can't hurt ourselves. You're good. You ~~gotta you~~ gotta stay. ~~I can't~~

The other day, I was waiting. Trying to see if I just needed to take a shit and get another letter from you but nothin was comin and I just kept tryin and tryin and nothin was happenin and I got so mad I couldn't eat and when they tried to bring me more food I took the tray and threw my food everywhere and started bangin the tray on the doors and on the walls and I couldn't stop. I knew what I was doing. I saw myself doing it, but I couldn't stop. It was like my old self took over. My out-there self.

That Quincy was always angry. Even when I was laughing and havin fun and all of us was hangin out at that abandoned house on Pico and one time we locked the homie in a shed and he was poundin on it for like hours and we finally let him out and we was laughing our asses off, even at that time I was angry. Then there's the Quincy that did everything he could to take care of his mama. Maybe I go to school but that don't work so maybe I slang on the corner and that don't work so you just fall into the gangbangin and everybody already go into that angry so it ain't nothin to pop somebody or to give them the whoop-dee-whoop. Then there's the Quincy that loves reading and kinda likes writing and is tryin to get good at it but they make it so hard for a nigga to learn in here, and it's like there are all these Quincys inside me and they all tired. They all tired. And the only time they all feel glued together is when I'm readin your letters.

I don't know that I can stick it out in here if I ain't got your letters. You're saving my life, man. You can't go. I'm beggin you. Please.

I been trying to see if I can do that trick again. Where I see a place I ain't never been to before. But I haven't been able to do it since that one time. Sometimes I wonder if it was really real. Like I musta dreamt it. But it was the realest dream ever. And it wasn't no part of Cali I'd ever been to before. That's the thing. It was a new place. So I been tryin. Like, I tried it with the Rimal place you told me about. And I could almost get there but not quite. It still felt like there was this fence between me and that spot.

(Sorry, I had to take a walk. I almost ripped up what I wrote so far, but I want you to get all of this if the letter gets to you. I'm sorry. I can't keep you from doin what you need to do. You fightin your fight is inspirin me and all. But you know what too? It's like the songs say: if you love somethin, you gotta be able to let it go. I just . . . I just don't want you to die, homie. On the set, you the best thing that ever happened to me and I don't know that this coulda happened if I didn't wind up here in solitary. Someone catches me shittin out a whole piece of paper they gon take me straight to the hospital, you feel me? Haha. But you a real nigga for what you doin. That's on the set. Out there, niggas die over all sorts of petty shit and it's like we don't see the bigger things that's above us, you know?

Like the homie who got asthma because his house is right by that coal plant and that's why the property value low enough for black families to buy it in the first place. And his mama and em was always tellin him to sleep with the window shut but he liked the breeze on his face so he'd always open it every night till one night he fell outta bed and couldn't breathe and they took him to the hospital and told him he had asthma. See, I wasn't thinkin bout none of that before I got in here. I was seein it. I was seein kids get jammed up over ridin trains without payin the fare then windin up behind bars over that shit and I just figured it was normal, but I wasn't seein the bigger thing hangin over it. I don't know. You opened my eyes to thinkin that kind of way. And that's why I'ma get out. That's right. I'ma get outta here. I'ma get outta the Box and I'ma beat my case and I'ma be clean on probation and I'ma make it so kids don't be gettin locked up over bullshit fare evasion and so kids don't get asthma from living to close to the coal plant and so ppl stop getting shot over bullshit. I'ma get out.)

And when I get out, I'ma find you, and we're gonna go swimmin.

And I'm gonna ask you what that last word meant. Habibi. It sounded important but it didn't translate in my brain when I read it. I hope that don't mean my powers is fading. Haha. Cuz I still gotta make it to you. And I think Gaza's a long way from Cali.

There's another reason I need to see you. And I wasn't even sure I was gonna write this, but whatever.

When you were talkin about my hands . . . I felt . . . I don't know. I felt Good. Like, Good good. Ain't nobody ever told me about my hands like that. And it ain't feel weird either. It felt right. I don't know. I just wanted you to know that.

Quincy—

Beloved. Habibi means beloved. I hope this letter gets to you in time.

Find me.

Habibi—
I'm coming.

ABOUT THE EDITOR

Dhonielle Clayton is the COO of We Need Diverse Books. She is the *New York Times* bestselling author of *The Belles* and the coauthor of the series Tiny Pretty Things, upon which the Netflix show is based. She is the cofounder of the diversity-focused story kitchen Cake Literary, whipping up decidedly diverse books for a wide array of readers. She makes her home in New York City.

ABOUT THE AUTHORS

Samira Ahmed is the *New York Times* bestselling and award-winning author of *Love, Hate & Other Filters; Internment;* and *Mad, Bad & Dangerous to Know.* Her poetry and short stories have appeared in anthologies including *Take the Mic, Color Outside the Lines, Ink Knows No Borders, Who Will Speak for America?,* and *Vampires Never Get Old.* She was born in Bombay, India, and grew up in Batavia, Illinois, in a house that smelled like fried onions, spices, and potpourri. A graduate of the University of Chicago, Samira has taught high school English in both the suburbs of Chicago and New York City, worked for education nonprofits, and spent time on the road for political campaigns.

samiraahmed.com

When she was in high school, **Jenni Balch** decided she wanted to grow up to be a physicist, like her grandfather, and an author, like her favorite storytellers. So she did. Jenni double-majored in physics and history, and wrote her first novel-length story while writing her honors thesis in physics. She earned a master's in mechanical engineering and now lives and works in western Massachusetts. While in college, Jenni was diagnosed with immune thrombocytopenic purpura, an autoimmune disorder where platelets are targeted as foreign antibodies. One of the main characters in her story shares this diagnosis.

jennibalch.com

Libba Bray is the #1 *New York Times* bestselling author of the Diviners series, the *Los Angeles Times* Book Prize finalist *Beauty Queens,* the Printz Award–winning *Going Bovine,* and the acclaimed Gemma Doyle trilogy. She divides her time between Brooklyn, New York, and Los Angeles, California.

libbabray.com

Zoraida Córdova is the author of many fantasy novels for kids and teens, including the award-winning Brooklyn Brujas series, *Incendiary, Star Wars: A Crash of Fate,* and *The Way to Rio Luna.* Her short fiction has appeared in the *New York Times* bestselling anthology *Star Wars: From a Certain Point of View, Come On*

In, and *Toil & Trouble.* She is the co-editor of *Vampires Never Get Old.* Zoraida was born in Guayaquil, Ecuador, and raised in Queens, New York. When she's not working on her next novel, she's finding a new adventure.

zoraidacordova.com

Tessa Gratton is the author of the science fiction fantasy titles *The Queens of Innis Lear* and *Lady Hotspur* for adults, as well as several YA series and short stories that have been translated into twenty-two languages. Her most recent YA novels are the original fairy tales *Strange Grace* and *Night Shine.* Though she has lived all over the world, she currently resides alongside the Kansas prairie with her wife.

tessagratton.com

Kwame Mbalia is a husband, father, writer, *New York Times* bestselling author, and former pharmaceutical metrologist, in that order. His debut middle-grade novel, *Tristan Strong Punches a Hole in the Sky,* received a Coretta Scott King Author Honor award. A Howard University graduate and a midwesterner now living in North Carolina, he enjoys impromptu dance sessions and Cheez-Its.

kwamembalia.com

Anna-Marie McLemore (they/them) is the queer, Latinx, non-binary author of *The Weight of Feathers,* a William C. Morris YA Debut Award finalist; Stonewall Honor Book *When the Moon*

Was Ours, which was longlisted for the National Book Award for Young People's Literature; *Wild Beauty,* a *Kirkus Reviews, School Library Journal,* and *Booklist* best book of the year; *Blanca & Roja,* a *New York Times* Book Review Editors' Choice; *Dark and Deepest Red,* an Indie Next List title; and *The Mirror Season.*

author.annamariemclemore.com

Tochi Onyebuchi is the author of the young adult novel *Beasts Made of Night,* which won the Ilube Nommo Award for Best Speculative Fiction Novel by an African, and its sequel, *Crown of Thunder;* Locus Award finalist *War Girls;* and his adult fiction debut, *Riot Baby.* He holds degrees from Yale, the Tisch School of the Arts, L'institut d'études politiques, and Columbia Law School. His fiction has appeared in *Asimov's Science Fiction, Omenana, Uncanny, Lightspeed,* and elsewhere. His nonfiction has appeared on Tor.com and in *Nowhere Magazine* and the *Harvard Journal of African American Policy,* among other places.

tochionyebuchi.com

Mark Oshiro is the award-winning author of *Anger Is a Gift* and *Each of Us a Desert,* and their forthcoming middle-grade debut *The Insiders.* When they are not writing, they run the online Mark Does Stuff universe and are trying to pet every dog in the world.

markoshiro.com

Natalie C. Parker is the author and editor of several books for young adults, among them the acclaimed Seafire trilogy. Her work has been included on the NPR Best Books list, the Indie Next List, and the TAYSHAS Reading List, and in Junior Library Guild selections. Natalie grew up in a navy family finding home in coastal cities from Virginia to Japan. Now she lives with her wife on the Kansas prairie.

nataliecparker.com

Rebecca Roanhorse is a *New York Times* bestselling and Nebula, Hugo, and Locus Award–winning speculative fiction writer. Her novels include *Trail of Lightning* and *Storm of Locusts* (both part of the Sixth World series), *Star Wars: Resistance Reborn,* and the middle-grade novel *Race to the Sun.* Her latest novel is the epic fantasy *Black Sun.* Her YA short fiction can be found in various anthologies, including *Hungry Hearts, A Phoenix First Must Burn,* and *Vampires Never Get Old.* She lives with her husband and daughter in northern New Mexico.

rebeccaroanhorse.com

Victoria "V. E." Schwab is the #1 *New York Times* bestselling author of more than twenty books, including the acclaimed Shades of Magic series, Villains series, Monsters of Verity duology, Cassidy Blake series, and *The Invisible Life of Addie LaRue.* Her work has received critical acclaim and been featured in the *New York Times, Entertainment Weekly,* the *Washington Post,* and more, translated into over two dozen languages, and optioned for television and film. When she's not haunting Paris streets or trudging up English hillsides, she lives in Edinburgh, Scotland, and is usually tucked in the corner of a coffee shop, dreaming up monsters.

veschwab.com

Tara Sim is the author of the Timekeeper trilogy and *Scavenge the Stars*. She can typically be found wandering the wilds of the Bay Area, California. When she's not chasing cats or lurking in bookstores, she writes books about magic, murder, and explosions.

tarasim.com

Nic Stone is the author of the #1 *New York Times* bestseller and William C. Morris YA Debut Award finalist *Dear Martin* and its companion novel, *Dear Justyce.* She is also the author of *Odd One Out,* an NPR Best Book and Rainbow Book List Top Ten selection, and *Jackpot,* a love-*ish* story that takes a searing look at economic inequality for young adults. Her middle-grade debut, *Clean Getaway,* is a *New York Times* bestseller and received two starred reviews from *Publishers Weekly* and *Booklist,* which called it "an absolute firecracker of a book." Nic lives in Atlanta with her adorable little family.

nicstone.info

ABOUT WE NEED DIVERSE BOOKS

We Need Diverse Books (WNDB) began as a hashtag in 2014 and has since grown into a 501(c)(3) nonprofit with thirteen initiatives that advocate for increased diversity within the publishing industry—in the books we read, the authors and illustrators who create them, and the people who edit, design, produce, market, publicize, and sell them. Our mission is to create a world in which all young people can find themselves in the pages of a book.

With the stories in this anthology, you moved into magical worlds and found the magic inside *you*. You commanded the failing spaceship. You broke the powerful enchantment. You can change our worlds—both fictional and not—for good. This is the mission at WNDB. We invite you to learn more about WNDB programs at diversebooks.org.

For more fantastic fiction, author events,
exclusive excerpts, competitions, limited editions and more

VISIT OUR WEBSITE
titanbooks.com

LIKE US ON FACEBOOK
facebook.com/titanbooks

FOLLOW US ON TWITTER AND INSTAGRAM
@TitanBooks

EMAIL US
readerfeedback@titanemail.com